CHARITABLE
INJUSTICE

Otto L. Wheeler

Copyright © 2021 by Otto L. Wheeler

ISBN: 978-1-7356251-1-9

Dedication

To my wife, Suzy

TABLE OF CONTENTS

CHARITABLE INJUSTICE

1

THE SOUND OF THE DOORBELL chime coming through Anne Wentworth's cell phone startled her. Expecting no one at this early hour, she tapped the Ring app on her phone to get a view of who or what was outside. No deliveries were expected, and no appointments had been set. She saw a slightly built young woman standing beside a large suitcase. Anne looked back at her computer screen, clicked the mouse down and pulled the red jack of diamonds over to the black queen of clubs. She got up and scurried from her small office above the garage, down the hall and to the twin curved staircase leading to the front doors. A few steps down the stairs the doorbell rang again.

Wearing her favorite robe and a pair of L.L.Bean mule slippers, Anne remembered her total lack of makeup. Rarely, if ever, did Anne Wentworth go into public without at least a little makeup. And opening the front door constituted going out in public.

She crossed the foyer leading to the antique leaded glass front doors and the covered entry. Through the glass she could see the young lady silhouetted against the gray Georgia morning sky. It had been drizzling since six that morning when Jason left for the office. At only fifty-two degrees, the moisture made it seem like forty.

Anne opened the door to find a pathetic creature. Maybe five-two, she couldn't weigh one hundred pounds soaking wet, and she was. Wearing a light blue sweatshirt with Sylacauga Aggies on the front, a pair of too large blue jeans and worn out sneakers, pathetic fit her description to a tee. She clutched a piece of paper. However, her most noticeable feature covered her head and flowed down well past her waist. Long, wet, tangled, red hair. No part, no clips, no pins. It just hung there. The ends, uneven and split, looked as though they had been cut with a hand ax. Well, maybe not that bad, but pretty damn close. Anne had no recollection of this person, not even a flicker of familiarity. A word Anne's mother would use came to mind – ragamuffin.

Anne couldn't help noticing the suitcase. Hard shell, vinyl, Samsonite, avocado green, circa 1970. Where in the world did that thing, and she, for that matter, come from?

"May I help you?" Anne asked, as she opened the door.

"Yes, ma'am," the young lady whispered. "I'm here to go to work."

"Go to work? I'm afraid I don't have any work. I have people who help me out and I don't need anyone right now.

What brings you to my door? How did you pick my house?" Anne inquired.

The young lady held out the piece of paper and said, "The man said I could get help here. I thought he meant I could get work."

"Let me see," Anne said. She took the piece of paper and unfolded it. There was her address with the words 'You can probably get help here' written underneath. "Who gave this to you?" Anne asked.

"A man over at a convenience store on Peachtree," came the reply, pointing away from the house.

"Well sweetie, there must be some kind of mistake. I'm sorry, but I can't help you." With that farewell, she closed the door.

2

ANNE STARTED UP THE BEAUTIFUL curved mahogany stairway on the right side of the foyer, its seldom-used matching twin on the left. The rich, thick carpet muted the sounds of her steps until her footsteps stopped midway to the top. At that point, either compassion or curiosity overcame her. She turned and descended the steps and approached the front doors.

Somehow, she thought, if the young lady had left, she could at least think she had tried. This initially appeared to be the case. Then Anne once again saw that slim silhouette, this time lower to the porch surface. She opened the door to see the young lady seated on the top step of the porch, face in hands, crying.

"Honey, why don't you grab that big suitcase and come into the house? It's cold out there."

With hesitation, the redhead stood, wiped the tears with the backs of her hands and picked up her suitcase. "Thank you, ma'am. I can go after I warm up some. I don't want to be a bother to you."

"If I thought you were going to be a bother, I wouldn't have opened the door. Now come in here and tell me what is going on."

Anne invited her to sit on the antique, red-stained, beech and pine Shaker meetinghouse bench that inhabited the space against the wall on the right side of the foyer. Above it was an expensive oil painting the designer assured Anne would "go well there." The bench had cost a little over twenty thousand dollars. No one at the Wentworth household, to her knowledge, had ever sat on the piece. That's what the interior designer called it, a piece.

"Now let's start from the start. Well, at least my start anyway. Exactly where did you get my address and who gave it to you?"

"Like I said, this man just volunteered it. I was at that convenience store over there on Peachtree Street. I asked if he knew where I might get some work. He was dressed real nice, wearing a tie and all. I thought he might be a banker or a lawyer. He got this sheet of paper out of his briefcase and wrote your address on it. I don't know his name or anything. Ma'am, I don't even know your name."

"Well, I guess that makes us just about even, because I don't know yours either. But my name is Anne, with an E, Wentworth. I don't know why I threw that E in there, just habit, I guess. And you?"

"My name is Becky Lynn Gregor."

"And, what's the rest of the story Becky Gregor? Did you just materialize on Peachtree this morning?"

"No, ma'am. And people call me by both names, Becky Lynn."

"Well sweetie, Becky Lynn, if you have a story, now is the time to tell it."

"Yes, ma'am. I got here in Atlanta last night on the bus. I come from Hollins, Alabama, in Clay County. It's near Sylacauga."

"Ah ha!" Anne exclaimed. "That accounts for the Sylacauga Aggies on your sweatshirt."

"Yes, ma'am. Sylacauga is in Talladega County. Maybe you've heard of the Talladega racetrack and all that? Well, anyway, that's where I'm from, and I left to start a new life. Do you have a bathroom I can use?"

"Yes," Anne said. "Go down that hall near the end and you'll see a bathroom on your left."

"Thank you," Becky Lynn said as she rose to enter the hallway.

Anne, sitting on the meetinghouse bench, picked up the piece of paper left there by Becky Lynn. On it was her address, 1716 Reid Lane NW, written in blue ink by an ink pen with a broad nib. The writing was bold. The figure seven in her address had a slash through it like the Europeans make when they write a seven. Somehow it reminded her of the F in the name on a Fender guitar. She held the plain white paper up to observe the watermark. It was Strathmore Writing business stationery twenty-five bond paper, quite common in the world of commerce. Nothing else seemed unique.

3

"HAVE YOU HAD ANYTHING TO eat? When was the last time you ate?"

"I had a Snickers earlier this morning at the convenience store, but that's all."

"Good-ness. I'll bet you're starving. Let's go into the kitchen and get you something to eat. Do you like eggs and bacon?" Anne asked as she walked through the foyer, through the stair hall and the edge of the great room to arrive at the kitchen, talking all the while. "How about an omelet? And I have some sourdough bread, we can make some toast. And coffee. Do you drink coffee? Do you drink it strong or mild?"

"Ma'am, I don't want to be a bother."

"Becky Lynn, to me a bother is the same thing as a nuisance, and you aren't a nuisance. I would like for you to sit down over there at that table and relax."

Becky Lynn settled in at the breakfast table, observing everything around her as Anne began accumulating the ingredients for the upcoming meal. She had never seen such elegance, and this was just the kitchen and the breakfast area. The copper-clad pots and pans hanging from the bronze kitchen pot rack chandelier, the hand-woven Persian runner rug separating the kitchen from the breakfast area, the glass-doored double-wide Sub-Zero Pro 48 refrigerator, and the table and chairs themselves where she sat, obviously old and expensive.

They sat and quietly ate, Anne not so much as she had eaten just an hour before, and Becky Lynn, eating like she hadn't in two days. Becky Lynn, being more focused on the meal and not light conversation, hardly spoke at all.

"Now, where is it you're from? Suskalula?"

"No, ma'am, it's Sylacauga, but I'm really from Hollins. Alabama."

"Now, I'm going to ask you a few questions, and I want you to be dead honest with me. There's a lot depending on your answers. Okay?"

"Yes, ma'am. I tell the truth. What are your questions?"

Anne set forth with a series of questions that tied together Becky Lynn's story, her credibility, her honesty, determined by how she answered repetitive questions, and her character. Have you ever been arrested? Do you do drugs of any kind? Do you drink, or do you have a drinking problem? Do you have brothers and sisters? What do your parents do for a living? What would appear on a search of county or state records about your background? How far along did you get in school? What did you do for a living in Alabama before coming here? Why did you pick Atlanta? And on and on.

Becky Lynn gave quick, concise answers, not mixing up her responses or averting her eyes away from Anne at any time. She didn't cover her mouth when she spoke. She didn't repeatedly clear her throat. She didn't touch her face or other vulnerable parts of her body. She didn't groom her hair. All tells of when someone is lying. She sat still. Her breathing steady. Anne thought Becky Lynn to be honest.

After the inquiry, Anne pushed slightly back from the table. "Here is what I want you to do. Get that big green avocado you're dragging around and take it to the bedroom at the end of the hall where you used the bathroom. Then, I want you to take a bath or a shower, whichever you prefer, get cleaned up and put on some clean clothes. Do you have any clean clothes in your suitcase?"

"Yes, ma'am."

"Okay. Now we're going to stop saying ma'am with each and every response, and we are just going to say yes or no, or even uh-huh or uh-uh. And when you are done in the bathroom, I want you to come back here, to the kitchen, and I'll be waiting for you."

"Can I help you clean up before I go?"

"No, that will give me something to do while you bathe."

4

BECKY LYNN WAS NOW FULL, clean, and warm. She stood at the entrance of the kitchen wearing a simple white cotton front-buttoned blouse, a black knee length pleated skirt, and black flats. She looked like a cross between a charter school student and a carhop from the 1950s. Of her long red hair, one might say it to be "all over the place." She was not pretty in the fashion or social sense, but she had a certain composition that drew attention. Maybe the smile, or just the pleasant oval shape of her face. Her red hair, brown eyes, and abundant assemblage of freckles gave testimony to her Scots-Irish heritage.

"Come and sit," Anne said. "I would like for you to tell me more about yourself."

And she did.

Becky Lynn Gregor came into this world in Sylacauga, Alabama, the daughter of a promiscuous sixteen-year-old high school girl, Bonnie Gregor, who found drinking, drugs, parties, and sex much more exciting than the drudgeries of schoolwork and discipline. Upon learning of her pregnancy, her family, both close and extended, insisted that she give birth and keep the child. On the child's birth certificate, the word "unknown" appeared on the line requesting the name of the father. Soon after giving birth, she fled her home and daughter. The bonds and the bondage of motherhood did not fit into her dreams and schemes. She gave the baby a name and nothing else. The most popular suggested name, and dark joke, among the males of the community turned out to be Bananas, after the bunch.

Becky Lynn's maternal grandparents, as all expected, took the baby girl into their home in Hollins, Alabama. For the first five years of her life, all went well. Then her forty-four-year-old grandfather, Braxton Gregor, developed pancreatic cancer and died within months. In the years following, at age eleven, she experienced the death of her grandmother, Loretta Gregor, brought on by a chronic lower respiratory disease that went specifically unidentified. Fortunately, and at the same time unfortunately, her uncle Stanley, the brother of her grandfather, took her into his care as guardian.

Stanley Gregor, age fifty-four at the time, carried a reputation around Hollins of being a religious zealot, or maybe even a fanatic. He also had the reputation of being the hard-working proprietor of a dry cleaning and laundry business. Stanley had never married. His devotion to his business aligned evenly with his devotion to the Evangelical Church of Jehovah. Becky

Lynn endured the wrath of his enthusiasm for the next seventeen years of her life, until she exercised her right to freedom.

Uncle Stanley was strict, demanding, and abusive. Strict in that he required her to attend any and all church services, tithe ten percent of her meager wages earned at the laundry, never make an error at work, or have a meaningful relationship with a man. He limited her dress to simple, monochrome garments, required she not cut her hair or have access to a computer. Television viewing was also monitored and limited. Demanding in requiring her labors six days a week at the dry cleaning and laundry business with no vacation and few holidays. Abusive in the sense that mental and physical abuse can be administered without the knowledge of anyone but the recipient of the abuse.

Uncle Stanley doled out both physical and mental abuse with the use of harsh language and open-handed hitting. Sexual abuse never occurred that would violate the underpinnings of his religious beliefs. The totality of the conditions and abuse, coupled with the limited exposure to the world beyond Hollins, kept her in a state of fear.

Naturally, this begs the question – why? For years, the answer in Becky Lynn's mind was simple enough. She owed it to him. For in all of those many years, hardly a day went by without a reminder from Stanley of his benevolence, sacrifice, protection, and care. Yes, she thought she owed him.

"I just had to get away, and get away from Uncle Stanley. My good friend, and nearly only friend, Teresa Jones, had been telling me to leave for a couple of years. I finally made up my mind to do it. Uncle Stanley went to Sylacauga yesterday afternoon to deliver laundry and cleaning to the shop outlet there where customers could pick them up. He spends more time there on Mondays. The Greyhound left Sylacauga for Atlanta at two-fifteen. Teresa came by after Uncle Stanley had gone. She took me to the bus station, well, the Exxon station, where the bus stops. I bought a one-way ticket for twenty-three dollars and got on. Goodbye Hollins, and goodbye Uncle Stanley. Mrs. Wentworth, I'm scared to death."

"Not in my house," Anne said. "What time did you get here from Sylacauga? And where did the bus let you off?"

"I got here at nine-fifty-five, ten minutes ahead of schedule. The station is on Forsyth Street, just a block or so from Peachtree."

"Really?" Anne quipped. "I didn't know that."

"Well, me and Teresa had studied the lay of the land, you might say. She said, and I agreed, it would be good if I first went to one of the more established locations here in Atlanta, if you know what I mean? The MARTA train runs right along Peachtree, so I got on and came out here."

"You were on that bus for eight hours? Goodness gracious. Where did you spend the night?"

"Actually, I slept behind the convenience store since there was a bathroom there. It wasn't too bad until the rain came. I didn't want to sleep in a hotel because I don't have all that much money to spend."

Anne looked at Becky Lynn for about fifteen seconds. An eternity for Becky Lynn because she didn't know what was coming next.

"Would you like to tell me where and how you got the bruise on the side of your neck? I don't think that's a hickey if you know what I mean."

"No, ma'am, I know what a hickey is and it's no hickey. I must have gotten it rough-housing with Uncle Stanley. He's a lot stronger than I am."

"Those days are over, and you've come here to start a new life," Anne stated. "And that's exactly what you are going to do. Goodbye Hollins and goodbye Uncle Stanley. Go get that big green suitcase. We have work to do."

5

BECKY LYNN LUGGED HER BIG green suitcase from the front bedroom to the back door of the house where Anne stood and waited for her. Anne opened the door and said, "We're going right over there." 'Over there' stood the Wentworth guest house, all eighteen hundred square feet of it. To Becky Lynn it was a mansion. But compared to the main house and its sixty-five hundred square feet, the guest house looked like a bungalow. Anne inserted a key into the lock and opened the door.

"This is where you will be staying Becky Lynn. You can have your choice of bedrooms. I doubt if Ava has any food in the fridge, but we will fix that."

"Ma'am, you are awfully nice, but I can't afford to stay here," Becky Lynn said.

"Oh, I'm sorry if I even implied that I expected payment of any kind. This is our guest house and you are our guest.

So, for now, here is what I would like for you to do. First, make yourself comfortable. Unpack your suitcase, get 'the lay of the land,' as you say. I have to go back to the main house to wrap up a couple of things. Since you are starting your new life, get some paper and a pen out of the drawer over there and write down the three most important things you feel you need to do, or want to do, right now. No long-range stuff. I'm talking about the now.

"I also want you to give me your cell phone number so we can communicate by texting. It beats running back and forth."

"I don't have a cell phone. Uncle Stanley wouldn't let me have one. He said they are the direct dial-up to sin, maybe worse than a computer."

"You have got to be kidding me! Well, we are going to fix that, too. Let's say you just come back to the house for lunch at twelve-thirty. Is that alright with you?"

"Yes, ma'am."

"Excuse me," Anne said politely.

"I mean, yes."

Anne departed to finish her chores, as she called them. Chores meant twisting the arm of big business for contributions to her primary charities of choice, Atlanta Primary Education Foundation and Mercy Care. Healthcare and education for children. For Anne, that's what mattered the most.

At exactly twelve-thirty Becky Lynn approached the back door. She didn't have to knock as Anne saw her coming across the flat, river stone, walkway to the main house. The sun had popped through the clouds and its rays highlighted Becky

Lynn's long red hair. It still lacked luster and was a bit in disarray as the breeze lofted it to and fro. She carried a piece of paper in her right hand.

"Come in, come in," Anne said. "Let's go sit at the table, have a bite to eat, and look at what you came up with for your list of things to do."

Both women took pleasure in a grilled American cheese sandwich and a cup of tomato soup. They drank San Pellegrino sparkling water, and each enjoyed a Biscoff cookie for dessert. The conversation was light, each asking questions and giving answers. Finally, Anne said, "Let's take a look at your list."

There, in black and white, printed in neat, blocked letters, appeared Becky Lynn's to do list:

1. Buy some new clothes.
2. Find a job.
3. Get my hair cut short.

"Those are excellent goals. I am, however, surprised by number three. I thought your hair kind of made a statement about who you are."

"My hair makes a statement about the control Uncle Stanley had over me. It's time for it to go."

"Very interesting, and good for you. That takes courage. How short do you want to get it cut?"

"Not quite as short as yours, but close. Maybe shoulder-length."

"Now that we are on the subject of cutting things short, and the fact that you are looking to start a new life, what do you think about truncating your name by dropping the

Becky? I don't mean to be rude, but when I hear the name Becky Lynn, I keep waiting for you to break out singing a country song."

Becky Lynn laughed as Becky Lynn for the last time. "I think that is a wonderful idea, Lynn it is."

"We will start those projects tomorrow, with gusto. And this evening I expect you to come to dinner and meet my husband, Jason. Now I suggest you go back to the guest house and take a nap. You must be worn out from the trip and spending the night behind a C store."

6

Anne sat at her 1885 antique oak English Tudor dining set that cost nearly twelve thousand dollars, plus the designer's commission, plus sales tax. The designer said the set was just begging to live in the Wentworth's breakfast nook, if nearly one hundred-thirty square feet constituted a nook. She sat there sipping tepid black coffee, mindlessly staring at a small stand of pines that hugged the eastern edge of the property line. The pines reminded her of her roots in northern Georgia. Her thoughts soon focused on Becky Lynn, now Lynn. What was her complete story? Near poverty, abused, undereducated, suppressed and obviously cowered. Anne, unlike Jason, did not win "the lucky sperm game" as some of Jason's friends kidded him. Raised in northern Georgia in a middle class family of seven, she never went without the staples of life, but she also didn't share in the grandeur. Far from it. But she had never been pushed around, except by her four older brothers for "gettin' in their stuff" or snitching on one of them for getting out of line with the family rules. Anne was a rule follower. No one had ever yelled at her, except her brothers, and no one had ever laid a finger on her, period. Had such an event occurred, the perpetrator would have most certainly received a visit from not one, but all four brothers.

Fate, luck, timing, God's hand. What did separate her from someone like Lynn? She knew the question would never be answered, but at the same time she felt like it was somehow not rhetorical.

One could certainly say that Anne Willis Wentworth came from a humble beginning. The headline to that fact: Being raised in Mineral Bluff, Georgia, a postage stamp sized burg of only 150 people on the Tennessee border, right in the middle of some of the heaviest timbered lands in the country. Her father, a botanist, frequently consulted with the federal government about timber preservation in the sprawling Chattahoochee National Forest. At other times he worked as a forestry agent for private landowners, serving as the liaison between the owners and the timber mills. Wishing to follow in her father's footsteps, she enrolled in the University of Georgia in Athens where she initially majored in botany, and forestry and natural resources. After one school year in Athens, she learned two things: one, she knew she would never return to Mineral Bluff or any place resembling it, and two, she had no desire to be a forester. She changed her major to landscape architecture.

It took Anne little time to adjust to the more rewarding life college had to offer. Between her academic scholarship for being the valedictorian of her senior class and a partial scholarship for playing tennis, she never had to be concerned about money for tuition, meals, and boarding so long as she lived in a university dormitory on campus. The responsibility for her books rested with her. Between her studies, playing tennis, and enjoying her membership as a sister of Kappa Kappa Gamma, she considered her college experience perfect.

Upon graduation, she accepted an offer to work for Land Architecture Studio, the largest, and most successful landscape design firm in Atlanta. She was so pleased to call her father to tell him she had a position with Land Architecture. He said, "Sweetie, what you have is a job, not a position. You have to earn the position." She dedicated herself to two activities, work and physical fitness. She never shied away from an assignment and never let the masculine atmosphere of landscape architecture interfere with her decision making. She continued to play tennis and run, utilizing her five-seven frame and slender, athletic body.

Assigned with her group to a challenging project for the grounds of an office complex being bid by Wentworth Construction, she met a sandy-haired, blue-eyed project manager named Jason. There were a lot of people being introduced at the same time and she didn't catch his last name. She did think about him that evening. The next day she learned his last name. Ironically, she didn't connect it with the construction company. She boldly asked him to join her for lunch under the guise of business development. They never dated anyone else and were married eighteen months later.

Anne possessed what some would call timeless beauty. She would still be stunning at age eighty. Unlike the silly Hollywood types who try to perpetuate their attractiveness by going under the scalpel of a plastic surgeon, Anne's flawless features would endure, even with age.

Anne's dark brunette hair, cut in a blunt off-the-shoulder-length bob, showed a few dozen gray hairs. Not uncommon for someone who had attained the age of forty-six. This matter, brought to her attention one day by Jason, seemed to worry her not.

"Do you think you'll do something about the gray hair?" Jason asked.

"Like what? Dye it? Why, are you afraid of gray hair?" she inquired.

"Well, don't you think gray hair might make you look old?"

"Oh, let's see Jason. I believe you, shall we say, appreciate the looks of Emmylou Harris, the singer."

"Well, yeah. She's, uh, pretty hot."

"'Nuff said."

7

JASON WENTWORTH WHEELED HIS COMPANY owned navy blue Cadillac Escalade, with the specialized Georgia license plates that read STINGER, into the third bay of the three car garage at the house on Reid Lane NW. At age forty-eight, he sat as Chairman of the Board and President of Wentworth Construction, the biggest privately owned commercial construction company in the South. Although quite an accomplishment, it hadn't hurt that his grandfather, Joseph Wentworth, had started the company thirty years before Jason was born. A good number of people said Jason was born on third base and thought he hit a triple. However, the evidence would show that the company had expanded tenfold after Jason ascended to its top positions.

As an honors graduate of the Georgia Tech School of Civil and Environmental Engineering and recipient of a Master of

Science in Building Construction and Facilities Management degree, he held the educational credentials to justify his position. But formal education alone did not pave the way to his success. It was his education from the school of hard knocks that truly gave him the competitive edge and skills to command the organization. At the age of sixteen, too young under the Georgia insurance laws to hold such a job, he went to work for his grandfather, or better stated, his grandfather's company.

He worked summers, long days in the heat, and part-time during the school years as a blue-collar laborer. He was paid as little as the law would allow. He had a "farmer's tan," calluses, and dirt under his fingernails. He started as a gofer, then as a member of the road flag crew, ascending up through the chain of responsibility and trades. He learned to weld, to plumb, to paint, to wire, to pour concrete, to shoot a line with a surveyor's transit level. As an understudy, he put his hands in, or on, nearly every phase of the business at a job site. By age twenty-four, with his on-the-job training and his educational background, he knew as much about the commercial construction industry as any experienced superintendent with the company.

Upon graduation from Tech, he was ready to begin his career as a contractor in the field. That's when he learned about the other phases of the business. Although Jason knew he was ready for the challenge in the field, his grandfather had other plans. Jason's first assignment with Wentworth Construction shocked him, being placed as a full-time employee in the accounting and business offices. He suffered a one-year apprenticeship before finally being reassigned to the bid department, all the while being paid the least acceptable wage for a college graduate with his credentials. Finally, after two years of what he considered pure torture, he received his promotion to the construction division.

His grandfather told him that understanding the workings in accounting, and the business office, and the bid process was just as important as building structures. He personally saw to it that Jason built a solid foundation for his future in the business. By Jason's fortieth birthday, he had reformed the company and made it wildly successful. However, Joseph's fingerprints could still be found in the fabric of Wentworth Construction: honesty, integrity, quality, and safety.

Jason's father, Troy, had no interest in the construction industry. Instead of construction, music intrigued him, even at a young age. His father, in turn, had the character and thoughtfulness to allow Troy to follow his own rising star. With no real interest in material wealth, Troy informed his father, in no uncertain terms, of his lack of interest in the business. Troy obtained a Ph.D. in music and became a tenured professor at Georgia State University in Atlanta, where he ultimately accepted a promotion to Director of the School of Music and later to the dean of the College of Arts.

As the only child of Joseph, Troy's choice of career stymied the plans of succession. Fortunately, Joseph learned early on that Jason, the only son of an only son, had an aptitude for construction. The thought never entered the grandfather's mind that Jason would not succeed him. At Joseph's death, he owned only twenty percent of the company, which he left to his son, Troy. He had informed Troy that he wanted him to enjoy a comfortable life in his retirement years, without the worry of money. The major interest in the company, eighty percent, had been gifted to Jason over many years. He bequeathed the balance of his fortune to numerous charitable institutions in and around Atlanta. His millions improved the lives of thousands.

At age forty-eight, Jason felt as though he was just hitting his stride. The company was still growing as Atlanta and the surrounding states continued to grow at what seemed to be a linear progression. The push provided by the 1996 Olympics in Atlanta could not have been scripted better in helping the company. He had expanded the company's footprint into most of the surrounding states and a good-sized chunk of central Texas. The positive economic impact of the business could not be understated. People thought Jason Wentworth constructed buildings; what he did was create jobs.

One of his many positive attributes was his focus on health. He maintained his body in excellent physical condition. His six-foot frame carried his two hundred pound weight quite well. He golfed, rather well, cycled, played racquetball, and practiced yoga. He consumed alcoholic beverages very infrequently and followed a healthy eating plan. He strongly encouraged his top executives to manage their physical health and provided the opportunities for them to do so.

As with most people in their forties, Jason progressively developed presbyopia, or simple farsightedness. He joked that being a Presbyterian caused the problem. His remedy: place one pair of 1.25 diopter reading glasses just about everywhere. He had a pair in his office, the Escalade, his field pickup truck he kept at the office, the bedroom, his study at home, in the den, and in the breakfast nook. He disliked carrying them around.

Jason Wentworth was rich, owned an extraordinarily successful company, had a beautiful wife, and lived in a home that would be the envy of nearly anyone. From the outside looking in, Jason had a perfect life.

8

JASON ENTERED THE HOUSE THROUGH the door from the garage, passed by the pantry, and into the kitchen where he found Anne preparing the evening meal. From the smell he discerned something special. He did not approach Anne. In a time before, he would have gone to her and kissed her on the forehead.

"What's up with the lasagna?" he asked. "It smells great."

"We have a special guest joining us for dinner this evening. I hope you don't mind?"

"Why would I mind? I get to eat your lasagna, and if it's one of your ladies from the League or one of your beloved Kappa sisters, I can head to the study and leave you to your own designs," Jason said.

"No, our guest is Lynn Gregor from Hollins, Alabama. I think you will find her very interesting."

"Hollins, Alabama. Where is Hollins, Alabama?" Jason asked.

"Near Sylacauga."

"Boy, that really clears things up," Jason said with mild sarcasm. "Never heard of it. So, what's the story on Lynn Gregory?"

"Gregor," Anne said. "Her name is actually Becky Lynn Gregor and she's here in Atlanta to start a new life. She'll tell you all about it at dinner. Now go wash up and relax for a bit. We'll eat in thirty minutes."

With those instructions, Jason wandered off to the master bedroom and then his study. He ran a couple of scenarios through his mind about the mystery guest. Was this going to be another fiasco like the one they had with the Haitian woman? Or maybe the Vietnamese nail technician?

Being an informal dinner, they would eat in the nook. The nook had become the primary place to gather since the formal dining room no longer fit many needs.

Lynn knocked on the back door at six-thirty sharp. Anne invited her inside. She wore a long-sleeved blue blouse, gray slacks, the same black flats she wore earlier, and red hair that seemed to be all over the place.

"Would you like a hairband or barrettes? I have some in my bedroom."

"No, thank you," Lynn said. "This is the way I wear it. My uncle said it shouldn't be cut, braided, pulled back in a ponytail or bound in any way. So, I don't. If I had, I would have paid for it with a lot of yelling and maybe a good swat.

I thought since I'm planning on cutting it, I'd just keep it like, you know, I always have."

"Okay," Anne said. "I think I understand."

Jason entered the room and was introduced to Lynn. During dinner, Anne informed Jason of everything she knew about Lynn. About her trip to Atlanta, sleeping behind the C store and having been given the note with their address. Lynn filled in some gaps since she was the one with the firsthand experience.

Then it was Jason's turn for a rather detailed, but friendly, interrogation. He asked about her background, her family, her education, and nearly anything else that flowed into such conversations. She explained how her uncle's involvement in the church guided his staunch belief system and impacted her. How the church seemed to consume her life.

"Did y'all handle and worship rattlesnakes?" Jason asked.

"No!" Lynn exclaimed. "I'm from Alabama, not Kentucky."

The conversation went on for nearly three hours. The more Lynn discussed her upbringing and life situation, more questions came to mind. She told of the creature comforts of today's world that she had done without. No car, no cell phone, no pets, censored television, no haircuts, and very few friends. Like Anne, Lynn's answers and comments intrigued Jason. The conversation covered the spectrum, from light laughter about humorous stories to heartfelt sorrow for the lack of civility she endured.

Then Lynn asked, "When will your children be home? I've seen their pictures around. They are so adorable."

"The children won't be coming home," Anne said, with little inflection in her voice. And with that she rose to clear the table. "Lynn, why don't you meet me here at eight-thirty tomorrow morning because we have a lot of work to do."

Jason helped Anne clean the kitchen and asked what her plans were regarding her new charge. "Don't get too involved," he said.

"Jason, sometimes you do have to get involved. That poor girl needs some help. She's lived a horrific life up to this point and she needs a break. We have enough money to burn a wet elephant, so don't be concerned about what I might spend. She needs help. If I can get her straightened up and employed, I'll be happy. And yes, I know, I can't save the world one person at a time, but I can try."

"I just hope you have better luck than the last two excursions you've taken into saving the world. It's not the money. I just don't want you to get hurt, any way you cut it."

9

THREE RAPID KNOCKS BROUGHT LYNN quickly to the front door of the guest house. Upon opening the door, she saw a solidly built, middle-aged, black lady wearing a light brown, double-breasted pincord house-keeping dress. From Lynn's experience at the cleaners, she knew the garment was expensive compared to simple woven cotton.

"Good morning, my name is Ava, and Miss Anne asked me to check to see if you need anything," Ava said.

"I don't think I need anything right now," Lynn replied.

"Well, do you have anything to drink in that refrigerator?"

"No, ma'am, I don't think so."

"And do you have anything in those cabinets you can eat, like a snack or something?"

"No, ma'am, I don't think so."

"Well, to me it sounds like you need a few things, and I'll take care of it. I'm Miss Anne's day help. And you can dispense with the ma'am business, I'm just the help. I work on Monday, Wednesday and Friday. Now for you, I'll be checking to see that everything is okay and if you need anything. I won't be messin' with your stuff, so you don't have to worry about that."

"I don't have any stuff," Lynn said.

"You will. Now, I'll be changing your bed linens on Mondays and Fridays. And Wednesday, today, is wash day. If you have anything you want washed make sure you put it in the dirty clothes hamper there in the bathroom. And general cleaning can take place anytime as long as I don't interfere with what you're doing, and I always knock."

"Well, thank you very much Ava. My name's Becky Lynn Gregor. I mean Lynn Gregor. Right now, I'm doing just fine, but I appreciate you telling me everything."

"I'll be bringing you some soft drinks, iced tea, and snacks. If there is something you need, just write it on a piece of paper and leave it there by the kitchen sink. I'll see it and take care of it."

"Thanks again," Lynn said.

"You're welcome. Just let me know if I can help you in any way," Ava said as she reached to close the door. 'My goodness that girl has a mess of red hair,' she thought as she headed back to the main house.

Thirty minutes later, and right on time as Anne had requested, Lynn appeared at the back door and knocked. She was wearing a light green, knee length, unpleated dress, her black flats and a lot of red hair.

"Come in, come in," Anne said. "Let's get you some breakfast."

As Lynn ate, Anne made a few inquiries about Lynn's background, and Lynn, starting to feel more comfortable, asked questions about Anne and Jason, but nothing about children.

At nine o'clock Anne picked up her cell phone, tapped it three times and put it to her ear. "Can I speak with Alana, please? Alana, this is Anne Wentworth, and I have an emergency. I have a young lady who needs her hair cut in the worst way. Is there any way we could get in to see you today? Now I don't want to be a problem if you can't do it."

Alana Holiday, who had cut Anne's hair for at least fifteen years, said, "Hold on, let me check. In fact, can I call you back in about five?"

Alana dropped the phone back in its cradle on the wall. She got a pencil, picked up the receiver and started dialing. "Mrs. McMurrey, Alana here. I'm really sorry, but I am going to have to reschedule your appointment."

This transpired two more times as she cleared the boards for whatever time Anne Wentworth might require. Anne was her top paying customer, a mover and shaker in Atlanta, as Alana referred to her, and she made quality referrals.

Alana then dialed Anne's number. "Anne, I'm available right now, and will be whenever you come in. Thirty minutes. Yes, ma'am."

Anne put down the phone and looked at Lynn. "You are getting a haircut in about thirty minutes. I think Alana will know exactly what you need. Let's go."

Anne and Lynn entered the waiting room of the Soren Salon, one of the top hair salons in Atlanta, and asked to see Alana. They were asked to have a seat, asked if they would care for coffee, tea, water, or a soft drink, and told that "Alana will be with you shortly."

"Shortly" was about thirty seconds. She came out of the door leading to the salon floor. "How can I help you Anne? Good lord girl, what are you doing with all that hair?"

"This," Anne said as she brushed the hair back out of Lynn's face, "is why we are here. This is Lynn Gregor, and she needs a haircut."

"What do you have in mind?" Alana asked, generally to both women.

"I want to get it cut short, but not as short as Anne's. But that's all I know."

"Okay, you come with me. Anne, have a seat. This is going to take a while." To Lynn she said, "You are a before and after dream come true. Do you mind if I take a few pictures before we begin this project, and I'll take some more when we're done? You won't even know yourself when we're finished."

"I'm actually afraid of that," Lynn said.

A little more than an hour later, Alana stepped through the door into the waiting room, held out her right arm toward the door in presentation fashion, and said, "Abracadabra."

With that introduction, Lynn stepped through the door and stood in front of Anne. Her hair, cut in a layered mid-length style, looked soft and conditioned. Medium-length bangs, angling down from right to left, shaded her brown eyes. Alana had applied just a touch of makeup. Anyone looking at her would not notice the plain light green dress she wore. Lynn, shy and reserved, blushed at the attention.

Alana said, "Wear it for a few days, and if you don't like it, come back in and I'll work on it some more. I can take more off, but I can't put more back on. That just takes time,"

"Lynn, that is a beautiful cut. Alana, you are just a magician. Now let's even up the score and hit the door. We're going to go buy a cell phone and get lunch, and buy clothes, and buy shoes, and buy underwear and maybe a bracelet, and whatever else we want."

As Anne and Lynn made their way out the front door, Alana watched and wished she could be Lynn for the day.

10

THEY JUMPED IN THE LAND Rover and began their quest. Anne headed east, in the direction of Lenox Square, the premier shopping mall for Buckhead and Atlanta. Generally speaking, if you couldn't find what you were looking for at Lenox Square, you probably didn't need it. Lenox Square consisted of nearly 200 different stores or shops on four levels. National brands to local merchants, the variety seemed limitless. Anne found a parking spot close to Neiman Marcus as luck would have it, and off they went.

"We are first going to the Apple Store and get you a cell phone. You'll wonder how you made it through life as far as you have once you get it and learn how to use it. You get the phone and then get a line at T-Mobile. Dang, it's already eleven. Let's try to get the phone business taken care of, and then we'll eat a light lunch at NM Café in Neiman's. I think we'll make some good progress today, but I can promise you we'll have to come back tomorrow. This is going to take some time to complete."

For two days they shopped. Neiman Marcus, Ann Taylor, Gap, Macy's, Calvin Klein, New Balance, Cole Haan, Ray-Ban, Anthropologie, Bloomingdale's, Levi's, and more. They had to make numerous trips from the mall to the Land Rover. Active wear, business attire, shoes, workout clothes, skirts, blouses, sweaters, pajamas, underwear, jackets, pants, shorts, and tops. Purses, belts, a wristwatch, and other accessories.

"Lynn, if whatever you try on doesn't make you feel wonderful, we won't buy it. Don't buy anything that you think you like, make sure you love it," Anne told her. "That's the only way you get what you want, and you'll feel good about it when you get home."

Simply going into the mall was an adventure for Lynn. She had heard of Lenox Square, but to see it was an experience. Shopping to her was getting to spend an afternoon in Sylacauga with a couple of female friends from church. Finding something in Sylacauga was an entirely different story. She had two burdens to overcome while shopping there. First, she wore a size zero. Size zero didn't exist in plentiful quantities in Sylacauga. Looking for a size fourteen, not a problem. Secondly, she had to satisfy the peculiar wardrobe requirements of Uncle Stanley. Simple, plain, dull, shapeless, and boring were not redundancies to Uncle Stanley. He reviewed all of Becky Lynn's purchases. He would also snoop through her belongings when she was away from the house and destroy whatever he found that he deemed to be unfit. Lynn found Lenox Square to be a wonderland.

"We got your north end taken care of this morning, so now let's work on the south end. Let's find you some shoes," Anne said. "Good shoes just make you feel better, both mentally and physically. And believe it or not, people really judge you by the shoes you wear. We're going to buy shoes that give you the edge."

The first shoe store they entered, called Ped-Appeal, showcased shoes in the window that Anne felt would be age-appropriate for Lynn. Personally, she had never been in the store. They looked at the various single shoes on display, all for the right foot, to determine if they were in the right type of store. After finding an interesting selection, a salesclerk, in true 'I could really care less' millennial fashion approached. "Are you interested in those shoes?" Her dilated pupils indicated she had either been to the ophthalmologist or she was stoned out of her gourd. If Anne had been placing a bet on the likelihood of either, the second won the day.

Anne, already put off by the lack of attentiveness when they entered the shop, wanted to say 'No, what we're looking for is a box of Mason jars, but these shoes may do.' Instead, she just politely stated, "Yes. For this young lady."

"Do you know, like, what size? You don't have very big feet."

"Why don't we measure her foot just to determine the size?" Anne asked.

The clerk asked Lynn to sit in one of the side chairs and she set about finding the measuring device. Lynn removed her shoe and stood on the measuring device, once provided.

"Oh, you wear a size five, and your foot is, like, narrow. I can tell you right now there's nothing in this store your size. And you'll have a hard time finding any shoes that will fit in hardly any of the stores here. I suggest you go to Nordstrom. They have, like, everything."

And so it went: shoes (later at Nordstrom), casual wear, blue jeans, athletic gear, and dresses for what Anne called "nicer occasions." Lynn said she had no desire to purchase jeans with holes cut across the legs. Anne understood why. They shopped store after store until Anne's feet hurt and Lynn's ability to comprehend the options and alternatives available to her seemed to blur.

While looking through the clothes racks in Macy's, Lynn noticed some T-shirts on hangers. Each T-shirt had a pocket that was stretched and out of proportion. The collar was stretched and frayed. There were little holes all over the shirt, looking like it had been sprayed with drops of acid. The price tag on the garment was eighty-five dollars.

"Would you look at that? That wouldn't have been thrown in the rag bag in Hollins, it would have gone straight into the trash. And they want eighty-five dollars for it?"

"If you want a worn out T-shirt, we have lots of them at home. Jason can't stand tossing out an old T-shirt. They all seem to be his favorite and he says they are more comfortable the older they get. I'll give you one."

After two days of exhaustive shopping, Anne declared them done, unless something else popped up that might be needed. Lynn's knowledge of clothes and fabrics acquired from years at Gregor Dry Cleaning and Laundry had impressed Anne. She would point out the variance in quality as to construction and materials. She selected the superior items, often priced less than the lower quality ones.

The evening of the second day, Anne spent several minutes telling Jason about the shopping spree and describing some of the items purchased. She told Jason how Lynn had marveled at the horn of plenty that was Lenox Square.

"She kept comparing everything to what more or less didn't exist in or around her hometown there in Alabama. I understand rural, and I know exactly how she feels. Believe me, Sylacauga had a lot more to offer than Mineral Bluff and 'surrounding communities' as they like to say. These last two days have made me feel like I have helped to defeat evil."

"Anne, I'm truly pleased that you feel like you do. And I'm glad you are able to help Lynn. But don't you think you might be getting a little ahead of yourself? You've only known this girl, what, two days? And you've spent thousands buying her a wardrobe and heaven knows what else. But it's not about the money, I'll state that up front."

"Jason, I know you're concerned. But there is just something about this young lady that I like. I think she has something to offer, and she just needs a little help getting there. My goodness, she's twenty-eight years old and way behind the curve, whatever the curve is. She has put up with and endured shit that I have a hard time even imagining. It's going to be okay."

"Well, you have to admit you have had a few misses with your charity endeavors. And yes, you have had some successes.

I don't want to see you getting burned. What if I send Jay Comsi over there to...."

"Hollins, Alabama."

"Hollins to check out her background. See what's going on with her?"

"You want to send your snoop-dog all the way over there? I guess it couldn't hurt. When do you think he can do it?"

"I don't know," Jason said. "I'll call him tomorrow. I know the company is his biggest repeat customer, so I expect he will be responsive. Jot down what you do know about her and I'll pass it along to Jay."

Jay Comsi, a private investigator frequently retained by Wentworth Construction, held Jason's confidence. Jay had a great rapport with Jason. As a former FBI agent, Jason actually envied Jay's skills and apparent freedom from stress. Jason would have him do what Jay called a "work-up" on new subcontractors bidding on work with the company. Jason didn't like incompetent subs and an investigation was the best way to avoid a problem before it started. Becky Lynn Gregor seemed to be the perfect candidate for a "work-up."

At the same time as the Wentworths discussed Lynn's prospects, she sat in the living room of the guest house surrounded by the bounty she received. In her mind she could not imagine the treasures around her, much less owning them. She cried.

11

ON MONDAY MORNING JASON TAPPED Jay Comsi's cell phone number in his contact information and waited. "Jay, good morning. I have a little project I'd like for you to do for me."

"When, what, and where?" Comsi responded.

"This one is a little out of the norm. I want you to do a background check on a woman from Hollins, Alabama. Her name is Becky Lynn Gregor."

"What's her line of business, and where in hell is Hollins, Alabama?"

"She's not in business, she's Anne's new protégée. I want to make sure she's not an ax murderer or something. When do you think you can do this for me?"

"I can't do anything today, but I'm open tomorrow. Just where is Hollins?"

"Apparently it's about one hundred and thirty miles kind of southwest of here," Jason said.

"How am I getting there? I'm guessing I'll be driving."

"You guessed right. I know you're not going to fly, but I understand you do have the Greyhound bus as an option," Jason said.

"Sounds like I'll be driving. What's it near?

"Sylacauga."

"How silly of me," Jay exclaimed. "That's between Mudville and Whoville, right?"

"Look, I'll send you an email with everything I know about her, which isn't much. That's why you're getting the job. But here's the good news, I think you get to drive through Talladega."

"Woohoo! And are you wanting a written report on this?"

"No, just take good notes, like I know you will, and give me an oral report. That should suffice."

That evening Comsi scoured the internet trying to find information about Becky Lynn Gregor or any combination of the name. He found nothing more than the fact that she held a valid driver's license. Now, more interested, he looked forward to his trip. Comsi liked face-to-face interviews the best because the interviewees give facial expressions and show reaction to the questions asked.

He left early the next morning, heading west on Interstate 20 to near Hobson City, Alabama, where he turned onto State Highway 21, taking him through Talladega as Jason had said and on into Sylacauga. He had done his homework, knowing that Sylacauga was the metropolis and Hollins the suburb, if you will. Knowing small towns and strangers do not mix well, he pulled into the Sylacauga police station for his first stop. If the local authorities are aware of your presence, and know what you are doing, life goes by much more easily.

Jay extended his hand in greeting to Chief Steve Hall of the Sylacauga police force. "Chief, I wanted to introduce myself and let you know what I'm up to. My name is Jay Comsi and I'm a special investigator from Atlanta. I'm licensed to work and carry in Alabama, but I left my weapon at home. I'm here today to do a background analysis on a young lady named Becky Lynn Gregor, who I believe lives near your community."

The name caused the chief to focus a little sharper on Comsi. "Do you know something about Becky Lynn? See, she's been missing for a couple of days and her uncle has been looking for her and is worried sick about her. She seems to have just wandered off. Left just about everything she had and disappeared from over in Hollins. Now just exactly what do you know?"

"First of all, she is apparently well, and safe. She is currently visiting with a very respectable family in Atlanta, and I think she's quite comfortable. I'm sorry that I can't divulge the name of the family."

"Well, she's over eighteen and if she's safe, that's all I need to know. I can inform her uncle Stanley and then it's up to him if he wants to pursue the matter further. If you're gonna check out Becky Lynn, you might get some insight if you look into Stanley. He's as goofy as a peach orchard boar."

"I appreciate the input and it's a pleasure to meet you. Where's the best place to eat lunch?"

After enjoying the "Dirty South," an open-faced meatloaf sandwich with pimento cheese, sautéed spinach, a fried egg, and balsamic barbecue sauce, Jay first drove around Sylacauga before heading to Hollins. He wanted to get a feel for the place. Sylacauga had a population of about twelve thousand. Known as "the Marble City" for the white marble that was mined from a giant quarry west of town, the quarry had been a major provider of jobs in Sylacauga for many decades. He drove by the Gregor Dry Cleaning and Laundry building, which he found to be very old, but very well maintained.

He drove the ten miles to Hollins on a narrow, two lane, country road. If he had blinked when he drove through Hollins, he might have missed it. Hollins had little to show for itself. Two churches, no schools, a downtown that looked like it died in about 1919, which it did. Even the post office had closed in 2011. The burg offered two service stations with convenience stores and the world headquarters of Gregor Dry Cleaning and Laundry, Stanley Gregor, proprietor. The cleaning and laundry business seemed to be the largest employer in town with a high of twelve employees, now eleven.

Jay made a few quick inquiries with the people he came across. He asked about Becky Lynn first, not mentioning her location or well-being. As general knowledge, everyone Jay encountered knew of Becky Lynn's absence from Hollins. People were genuinely concerned for her safety and interested in her whereabouts. The recurring responses to Comsi: Becky Lynn is smart, friendly, and a hard worker. According to the interviewees, Becky Lynn ran the dry cleaning and laundry business.

He also queried people about Stanley and his reputation. Odd, introverted, controlling, miserly, and unorthodox seemed to hold true. Having determined Stanley to be odd but harmless, Jay, now prepared to interview him in person, entered the laundry building.

He was directed to a small office where the interview would take place. Comsi, after introducing himself, found Stanley Gregor to be about as cheerful and uplifting as a Tennessee Williams play.

"I would like to ask you some questions about Becky Lynn Gregor," Comsi began.

"Is she all right? Where is she? I need to get her back here. She's important to this business. I'm a person short right now."

The interview lasted about thirty minutes. He assured Stanley that Becky Lynn was in good health and not being held against her will. Uncle Stanley seemed willing to accept that.

He also interviewed Teresa Jones, Becky Lynn's friend who helped steal her away on the Greyhound to Atlanta. Teresa, thrilled to know of her friend's status, cried tears of joy. She withheld nothing of her opinions regarding Stanley and his relationship with Becky Lynn. According to Teresa, Stanley was oppressive with his fervent and adamant requirements regarding church attendance, his stifling control over her appearance, her relationship with others, and even her money. Teresa said she had been begging Becky Lynn to escape for years. She just knew that Becky Lynn would be turning her life around the day she stepped onto the bus for Atlanta.

Jay called Jason Wentworth from his car that evening. "I'm about twenty minutes from your house if you care to hear about my findings tonight. I know it's eight-thirty, but I have a lot on my plate tomorrow."

"That works for me, and it should be okay with Anne. Lynn is in the guest house, so you won't be seeing her."

Upon his arrival at the Wentworth's and greeting them with brief cordialities, Jay got down to business. "I started out in Sylacauga. It took me five minutes just to get the spelling correct. The police chief there was aware of her absence but didn't seem at all concerned when I explained her situation. He said based on her age and her apparent desire to leave, he had no further interest in the matter. He even said Stanley Gregor was a bit of a kook and he didn't blame her for leaving.

"Hollins," Comsi said, "is a completely different deal. It's not even a legal town. It's a census-designated place. Unincorporated. The population is about five hundred and fifty in the area if you don't count the dogs.

"Two of the people I interviewed, and not together, had interesting comments about Stanley. Both mentioned his, what they called 'religious fanaticism,' but each one also brought up mention of a shelter Stanley had built in his backyard. According to the interviewees, Stanley was an alarmist of un-known events. He thinks we will be hit by some uncontrollable pandemic at some point in the future. He just doesn't know when. He built this shelter, like a bomb shelter, in his back yard and he has been stocking it for years with non-perishable food products and stuff like soap and toilet paper. It sounded a little goofy to me, and I didn't bring it up in my interview with Stanley. I didn't see how it related to Becky Lynn.

"As for the girl, most, if not all, of the people I interviewed who knew her felt sorry for her. I didn't hear one word of complaint or criticism. They all seemed to be pleased that she had vacated the place. One lady said if Becky Lynn needed any help with money for her to get in contact and she'd send her what she could. Not your everyday runaway.

"Her uncle showed more interest in her as an employee instead of being a blood relative. That was obvious. He talked about her duties and responsibilities at the shop. To me, it sounds like he's sour because he's having to put in more hours himself.

"I found no record of anything. She does have a driver's license, she's never gotten a traffic ticket, she's not registered to vote, she graduated in the top ten percent of her class of sixty-six, she has no brothers or sisters. Her mother, a druggie, skipped out on her when she was born. She was raised by her grandparents until they passed of natural causes, and that's how she wound up with Stanley Gregor. She doesn't drink, she doesn't chew, and she don't go with the boys that do, if you'll excuse the expression. My summary on Becky Lynn is that she does four things: eat, sleep, work, and go to church. Her activities other than work and church are virtually nonexistent.

"Oh, there's one other item of interest I need to leave you with. Sylacauga is the hometown of Jim Nabors, AKA Gomer Pyle. Surprise! Surprise! Surprise!"

He had given a detailed reporting of his interviews, observations, and thoughts. He covered the results of his interviews with various members of the citizenry, Ms. Jones, and Uncle Stanley. His conclusion: Lynn is trustworthy, everyone was pleased to know her situation except Uncle Stanley, and no one expects her to return to Hollins, or Alabama for that matter. Uncle Stanley's biggest complaint seemed to be the loss of an underpaid employee. Now he had to replace his niece with a market-priced substitute.

12

LYNN HEARD THREE QUICK RAPS on her front door and she instinctively said, "Come in."

It was Ava, who greeted Lynn with a good morning and said she had come to pick up the laundry. It was Wednesday after all. Lynn darted to the clothes hamper to gather what she had.

"Ava, can I ask you a question?" Lynn asked.

Ava chuckled and said, "You already have. Do you have another one?"

"Yes, can you tell me about Anne's children? I assume the pictures of the kids in the house are her children. But I certainly won't ask her about them, or what might have happened. I can tell something happened."

"Well, Miss Lynn, I will tell you. But you better first come and sit at the table, it could take a few minutes. Oh, those beautiful chilren. Cole and Emma. Lord have mercy. I first came to work for Miss Anne sixteen years ago when her first child, Cole, was born. Emma, the little girl was born just twenty-two months later. It all happened six years ago when the chilren were at camp. It was their third day there...."

Cole Wentworth, age ten, and Emma Wentworth, age eight, would easily fit into any picture that purported to show members of the proverbial perfect family. Cole, a blonde haired, blue-eyed scrapper of a boy, had a competitive nature, a quick mind, and loved sports. His younger sister, Emma, with brunette hair and bright blue eyes like her mother, was more reserved, and more studious, but could take Cole to task when the challenge warranted it.

On a Sunday, in mid-July, Jason and Anne had driven their children to an athletic and adventures camp just north of Rome, Georgia, about eighty miles from Atlanta. The camp sat at the foothills of the southern end of the Appalachian Mountains range. Camp Action, for ages eight through fifteen, had been providing fun and summer activities for children for over fifty years. The camp offered specific sports for skill-building: football, basketball, baseball, tennis, volleyball, tumbling. A child could test them all, or just focus on one sport. There was no soccer. The owner could not tolerate the sport. For the non-team sports minded campers, the other activities included hiking, climbing, swimming, horseback riding, archery, and more. Cole was a repeat camper. It was Emma's first year.

Cole relished football and baseball. He intended to play in both the NFL and MLB, also the dreams of hundreds of thousands of other boys. Given the option, he would have invested most of his time in those two sports. His parents had a different plan. Their instructions included the necessity of Cole participating in events with his sister. Being as selective as possible, he spent at least one event period with his sister each day. He knew he would have to include this in the dreaded "letters home" each camper had the duty to write. The activities could not be conveyed verbally as all cell phones had been confiscated by the camp counselors. The children would not hear or see their parents until the first Sunday following opening day when the parents came to visit and enjoy lunch at the camp. Anne could hardly wait until Sunday.

"Friday at camp was a day when the chilren got to go to the Coosa River, where it flows out of Wiess Lake on the Alabama border. It was special. The chilren got to ride on inflated tubes that were pulled behind boats. All the chilren loved it," Ava said.

Cole coveted the thrill of being pulled behind the boat on a towable water tube. It was one of only three activities he had previously participated in other than football or baseball. He desperately wanted to go again and thought it would serve as a great dual-participation event with Emma. The problem, Emma did not want to go. After much begging and arm-twisting, Cole finally convinced her it was a fun thing to do. He told her even if she chose not to ride on one of the inflated tubes, she would have a great deal of fun just riding in the boat. He finally won her approval and participation, at least to go. She still had major reservations about the inflated tubes.

The day trip required a twenty-two mile bus ride to the Coosa river. Camp Action had three small-sized buses that would accommodate sixteen riders and the driver. The bus boarded by Cole and Emma, named Charger, led the pack. The campers were singing along with the counselor and having a big time, traveling south on Georgia State Route 100 where it intersects with Holland Chattoogaville Road. At this intersection, souls were lost, and hearts forever broken, for the Wentworth family.

Jeremy Lamb, a forty-one year old mill worker, driving east on Holland Chattoogaville Road, ran through the stop sign posted at Route 100. He had partied too much and too late the night before and had consumed two beers that morning to "shake out the cobwebs." He didn't want to be late for work. He needed his job. He had lost his last two due to alcohol consumption and tardiness.

The Ford F-150 pickup truck driven by Lamb hit Charger broadside. The truck hit the bus with such impact that the bus left the ground and flipped over and over, rolling down the embankment on the far side of Route 100, where it hit a large pine tree and came to a rest. Uncharacteristically in such a collision, the pickup followed the path of the bus. Lamb, knocked unconscious, somehow continued to press the accelerator to a still-running engine. The pickup slammed into the side of the bus a second time, crushing it against the tree.

The carnage was horrific. Twelve of the sixteen children on board lost their lives. The remaining four children were severely injured, one crippled for life. The quick action of the driver, badly injured himself, was instrumental in saving the lives of the remaining children.

Jeremy Lamb, as it too often seems, walked away from the accident after he regained consciousness. His seatbelt and airbag saved his life. However, he would never be late for work again, now employed as a janitor, so to speak, by the Georgia Department of Corrections. Sadly, he had been arrested five times for driving while intoxicated and his driver's license had been revoked for over two years. He was accustomed to prison life however, having served an eighteen month sentence for beating his third ex-wife. In Georgia, the penalty for first-degree vehicular manslaughter, a felony, can carry a sentence of three to fifteen years. If a driver is a habitual violator, the sentence is typically five to twenty years in prison. Ironically for Mr. Lamb, that stiffer sentence is per death. Lamb was sentenced to ten years in prison for each of ten deaths. The Chattooga County prosecutor reserved charging Lamb with two deaths in the very unlikely event that he may be paroled at some point in the future. At that time, additional charges would be brought. In essence, Lamb received a life sentence.

"It was horrible. So horrible. I was here when the DPS troopers came to the door. I greeted them and let them in. I knew right away something bad was wrong. They asked for Mister Jason and Miss Anne, but she was the only one here. I went to find her after having the troopers sit in the big room. When Miss Anne came into the room and saw the two troopers her face went ashen. One of the troopers suggested that she sit down. She also knew something bad had happened because two DPS troopers don't just drop by to visit. The first words out of her mouth were 'Is it Jason?' Mister Jason was returning from Charlotte where the company was building a building. He was in the company plane, which Miss Anne hated. She worried every time he flew in it. When one of the troopers said no, she closed her eyes. They told her, in the kindest and most tender way possible, about the wreck and the loss of lives, and that Cole and Emma were among them. One of the troopers pulled a white linen handkerchief from his pocket and gave it to her. I was shaking.

"In a very soft voice Miss Anne said, 'My God, what do I do now?' The troopers, as best they could, explained that the Chattooga County coroner in Rome had the chilren, but arrangements would have to be made. The troopers excused themselves and Miss Anne sat on that couch rocking back and forth and seeing or hearing nothing. She didn't move from that spot for three hours until her husband got home.

"It was the worst day of my life."

Lynn was stunned.

13

EACH SPRING, FOR ABOUT THE last twenty-five years, the ladies of the Junior League of Atlanta sponsor an affair titled Tour of Kitchens. The concept is simple. Ask twelve to fourteen prominent Atlanta ladies for permission to use their kitchens for public viewing. Charge a small fee for the privilege to wander through the monstrous homes that permeate the 30305 and the 30327 zip codes. It sounds pretty simple. But wait, there's more. There is a gala to be enjoyed by the League members, for a fee. There are luncheons to be enjoyed by anyone interested in attending, subject to seating availability, and a fee. Culinary demonstrations and tastings occur during the course of a day, for a fee. Each kitchen is opened for viewing just one day out of the two, and a time-slot of two hours is assigned to each. Often the designer of the kitchen, with a stack of business cards in hand, is available for questions, and show and tell. Looking from the bottom up at the Tour, it's a wonderful way for wealthy Atlantans to showcase their homes. Looking from the top down, it's a low cost, fundamentally simple activity to fill the coffers of the League. Each year the net proceeds come in at around $180,000. This money, in turn, flows outward to some twenty-seven selected Atlanta charitable organizations, most of which provide health or educational services.

The Tour is a self-guided, two day affair that focuses a lot of attention on the Buckhead subdivision. Buckhead is comparable to the Garden District in New Orleans, River Oaks in Houston, and Highland Park in Dallas. A requisite amount of green must be abundant to abide in any of these neighborhoods, and the reference is not to the lawn. The inhabitancy of Buckhead has a little better life and a much higher tax bracket than the average resident of Atlanta. Anne Wentworth's home, located in Buckhead, fits the model of what the League looked for in a home. Her kitchen, completely remodeled earlier in the year, became a perfect candidate for the Tour. Given all the coincidences of the remodel, the physical location of the 6,500-square-foot house, and Anne's willingness to participate, her kitchen won the honor as one of the selected few.

Jason hated the idea personally. Being cautious, conservative, and rich, he felt as though the Tour provided the not-so-worthwhile citizenry an opportunity to case the homes of Buckhead and return later for a Smith & Wesson funded shopping spree. In actuality, this dreadful suspicion concocted by Jason had never come to fruition. To give Jason comfort,

Anne enlisted the help of her near lifelong friend to come the day of the Tour to scout out the guests. Of course, the League had a bevy of volunteers on hand to aid with parking, questions, and direction to the toilet.

Paige Buchanan, locally known in close circles as Anne's best friend, jumped at the chance to observe people, make Jason feel comfortable and help the League. Any time Paige jumped in to help, the concentric circles from her splash reached far, and often touched many. She was a virtuoso at shaking down corporate leaders, and "the rich folks that live around here," as she was inclined to say, for money for good causes. She always said, "I'll put my money where my mouth is," and contributed hundreds of thousands of dollars to her charity du jour.

Anne's kitchen, on display during the ten to twelve time slot, sparkled. Everything from floor to ceiling had been replaced within the year except for the pot chandelier that hung over the location occupied by the range island. Anne's kitchen designer, retained by Anne's interior designer, had informed her that pot chandeliers were out of style in the modern kitchen. Anne informed both designers that the chandelier, being the most convenient and efficient fixture in her kitchen, would be staying. They both conceded, but of course a new design would be required. The interior designer, Brianna Stafford, and the kitchen designer, Dawn Phillips, had called to inform Anne that they were on their way and would arrive shortly, eager to answer any questions that might be thrown their way.

Lynn Gregor rounded out the kitchen crew. Dressed in her Neiman Marcus conservative two button navy blue blazer with matching slacks and a light blue tank top, she could have fit well anywhere in Atlanta. What didn't show were her nerves. So uncertain of herself in the situation, she wanted to return to the guest house.

"Paige, I want you to meet Lynn Gregor. She is who I told you about on the phone," Anne said.

"Lynn, it is so nice to meet you. I've heard a lot about you."

"Thank you, it's so nice to meet you too," Lynn replied, wondering all the while what Paige could have heard about her, as her story is not long to tell. At the moment, this added to her uneasiness. She felt like the object under a microscope.

"We're going to have some fun this morning and I'd like for you to help me if you don't mind. That outfit is the cutest. And I just love your hair. I wish my hair would behave like that."

Anne watched and listened from a few feet away. She had asked Paige to interact with Lynn to see how she reacted around other people. At this point, Anne had only seen her converse with salesclerks, Alana, and Jason. This could be the measure to determine how far into her shell she might reside.

Paige put Lynn at ease. By the time the designer bandits and the patrol squad from the League had arrived, Lynn, in the midst of it all, appeared as comfortable as if she owned the home herself. She followed the designer bandits around with the first two waves of viewers, then took tours by herself, never missing a beat as to product, function, or brand. "This is the forty-eight inch wall oven and cooktop combination..." "This is the double-wide Sub-Zero Pro 48..." "The black granite countertops are sourced from Maine..." "To start the fire, you just push this little doohickey..." The designer bandits by the end of the tour just stood back and watched.

"Lynn," Anne said, "I must say I am impressed with your composure and confidence in dealing with all these people here today. Given your situation, I know I couldn't have accomplished what you did. I think you have a future here in Atlanta."

14

PAIGE BUCHANAN, ORIGINALLY FROM SAVANNAH and a Simmons
by birth, had three things that many others coveted: head-turn-
ing beauty, a highly functioning mind, and extreme wealth.
The Simmons family, a multigenerational clan, owned and
operated ocean-going freighters. The business flourished and
had for centuries dating back to 1787. A pure Southern Belle
and former debutante, Paige possessed the class, the style, and
accent that set her apart from anyone else in a room. At the
same time, she had the charm and unassuming nature to make
anyone feel comfortable in her presence in just about any situation. With attribution to her family's seagoing history, she could
also cuss like a sailor when she felt as though a particular situation might warrant it. The fact that she stood only five-three,
according to her, never diminished her willpower. She would
stand toe-to-toe with anyone. She would not be intimidated.

Fortunately for Anne, and for Paige, they met the first day of sorority rush at the University of Georgia. Paige, a Kappa Kappa Gamma legacy, but sought out by all of the other sororities on campus, loved meeting the people. Anne, having been persuaded to participate in rush by her great aunt, felt as out of place as a dedicated Baptist preacher at a craps table in Las Vegas. They instantly bonded, forming a friendship that would endure a lifetime. After Anne pledged Kappa, Paige intended for them to live together at the Kappa house once they were initiated. In the meantime, perhaps they could live together in the dorm. At that juncture, Anne felt the concept of living together might be coming to an end. Anne's scholarships required that she live on campus in the least modern, least expensive dorm. Anne could not afford the school otherwise. But true to her nature, Paige changed her dorm residence from the newest, classiest, most expensive dorm on campus to move into the old dorm with Anne. Unknown to Anne, Paige prepaid the rent differential for Anne's originally assigned roommate so she could afford to live in the higher costing facility.

The two scheduled some core classes together their freshman and sophomore years, but that ended when their major study classes became necessary. Anne, the landscape architecture major, gave the time needed to accomplish her goal of graduating at the top of her class. Paige, after changing majors three times, finally settled on philosophy.

"Well gee Paige, that's a little variance from physics. But let's see. Both words start with ph and they're Greek based. Other than that, I don't see a lot of correlation."

"Physics, I'm told, is natural philosophy. It's a science dealing with the properties, changes, and interaction of matter and energy, right? On the other hand, the study of philosophy permits you to see the connection between ideas, and to explicate that connection in a reasoned and logical manner. Very simply put, in physics, I have to prove to the professor that I'm right, but in philosophy, the professor has to prove me wrong. I like my odds with philosophy. Besides, all the great thinkers were philosophy guys, and it will drive my dad nuts."

"I never asked. What does your dad want you to major in? Or does he have a preference?"

"Finding a husband, I think. Preferably one that plays football and wants to be in the freighter business."

"I think it's time for pizza and beer. Let's go, Socrates."

Anne and Paige were in lockstep with just about everything, except music. Anne's favorite singer was country star George Strait. Paige told Anne she had grown up too close to Tennessee and had too much country in her blood, or maybe hillbilly. Anne took no offense. Paige, on the other hand, enjoyed and admired the music of Elton John. Both easily tolerated each other's choice of musicians.

For four years they were nearly inseparable, except during the summers. Anne went back to Mineral Bluff where she strengthened her resolve to never return once she graduated and Paige would return to Savannah where she "helped my mom buy more crap we didn't need." They stayed in touch by telephone, long distance back in those days, and talked every night they could. Paige always initiated the call because she could afford the charge.

Most students abandoned the campus dorms starting their third year. Anne had a collar around her neck that kept her on campus, her scholarships. Paige, anxious to move away from dorm life, offered to pay for Anne's expenses if she would agree to move into an apartment. Anne vehemently refused. Anne had grown quite accustomed to Paige's wealth, especially after her first trip to Savannah with Paige. But she would not forego what she had worked so hard to achieve at anyone's expense.

Paige saw the remedy as quite simple. She chose to rent an apartment off campus to serve as a gathering point for weekend fun and frolic. She had convinced her father that the need for the apartment was scholastic. Studying in the dorm was troublesome with the interruptions. Besides, she couldn't abandon her friend Anne. Her father approved the rental of the apartment. In true seamanship form, the apartment was christened Safe Harbor.

At graduation, each regretted the parting of their ways. Anne, with her job offer from Land Architecture, moved on to Atlanta. Paige, because she thought it might be interesting, enrolled in law school at Columbia in New York City. They continued to talk frequently, based on predetermined times, as the availability of both became more limited. Anne felt like she was soaring. Paige felt as though she was floundering. She hated the northeast; she certainly didn't have a fondness for the attitudes of New Yorkers, and she missed the warm weather of the South.

"I met a guy named Jason today at work," Anne said. "He has some promise based on the five-point scale. He's an engineering construction guy with the big construction company here, Wentworth. We're making a proposal on a big project with Wentworth and we're meeting again tomorrow, our people and their people. I'm going to check him out more closely, and no, he's not married."

"Well, do I have news for you. I dropped out of law school today."

"You what? Are you out of your mind? You're half-way through your last semester. Why would you want to drop out now?"

"I was sitting in a class on remedies. Sounds exciting, huh? Anyway, I'm sitting there thinking what a crock of shit. I was looking at my fellow students trying to think of exactly why we were all there. Some truly want to be lawyers. Some are following a family tradition. Some of them are there because their mommies rode their asses making them go to law school. But I thought, there's one common thread – money. They all want to make money. What a bunch of horse shit. And then I'm thinking, what the hell, I have all the money I'll ever need. I better find something to do that gives my life a little more meaning. It's not the law. So, with your permission, I think I'll just pack up my shit and move to Atlanta. What do you think of that?"

"I think that's the most wonderful thing I've heard in nearly three years. The welcome mat is waiting for you."

"I guess you wouldn't happen to know another guy like this Jason you met? Everything I've caught up here I have thrown back. Bottom feeders and sponges. I know there's one out there somewhere worth keeping."

Paige, true to her word, left law school and moved to Atlanta. At the age of twenty-four she began testing the city looking for the connections and activities that would most fulfill her goals and desires. She persuaded the trustee of her trust to advance $1.3 million permitting her to purchase a secure townhouse just off Peachtree. Her distributions from the family business provided more than sufficient funds for her to live without a financial care in the world. She had no inclination for commerce. She found it boring. She didn't need a job because she had money, and in one year she would become the unbridled trustee of her own trust, which at the time would have amassed cash and securities in excess of $63 million. When someone asked her grandfather why the age of control was selected as twenty-five, he said, "People were either meant to have money or not. Paige can piss it away just as easily at age thirty-five or forty-five as she can at twenty-five. This way she gets a quicker start. If she's a good steward of her money, she'll be fine." Paige told Anne her simple goal consisted of two things: find something interesting to do and find a man.

A year and a half after arriving in Atlanta, she had the pleasure of serving as Anne's maid of honor. Anne would enjoy the distinction of being matron-of-honor two years later at the wedding of Paige and Eric Buchanan. Eric, eight years her senior, highly educated and handsome, had been raised in an affluent Atlanta family which complemented Paige's aspirations in life. Eric met Paige at Anne's wedding when he served as a groomsman for Jason.

Paige and Anne continued their close friendship as the years passed. Children, new homes, PTA, Junior League, and whatever life threw at them. Any disagreement, large or small, between them would be resolved over glasses of wine and stories of life-to-date.

15

ANNE FIRED OFF A TEXT to Lynn late in the evening.

AW: *Nearly forgot! Mercy Care exec mtg tomorrow morning at 10. Care to join me?*

The text could have stated the event involved picking up trash along the side of a country road and Lynn would have accepted the invitation.

LG: *Yes. What do I wear?*

AW: *Go with casual business attire. You'll get it right. C u at 9:30 tomorrow morning. Sorry about the late notice.*

At nine-thirty sharp Lynn appeared at the back door wearing a blue cap-sleeved crepe sheath dress with a cream V-neck cardigan over her shoulders and ring loafers.

"You look super. I didn't ask permission to bring you along today, but I think it'll be okay with everyone. I'll explain in the car."

Driving through congested Atlanta traffic, Anne talked about Mercy Care and her relationship with the non-profit. Mercy Care and the Sisters of Mercy, with roots going back to the 1880s, provided healthcare for the uninsured and underinsured. Patients could receive treatment or care from a variety of disciplines including general medical care, vision, dental and social services. Mercy's facilities saw 60,000 patients a year on average. Of those patients, seventy-five percent measured below the federal poverty level.

"I got involved with Mercy a few years ago when Paige came across it and selected it as more than worthy of her attention. She made a pretty substantial contribution and then asked what else she might do to help. After discussing options with some members of the board of directors, it was concluded that she could have her own little area of operation, you might say. Mercy created what is called The Rainy Day Board, or RDB for short. Paige took it upon herself to develop a funding program with the goal of accumulating a thirty million dollar nest egg to shore up any shortfalls that might occur with Mercy. She says for Mercy, it's like having a big savings account. Right now, she's about seven million short of the goal, but at the same time the fund has provided nearly nine million dollars in funding to Mercy's general operations. Sometimes I wonder if that thirty million is a mirage."

Lynn listened as Anne talked about millions of dollars here and millions of dollars there. She could not comprehend one hundred thousand dollars, much less a million. But if Anne wanted to introduce her to the world of significant charitable giving, she wanted to learn. There had to be opportunities for her.

"So today, we will be meeting with the cozy little board of five. It's called the Special Board by the administrators. Paige, myself, and three other ladies. I think you'll enjoy the meeting.

"Oh, I have been intending to ask you if you would be interested in attending church on Sunday with Jason and me? The last thing I want to be is pushy in that arena. We attend Northwest Presbyterian. It's just up the road from the house."

Nearly as quickly as Anne ceased speaking, Lynn responded with a hushed but resounding, "No."

"I'm sorry." Lynn said more calmly, "I meant to say no thank you. I'm not ready to go to church and I don't know if, or when, I ever will be. I've spent the last seventeen years of my life at church every time the doors were opened. Sunday morning, Sunday evening, Wednesday evening, revivals, special parties, fundraising dinners. You name it, I participated. I have listened to preachers yell at me and tell me I was going to hell, and I just don't need that anymore."

"You're not going to find that type of religion at Northwest. The ministers actually speak in a calm voice. You won't be yelled at. But that decision is yours. If you ever want to attend one Sunday, just let me know."

The board meeting took place in a small room on the third floor, away from the daily hustle and bustle of Mercy Care. The single perpetual feature of Mercy Care was activity. Patients were taken on the first and second floors. Administration, on the third floor, seemed to be in constant motion.

The five Special Board members, Paige, Anne, Julie Oatman, Andrayah Brewer, and Caroline Tochman formally welcomed Lynn to the meeting. After some idle chit-chat and catching up, the board got down to business. The order of the day, as it appeared to be with every such meeting, addressed the issue of how to raise money. Not how to spend the money. Not how to invest the money. Only how to make the money.

"I still haven't given up on the idea of having a special gala," Julie Oatman said.

"I think it would be fun, but that would be stepping on the toes of world headquarters over there," Paige said as she thrust her thumb over her shoulder toward the opposite end of the building. "We have to remember, we can't compete with what the primary operation does, or wants to do, if they tell us first."

"Okay," Anne said. "How about a golf outing? A scramble. I could persuade Jason to get behind it. Maybe we could convince a couple of Braves or Falcons to play. That's always good for a premium contribution."

And so went the morning. They measured the feasibility of a fashion show, a treasure hunt, an 80's disco party, a 5K race, and the list went on. Some had merit, most didn't.

Lynn sat and listened, captivated by the quick minds and energy around the small table. She wanted to add something to the conversation, not just be a piece of furniture. Yet she didn't want to step across the invisible line that she felt separated her from the others. She wanted to stay in bounds. After several minutes of thought, she asked to speak and permission was granted, accompanied by five smiles.

"When high school students apply for college, or several colleges I guess, they submit a personal résumé with their admission papers, is that correct?" Five nods silently responded yes. "Okay, one of the hot buttons to draw attention to a student is volunteer work with a charitable organization. Here at Mercy the patients are indigent or even homeless. This is common knowledge. This is where the Junior League comes in."

This comment brought five peculiar looks, but no verbal responses.

Lynn went on elatedly to explain that Mercy was the perfect platform to join with the League to create what she called "charitable work credit." For a fee, the high-school-aged sons and daughters of League members would be assigned an individual patient to assist for a limited period of time. After that patient's needs were met, as defined in the "help pledge" the student would sign, another patient would be allotted for care. The "contract" would auspiciously expire after the student had accumulated enough "credits" to help satisfy the requirements of the college admissions officers.

"You kill four birds with one stone. Mercy gets some money, a patient will receive some additional care, the kids are a step closer to getting into the colleges they want and, they, the kids, might even benefit from an experience that could positively influence them for a lifetime."

When she finished not a sound could be heard. Five faces just stared at her as though she had just explained the Pythagorean Theorem to them in a fashion they could understand, except for Paige of course who could handle it on her own.

Finally, after what seemed an eternity for Lynn, Julie Oatman spoke. "And just where is it you come from? I think you just gave us something new that we can work with. Thank you."

The pride welled up inside of Lynn. She felt one step closer to achieving the confidence that Anne had seen in her. The acceptance by these five women, to her, could not be expressed in words.

On the way back to Buckhead, Anne complimented Lynn on her contribution to the meeting.

"I just have to ask, where did you come up with that idea, for the charitable works credit? I remember you saying you went to high school, but that was the limit of your education."

"Just lucky I guess," Lynn said. "I was looking online on the computer in the guest house. Looking at what it took to get into college. That's where I saw the public service issue being good to have on a résumé. I just put two and two together."

"I think you did more than just add two and two today. Are you thinking about going to college? This is new news."

"I don't know about college. That's kind of a dream. I do have a question though. If the RDB was created to raise money for Mercy, does it help if Andrayah Brewer is on the board? The black people I know don't have much money."

"Before I explain that situation, let me ask you a question. How many people live in Hollins, no, let's say Sylacauga? How many people live in Sylacauga?"

"About twelve thousand or so."

"And out of that twelve thousand, about how many are black, or African American?"

"It's something like seventy percent white and thirty percent black," Lynn said.

"And of that thirty percent black population, how many families would you say are rich, or well-off? Or just have a standard of living equal to the average standard of living there?"

"Not many. I'd say maybe ten families."

"Okay. Now let's talk about Atlanta. The metro area here has nearly six million people. Of that six million, about fifty-one percent are black. Atlanta is the second largest majority black metro area in the country. Atlanta has about eight thousand African American owned businesses and higher than average home ownership compared to the rest of the country. So, there are some wealthy blacks here in Atlanta. The lady you just met, Andrayah, her husband is an orthopedic surgeon and believe me, they do quite well. At Mercy, nearly eighty-percent of the patients are black. That's why we have black involvement. Half of the Mercy Board of Directors are black. What I'm saying is, don't be influenced by the surrounding in which you were raised. Atlanta is a different animal."

On the way home, Lynn made an interesting, but not unexpected comment. She said, "It must be nice to be rich, to be happy."

Anne did not look in Lynn's direction when she responded but continued looking straight ahead at the road. "Money does not make you happy, it only makes you comfortable. Never forget that."

16

LG: *Anne, I need to go to the drug store and buy some things. Do I need to call a taxi?*

AW: *No, come into the house.*

"What do you need from the drug store? I'll be glad to run you over there. There's a CVS just a couple of miles away."

"No, thank you, I take up way too much of your time as it is. I know you have a lot to do. And besides, I need to start doing some things on my own. I can't be relying on you for everything," Lynn said.

"Okay. Well, you don't take a taxi. I'm guessing they didn't have Uber in Hollins, Alabama? Uber is going to be the best way for you to get around until we get you a car."

"A car? No, you don't have to do that. You can't do that. You've already done more for me than I could expect in a lifetime."

"Oh, I was just thinking we would get you an old Lexus SUV or something. You know, a couple of years old, low mileage. Real dependable, but not costing a fortune. We'll discuss it later. But for now, give me your phone and we'll download the Uber app. You'll love Uber. I use it all the time when I have to go downtown and don't want to mess with parking my car."

Within no time the Uber driver confirmed the fare and Lynn readied herself for her first solo excursion into Atlanta since stepping off the MARTA coach on Peachtree.

As the Uber drove into the driveway and approached the house, Anne asked, "Do you have your credit card with you?"

"Yes, ma'am, but I have my own money. I planned on using some of it because I don't want you to think I'm a freeloader, and I don't want to be a freeloader."

"Lynn, you're not a freeloader, I'm just a free giver. I think the only things you have asked me for since you've been here were to use the bathroom and see if you needed to call a taxi. I wouldn't call that freeloading. However, I'm pleased that you want to venture out. That's a good sign. But don't spend any of your money, you may need it someday. I don't mean to be impolite, but how much money do you have?"

"I have six hundred and seventy-three dollars. Ha, my life savings at age twenty-eight."

"You just hang on to it for now. Maybe a great opportunity will pop up and you'll have the money to invest. Now, go get into your Uber, and tell her to wait for you while you're in the drug store. Then I would like for you to find out if she is from Atlanta, and if she is, ask her to drive you around town. Tell her you just moved here, and you want to see how Atlanta is put together. If she's from here, she'll be glad to do it. Maybe have some fun and get an easy fare. Don't worry about the cost. Invest a couple of hours if the driver's game. You'll enjoy it."

That night as they went to bed, Anne told Jason about Lynn's excursion and that she thought she was getting her "city legs." She told him about the meeting with the Rainy Day Board at Mercy and how Lynn had wowed the board members with her suggestions. Lastly, Anne mentioned Lynn's possible plans of attending college.

"Boy, I hope she doesn't want to go to Stanford," Jason said in a slightly cutting fashion. "She's been here for what, about three weeks. We need to find her a job, and no, I won't hire her at the company. And please don't offer her a job at Democycle. If something should go awry with your relationship, you don't want employment to be an issue. Why doesn't she just apply for a job at Peachtree Cleaners and Laundry? She has experience in that line of work. She needs to be planning on getting an apartment after she finds a job."

"The whole point of this exercise is that she shouldn't be working in the dry cleaning and laundry business. She's trying to change her life. And we need to discuss getting her some kind of little car or something. She needs to be able to get around on her own."

"A car? Really? Why don't we just buy her a two million dollar annuity and she can start drawing down on it now? Holy mackerel! Do you think it's efficient and cost effective to save the world one person at a time?"

"Is that what it boils down to? Efficiency and cost effectiveness? I'm not constructing a building, and no, I'm not trying to save the world. I'm just trying to help someone. One person can make a tremendous difference in another person's life. Didn't you have someone, and I do mean one, who helped you become the person you are today? Like, your grandfather?"

"But he was my grandfather."

"Had he not been your grandfather, and you were just out of college and in his employ, don't you think he would have had some influence on your life?"

"Unquestionably. He set my compass."

"Well, I'm unquestionably trying to help Lynn improve her life. Look what your grandmother did for me. When you and I became engaged, Lillian took me under her wing and instructed me on how to be a lady. Coming from the back woods, I wasn't exactly Amy Vanderbilt. I learned a lot at UGA, and as a Kappa, but not what your grandmother taught me. It was on a whole different level. And she instilled in me the understanding of truly helping someone, not just handing over a dollar and driving on down the road. Deep down inside I may still be a hick or a redneck, but without Lillian it would still shine through. She taught me a whole lot more than just saying 'amazing' instead of 'no shit.' That's what I'm trying to do for Lynn.

"Now, to change the subject, I assume you're playing golf tomorrow?"

"Yes, teeing off at ten-thirty."

"Who's playing?"

"Eric, Scott Brkic, and Mark Ingram."

"Why are you starting so late?"

"Because it's Saturday and Scott won't drag his ass out of bed to get an earlier tee time."

Jason rolled over on his right side to go to sleep, his back toward Anne. This had become the standard, not the exception.

17

ERIC BUCHANAN SAT HIS GOLF bag down at the driving range well behind Jason to watch him tee up a ball and lay into it with his driver. The ball, hooking like a banana, traveled about three hundred yards to what would be way out of bounds to the left if Jason's shot came at the first tee. Eric watched as Jason teed up again and sliced the second ball about three hundred and twenty yards to the right.

"I don't think you're going to hurt those golf balls, but you sure may wrench your back. What's going on with you?" Eric asked.

Eric Buchanan, masterful banker, superb golfer, and true friend, played golf with Jason nearly every Saturday at the Capital City Club. Eric became acquainted with Jason when T Bank, Eric's employer, retained Wentworth Construction to erect the building that became T Bank's primary office location. Such a friendship developed that Jason served as best man at the Buchanan wedding, with Anne shoring up the other side of the program as matron of honor. Eric, a third-generation banker, obtained his undergrad at Duke and a Master of Business Administration from Wharton. Upon graduation, he spurned a position with a multi-state banking institution to begin his career with a startup, a very risky venture. The risk had its reward, as T Bank of Georgia grew in an explosive manner.

T Bank came into existence after Harvey Tullis sold fifty-three automobile dealerships throughout the South for an after-tax sum of $432 million. Instead of investing the funds in tax exempt bonds, his sons convinced Mr. Tullis a bank would provide a better return on the capital. It had. And Eric had been along for the ride. In most respects, he drove the truck. The bank itself expanded into a multi-state operation. Eric became wealthy, at least by typical business standards. This fact sat well with Paige when they met. He had no need to pilfer her wealth. Paige also judged their eight-year age differential as a blessing, believing he had sown his wild oats and was ready to settle down. Their friends said the two matched up like bacon and eggs.

The business relationship between Jason and Eric commenced after Eric swayed Jason into moving all of the Wentworth Construction banking relations to T Bank. It turned out to be a win-win for both institutions. With the well-established friendship between Anne and Paige, the Wentworth and Buchanan families capitalized on their time together.

"Anne's new cub socialite is settling in for the long haul it appears. I said something to Anne that it might be time for the young lady to get a job and an apartment and Anne got all defensive."

At this time Scott Brkic and Mark Ingram came strolling up to the driving range.

"Have we missed any good stories?" Ingram asked. "Like a new joke?"

Buchanan, known for his humorous stories and jokes, said, "Jason, do you want to tell us about the new apprentice Anne has brought home? He's betting it's going to be better than the last two efforts Anne experienced," Eric said as he looked at Scott and Mark. "You guys know about those, don't you?"

"I do, but Brkic doesn't," Scott said. "Give him the CliffsNotes version."

"What do you say, Jason?" Eric glanced over at Jason, who gave him a half-hearted go ahead look. "The first adventure came in the form of a woman from Haiti. Anne felt sorry for her economic conditions and wanted to help her out. After about four days, the lady had sized up her good fortune and made off with all of Anne's sterling silver flatware. But insurance covered a lot of that, right?" as he looked toward Jason. "Would you like to tell the next one?"

"Oh, hell no. Go ahead. It sounds better when you tell it," Jason said.

"Okay. Well, there was this Vietnamese lady who did Anne's nails, and Paige's too for that matter. The lady, her name was Hang believe it or not, lived upstairs at the store, the nail place. She told Anne the owner was closing the business because of a rent increase, and she, Hang, was going to lose her place to live. Anne told her she had a temporary solution to the problem. Hang could occupy the Wentworth guest house. But only for the time Hang needed to secure gainful employment and a new place to live. Hang moved her meager belongings into the guest house two days later. All appeared to be working as planned. But by the end of the third day, there were thirteen Vietnamese living in the guest house. How long did it take you to get them out?"

"Too damn long," Jason said.

"What's the new one like?" Eric asked.

"This one's different. She's from a little town in Alabama and has come here to 'start a new life,' as she puts it. You'd think she'd be as country as a henhouse, but she seems to be smart. And she's actually pretty damn cute. She's twenty-eight."

"Cute?" Scott asked. "Do you mean she has a nice pair of titties?"

"Cute in the face, dumbass. However, she does have a tight little body," Jason said with a grin. "Let's head over to the first tee box. You guys squandered your warmup time listening to goofy stories."

At the first tee box, the starter informed the foursome it would be about ten minutes before they could tee off. Eric offered to tell a new joke, if the other three were agreeable, and they were.

"This guy joins a country club and at the new members party meets three other members who invite the new guy to play a round on Saturday morning at nine. He accepted but said he may be fifteen minutes late. The other three said they were okay with that.

"On Saturday, the guy shows up at nine, and shoots two over. A foursome is arranged for the next Saturday at nine and all agree. Once again, the new member says it's possible he could be fifteen minutes late. But he shows up at nine, and shoots even par, this time lefthanded.

"One of his fellow golfers, after the round, said, 'Last week you played righthanded and shot two over. Today, you played lefthanded and shot par. What makes you decide to shoot right or lefthanded?'

"The new member smiled. 'When I wake up, if my wife is sleeping on her right side, I shoot right handed. If she's sleeping on her left side, I use my lefthanded clubs. If she's sleeping on her back, I'll be fifteen minutes late.'"

On the walk up to the tee box, Buchanan said to Brkic, "Scott, if you'll come by the bank on Monday we'll see if we can find an additional vowel or two you can throw into your last name."

18

Anne sent a text to Lynn on Tuesday night.

AW: *Can u come to the house tomorrow morning at 9? There are a few things I want u to learn. Just u and me and Ava. Casual. Sweatpants and t shirt if u want.*

Lynn's response.

LG: *See u at 9.*

The next morning Ava arrived at eight and came into the kitchen through the back door, not because it was "her place" to enter through the back door, but because it was convenient. She parked her car in the driveway beside the garage, which was closer to the back door than the front. It also afforded her easier accessibility when she brought in groceries. Ava Bolander could enter the front door of 1716 Reid Lane NW at any time, day or night.

"Ava, we are going to have a little etiquette lesson here this morning. I would like for you to lay out a formal table setting for one, in the formal dining room. Why don't you set it up on the end of the table. Use the good china and silver flatware. And let's use crystal, too. And a fine linen napkin. Very formal. Then on the other end of the table we are setting up an informal table setting. Our student today is Lynn. She's going to a dinner with me tomorrow evening and I want her to be aware of what to expect when she sits at the table."

"It'd probably help if we had some biscuits and gravy to put on that plate," Ava said.

"Now Ava, don't forget that I came from the same type of backwater town as Lynn, and I was fortunate to have someone help me learn a good deal about etiquette. And for that little smart remark, you get to do the instructing this morning," Anne said.

"Now Miss Anne, I can't..."

"Oh, yes you can. You could give an etiquette lecture at the Governor's mansion. A little practice will do you good. You never know when the governor's wife might call."

"Yeah, uh-huh," Ava mumbled as she went over to the lighted rosewood breakfront china cabinet to retrieve the necessary components for the table settings.

It took Ava, with some help from Anne, about ten minutes to gather and assemble the various ingredients to the settings.

Lynn came through the back door at nine o'clock sharp. Anne appreciated her promptness. Days before, Anne had instructed Lynn to enter the back door of the house without knocking if it was unlocked. "I'm going to let you in anyway, so just come on in," Anne had told her.

True to Anne's comment on being casual, Lynn came dressed casually. She wore blue Lululemon yoga pants and an old, stretched out, faded gold T-shirt with Tech in dark blue lettering across the front that Anne had given her. She was certainly casual.

"Lynn, today..., and I don't intend to insult your knowledge, but I thought we would review some basic etiquette in preparation for the dinner tomorrow evening with the Atlanta Primary Education Foundation. We will be dining at Buckhead Club and the setting will be formal. It'll be only women in attendance, and you know how critical they can be with just a sideways glance and not uttering a word. So, I want you to have your best foot forward, whatever that means.

"The dinner is a board meeting and fundraiser of sorts. The Foundation, which is pretty small by Atlanta standards, doesn't go around spending its money on five-star dinners, so everyone chips in a couple hundred bucks a plate and a couple hundred bucks for the Foundation. The dinner part isn't a reported event, so the staunch old hussies who monitor charitable activities here can't have anything to gripe about.

"Now, just like you, I grew up in a podunk little town where the standard of the day was one spoon, one fork, and one knife, when necessary. A napkin was generally paper, unless you were wearing blue jeans like my brothers who said they could wipe their hands on their pants. And the glassware occasionally fell into the plasticware category. Am I hitting pretty close to home?"

"Yes, ma'am. I mean, yes."

"Now, on that 'yes, ma'am' business. I don't want you to think it's inappropriate. Use it, just like I do, when you want to be respectful. Particularly with an older lady. I know you know what I mean."

"Yes, ma'am I do, older lady," Lynn replied in a joking fashion.

All three women laughed. The comment indicated Lynn's developing comfort level with her new teacher and benefactor.

"Ava, now if you would, please give Lynn some instruction on proper dining etiquette."

"Okay, young lady. I would like for you to have a seat, please," Ava said. "This is a formal dining setting. You will observe there are fifteen different items in front of you. We're going to discuss each one and how it comes to be used while you are dining. What you don't see, and in a formal setting you probably will, is a dinner place card or a name card with your name on it indicating where you should sit. If there is no dinner place card, look to the host or hostess to direct you. If you get no direction, hustle up and sit by the best lookin' single man you see. Oh, I'm kiddin'."

"No, she's not," said Anne with a smile.

"There is one fundamental rule that will generally keep you out of trouble. Work from the outside in. The salad fork will be to your far left. So, remember, outside in.

"Your first move will be to pick up your napkin. Don't shake it out. Unfold it and place it in your lap. It will remain there throughout the course of the meal. If you excuse yourself from the table, fold your napkin and place it on either side of your plate. Don't put it in your seat. And, lord forbid, don't use it to wipe your face or blow you nose.

"Up to the left you see this small bread plate. That's the butter knife across it. When the butter is passed, if you want any, use the butter knife to place a patty on the rim of the bread plate; don't spread it on your bread. The butter goes from your plate to the bread. And don't butter more than one bite, after you've broken off a piece."

And on she went, explaining in detail the function and use of each plate, glass, and utensil.

"Now, when you're finished eating, here's what you do. You take your dinner knife and fork and place them on your plate where the handle ends are sitting at four o'clock, like this, and the blade of the knife and the tines of the fork are pointed toward ten o'clock. The cutting edge of the knife should be facing you. This will tell the waiter you're finished. Don't expect the waiter to take your plate just because you quit eatin'. If you still have food on your plate, that plates not goin' anywhere until you properly set your knife and fork."

After the thorough instruction about the formal setting, Lynn moved to the other end of the table where she got the junior instruction version while looking at the informal setting.

"Now let's cover some of the etiquette rules that apply to every situation. First, sit up straight. Don't slouch. It makes you look lazy. Don't put a used utensil back on the table or tablecloth. If you get butter fingers and drop anything, let it lie. The server will notice and get you a replacement. If the server doesn't notice, quietly ask. Don't put your elbows on the table. My grandmother said, 'the only bones or joints on the table should be cooked.' Don't reach, but ask. Pass the food from your left to the right. Stemmed glasses should be held by the stem. Any glass on your right is yours. Don't blow on your food to cool it down. Chew with your mouth closed and don't talk with your mouth full of food. Cut your food one bite at a time. Don't gesture with your fork or knife when you're talking. Eat slowly. If the table has eight or fewer people, wait until everyone is served before you begin eating. If the host or hostess is at your table, let one of them begin before you do. If the table has more than eight, you can begin when the people on either side of you have been served. And don't burp. That's about all I can tell you," Ava said. "I guess there is one more thing. If you have a doubt, let a couple of other people go first and watch what they do."

"I think that about covers it," Anne said.

"Oh, there is one other thing," Ava said. "I probably don't have to say this, but don't be takin' anything home with you from Buckhead Club. It's not Dairy Queen."

"I wouldn't dare. But it sounds like it's a lot easier to eat at Dairy Queen," Lynn said.

"Yes, it is," said Anne. "But in the future, maybe you'll be going to Dairy Queen only for very special occasions, like I do. I love Dairy Queen."

19

BUCKHEAD CLUB OCCUPIES THE 26TH floor of the Sovereign
Building, just slightly over four miles from the Wentworth residence. A prestigious dining club opened in the mid-1980s, it is
the frequent facility of choice by Atlanta business and societal
leaders. Finely appointed, with leather wingback chairs, walnut
paneling, and a panoramic view of the city, it offers both a
large, open dining area and private dining rooms. The board
members of the Atlanta Primary Education Foundation would
be gathering in a private dining room that comfortably sat
twenty. There were only twelve members on the board. On this
fine spring evening the board members would be dining on a
warm spinach salad, petit filet of beef with fingerling potatoes,
seasonal vegetables, and brandy au jus. For dessert, key lime
pie. A grand selection of drinks and wines was available for
the personal preference of each guest.

Cruising along Powers Ferry Road toward Buckhead Club, Lynn inquired about the purpose of the meeting and the group in general. She thought it odd that Anne just assumed she would be willing and desirous of attending Anne's functions.

"What's the purpose of the meeting tonight?" Lynn asked.

"Like the others, our attending has a dual purpose. One purpose is to introduce you to my friends and the people of the city, and the other is to participate in a charitable event that I consider worthy. It's a board meeting for the Atlanta Primary Education Foundation. Didn't I tell you that? Well, if I didn't, I'm sorry. The foundation was created about forty years ago to assist students and teachers at elementary schools. The school district here doesn't have enough money to provide the level of services necessary for today's educational demands. We, the foundation, collect money to provide help to the students and classroom teachers of the less privileged primary schools.

"We will contribute anywhere from two to two and a half million dollars a year into helping students with materials and supplies, and teachers for their classroom needs. We distribute the funds on a 'grant request' basis. In other words, a request for need must be submitted, reviewed, and approved before the money is spent. Tonight, we are going to discuss plans for next fall when the money will be distributed, and we will discuss fundraising activities. It's similar to the meeting you attended at Mercy Care, but here the dollars aren't as big.

"The executive director of the foundation, Letitia Thomas, is a former elementary school teacher from one of the most disadvantaged schools in the district. She is battle-tested and sharp as a tack. She has direct contact with the teachers, the parents of these children, and the school administrators. She is responsible for receiving the grant forms and reviewing them for us. On the spending side, she is amazing. She has more contacts than Bausch and Lomb. She knows the point people at Dell Computer, HP, and Apple. She's a jewel."

When Lynn entered the dining room she did not feel out of place. She wore her floral, short-sleeved wrap dress with trendy dark blue mid-heels. She had long since concluded Atlanta to be a moving fashion show, put on by the ladies whenever six or more gathered. The events she had attended were certainly not clothing competitions only because no trophies were awarded at the end of the evening. She wondered if everyone thought they went home the winner.

The board members enjoyed a cocktail prior to the meeting which gave Anne the opportunity to introduce Lynn to all of the attendees. Conversations about kids, and school, and up-coming trips swirled around the room. Lynn, having nothing in particular to throw into the mix, stayed on the edge of the action and enjoyed her tonic water and lime. She answered questions tossed her way as simply as possible without being too evasive. She didn't think the ladies would be very interested in Hollins, Alabama, or how long it took to get from there to Atlanta by bus.

When it came time to eat and everyone was asked to be seated, it came to Lynn's attention that, sure enough, name cards had been placed above each place settings. The setup consisted of two tables with six people per table. And to her horror, her name rested on one table and Anne's on the other. She was, more or less, on her own. Outside in, she thought, outside in. She made eye contact with the head waiter, who somehow instinctively knew her plight – fear. As she ate, she would look toward the head waiter, who remained in the room during the meal, for reassurance that she used the proper fork or reached for the proper glass.

The chit-chat continued as dinner was served and eaten. Anne, interested in Lynn's involvement in the conversation, tried to listen, but found herself too removed to hear well. She had confidence that Lynn could hold her own, but unsure as to what level. Then Anne heard the laughter coming from the board members at the other table. And she heard that distinctive Alabama accent coming from Lynn's mouth and could not tell if her fellow members were laughing with Lynn, or at Lynn. Anne turned without being too conspicuous to grasp the essence of the situation. Then she heard Lynn say, "And I think the only reason they have schools in Alabama is so that no other state would be ranked last, charitable souls the citizens of Alabama are."

Thank God they are laughing with her, Anne thought.

After the meal Holly McGuire approached Anne. "Where on earth did you meet Lynn, she is just delightful. And funny," she said.

"I guess you could say she was introduced to me by her guardian angel," Anne said.

"She has such a quick wit. And she's dressed to the nines. She's just as cute as a bug. I know a young man who works with my husband that certainly might be interested in meeting Lynn. Is she, shall I ask, connected with anyone in particular?"

"No, she's free as a bird. But I do know Lynn is going to be busy for the next month, so maybe after that we can introduce the two."

"Okay," Holly said. "But don't let some old hairy-legged critter run off with her first."

"I can make no promises."

On the way home Lynn chattered about what a good time she had. It made Anne feel good to know Lynn was progressing well. However, she didn't make mention of Holly's male friend. What impressed Anne came from Lynn's ability to apparently name each and every person in attendance at the meeting. She asked, "Lynn, would you name for me everyone you can think of who was there tonight? Last names too if you can remember."

Lynn named the ten ladies who attended the meeting, first and last names, with no mistakes.

"How do you do that?" Anne asked.

"When you're in the dry cleaning and laundry business I guess you associate faces and clothes. I really don't think about it. That's all I can think of. But once I learn someone's name, I can usually remember it. I know that somebody said one time 'the sweetest thing someone can hear is their own name.' I believe that."

"But you never learned the name of the man who gave you my name and address?"

"He never gave me the chance."

20

SOON AFTER LUNCH ON THE day following the meeting at Buckhead Club, Anne received a call from Jason.

"Hey, I've got the tickets for the Braves game tonight, what do you say we go?"

"Really, you've waited until the day of the game to tell me this. I can't go," Anne said, not willing to mention the fact that she had no interest in attending a game that evening. "I told Letitia Thomas I would go over some stuff with her this evening for Primary Education. It's important and has a short fuse, and tonight is apparently the only time the two of us could get together. Why don't you call Eric and see if he can go."

"I already have, and he can't make it. Since it's my turn to use the tickets, I'd like to go."

"Oh, so you called Eric before you called me? That's a real compliment," Anne said. "Why don't you take Lynn? I bet she would really enjoy the game, and it would give her an opportunity to get out of the guest house."

"Really? I don't know her well enough to take her to a ballgame. Besides, if I ran into someone we know, you wouldn't want them to think I was out with a younger woman."

"Let's see. She's twenty-eight. You're forty-eight. Don't flatter yourself. I don't think anyone will be confused. You're nearly old enough to be her father. It will give you a chance to get to know her better. She's a sweet young lady."

"Whatever. You check to see if she's interested. If she wants to go, we'll leave the house at six-fifteen and eat at the ballpark. Let me know ASAP."

Not to Anne's surprise, Lynn jumped at the chance to go to the game. She had never attended a sporting event larger than a high school football game. She had seen the Braves on television, and they were everyone's favorite team back in Alabama.

"What should I wear?" came the standard question from Lynn.

"Blue jeans, a shirt, sneakers and take a jacket because it can get chilly at the ballpark this time of year."

Lynn bounced into the kitchen at six-fifteen wearing blue jeans, a collared beige flax linen shirt and white Brooks running shoes, and carrying a red North Face lightweight jacket. Jason, ready to go, signaled for Lynn to follow him to the garage for departure. The seven-mile trip to the ballpark took less than fifteen minutes. Parking the Escalade in the season ticket holders' reserve parking section near the entrance gate on the first base side of the stadium, they were inside thirty minutes before the game started.

Lynn had never seen such a sight. The magnificent size of the stadium, three stacked levels of row after row of seats surrounding a brilliant green, perfectly manicured, playing field. People, all shapes, sizes, ages, and races flowed into the stadium. The fans, both male and female, wore a variety of garments, from jerseys to T-shirts to business shirts. Sweaters, an occasional skirt, slacks, shorts, and jeans. They carried jackets, ball gloves, and backpacks and some had rolled up paper sheets that appeared to be signs seized by large rubber bands.

They walked to the entrance of the stairs descending toward the field. From that location Lynn could see the infield, the pitcher's mound, and the visitor's dugout across the way on the third base side. Players from both teams were running or throwing balls in preparation for the action to come.

"Our seats are right down there, thirteen rows up, seats twenty and twenty-one, on the aisle. Let's walk around a little so you can see the stadium, then we'll grab something to eat."

They strolled along the concourse mixing with the thousands of fans. Venders hawking pennants and foam tomahawks, beer sellers, souvenir shops, and food venders. On one hand it seemed to be a disorganized circus, but on the other, it proved to be a well-orchestrated, time-proven ballet of activities. The smells, sights, and sounds coming from the fans, the shops and the eateries that lined the outside of the concourse filled the senses. The odor of grilled onions permeated the air.

"Those onions smell good," Lynn said.

"Yeah, they put them in the Philly cheesesteak sandwiches. It's a good sandwich, but here in Atlanta they should change the name."

"That sounds like a real Southern thing to say," Lynn said, forming air quotation marks with her fingers when she said the word Southern. "Are you still having issues about the war?" she asked with a grin.

"No, it's not that, although some rebel blood flows deep around here. I get perturbed with the Northerners who move down here fleeing the mess they have created in the northeast but want to bring their concepts of doing business down here with them."

"Sounds like you have a protectionist attitude to me," Lynn said. "Based on what I've read, the flood gates are open, and the flow won't stop anytime soon."

Jason, a little surprised by her perception of the issue said, "In twenty years, maybe less, the South will hold the reins of power; banking, commerce, real estate, positive population growth. You name it. The South is going to rise again."

Jason chose the quarter-pound cheeseburger for his entrée, accompanied by an order of fries. Lynn chose the footlong chilidog with kettle fries because it seemed like the right meal to have at her first baseball game. Jason said they would get something to drink when they got to their seats. They had plenty of time to eat before the first pitch.

Once in their seats, Jason waived his hand at a beer vender who hustled over with a full box of ice cold beer, water, and soft drinks. Nearly instinctively, Jason ordered two Coors

Lights, which came in sixteen ounce cans, handed the vender thirty dollars and said, "Keep the change." The vender opened the two cans of beer and handed them to Jason and Lynn. She had reservations about the beverage, but aren't you supposed to have a beer with your hotdog at a baseball game?

They both dove into their dinners. Food of this nature tastes better when eaten at a ballpark. Jason took a big gulp of his beer, and Lynn took a little sip. Jason observed her response of showing to be a little surprised. He couldn't tell if it was the carbonation or the taste that caused the reaction. She halfway smiled and said, "Oh." It never dawned on Jason that this was the first beer she had ever had in her life.

As Lynn went to take a bite, a light gust of wind blew her hair toward the chilidog. Jason shot his hand up and pushed the hair back before it got a good coating of chili. "Sorry about that," he said. "I didn't want you to get that in your hair."

"Thank you," Lynn said. "I don't know if anyone would have noticed with this red hair."

"You sound like you don't like your hair."

"Oh, it's okay. It's my brown eyes I don't like. I wish I had blue eyes like Anne," she said. "Cows have brown eyes. Do you know that over seventy-five percent of the world's population has brown eyes? Maybe more."

Jason leaned over a little and looked square into Lynn's eyes. "They're not all that brown anyway. They're closer to being hazel. You've got pretty eyes."

"Thank you," Lynn said, then she blushed.

The game ebbed and flowed, displaying well-played professional baseball with no scoring until the bottom of the fourth when the Braves got two runners on base and the cleanup hitter pulled the ball into the right field corner for a double, scoring the two runners on base. The Braves took a two to zip lead.

This action brought Lynn more into the game as she cheered with the other thirty-six thousand Braves backers over the result of the hit. She turned to Jason and said, "We got the first two points of the game."

Jason put his arm around Lynn's shoulders and said, "Those are runs. Runs are scored in baseball. Every other sport has points. Football. Basketball. Soccer. Tennis. But in baseball we have runs. Got it?"

She replied, "Yes, sir. Got it, sir," and saluted. "I'll never speak those words again," she said as she lifted her beer and motioned with it like she was toasting Jason before taking another sip.

In the bottom of the fifth inning three events occurred. First, the wind shifted from out of the southwest to coming in from the north. This brought about a quick drop in the air temperature, from around seventy degrees to sixty-four. This decline in temperature, in turn, caused a change in Lynn's physique, signifying the fact that she was braless. She did slip on her jacket. The linen shirt, more lightweight than she thought, left little to the imagination. Jason could not help but notice.

In the top of the seventh, the Mets put two runs on the board, tying the game. Lynn took her last drink to finish the beer. Jason's arm covered the armrest that separated their seats.

Lynn, with a slow push against his arm and pushing it off the armrest toward him, said, "It's my turn to use the armrest."

Gently pushing back, Jason said, "Your arm's not big enough to need all that space." He re-established his position atop the armrest. Lynn simply snuggled her elbow in behind Jason's at the back of the armrest. Jason made no effort to move.

In the bottom of the ninth, with one away and a runner on third, the batter sent a long flyball into deep centerfield. The centerfielder caught the ball but had no chance to throw out the runner tagging from third to score the final, and winning, run for the Braves. As they left the stadium, heading for the Escalade, Lynn seemed a little tipsy and asked Jason if he would hold her arm to steady her. She ran her arm under Jason's and pulled it to her body. Jason could feel the firmness of her breast and the hardness of her nipple. He made no effort to adjust the position of his arm.

Anne, in bed but not asleep when Jason arrived home, asked, "How was the ballgame?"

"The Braves won three to two in the bottom of the ninth."

"Good, but I don't mean that. What I meant was did Lynn enjoy the game?"

"Oh, yes, I think she did. When do you think she'll be getting her own apartment?"

"That was a great segue. What's the problem? Do you think I'm spending too much money on her?

"That's part of it. I think it would help her development, as you call it, if she had her own place. She shouldn't be too dependent on us."

"Let her get a job first. She's been looking, and something will pop up. And as far as the money, I just have one word in that regard, Democycle."

"Yeah," Jason said as he rolled over on his side with his back to Anne and went to sleep.

21

"Hello, Anne. This is Amber Sessions. Do you have a minute to talk?"

Amber Sessions was the executive director at Mercy Care. She had cultivated a great rapport with Anne over the past five years. She treasured Anne's enthusiasm and contribution to the operation of Mercy Care through her involvement with the Rainy Day Board.

"I have all the time you need, Amber, how may I help you?"

"It's more of a question. I had a conversation with Julie Oatman and Andrayah Brewer after the Rainy Day Board meeting last month. They both seemed to be extremely impressed with the young lady you brought to the meeting. Lynn Gregor, I believe. Well, they told me how she brought such good ideas to the meeting, and how anxious she was to participate.

I think I would like to interview her for an opening that just came up in the financial development group."

"Amber, I don't think you could have called at a better time. As you may be aware, she is new to Atlanta. She has just started to investigate the job market here. She is just as nice as she can be, and she's sharp. But there's something you need to know up front if it's going to make a difference. She only has a high school education, but she has spent a lot of years working with the public. She has a knack for getting along with people."

"Anne, I don't have a college education, so that's not going to trip her up around here. We don't always look for people with educated brains; we like to hire people who know how to use their brains."

"Okay, what do you have in mind for her?"

"Sydney Collier, in our grant request section, announced that she and her husband are expecting their first child and she will be leaving to be a full-time mom. She said she was going to leave now to get some free time in before the baby comes. She gave her two-week notice. Her leaving early was a big surprise to us, but it is what it is. However, based on what Andrayah and Julie said about Lynn, she sounds like she might be the perfect fit for what we need."

"Let me ask you, what is the pay level for the job?"

"You know how that goes, commensurate with experience. Off the cuff, I'd say about thirty-six hundred a month."

Anne, sitting at her desk in the small office above the garage, punched in a few numbers on her calculator. She estimated the take home pay would be about twenty-eight hundred a month.

Not enough to support Lynn in the fashion to which she had become accustomed, but with a small stipend from Anne, it might work. After all, Anne thought, she has to start somewhere.

"Amber, this sounds like it might be a wonderful opportunity. I'll send you her contact information by email but give me some time to visit with her about it first."

"There's no rush. Why don't you send me an email when you think the time is right."

"Thank you so much Amber. Goodbye."

Anne pushed her chair away from her desk and leaned back. Is this what Lynn should be looking for? For someone with a high school education and no experience other than the clothes cleaning business, could this be her best opportunity? And just because she might get a job doesn't necessarily mean she has to move out of the guest house immediately. Lynn still had a lot to learn.

Anne sent a text to Lynn.

AW: *Do u have a minute to visit about something now?*

Lynn looked at the text and wondered if her trip to the ballgame might be a matter of discussion with Anne. Having thought about her actions at the game with Jason, she knew she had gotten a little too cozy. But had she gotten so cozy that Jason would have brought it to Anne's attention?

The total of Lynn's responding text was short.

LG: *Yes.*

AW: *Great! I'll c u at the breakfast table in 5.*

That response didn't appear to be too ominous. So off she went to the nook.

"I have some wonderful news. You have a job interview. Wait. Let me slow this down a little. I was told that Mercy Care, the main institution, not the Rainy Day Board, would like to interview you for a job. You would be working in the grant request section if you get the job. Are you interested?

"I don't know what to think. How did this happen? Did you pull some strings to get me the interview?"

"No. None whatsoever. You've gotten this opportunity all by yourself. It's that Alabama charm that won the day."

"I doubt that." And then with excitement, Lynn said, "So tell me, tell me. How has this happened?"

Anne went on to explain that Amber Sessions had called to see if Lynn would like to interview for a job as a grant writer, which Anne described as best she could. She briefly explained to Lynn how grant requests were critical for many charitable organizations. That certain well-funded charities and foundations existed for the purpose of providing funding to other needy charitable organizations, like Mercy Care. That the funding charities and foundations required sophisticated requests for money. These requests were called grant requests. She told Lynn there would be no guarantee that she would get the job. The job would be won on merits, not who the applicant knew. She told her what she thought the compensation might be and that she would receive other benefits as well. "This could be the foundation of the building blocks you're looking for."

Lynn began firing questions at Anne, most of which she couldn't answer.

"You need to write those questions down so you'll have them at the interview. It will help make you seem interested and prepared," Anne said. "But am I moving a little too fast? Are you truly interested in interviewing for the job? You shouldn't go to the interview just to please me."

"Oh, yes. I want to go to the interview. I have to start somewhere and this is my first step. I do have one question for you though. Does this mean I have to move out?"

"Absolutely not. I would expect you to stay here until you become self-sufficient. I don't think you are there yet with this job. But let's not get the cart before the horse. You have to get the job first. And I'm guessing your résumé at this point is nonexistent. Right?"

"I've never had a résumé. What would I put on a résumé?"

"You're about to find out. But first, let me email Amber and let her know you're interested in the job. She'll contact you to set up a time for an interview. Then we'll get on the résumé."

At four in the afternoon, Lynn's cell phone rang. It startled her a little, not being accustomed to receiving calls. Teresa Jones from Hollins called every few days with the Hollins update. Teresa called her Becky Lynn, which she began to abhor but said nothing because she didn't want to hurt her friend's feelings. The caller was Amber Sessions.

"Lynn, my name is Amber Sessions." And she went on to explain who she was and why she was calling.

"Yes," Lynn replied. "Anne told me about you and a little about the interview opportunity."

"Well, we usually post these jobs and we may interview up to twenty candidates. Then we go through the second round of interviews and reduce the number of candidates to three. Then the three candidates are interviewed by at least five board members before a final selection is made. But, because of the stellar recommendations from two Rainy Day Board members and your relationship with Ms. Wentworth, we will forego posting the job at this time and just interview you. How about Thursday afternoon at two o'clock, here at Mercy downtown?"

"I will be there on Thursday and thank you."

After Lynn terminated the call, Amber's words seemed to echo in her head. "And your relationship with Ms. Wentworth."

22

LYNN BOUNDED ACROSS THE CURVED line of flat river stones that connected the guest house to the main house, and into the kitchen. "Anne," she yelled with excitement, anxious to tell her the news about the job interview.

From outside the kitchen, and barely audible, she heard Anne respond, "I'm up here in my office. Come on up."

Crossing the threshold into Anne's office and nearly out of breath, Lynn said to Anne, "Guess what? I have an interview with Mercy Care on Thursday afternoon at two. I'm the only person they're interviewing for the grant writer job. I can't believe it. Oh, thank you."

"You don't have to thank me, you've done this all by yourself."

"No, you've done more for me than anyone in the whole world. There's no way I can thank you enough."

"Lynn, you thank me by working toward accomplishing the goals you set for yourself in life. You came here wanting to improve yourself and I have to say, so far, so good."

"Anne, I'm actually a little scared about this interview because I have a general idea what a grant writer might do, but as far as specifics, I don't have a clue. I can't just fake it."

"If you get down to the brass tacks, the purpose of a grant request is just a request for money. You'll provide a detailed background of Mercy. The request will have information about Mercy's current financial status and indicate explicitly how Mercy will use the funds. You'll provide goals and objectives about the need for the money and a detailed budget is usually included to show how the funds will be used."

"But I've never even thought about doing something like that, much less do it."

"There will be plenty of examples and someone will be looking over your shoulder. Now I guess I should have asked you this earlier, but how is your English? Your writing skills I mean?"

"I'm confident with my English and writing," Lynn said. "After all, you haven't heard me say something like, 'We ain't got no more of them thangs', have you? I think I can hold my own. Believe it or not, good Uncle Stanley was a stickler on proper English. He said the better you could speak, the more intelligent people thought you to be. I know he was right. And I can transform proper thoughts into written words."

"Wonderful," Anne said. "Now is the time to start working on your résumé. We can find some simple outlines on the internet. Let's take a look. Here's a straightforward example. See, it takes only one page and doesn't have a lot of detail. That's good. You want to say enough to get your foot in the door. Well, you already have your foot in the door. But keep the résumé short so the interviewer will have to ask you questions and you can expound at that time. And the fact that you have worked at one location for more than ten years is a big plus. Employers like commitment. You don't have to put down that you worked for Uncle Stanley." Anne felt some excitement herself as she discussed the planning of the interview.

"Now, how are you going to get there on Thursday?"

"Uber?"

"Yes, Uber. Here, jot this down. Four twenty-four Decatur Street, Southeast. That's the address. It's seven miles from here and it will take about twenty minutes to get there. You need to allow for traffic, so plan on having Uber pick you up at one-thirty. It's much better to be early than late. Uber will serve you well, but we still need to look into getting you a car. But before we do that, I guess we better get you a Georgia driver's license. I assume you have a driver's license."

"Yes, ma'am, I do, and a commercial license at that. I had to drive the laundry van occasionally, and a commercial license was required."

"Can I guess your next question?" Anne asked. "What am I going to wear? The answer is whatever makes you feel comfortable, but not one of your outfits from your days at the laundry."

"Oh, lord no. Those things are long gone. Ava took them away weeks ago."

The Uber arrived at one-thirty. Lynn took no chance that she might be a second late for the interview. She arrived a quarter until two and entered the building. If she had to wait because she arrived early, she would sit and wait for her appointed hour. She wore light gray slacks, a fitted white cotton shirt and her blue blazer. She had seen what the staff wore during her trip to Mercy to attend the Rainy Day Fund meeting. Generally, very casual; cotton print dresses, slacks, some blue jeans. She knew her outfit was at the top end of casual, but she wanted to present herself as a cut above the norm. She could always dress down, appropriately, if she got the job. She wanted to fit in, not stand out.

She waited only about twenty minutes until Amber Sessions came to get her. They entered a small conference room, smaller and not as nicely appointed as the room where the Rainy Day Board meeting was held. The furniture and fixtures in this room could easily have come from a secondhand office furniture store. The decor made the statement that Mercy Care spent its dollars elsewhere. They sat at the small table and Lynn handed over her résumé after a couple of minutes of cordialities.

Amber asked the questions that would be expected in an interview. Tell me about yourself. Tell me about your prior employment. Tell me what you think you can bring to our organization. Tell me. Tell me. Lynn answered each question succinctly and quickly. The questions came one after the other for twenty minutes.

"Lynn, I'm aware of your limited experience in the area of non-profits. But you seem to have made quite an impression on a couple of the Rainy Day Board members. And knowing you have a relationship with Anne Wentworth is a big plus. Here's what I would like to do. I'm offering you a job as a grant writer on a probationary basis for sixty days. That means you'll be employed temporarily, giving us a chance to check you out, and you get to do the same with us. If, at the end of the probationary period, we like each other, and you're still interested, you have a fulltime job. If for whatever reason either of us think it's not a workable deal, then we terminate the temporary employment agreement and we both go our separate ways. Your compensation during the probationary period will be three thousand dollars a month, with no other benefits. If you become fully employed after sixty days, your compensation will be adjusted to four thousand per month and you will receive the same benefits as everyone else here, which includes health insurance."

"Ms. Sessions, I could not ask for a better opportunity today. I will not disappoint you. When can I start?"

"I think we'll wait until next month. Sydney Collier, who you'll be replacing, will be here for a couple of more weeks. We don't want to strain the budget with two paychecks for the same job. I hope that's okay with you. And as far as your start date, how about Monday morning, May seventh? That would be good. We start at eight. And please call me Amber."

Lynn could hardly wait to get back to Reid Lane to tell Anne. Not that Anne probably didn't know the situation, but still it was her first job in Atlanta. In fact, she couldn't wait and texted a quick message to Anne.

LG: *I got the job!*

Anne texted back the image of a thumb up and wrote a quick response.

AW: *Great news! Come into the house when u get here. Up to the office.*

Lynn, still excited about the interview, gave Anne a blow-by-blow description of the whole affair. She joyfully stated that May seventh would be her first day, "at a real job."

"We now need to think about getting you a car, and a Georgia driver's license. Let's look at the Department of Driver Services website for what you'll need. Oh, look, you can make an appointment. This is unbelievable. How about tomorrow morning at eight-fifteen? Here, I'll print the application and you fill it out tonight. You'll need your Alabama license and your social security number. Georgia grants reciprocity as long as your license from Alabama is still valid. Is it?"

"Yes, and I have my social security card."

"Then you should be good to go. Let's leave at seven forty-five in the morning to beat the rush. It's located over on Whitehall, so it's not too far."

That night, Anne told Jason about Lynn's good fortune. "We are getting her a Georgia driver's license tomorrow and we need to start looking for a car."

"The job sounds great. Maybe she can get her own apartment. And she can buy herself a car, too."

"So you're still having problems with the money aren't you? Tell me, do you know how Democycle's doing so far this year?" Anne asked as she slipped into bed.

"It's doing okay, I guess. I'm going to my study to read."

"Year-to-date it has a profit of eight hundred thousand. I'm buying her a car tomorrow," is the last thing Jason heard as he walked out of the bedroom.

23

AT SEVEN FORTY-FIVE, AFTER LEAVING a note for Ava, Anne and Lynn hopped into the Land Rover and headed to the Georgia DDS. Anne, again astounded by the early appointment time, pulled into the parking lot.

"I didn't ask before we left, but I assume you filled out the application and you have your Alabama license and your social security card?"

"Yes, I do. And thirty-two dollars to pay for it. And I want to pay for it myself."

"Fine, let's hit the door."

Inside, after passing security, they still got the privilege of standing in a governmental line. Once at the service desk, Lynn submitted her application and social security card.

"Do you have proof of your current residence here in Georgia?"

"I'm that proof," Anne said. "Miss Gregor lives at my residence at 1716 Reid Lane, Northwest. And here is my driver's license. What else will you need?"

"I think this will do it."

"Do I have to take a driving test?" Lynn asked.

"No, ma'am, that's waived because your Alabama license is current. First, we need to get your fingerprints. If you will put your thumbs on those two squares. Okay, now each finger starting with your right index...Now if you'll put your feet on the mark behind you, we'll get your picture. Now don't smile. We don't want no smiles. After you pay the fee at the checkout desk, you'll be given a temporary license. The original will be mailed to you in about four business days. But first, you have to surrender your Alabama license. It's kind of a trade-in deal, not two for one. It's the law."

Back in the Land Rover, Anne said, "Now it's time to go shopping for a car. What do you think of the Lexus?"

"Oh, no. You don't have to buy me a car. And it doesn't have to be a Lexus for sure."

"How about a pre-owned one, as they like to call them. Sounds much better than saying used car. I think it'll work just fine. We'll get one at the dealership because they'll provide a warranty plan that others won't. So if you need to get the car worked on, you'll take it there."

At the dealership's pre-owned car lot, and trying to avoid a salesperson, they found a used GX 450 SUV. Blue with beige interior, it had only 36,000 miles. The listed price was $33,850.

"Do you think you could get used to this one?" Anne asked. "That's low mileage for one this age. That's what my brothers would say."

"Yes, but not for that much money. You can't spend that much."

"Watch me," Anne said. "Besides, I'm not spending that much, just watch. Now let's find a salesman."

Eugene Jackson wasn't that hard to find. He had been birddogging them since they had gotten out of the Land Rover.

"That's a fine automobile and a heck of a deal," Eugene said as he approached Anne.

"I'm not looking for a car, she is. But I'm here to help her along."

"Okay, great. I'm Eugene," he said, as he turned to Lynn. "And you are?"

Eugene provided a glowing review and inspection of the SUV, inside and out. He went over all the features and then popped the hood so the engine could be examined. He could have just as easily taken the back off a GPS device as to what it meant to Anne and Lynn.

"I'd like to see the dipstick please," Anne requested.

Eugene stretched over the fender, extracted the oil pan dipstick, and showed it to Anne.

"That oil looks dirty. When was the last time the oil was changed in this thing?"

"Ma'am, I don't know the last time, but I know the next time, and that will be today."

As they walked around the car away from Eugene, Anne whispered to Lynn, "I learned that from my brothers, too."

Next came the test drive. With Lynn in the driver's seat and Anne in the back, they pulled out onto Interstate Highway 20. Eugene, sitting shotgun, fired questions at Lynn and at the same time continued to mess with the features on the dashboard.

"What type of music do you like?" he asked.

"Country, I guess," Lynn responded.

Eugene pushed a couple of buttons and up came Blake Shelton's voice filling up the interior of the SUV.

"Excuse me," Anne said, "we're here to buy a car, not a sound system. Would you please turn that off. We need to listen to the car, not the music."

At that point Eugene knew his customer had more knowledge than most.

Eugene discussed the warranty situation and the pride of driving a Lexus. Now it was time to return to the dealership and sit in that miserable little closing office and listen to Eugene play "Let's Make a Deal."

"Lynn, we have a very favorable financing and insurance package. Your first payment won't be due until three months from now. How does that sound to you?"

"Eugene, this is where I take over," Anne said as she scooted her chair closer to the desk. "Now, how much do you want for that SUV?"

"Yes, ma'am. It's listed at thirty-three eight I believe. No, thirty-three eight-fifty," Eugene said after looking at the inventory card.

"Oh," Anne said. "I must have misunderstood. I thought you wanted to sell that car. Obviously, you don't. Lynn, it's time for us to head over to the BMW shop." She stood, and so did Lynn.

"No. No, ma'am. That's just the list price. I think we can work something out here."

"Okay, Eugene, here's what you're going to do. You're going to go into your sales manager's office and tell him we are about to walk. Tell him you want a number to present to me that's his best offer. I'm not going to sit here and play that run-back-and-forth bullshit car sales game. If I like the number, we'll buy the car. If not, Lynn will be driving a BMW tomorrow. Isn't that right Lynn?"

"Uh, yes, ma'am."

"Now, Eugene, I'm guessing that your sales manager works for a salary, but you probably get paid by commission. So what that means is, your sales manager probably doesn't give a big rat's ass if we buy this car or not. But for you, you're about to watch some percentage of some sales price walk right out those doors."

"Yes, ma'am. I'll be right back."

"And don't bring him over here. I like dealing with you."

"Did you learn that from your brothers?" Lynn asked.

"No, I learned that when I bought my first car out of college and I had to deal with some chauvinistic assholes who thought they could take advantage of me. They didn't."

Five minutes later Eugene reappeared with a piece of paper in his right hand. "He says we can go with twenty-nine seven fifty, but that's it."

"Okay, Eugene. You have a deal. Now wasn't that easy?"

"Let me take you over to the F and I guy where you'll get the paperwork done."

As they walked toward the main building, Lynn asked Anne what the salesman meant by F and I.

"That stands for finance and insurance. That's where they take the unwitting customers to rub salt into the wound after screwing them over out here on the lot. We won't have to put up with their BS."

When Anne sat down with Larry, the F and I guy, she had no plan of spending any more time with him than was painfully required.

"Here's the deal Larry, we don't want or need financing or insurance. This young lady is going to be the owner of the car. I will pay for it. I want you to complete the registration papers and whatever else you have to do and let us be on our way. I'm going to write you a check for the purchase price, tax, title, and whatever else the law requires. The check will be drawn on T Bank. I don't expect you to accept it as good, even knowing you could call the bank to see if the thing would clear. So here's what we're going to do. After we finish up here, you, or one of your trusted colleagues, can hand deliver the check to the nearest T Bank branch and trade it in for a cashier's check. That way you'll know you're getting your money. We don't expect to take the SUV with us today, but we'll be back here tomorrow morning at ten to get it. And make a note that the oil is to have been changed, at your expense, before we pick it up. Eugene made that deal. If for whatever reason you can't turn the car over to Lynn tomorrow morning, I will get my money back and Lynn will be driving a BMW on Monday. Now, unless you have some questions, it's been a pleasure doing business with you. Oh, I don't want to be presumptuous, but won't the gas tank on that SUV be full when she picks the car up tomorrow?"

Heading back to Reid Lane, Lynn said, "I can't believe how you handled that whole thing. I mean, you were, uh, a little abrupt."

"Lynn, sometimes the people we deal with in life can be snakes in the grass and they'll bite you the first chance they get. If you know that going in, you can avoid being bitten. That's all I was doing."

That night, Anne informed Jason about the SUV purchase. She told him she had gotten a good deal.

"How much did you pay for it?" he asked.

"A little over thirty thousand with all the taxes and stuff."

"Thirty thousand? Holy shit Anne, you know money doesn't grow on trees. What else are you going to buy her, a house?

"It's only thirty thousand, Jason. Don't you remember how much Democycle netted last year? It made two point nine million before income taxes, so the net will probably be around one point nine after tax. So, if we're making a million nine off of a side business, I think I can use my own discretion in spending a few of those dollars. I don't think we're going to be eating cat food anytime soon."

"I do have a question though," Jason said. "Just exactly what does she do all day now? Follow you around?"

"I thought you would never ask. Interestingly, when she's not 'following me around,' she's studying. After you leave for work, she takes the newspaper to the guest house and reads it from front to back. She just absorbs it. How do you think she can ask you those questions about next-year's Yellowjacket football team? Or about expanding the police force? And she spends a good deal of time on the computer, surfing the internet. She has a thirst for knowledge and she is becoming very well informed."

24

ON A SUNDAY MORNING IN 2006, two years after Emma's birth, Jason asked Anne to skip church and have Ava come to the house to watch the kids. He wanted to take her to downtown Atlanta to observe the demolition of a 62-year-old, 15-story brick structure known as the Butler Building. The land upon which the old building sat would be the location of a new 54-story tower to be built by Wentworth Construction. The building, at the intersection of Courtland and Auburn Avenue, had been abandoned for years and stood as an eyesore to the city. The approval for the demolition came quickly, as the City Council saw the opportunity for economic growth and a bigger tax base.

Jason parked his Tahoe on Auburn, about a block away from the Butler Building. The street at that point had been barricaded to keep the area clear of unauthorized bystanders. An

Atlanta police officer came over to the Tahoe to inquire about his reason for being there. Jason explained that Wentworth Construction was the general contractor of the project and he wanted to observe the demolition.

"Sir," the officer said, "it's going to get real dirty around here in about forty-five minutes. I just want you to know that if you stay here, your Tahoe will probably change from blue to the color of dust."

"Thanks officer, I'm well aware, but I appreciate the heads up.

"That's the old Butler Building I've been telling you about," Jason said turning to Anne. "It's been there for sixty-two years, but in about forty-five minutes it won't be there anymore. I thought you might like to watch it come tumbling down," Jason said.

"Are they going to blow it up?" Anne asked. She had been involved in numerous commercial construction projects while she worked at Land Architecture, but never on the demolition segment because the landscape development came at the end of a project.

"More like implode it. Do you see the plastic sheeting encompassing the ground floor and the seventh floor? That's heavy duty plastic that protects the surrounding area from debris that might fly out when the charges are exploded. Those are the floors that have the dynamite charges. The pyrotechnic guys drill holes deep into the support columns of the old building and the holes are packed with dynamite. There's about two hundred and fifty pounds of the stuff embedded in the building."

"To me, that doesn't seem like a lot if the goal is to implode the building," Anne said.

"It's plenty," Jason said. "The trick is to let gravity do the work. Once the charges are set off, the columns that support the building's skeletal structure are blown apart, but only where the dynamite is located. Once those columns are gone, there's nothing to support the building, so gravity takes over. That's what a lot of people don't understand. I guess you could say the dynamite is the catalyst and gravity is the force that takes the building down. You'll see what I mean in a few minutes.

"The dynamite is strategically placed so that when the support columns are destroyed, the outer walls will fall inward, toward the center of the structure. Besides dealing with the high explosives, the angle of the collapse is the most critical aspect of the demolition job. If the walls don't fall inward, it can be a tremendous hazard to the streets and surrounding buildings. If the structure doesn't tumble all the way down, it creates a real mess. The clearing away of the debris becomes more complex and more dangerous. That's why it's so critical to get the explosive set in the proper location. There's also a firing sequence that's important. You want different segments to collapse at different times. That's above my pay grade, so I can't tell you much about the physics of the timing."

"Speaking of pay grade, what does it cost to bring the building down?" Anne asked.

"It's not just bringing the building down, it's also clearing the site. When these guys are done removing the debris, the lot will be flat from corner to corner. And as for cost, this one is going for about nine-hundred."

"Nine hundred thousand?"

"More precisely eight hundred ninety-three thousand I believe. It ain't cheap, as the old saying goes."

"Holy shit, Batman! That's a lot of money. Why are you having them do it and not the company?"

"First of all, they're pros. It takes knowledge. And the kind of knowledge no one at the company has. Secondly, there's obviously a liability issue involved, and I don't care to expose the company to it. Thirdly, you have to have a place to ditch the debris. These guys have access to landfills and we don't. There are a lot more reasons, but those should be enough."

"Have you ever heard of anything going wrong with one of these jobs?"

"I've never known of anyone getting hurt if that's what you mean. I saw a building that didn't come down all the way once. Couldn't re-demo with explosives because of the instability of the building. It was too dangerous. They had to take the balance of the structure down with wrecking balls. It took months and cost the excavator a lot of money."

"Who are these guys, the ones doing this job? Where are they from and what makes them so special? As in worth nearly a million dollars?"

"LeBlanc Demolition and Excavation, out of Metairie, Louisiana. They're the best in the South. One of the best in the business. They've taken down buildings, bridges, grain silos, brick smokestacks, coast to coast. You name it, they've taken it down. The company's reputation is impeccable. I really think they get a kick out of what they do. They're a great bunch to work with. We've used them several times. Never so much as a minor problem."

"What's the guy's name that's in charge of this job?"

"David Gallimore, why?"

"Just curious. These guys make a lot of money, don't they? And I mean individually. I'm betting their skillset doesn't come cheap."

"That's probably true. They're in a unique business."

"How old is David Gallimore?"

"I'd guess he's about forty. Why do you care?"

"Just curious. But for nine hundred thousand, there has to be a whole lot more to this business than just blowing up a building. Or imploding a building as you called it."

"Sure. Permits have to be obtained. Environmental studies have to be done. Asbestos abatement may be required. Rodent control and extermination may be an issue. Moving men and equipment. Disposal of the debris, which is a real biggie. Most of the bigger demolition companies today recycle the materials that can be salvaged. Copper, lead, iron, asphalt. The residue is taken to a landfill. Everything is under the watchful eye of Big Brother. City, county, state, and federal. OSHA, EPA, and the ATF. There's lots of components, with little room for error," Jason said.

"Why would ATF be involved in the operation of a demolition business?"

"Dynamite."

They both sat in silence and looked at the old building for a few minutes. Anne thought about the stories that could be told if the old structure could only talk. Jason thought about the first opportunity his crew would have to walk the property after the clearing of the debris. A series of short blasts then came from a siren near the property, followed by an announcement coming from a very loud bullhorn.

"We are at ten minutes and counting. Detonation will occur in ten minutes. You are to clear the premises. Again, detonation in ten minutes."

These warnings came at five minutes, three minutes, and one minute before detonation. Bright red lights, looking like the type that once sat atop police cars, spun and flashed at various locations around the perimeter. Not a sign of life could be seen. An eerie silence engulfed the entire area.

"Okay, here's where we run up the windows. You are about to see the biggest cloud of dust and dirt you have ever seen in your life. When that sucker comes down, the dust will climb as high as five or six stories, and spread out for blocks," Jason said as he started the Tahoe. "We'll be okay in here, and the air conditioner will be running to keep us cool."

The time had finally come. The bullhorn bellowed, "Ten, nine, eight,...one, zero. FIRE IN THE HOLE!" At that moment, a series of explosions reverberated from the building. Not as loud as a cannon blast, but much louder than a shotgun. And the sounds came in a sequential order, not all at once. Through the gaps between the plastic sheeting surrounding the first and seventh floors, Anne could see bright flashes of light. Within seconds, all four walls of the building started to move, leaning inward toward the center of the structure. It looked as though the building had been full of air and was now deflating. Then, up from what appeared to be ground level, a tremendous cloud of smoky white dust climbed into the air and billowed out to the four points of the compass. It came rolling toward the Tahoe, obscuring the sight of everything behind it. Just seconds after the rumble of the explosions had shaken the Tahoe, the cloud engulfed it in darkness. It took nearly ten minutes for the dust to settle to the point where Jason could turn on the windshield wipers.

"So, one of the biggest problems is the landfill availability, is that correct?" Anne asked.

"Yes," Jason answered, "in today's world, maybe the biggest."

Jason put the Tahoe in gear and the wheels started to turn. Anne already had her mind in gear, and the wheels were turning.

25

A FEW WEEKS BEFORE LEAVING her job at Land Architecture, and about three months before Cole's birth, Anne had sat in on a meeting about an abandoned granite quarry east of Atlanta. The owner, Thaddeus Hicks, had some ideas as to what to do with the property, but the plans never came to fruition. A lack of capital put a stake in the project. The property measured 15 acres. It consisted of a big hole, about four stories deep and consumed six acres, and a nine-acre plot of land that abutted the pit. The granite extraction played out in the 1960s and nothing had been done with the land since that time. Now, ten years after that meeting, Anne would follow up to determine the status of the property.

Everyone had encouraged Anne to "find something to do" after the bus accident. Perhaps the hole might be the answer to that "something to do."

Through a simple internet search she found that the owner of the property had died in 2008, leaving the property to his three sons: Arnold, Arthur, and Dwight. Fortunately for Anne, they each had one thing in common, they each needed cash. Anne directed her attention to the oldest son, Arnold, now age 63, who served as the executor of the father's estate. She found his telephone number and called him. Yes, the estate owned the property. Yes, they would certainly like to sell it. No, nothing has been done at all to improve it. Make an offer.

Anne told Arnold she had an interest in the land but could not make, or accept, an offer at the present time. "I need to do some research and talk to a couple of people. I'm very interested in the property and I'd like to secure it until I can make a fair offer. Would you and your brothers be willing to take a three thousand dollar deposit to hold the land from sale to anyone else for three weeks? If I come back with an offer to buy, the three grand is applied against the sales price. If I don't make an offer in three weeks, you can keep the money."

Arnold, trying to think of a way to screw his brothers out of their share, said he would be glad to hold the land for three weeks. Three thousand dollars would go a long way toward a new pickup.

"Give me your address and the check will be in the mail this afternoon," Anne said.

That evening, at dinner with Jason, Anne asked, "Do you remember what you told me a long time ago about the most critical part of running a demolition business? Having a place to dump the debris? What if I could buy a piece of property near Atlanta that you could use as a landfill? Would that advance the ball for the company doing its own demolition and keeping the nine hundred thousand in the bank instead of paying it to a bunch of Cajuns from Louisiana?"

"That sounds like a wonderful idea if it was just that easy. The red tape involved is staggering. The liability is horrendous. I could not, in good conscience, subject the company to that kind of liability. Demolition is a whole different business. We build buildings. Any knucklehead can build a building. We don't take them down," Jason said. "It takes an expert to take one down."

"What if the business is owned by a completely separate entity from the construction company, with no strings attached. Would that make a difference?"

"Yes, that's the only way I would be involved. But the amount of money required to capitalize a demolition business would be in the millions, to do it right. That's a lot more money than nine hundred thousand."

"And what about the recycling of the copper and iron and stuff? That could be a money maker, couldn't it? Someone somewhere is putting money in the bank recycling materials, right?"

"Yes, they are. So why are you asking me all of this?"

"Because I think I have found a piece of property that would be perfect for the landfill and maybe the recycling work, too. I think we should take a hard look at starting a demolition and recycling business."

"Okay," Jason said. "You run the proverbial numbers and I'll take a look at it."

That's all Anne needed to hear. The next day she telephoned a real estate appraiser to determine a value for the old quarry. She also called LeBlanc Demolition in Louisiana and got the cell phone number for David Gallimore. Anne already knew one thing. Jay Comsi had done his job. Both LeBlanc Demolition and David Gallimore had been checked out front and back and inside out, and they had passed the test. Otherwise, another company would have been razing the Butler Building for Wentworth Construction. By a stroke of luck, or perhaps fate, she learned that Gallimore was currently in Atlanta managing a demolition job.

The cell phone rang only once. "David Gallimore."

"Mr. Gallimore, my name is Anne Wentworth and my family owns Wentworth Construction. Is there any way I could meet with you for dinner some evening, since you're here in Atlanta, and talk about a potential business opportunity? The conversation will be extremely confidential for both of us, and if you can't give me your word regarding confidentiality, then we probably shouldn't meet."

"Ma'am, I'll sign a confidentiality agreement if you like, but I give you my word."

"No, an agreement won't be necessary. From what I understand, your word is your bond. And that's good enough for me. Could you meet me at Paschal's at seven on Wednesday night?"

Anne arrived at six fifty-five and found David Gallimore standing in the waiting area at the front of the restaurant. Mr. Gallimore had already earned his first star with Anne thanks to his punctuality. Having seen his picture on the LeBlanc website, she spotted him immediately. Anne thought if she would ever see the quintessential U.S. Marine out of uniform, one stood before her now. Square jaw, square shoulders, ramrod straight with an air of unmistakable confidence. The firm handshake and eye-to-eye contact complemented that thought.

After the introductions and some limited small talk, Anne got down to business. She explained that she had witnessed the demolition of the Butler Building several years earlier, and that the entire event fascinated her. But when her husband, Jason Wentworth, informed her of the cost to raze and remove the building, she started thinking of developing a business.

"Mr. Gallimore, if I could acquire a landfill location about twelve miles from where we are seated, that could absorb around a half-million yards of solid waste materials, would that provide a solid backbone for the creation of a new demolition and recycling business?"

"What's the size of the hole?"

"It's six acres. And it averages about sixty-six feet deep."

"Let's see. That's about four stories deep and the footprint would be about what? Six football fields or two and a half city blocks? That's a lot of hole."

"And you just did that in your head?"

With that tidbit as an opener, David Gallimore's interest sprouted and a serious conversation initiated. They talked for three hours. David getting what details Anne had about the old quarry. Anne asking questions about the industry and David responding. What type of equipment is required? High reach hydraulic excavators, bulldozers, front end loaders, a claw machine, cranes with wrecking balls, dump trucks, lowboy trailers. The list went on. Anne took notes and asked more questions. How many employees are needed for a base crew? How much money do they make? How do you find your business? What are the biggest hurdles? Well before the end of Q&A, they were just Anne and David.

Finally, Anne asked, "Would you provide me with a spreadsheet projecting the equipment needed to start the business and the necessary cash demand to operate for one year assuming no revenue for the first four months and a breakeven operation for the balance of the year?"

Yes, ma'am, I would be glad to do that. It's going to take me some time to do it right."

"Is there another way to do something?" Anne asked.

As they prepared to leave the table and the hardly-touched food, Anne asked another question. "David, what is your annual compensation, with bonuses and everything?"

"Right now, as a superintendent, I make one hundred and forty thousand a year."

"When you do your cash flow projections, write yourself in as president of the company and use a base pay of two hundred and fifty thousand. Because Democycle is an LLC, it will be taxed as a partnership, so your compensation will be called a guaranteed payment instead of a salary."

"That's very attractive, but being from Louisiana I need to be frank and tell you, I don't have time for bullshit."

"I don't either David, but if I can pull this off, you have the job. The critical component is the hole in the ground, which

I'm working on now. I do have a couple more questions. One, do you have any problem with former prisoners working for you? And two, were you ever, by chance, in the Marines?

"To the first question, no ma'am, not if they're willing to work and stay out of trouble. To the second question, yes. Infantry, First Marine Division. I mustered out of the Corps as a captain. Now, I have one question of interest. What are you going to do with that old quarry if you can't get the permits and approvals needed to operate a solid waste landfill?"

"There's a good flow of water across the floor of the pit. The walls of the hole provide a lot a shade over the base of the pit because of the angle of the sunlight as it comes into the hole. Simple. I'll put in a botanical garden."

26

TWO WEEKS AFTER CALLING THE real estate appraiser Anne received an appraisal expressing a value on the land of $712,000. She had specified that the appraisal be on an "as is" basis with no expectation for improvement. Two days later, she received an equipment acquisition list and a pro forma cash flow statement from David Gallimore. The total for the equipment and operating cash needs amounted to $2.6 million. She called David, asked him to get out his razor and shave $100,000 from the asset list, and to send her the amended spreadsheet.

The same afternoon, she put in a call to Arnold Hicks. She asked him where they might meet to discuss the possible sale of the old quarry property. He said the Wendy's in Stone Mountain would be a great place to meet. He said she could find it on South Hairston Road, about a quarter mile south of Redan Road. Anne thought what a better place for a meeting to discuss real estate sales and high finance than a Wendy's. The Wendy's was located just twenty miles from Reid Lane, and the quarry just a stone's throw away from the Wendy's.

"That works for me," Anne said. "Could you meet me there at three o'clock? And bring your brothers."

Anne arrived at two forty-five, bought a Coke, and staked out a table as far from the general population as possible. At five past three, the brothers Hicks walked through the door. Anne most certainly thought she was witnessing a scene from *Deliverance.* Arnold Hicks, the obvious spokesman for the brothers, wore a blue, button-down, long-sleeved shirt, and blue jeans. The others wore bib overalls and Wolverine steel-toed work boots. Each sported a jaunty redneck adjustable gimme cap, promoting John Deere, Jack Daniels, and NASCAR, respectively. Gauging from the length of their beards, the brothers had been at a loss to locate shaving paraphernalia for several years. Anne thought that if Wendy's had an air current, she should be up wind. She wanted to get down to business and get the meeting finished.

Anne stood, waived her hand, and invited the brothers to the table. The conversation went quickly as the brothers seemed anxious to leave, like someone from law enforcement might be pleased to find the three of them located in the same place.

"So, you wanna buy the pit, huh? How much you offerin'? Arnold asked.

"So much for the small talk. How much do you think it's worth?" Anne replied.

"We're thinkin' round a million, give or take."

"I do want to thank you gentlemen for getting me out of the house this afternoon. It's such a beautiful day. I think I'll just run on up to Stone Mountain Park. I haven't been up there in several years. Y'all have a pleasant afternoon." She stood.

"Whoa, whoa," Arnold exclaimed as he too, stood. "Now that was just a suggestion, you know, kind of a number to put out there to get the conversation started. You know, a negotiation."

They both reoccupied their seats.

"Fellas, I'm not going to beat around the bush. I don't think that old pit is doing you boys any good. In fact, how much money have you made off the place in the last, say, fifty years? I'm guessin' you probably have a little still set-up in that hole somewhere, and you're making a few bucks running hooch. Or maybe not. Who knows? But I'll tell you what I do know. I know the property taxes haven't been paid on the place in two years. I also know how much I'm willing to pay. That's five hundred thousand even. You can take it or leave it. Period. I'll give you some time to talk it over. But in ten minutes I'm going to get in my car and leave, deal or no deal, and you'll never see me again. And I'm betting you can sit here and eat a lot of French fries before another offer of any kind comes walkin' through that door. Let me make it easy for you. I'll just ease up to the counter and order another Coke. Give you boys some time to talk it over. And one other thing. If the title search is successful and we can close, you'll get your money in five days."

In four minutes Arnold raised his hand and motioned Anne over. "You have a deal. And you say you can get us the money in five days?"

"I guess I should have said business days. That will be next Tuesday."

Arnold looked at his brothers, then to Anne and said, "Okay, you have a deal."

"Great," Anne said. "Here is a card with my real estate attorney's name and number. He'll be in contact with you about the closing. Oh, and Arnold, remember the three grand I gave you will offset the purchase price, so at closing y'all will be getting four hundred and ninety-seven thousand. Oh, and less the property taxes you owe. The county will be getting that."

The two brothers looked at Arnold.

As Anne left it dawned on her that during the meeting, neither Arthur nor Dwight had said a single word to her at any time.

That evening, after dinner, Anne asked Jason to come to her little office over the garage. There she had started the plans to cultivate a demolition and materials recycling business. She just needed to sell the idea to Jason.

"Do you remember me telling you I might have access to an exhausted granite quarry? And you do remember me saying I'd like to investigate the creation of a demolition company, don't you? And do you remember saying, and I quote, 'You run the proverbial numbers and I'll take a look at it?' Well, I have the numbers and I want you to look at it. In fact, I have a commitment to purchase the quarry immediately."

"And just exactly how much of a commitment did you make for the quarry?"

"We'll come back to that in a minute. First, look at these aerial photos of the property. You can see the hole here. It's six acres and about sixty-six feet deep. And here is a nice level piece of ground, nine acres, that would be perfect for offices, shop, the recycling facility, and the apartments."

"Apartments? What do you mean by apartments?"

"We'll come back to that, too. But look here. That's an old railroad spur that was used when the quarry was producing. It's still good, and perfect for hauling in money and shipping out money. Did you ever think about this? People will pay to get rid of debris that can be broken down and parts of it sold off. We would be paid to take inventory that would then be sold."

"Slow down a little. I can tell you're excited about this, but slow down. Tell me about the land, the quarry. How much will it cost?"

"First, look at this. It's an appraisal by Jordan Pendergast. And I know you know Jordan. He put a value on the property of this," she stated, pointing to the $712,000 on the front page of the appraisal. "I have a locked-down price of five hundred thousand. The sellers started out at one million. Pretty good, huh?"

"Well yeah, that's great. But this business has to be approved, left and right. What if you can't get the approval you need?"

"I've actually already been over that. I'll put in a botanical garden. The conditions in the pit are perfect, and don't forget I do have a degree in landscape architecture."

"So, now what? What else do you have to show me?"

"After the Butler Building fell, do you remember me asking you about the superintendent, David Gallimore? I contacted David and we had dinner the other night. You probably thought I was at some board meeting. Well, David developed a real interest in the quarry and the idea of starting a new venture. He prepared these, an asset listing costed out and a one-year cash flow projection. It adds up to two point five million. So, for a mere three million, we can have this puppy up and running. And I believe David Gallimore will sign on as president."

"Anne, that's a tremendous capital requirement for an unknown commodity. How do you expect to pull it off?"

"Oh, come on, Jason. How much do we have socked away at Schwab? Ten, twelve million? We have the capital. But if that's a concern, I have plan B. You, and Wentworth Construction, will have nothing to do with this business. I'll own it myself. And I know this banker by the name of Eric Buchanan. I think Eric will work with me. He'll have the quarry, which is a deal compared to the appraisal, and the equipment as collateral. And I can use my share of our savings as backup collateral if necessary. And to protect Wentworth Construction, I'm putting it all in a new LLC. I'll own it one hundred percent. And think about this. It will be one of those historically underutilized businesses. You know, a HUB. As the sole owner, and being a female, I am betting we can get all sorts of work. The company will pursue all contracts that are attractive, not just contracts with

Wentworth Construction. And let me ask you a question, and I know you don't have a crystal ball, but do you think Atlanta and the South will continue to grow, and tear down, and rebuild? And won't all those contractors, like you, need somewhere to dump their shit?"

That night, more or less, Democycle, LLC, the best name Anne could come up with, launched, or better yet, ignited. It was time to go to the bank.

27

ANNE CALLED DAVID GALLIMORE FIRST thing Friday morning. "Good morning David, this is Anne Wentworth. Is there any possible way you could get away to go to the bank with me today?"

"What time?" David asked. "We're closing shop at noon today, so the crew can get back to Louisiana for the weekend. I can hang around if the meeting can happen after lunch."

"I think I can make that happen. I'll call you back."

She next called Eric Buchanan at T Bank and set up a meeting at two o'clock at his office. She quickly indicated the purpose of the meeting to be business, not personal, and that she would be accompanied by David Gallimore.

The two-story T Bank building, sitting on a one-acre lot on the edge of the Atlanta financial district, looked to have been constructed around 1900. A spectacular specimen of

Greek Revival architecture, the building's exterior of gray granite displayed six large granite columns which supported the roof. The six columns, weighing 23,000 pounds each, fostered an impression of safety, security, strength, and trust. The dome atop the building offered a touch of elegance that the competition could not match. Utilizing all of the electronic features available in the modern banking landscape, T Bank competed head-to-head with all of the large multi-state banking institutions.

"To what do I owe the pleasure?" Eric asked as he lightly kissed Anne on the cheek. "It sounded like you have business to discuss, which I find interesting." Turning to David, Eric introduced himself and offered them each a seat at a table in a small conference room adjacent to his office.

"Eric, I want to start a business and I need to establish a financing vehicle to accomplish that goal. I'm talking about a considerable amount of money and a business that I believe will generate substantial profit early on. Can I show you what I have in mind?"

For over an hour, Anne moved through what she believed to be the essential components of her plan, beginning with David Gallimore. She described the demolition of the Butler Building and how that got her mind to contemplate the opportunities, especially relative to her knowledge of the old granite quarry.

"Eric, I believe I have the quarry wrapped up. A professional appraisal indicates a value of a little more than seven hundred thousand. I'm buying the property for five hundred thousand. That's a savings of roughly thirty percent. The total acreage is fifteen, with six being a granite pit perfect for the solid waste landfill. The additional nine acres are more than sufficient for an office building, a shop, the recycling facility, and an apartment complex. The six-acre hole represents over a half-million cubic yards of fill capacity. Eric, that's the size of six football fields. And the hole averages a depth of sixty-six feet."

She then moved on to the equipment and facility needs for the demolition operation only. At that point she turned the discussion over to David, who fell in step with her commentary and described the functional operation of a demolition company. He expounded on the quality of the site, having walked it the evening before with Anne. He did not sugarcoat the obstacles that had to be cleared in order to obtain a permit to operate. He discussed the prospects for the business given the current economic conditions, the avid desire on the part of development companies to grow the South, and the ever increasing demand due to the growth in population south of the Mason-Dixon Line.

"What happens if we hit another building slowdown, which historically, will occur at some point?" Eric asked.

"Well, the hole, or what's left of it, won't be going anywhere, so we just wait for the market to turn, which, as you say, historically it will," Anne said. "And think about this. As a solid waste landfill, when the hole is full, and it will be someday, our little company will own a pristine fifteen-acre plot of prime real estate just twelve miles from here. And there will be no problems with methane gas. The market value for land like that is around eighty thousand per acre. So after we get paid to fill the hole in, the dirt gets sold for one point two million, in today's dollars."

The funding requirements for the company were reviewed in detail along with the collateral that would be available to protect the bank's loans. The initial amount of the financing needs came to two and a half million dollars, two million on a long-term basis and five hundred thousand on a revolving line of credit. Anne, confident in the potential of the company, told Eric she thought the company could repay the loan within five years and that she had made the mental commitment to not take any profit distributions until the loans were repaid.

"Anne, your total borrowing requirements on your spreadsheet appear to be two point five million. This doesn't account for the purchase of the land. Where is the purchase money for the land?" Eric asked.

"Oh," Anne said, "that's coming from me. I'm contributing half a million dollars in capital into the LLC, and it will be used to purchase the land outright. You can still use it as collateral for the bank loans."

"Anne, and David, I find this fascinating. Obviously, we have to go through the regular loops and hoops here at the bank to commit to and fund such a request, but with the collateral, the business plan, and David's hands on the wheel, I don't perceive any problems. And, naturally, our relationship with Wentworth Construction and Jason will go a long way in helping us with our decision."

"Eric, this is going to be our company. I don't believe I mentioned Wentworth Construction or Jason at any point during our presentation and conversation. Please give no consideration to either in the process of making your decision. And if you feel like you can't do that, let me know now because we have a hole to fill and 'time's a-wastin'.'"

"I understand and I will honor that request. I hope to get back to you by Thursday or Friday with our proposal."

On the way back to the car, neither Anne nor David said a word. But once seated and latched in, David spoke.

"More than once you used the term 'our company.' I thought this was one hundred percent yours. I didn't think your husband or anyone else was going to be an owner."

Anne, who had already put the Land Rover in reverse to back out of the parking space, returned the gearshift to park and looked straight at David. "When I say ours, I mean yours and mine. You will be a ten percent owner in the LLC."

"I appreciate the thought, but I don't have the kind of money required of an owner."

"Are you kidding me? We just sat in there and convinced that bank – and I can assure you they will – to fund our business. As of today, ten percent of Democycle, LLC is worth a big fat zero. In fact, it's insolvent because we owe the lawyer money for drafting the agreement, in which I instructed him to include you as a ten percent owner."

"I just feel like I should have some skin in the game," David said as he looked through the windshield at the granite columns in front of the bank.

"You do have skin in the game David. You and your family."

In the end, T Bank, with the encouragement of Eric Buchanan, agreed to fund ninety percent of the start-up costs, backed in part by the Small Business Administration, some of Anne's savings, and a collateral assignment on all equipment and real estate. Three days after signing the initial loan, Anne presented architectural schematics for the office and recycling building, and the apartment complex. The bank agreed to a twenty-year mortgage loan for three million dollars to be used to build the structures.

David Gallimore came on board as president, and thanks to his knowledge and acquaintances, he put together a team of industry professionals. By the end of the first full year of operations, the company enjoyed a positive cash flow. By the end of the third year, annual profits exceeded one million dollars after bonuses. By the end of the fifth year, all original debt had been repaid, with the exception of the additional three million dollars borrowed to complete the construction of the recycling and office facility, and the apartment complex.

Democycle built a twenty-one unit apartment complex constructed on the back side of the level ground. One-third of the units had only one bedroom, one-third had two, and the final third three. The apartments were built solely to house former convicts and their families while they worked for Democycle and got their lives back together. The applications for employment were many, and turnover virtually nonexistent. With good pay, affordable housing, and the promise of a job, old lives got new beginnings.

28

LYNN BEGAN HER JOB AT Mercy Care on Monday morning. Wearing a gray cotton-covered button front, fit and flared, short-sleeved dress with a round neck, she arrived before the designated starting time of eight o'clock. To assure her time-ly arrival, Lynn had driven from Reid Lane to Mercy three times the day before, taking alternative routes. She parked her car, entered the front door of the building and sat, waiting for someone to appear. At eight sharp, a young lady took her position behind the tall, walnut finished, glass-topped recep-tionist desk. With a smile, and an offer of a cup of coffee, she informed Lynn that someone would be with her shortly. Lynn declined the coffee, thanked the receptionist, and sat in a side chair awaiting further instruction.

At eight-ten, Amber Sessions popped out from behind the reception area, shook Lynn's hand and gave her a semi-hug.

"What a pleasure to have you here. To get things started I'm taking you up to personnel so you can fill out all those forms and papers that seem to be so important to some people. When you finish with that, I'll come and get you and take you to your new office."

Personnel, the place, and the requisite plethora of paper that came with it, provided the first real taste of organized corporate structure for Lynn. At Gregor Dry Cleaning and Laundry, forms were not a part of the hiring function, at least as far as she was concerned. Maybe controlling Uncle Stanley took care of all that for her, as she would expect. But here at Mercy Care, the forms seemed endless. Complete Form W-9 (am I a dependent or not?), health insurance (do I want a high deductible so I can open an HSA account?), 401(k) participation agreement (do I leave it to my estate or do I have a beneficiary?), confidentiality agreement, trade secrets and intangible properties agreement, parking lot information disclosure, background inquiry authorization, and a few more.

"And finally," the head of HR said, "here is our personnel manual. You will need to take it home and read it, and return this paper, signed by you, declaring that you have read the manual and that you will comply with it."

Just before ten, Amber came to take Lynn to her new office. Located near the top of the stairs on the third floor, the office, requiring a stretch of the imagination to call it such, more closely resembled a closet. Nine by twelve with a door, and elegantly appointed with a gray metal desk, a mesh back faux leather desk chair, and one metal side chair, Lynn looked in with a certain degree of pride. Atop the desk sat a telephone and what appeared to be a brand new Apple computer with a printer.

Lynn invested the time from ten to noon meeting people. One by one, they came. From development, from operations, from accounting, from security, from administration, from under the carpet, and from out of the tree that grew near the building's entrance. Then off to lunch with the two women she would be working with making grant requests.

Following lunch, one of the ladies, Joanne Vonderheide, spent the remainder of the afternoon with Lynn. They reviewed the functions and files held captive in the Apple, discussed the requirements and expectations of data presented in a grant request, examined a few old grant request binders, and discussed the various departments that made up Mercy. Lynn also learned more about Joanne's children and personal life than she really cared to know, but she knew to let it ride.

On Tuesday morning, Lynn received her first set of documents to start a grant request. Fortunately, a well-designed template existed in the Apple that cut through the confusion by using what Joanne called the boilerplate format. The recipient of the request, the newly announced Alexander Family Foundation of Macon, stood ready to provide funds to qualified Georgia charitable institutions. Mercy Care stood ready to accept the Foundation's money.

At four o'clock Lynn tapped on the door of Joanne's spacious fourteen by twelve office to tender her first go at grant writing. Uncertain and nervous, Lynn waited as Joanne thumbed through the written request and its attachments.

"Lynn, this looks very good. I'll need to go over it in more detail, but it looks good. It's four o'clock and you have completed something that I thought would take you the rest of the week. I would expect that I would have spent two days on this myself. How did you get it done so fast?"

"I just got with it. I guess coming from the laundry and dry cleaning business there is always a sense of urgency. When people give you their clothes, they want them back promptly. And I mean ASAP. That's the way I do things."

"Well, in the future, don't be getting in that big of a hurry. Okay?" Joanne said without making eye contact.

On Wednesday, mid-morning, a couple of fellow employees, Janet and Robin, last names currently unknown, invited Lynn to join them on their morning break. A Starbucks, not surprisingly, sat across the street and catty-corner to Mercy. It had become the "get-out-of-the-office coffee break place." The personnel manual specifically stated the morning and afternoon breaks were to consist of two ten minute periods of rest and relaxation. Tradition, complemented with no objections, had expanded the time to twenty minutes per break. Plenty of time to scoot over to Starbucks, grab an oatmilk honey latte with blonde espresso, chit-chat for a few minutes, and hustle back to the office to enjoy the balance of the drink.

Being on her first out-of-the-office break, and being in a Starbucks for the first time ever, Lynn laid back and let her two colleagues lead the way. She observed what seemed to be the standard procedure of ordering, paying, and waiting. When she stepped up to face the barista, she ordered a simple cup of coffee and provided her name upon request, Lynn.

"Hey, I like that name," came a masculine voice from directly behind her.

Lynn turned around to see an average-sized man, early thirties, wearing baggy shorts, flip-flops, an Atlanta Hawks basketball jersey, number 21, and a GQ fashionable scruffy three-day growth of beard. He had a mop of brown hair, brown eyes, teeth that were just a little too white, and a round face that indicated a little too much latte and not enough basketball.

"Hey, I haven't seen you in here before. Are you just passing through or do you think you'll be back, maybe about this same time tomorrow?" He stood just a little too close, getting into Lynn's personal space.

"Hey," Lynn replied, rather sarcastically, "I don't know you from Adam's off ox, and you're pretty snoopy for someone dressed like you just graduated high school." She retreated to her office companions.

Robin leaned over and whispered to Lynn, asking, "Don't you know who that is?"

"I haven't a clue. And couldn't care less."

"Oh, my god," she said, "that's Tatum Anderson. He's only worth about a gazillion dollars. And he wanted to launch a conversation with you and you shut him down. Wow."

"He may be worth a gazillion dollars, but he seems a little pushy to me."

As the women got their drinks and headed to the door, Tatum Anderson spoke, directing his comment solely to Lynn.

"I'm planning on being here tomorrow just about this time. I sure hope to see you here."

Crossing the street back to Mercy, Janet said, "I hope you're planning on going to Starbucks tomorrow morning, and if you do, can we come with you?" she asked enthusiastically.

"I'll think about it, and sure, I don't care if you come along. Maybe he'll hit on one of you."

"I doubt it Lynn. We don't have the cutes working for us like you do."

On the Thursday morning break, Lynn begrudgingly toddled over to Starbucks at the bidding of Janet and Robin. Tatum sat near the entrance where he had been waiting for forty-five minutes.

"There you are," he said as he got up and extended his hand. "I'm Tatum Anderson and I apologize if I seemed a little direct yesterday. I'm hoping we can get off on better footing today. Can I buy you and your friends' coffees?"

His wardrobe had overgone a renaissance moment during the night. Dressed in grey tweed trousers and a light blue long-sleeved casual shirt, his outward appearance had improved substantially.

"I'm Bec..., excuse me, I'm Lynn Gregor, and this is Janet, and Robin. So sure, we'll let you buy us a cup of coffee. That would be nice. We can all sit over here and chat. But, we only have a few minutes because we have to get back to work."

They, all four, sat and talked for about fifteen minutes. Most of the conversation centered around Tatum, coming from Tatum. Tatum held himself in rather high esteem, and demonstrated the fact that he had no reservations about promoting himself. When Janet stood and advised Lynn and Robin that the time had come to vamoose, Tatum kept his seat.

"Hey, Lynn, could I get your digits?"

"My digits?"

"Hey, your cell phone number."

Lynn complied with his request and he assured her he would be calling soon. Soon turned out to be ten minutes later.

"Hey, how about dinner and some partying tomorrow night, unless you're booked? We can go to Le Bilboquet for dinner and then we'll go to The Sanctuary Club for some dancing. How does that sound?"

Lynn complied with this request also, and provided her address and chose a time of seven. Tatum thought that to be a little early, but he would be there to pick her up.

29

UPON ARRIVING HOME FROM WORK, Lynn rushed to the back door, gave two quick taps and heard that ever-friendly "come on in" from Anne. Anne stood by the sink, preparing potatoes for dinner and Jason sat in the nook, reading a document.

"Guess what? I have a date. I have a real date and I'm going out tomorrow night. Can you believe it?"

"Lynn, that's super. Tell us all about it."

"He's a guy I met at work. Well, not at work, but while I was working. Oh, anyway, I met him at Starbucks and his name's Tatum Anderson."

The name floated into the stream of Jason's consciousness. "Excuse me, Lynn, did you say Tatum Anderson?"

"Yes, why? Is he okay? I just met him. A couple of girls at work told me he was rich, but I really don't know anything about him."

"Well, I think it's safe to say he has some money. He's one of these computer guys who seems to be able to think something up, put it on the internet or somewhere, sell it and make tons of money. At least that's what I've heard about him," Jason said. "And you have a date with him tomorrow night?"

"Yes, dinner and dancing."

"That sounds exciting," Anne said. "Now sit down and tell us everything."

Within five minutes Lynn had divulged everything she knew, which obviously wasn't much.

"I gave him this address. He's supposed to pick me up at seven. I hope that's okay."

"It's just fine," Anne said. "He can come and pick you up at the front door of this house like a gentleman. And I know your next question, 'What am I going to wear?' Since I know where you're going, I can get that together while you're at work. You'll have plenty of time to get ready after you get home tomorrow. I promise."

At long last, the Friday workday came to its finale for Lynn. She had been the talk of the office. By noon it appeared as if everyone at Mercy Care knew she had a date with Tatum. Numerous people, including two she had never met, stopped by her office to comment or wish her luck, which she thought extremely odd. For some intuitive reason, she lacked the excitement that others exhibited.

She arrived home at six, ready to prepare for the evening out. Anne, as promised, had laid out the appropriate attire for the date. Both destinations accepted nice blue jeans and a blouse on Friday night and that is what Anne suggested. She advised Lynn to wear her most comfortable pair of flats to avoid sore feet or blisters.

A few minutes before seven, Lynn, wearing blue jeans and a forest green, long-sleeved button-up chiffon blouse, V-necked with a fitted waist, paced the floor. After Anne told her Le Bilboquet was an upscale French restaurant, she reviewed the eating etiquette Ava had taught her. And how to dance. She didn't know how to dance, at least not in the big city.

"Don't worry Lynn," Anne said. "And you look great."

"You're going to fit in well with the uptown crowd," Jason chimed in for the first time. "You look hot."

"Jason, really!" Anne exclaimed.

"You have to admit, she doesn't exactly look like a country bumpkin anymore." He grinned at Lynn when he said it.

The low rumble from the exhaust of the car pulling into the circular drive got the attention of Jason. He would say the sound was intense. It was not the sound of a muscle car, it was the sound of speed. The kind of sound that comes from a Ferrari or a Lamborghini. He walked to the side window by the front doors to see a cobalt blue McLaren. He turned to Lynn and said, "Wherever you're going tonight, you're going to get there in a hurry."

"Now we get to meet Mr. Anderson," Anne said.

Just as she spoke, Lynn's cell phone dinged with the announcement of a text from Tatum Anderson.

TA: *Out front. Let's go.*

"So much for chivalry," Anne said as Lynn walked out the door.

After the door closed, Anne started to open it again and Jason put his hand against it to stop her.

"Don't dare ask her what time she'll be home. She's twenty-eight."

Tatum Anderson sat snuggly in the driver's side of the McLaren. He lowered the passenger side window and said, "Hey, put all four of your fingers along the bottom side of that ridge just below the window and slide them toward the front of the car. The door will pop open. When it does, just pull up."

The butterfly wing door raised smoothly, up and forward to the front of the car. The smell of the top-grade black leather upholstery wafted from the cabin. Lynn found her seat to be very low to the ground but comfortable. After she buckled her seatbelt, she could have reached out and touched the rough gray stone surface of the Wentworth drive.

"Reach up and pull there and the door will close," Tatum said, pointing.

Jason watched as the McLaren exited the driveway and turned left heading toward the freeway. "He probably has a little dick, otherwise he wouldn't need that car," he said to Anne.

30

"I GUESS THIS IS WHAT a spaceship feels like," Lynn said. "What kind of car is this?"

"It's a McLaren Seven-Twenty S," Tatum said over the rumble of the exhaust. "Do you want to go for a little spin before dinner? We have time. I can pop over to I-Seventy Five for a runabout."

"Sure, I guess. What's a McLaren? I've never heard of it."

"It's obviously a high performance automobile. It's made by McLaren Automotive, a British manufacturer. It has a four liter V-eight engine with seven hundred and ten horsepower. The engine's behind you. It will hit one hundred and twenty-four miles per hour in seven point eight seconds and has a top-end speed of two hundred and twelve miles per hour."

"Wow," Lynn said. "Do you mind saying what it cost? I know I shouldn't ask, but it's not every day I get to ride in a car like this."

"I don't mind. This little jewel cost me around three hundred and eighty thousand, before taxes and title."

Tatum pulled the car onto the highway and accelerated. Lynn felt the force of the engine as her body pushed against the seatback. He darted in and out of traffic, passing some cars as though they stood still. Lynn could not see the speedometer, but she knew that she had never sensed such speed before. Tatum slowed the car, exited and turned back toward Atlanta.

"You said this thing will go two hundred and twelve miles an hour? What good does that do you? The speed limit, lawfully, is seventy. My car will do seventy and it cost about thirty thousand. So, except for acceleration, I get the impression you paid about three hundred and fifty thousand too much."

"If that's the way you want to look at it." Tatum said.

"Oh, I'm just kidding you. But three hundred and fifty thousand dollars is more than I've ever made in my life."

"Based on where you live, somebody's raking in some coin."

"That's not my house. I don't live there, I'm just staying there for the time being. I'm staying in the guest house behind the big house. You don't seem to mind talking about your money. Jason Wentworth, who owns the house where I'm staying, said you made a lot of money with computers."

"Not with computers, per se, but with computer programs and old-fashioned capitalism. Computers are just dumb boxes until they're told what to do. I thought up an idea about how lower-wage employees could participate in IRA investing. It helped the employer, the employee, and the investment companies and banks holding the invested funds. I get tons of revenue from medium-size companies all over the country that are willing to pay fees to make their lives easier."

"That must be nice. I certainly wouldn't know. Where did you go to college? Where did you learn to do that stuff?"

"Ha, college," Tatum scoffed. "I had one semester of community college. I didn't have time for college, I had ideas to develop. How about you? Where did you matriculate?"

"Where did I do what?"

"Go to college?"

"I didn't go. I've spent most of my life making the world a cleaner place, but the pay wasn't that good so I came to Atlanta to take another grab at that brass ring people used to talk about. I have no idea what it means."

Tatum turned off of Buckhead Avenue onto Bolling Way and pulled into the valet parking queue. Two attentive valet service employees hustled over to the McLaren. The one on the passenger side of the car stood and stared, looking for a door handle to open the door to permit Lynn's exit. He might as well have been staring at a Rubik's cube. Through the window, Lynn instructed him to run his fingers along the bottom of the ridge as she had been told.

On the driver's side of the car, Tatum opened his door wide as the attendant approached. He tossed him the fob and said, "Take good care of her."

"Yes, sir. We will park it right here behind this Benz. They should get along well."

As a lot of upscale restaurants with valet parking are inclined to do, the very expensive automobiles seem to have a parking spot available on the street right in front of the restaurant. The cars make a silent announcement about the type of patrons who dine at those establishments. The McLaren joined the Friday night lineup already in place at Le Bilboquet, consisting of a Mercedes-Benz S-Class Cabriolet convertible and a Bentley Flying Spur. The cheap seventy-five thousand dollar vehicles were parked out of sight in a parking garage.

Le Bilboquet, a sleek, one-story structure on the corner, had an inviting presence. Around the front and one side of the building were two-top and four-top tables covered in white linen tablecloths and surrounded by wicker chairs. White patio umbrellas stood above the tables, affording the patrons some protection from the elements, if needed. The inside of the restaurant was bright, warm, and spacious, but not so big as to feel overly commercial. The attention to detail gave the restaurant an ambiance of a true French bistro.

Seated at a table next to an art-covered wall and well away from the clatter of the kitchen, the waiter, with a wine list and menus in hand, greeted Tatum and Lynn.

"Welcome to Le Bilboquet. We are so pleased that you have joined us. Can I interest you in a drink this evening before your meal, or would you care to see the wine list?"

"I think this is going to be a special evening," Tatum said. "Bring us a bottle of your best champagne."

"Sir, that would be our Krug Grande Cuvée NV. But I must tell you that a bottle costs six hundred dollars. We don't want there to be any misunderstanding."

"That will be fine. Like I said, I think tonight is going to be a very special night."

The waiter brought the champagne, as ordered, and poured a flute for both Lynn and Tatum.

"Here's to you," Tatum said, lifting his glass.

"Cheers," Lynn said. She took one small sip and put it down.

"Don't you like it?" Tatum asked. "It's the most expensive they have."

"I really don't care for it. Let's just say I never developed a taste for champagne."

The waiter returned and took their orders. Lynn requested an organic mixed green salad, seared Atlantic salmon, and substituted French fries for the lentils. She said she thought the French fries were important since she was dining in a French restaurant. Finding only one knife, one fork, and one spoon on the table gave her some comfort. Tatum ordered a kale and quinoa salad, braised veal cheeks with king trumpet mushrooms and spinach for his entree. For dessert they each had a French Napoleon pastry. At the end of the meal Tatum paid the check, tip included, with his American Express Black credit card. Lynn got a glimpse of the total, over nine hundred dollars.

"Let's go dancing," Tatum said as he pushed his chair back. "We're going to The Sanctuary. Have you ever been there?"

"No," Lynn said with some reluctance in her voice. Her dancing experience amounted to a few post-game parties in high school, coupled with the Senior prom, which took two months of begging before Uncle Stanley agreed to let her go. "It sounds like we're going to church."

"Let me assure you, The Sanctuary is not church. We are going to have a lot of fun."

They buckled up in the McLaren and drove what didn't amount to a half mile, where Tatum pulled the car into a strip mall parking lot. All of the businesses appeared to be closed for the evening, except for the club at the end of the facility. Even with sufficient parking available, Tatum pulled into the valet parking queue. Well, actually no queue existed as his vehicle represented the only taker. Once again, Tatum flipped the fob to the valet and barked some orders. Lynn had to guide the valet on her side of the car through the exercise of how to open the door.

Lynn heard the head valet say, "It will be right here when you return, sir," as they made their way to the door.

Tatum slipped the gatekeeper twenty dollars for the normal entry fee and they walked inside. Friday night was salsa night and Latin American music with its driving rhythm left no doubt as to the musical genre for the evening. The club operated on two floors, the first floor offering a bar, the only restrooms in the club, and free salsa lessons. A grand stairway led to the second floor where the big dance floor sparkled in the rainbow-colored rays from strobe lights that flashed with the beat of the music.

Tatum explained to Lynn that free salsa lessons were available on the first floor, and she accepted an invitation from an instructor without pause. The teacher made Lynn feel comfortable. Within minutes, she felt in perfect step and had cultivated the courage to go up the stairs with Tatum.

Tatum forked over another twenty to assure an acceptable seating arrangement and ordered drinks. He requested a Cuba Libre. Lynn, going on best guess, ordered a margarita. She had never had one in her life. After listening to a couple of songs and watching the fluid motion of the bodies on the floor, Tatum extended a hand for a dance. Lynn, ever thankful to the instructor on the first floor, felt like she could hold her own. The DJ on the platform against the back wall of the dance floor bombarded the room with *Yambeque*. Song followed song with no time gap in between. The fast beat and the fast movement of the dancers raised the temperature of the room. Patches of wetness showed on the shirts and blouses of the guests as their movements flowed with the rhythm. In Lynn's vernacular, Tatum got just "a little too gropey and a little too grabby" on the dance floor. After four songs she moved back to the table, followed by Tatum.

At the table they engaged in a little conversation as Tatum finished his drink and ordered another. Lynn's margarita transformed from slush to liquid as it sat untouched. The conversation eventually focused on money, seemingly Tatum's favorite subject.

"I just can't imagine having money like you," Lynn finally said. "It's just something, unfortunately, I've never had a whole lot of."

Tatum shoved his hand down into a pant pocket and extracted a folded stack of bills the likes of which Lynn had only seen in the movies. All hundreds, Lynn guessed there must have been twenty-five to thirty in the wad. Tatum thumbed off ten new hundreds, Franklin's face in directional uniformity. He pushed them across the table to Lynn.

"Here," he said. "Just put those in your little purse. That way maybe you can get used to the feel of having a little money."

"I can't take this money."

"I'm not giving you the money, I'm just letting you feel it. Take good care of it for a spell."

Lynn took the bills, counted them, and placed them in her Michael Kors metallic-plated clutch. She thought there they would stay until Tatum requested it back.

After another drink for Tatum, four more dances accompanied by another round of unwelcomed groping and grabbing, and a trip downstairs to the restroom, Lynn said she thought the time had come to call it an evening. Tatum, without objection, said he thought departing suited their needs.

They maneuvered their way into the McLaren, which waited for them in front of the club as promised. With seatbelts fastened, Tatum pushed the start button.

31

"Hey, what do you think about heading over to my condo for a nightcap? I live right over here on Peachtree, not ten minutes away. You'll love the place. Has a great view of downtown. I picked it up for a cool four point three mil. I think I could sell it for five and a half today. It's super comfortable."

"No, thank you though. My eighty-five dollar wristwatch says it's time for me to head home. It would be best if we headed that way."

"Hey, come on. Tomorrow's Saturday. That place you work, they're not open on Saturday. It's only eleven fifteen. I'll have you home by, say one-thirty. What do you say?"

Before Lynn could reply, Tatum reached across the console, put his hand on the nape of her neck and pulled. Hard. With Lynn weighing slightly over one hundred pounds, he nearly dragged her over the console before she could react. A flash of fear shot through Lynn's body and mind. The pain in her neck, sharp but bearable, could not overcome the sight in her mind's eye of Uncle Stanley. How many times had she been drawn to attention in this manner? As her head crossed over the console, Tatum attempted to kiss her on the mouth. She drove her right hand up to block his facial assault, then with all of her strength, she put her hands on his ribcage and pushed as forcefully as she could while jerking her head back toward the passenger side of the car. This freed her from his grasp.

"What are you doing?" she yelled at him.

"Hey, some chicks like it a little rough. I thought I'd give it a try. Nothing ventured, nothing gained, right?"

"Do not touch me again, and take me home, now," she insisted.

"Okay. Okay. You don't have to be such a bitch. After all, I did buy you dinner. There should be something in it for me."

"If you pull anything like that again, what's going to be in it for you is a trip to jail. Now I mean it. Take me home. On second thought, I'll just get out and Uber home. How do you open this door?"

With those words, Tatum slammed the car into gear and spun the tires exiting the parking lot. He turned left onto Paces Ferry Place to return to Buckhead. As he approached the Irby Avenue intersection, just a couple of blocks from the club, a black Chevy Tahoe pulled across the lane he occupied, blocking his way. Another black Tahoe blocked the other lane, keeping Anderson from turning onto Irby. Tatum slammed on the brakes and cursed. Another black Tahoe, coming from behind, off of Vieux Carre, pulled up within inches of the back of the McLaren. Then all hell broke loose. Red lights. Blue lights. White lights. In addition to the three Tahoes, Atlanta city police units, at least six of them, surrounded everything. Within seconds police officers and several men wearing windbreakers with the FBI, ATF, and DEA initials in plain sight circumscribed the car.

"FBI! Kill the engine and put your hands in plain sight on the steering wheel!"

Two policemen stood on both sides of the McLaren, pointing shotguns at its inhabitants. The other officers and agents, as best Lynn could see, held pistols. Being from "Smalltown," Alabama, she immediately recognized the pistols as nine-millimeter Glocks.

"What is going on?" she yelled at Tatum, who seemed to be rather smug about the entire situation. "What have you done? What have you gotten me into?"

As she sought answers, Tatum held up his left hand to show he held nothing and pushed his door open after having been instructed by the FBI agent to do so.

"Voxlow," the agent called him. "Your timeclock just expired. No overtime in this game, dude. Now get out of the car, slowly, get on the ground and put your hands behind your back."

"Voxlow? What does he mean by Voxlow? Who are you?" Lynn demanded before she heard a hard tap on the window to her right.

"Open the door ma'am," came the instruction from an Atlanta policeman after tapping the window with his Glock.

"I don't know how," Lynn yelled back at him through the glass. "Put your four fingers under that ridge and move them toward the front of the car."

After opening the door, the officer said, "Now slowly get out of the car, turn around and put your hands on the roof. Put your cell phone on the car seat. I'm going to frisk you, so don't move."

After exiting the car and being frisked, Lynn had both questions and explanations at the ready. She had not factored in the implications of being handcuffed and told to "stand still and keep your mouth shut."

Across the top of the McLaren she could hear the agent speaking in a very calm voice to Tatum. "Mr. Anderson, we have a warrant for your arrest. You are now under arrest. You are being charged with conspiracy to distribute narcotics, trafficking and distribution of illegal substances, wire fraud, money laundering, and a few other things that I'm sure will pop up when the DA has a grand jury convened to hear your story. You have the right to remain silent...."

Lynn, handcuffed and nearly in a state of shock, continued her unilateral conversation with the police officer. "What is going on and what have I done? I was just on a date. I just met that guy."

After several minutes, and what to Lynn seemed to be an eternity, an FBI agent came over to her and the police officer. He held Lynn's clutch purse in his hand.

"What are we going to do with her?" the officer asked.

"We have no interest in her. She's not on our radar screen, or the DEA's for that matter," the FBI agent said. "If you want to take her in on a local charge, it's up to you. I found a thousand dollars in her purse. Ten brand new hundreds. You can get this young lady on a money laundering charge."

"No, no way! He just gave me the money to hold, like some kind of stupid game. It's not my money. I haven't laundered anything."

"Ma'am," said the police officer. "You can explain it all to the judge tomorrow. You have the right to..."

"You're taking me to jail? Why? I haven't done anything. I don't even drink. Will you please get my phone out of the car so I can call someone? Please, I didn't do anything!"

"Yes, ma'am. And Snow White didn't know the apple was poisoned, but she ate it, didn't she? I've heard it all before. We'll gather your belongings, your purse, the money, and your cell phone, and take them to the station. They're now evidence and may, or may not, be returned to you, depending on how your case goes. You'll be given an opportunity to make a phone call after you have been processed."

"What do you mean, processed?"

"Really? You're not that naïve are you? How about booked? Same thing."

As two officers guided Lynn toward a cruiser for a ride to Fulton County Jail, she saw Tatum Anderson still standing and being lectured to about something. Afraid, bewildered, and shaking, she saw what looked to be her last opportunity to speak her mind. "Thanks a lot, you ASSHOLE!" she yelled at the top of her lungs.

32

THE STOCKY, THICK OFFICER OPENED the back door of
the Ford Interceptor and the tall, lanky officer held his hand
above Lynn's head as she entered the vehicle and slid across
the plastic seat. Neither officer wanted to answer to a police
brutality claim should Lynn have slammed her head into the
door frame.

"Now I'm going to reach across you and fasten your seatbelt so you'll be safe. Don't bite me, or this situation could
change in a hurry," the lanky one said.

"I'm not going to bite you Officer, I just want to go home."

"I can appreciate that ma'am," the stocky one said as he
crawled into the passenger's side of the Interceptor. "However,
that's not going to happen."

A thick piece of plexiglass separated Lynn from the officers, but she could easily hear them. The handcuffs, which

remained on her wrists, felt uncomfortable and pinched her skin. She could not lean back against the seat, so she leaned over against the door seeking some level of comfort. The unpleasant odor coming off of the door changed that line of thought and she sat up straight again.

"Where are you taking me?" she asked.

The stocky officer made a one-third counter-clockwise turn and looked at Lynn. "You've never been arrested before, have you?"

"Well, no, I've never been arrested. And I don't want to be arrested now, since I haven't done anything wrong."

"Let me go ahead and tell you, I'm betting this has just turned into the worst day of your life. You are about to have a very unpleasant experience. I'm not being mean, I'm just trying to get you ready for what you're about to face. But if there's any comfort in saying it, you will come out the other side in one piece. The jail's about seven or so miles south, so we'll have you out of here in about twenty minutes. Then we have to go fill out a report describing what went on this evening."

Within a matter of minutes the police vehicle approached an institutional-looking building, pulled up to a huge garage door, and parked. The stocky officer got out to talk to someone and the lanky officer said, "This is the jail and behind that door is the sally port. This is where you'll get out after the door is opened. I'll tell you that I believe you didn't do anything bad, but like you, my hands are tied if you'll excuse the play on words. I'm not in a position to determine your final disposition. I hope you understand." And with those closing words, the bay door opened and the vehicle took the one-way path into the sally port.

After the Interceptor pulled into the sally port and the garage door closed, Lynn sensed that her environment had just become transformed. The stocky officer opened the vehicle door, assisted Lynn from the back seat, and removed the handcuffs, telling her she would not get to keep them as a souvenir. Two rather large men met her at the bottom of a ramp and ushered her into hell.

At the top of the ramp and through a heavy metal door, Lynn met her new temporary companions for the evening, female Detention Officers Meadows and Townsend.

Officer Meadows informed Lynn that she and Ms. Townsend would be her escorts for the next thirty minutes or so, and they wanted to have a nice, peaceful experience, to which Lynn did not object. Ms. Townsend didn't appear to have a lot to say.

"I'm scared. I want you to know that."

"Oh, we know it, and you should be. You don't appear to be cut out for this type of entertainment. I'll do this for you. I'll tell you what's about to happen as we go along so you won't be getting no big surprises. How's that?"

"I would really appreciate that," Lynn said. "Can you tell me your first names?"

"We don't get that question often, but sure. I'm Mikayla and this is Alexa, and no, you can't ask her any question you want.

"Now, let's get to work. The first part is going to be the most unpleasant, I'll just go ahead and tell you that. Head right into that little room there and we'll be coming with you. This is the strip search area. This is how we make sure everyone in here is safe, as best we can. Now when I said strip search, I didn't say cavity search. That's a whole different deal and I doubt you'll be participating in that activity. At least I hope not.

"If you would, please remove all of your clothes. That means bra, panties, everything. I know it's embarrassing, but this is the way it is. But nobody is going to touch you.

"Now, I want you to squat down with your legs spread, like you were a catcher on a baseball field. Do you know what I mean? Okay. Now, I want you to cough three or four times pretty hard. Well, you passed that one girl, so put your clothes back on."

As she dressed, Lynn knew she had never heard the term exuberant humiliation, but she had just lived it. She prayed that Mikayla had told her the truth about this being the worst part.

"Now we're going to move clockwise around this big room to different stations. Let's go over here where this EMT is going to take you vital signs. It's just a quick health screening. We don't want you bringing something in that's not welcome."

The EMT took Lynn's blood pressure, examined her eyes, ears, nose and throat, and listened to her lungs and heartbeat. She passed and moved on to the next station.

"This is where we check your fingerprints to see if you have any warrants or such outstanding. It'll also tell us if you been in the system before. Some people just forget that they had been locked up before. Have you ever been fingerprinted?"

"Yes, ma'am. When I got my driver's license recently here in Georgia."

Lynn pressed her fingers, as told, onto the electronic scanner. As she had told the officers, no warrants or priors popped up.

"You're doing good girl. Now, we're going into booking. We have another medical review, but more in depth. This will be done by a medical records specialist. It's kinda like going to a new doctor and you have to fill out all that paperwork before you see the doc. It's about how your health has been for about your whole life. This is for your protection so you don't have any problems while you're here visiting with us."

The inquiries by the specialist were exactly as Mikayla had said. "Have you ever had, or do you currently have, allergic reactions to any medications, yes or no? Do you have, or have you ever had, ... And the list went on. Finally, after thirty-two "no's" and one minor "yes," Lynn moved on to the next station.

"This is where you get your picture taken, your mugshot to most people, and your fingerprints taken. Everything is electronic, so you don't get your fingers inky like in the old days. You can give a little smile when your mugshot is taken if you want to. But, if it turns out too cute, some asshole might put it on the internet, so I wouldn't look too cute if I were you."

Lynn did not smile.

"You have now been all checked in. This is where we say our goodbyes," Mikayla said. Ms. Townsend had yet to utter a word.

"Can you tell me what happens next before you leave?" Lynn asked.

"Yes. Everyone is reviewed to determine if they might get bailed out or released tonight. Those that do will be turned out. Those that don't will go to a holding cell."

"Do you think I will be released?"

"No, I'm sorry. You've been charged with a felony, so you'll have to go before a judge tomorrow. You'll be spending the night here with us."

At this point Lynn moved into what the officers called the holding cell, along with the other felons, drug dealers, thieves, rapists, and murders. The very marginal feeling of comfort Lynn had developed with Mikayla and her silent sidekick melted away like a snowflake on her tongue.

A service provider looked Lynn over and returned with a large plastic bag, which she handed to Lynn.

"These are your blues. Your jail garb. You will go into the shower area over there where you will take shower. When you're done, you'll put all, and I mean all, of your clothes into this plastic bag, which now holds the clothing you will be wearing. These are called the blues. You are provided with a shirt and a pair of pants. They're like pajamas. You also get a bra, panties, socks, and a pair of flip-flops. You will wear all of these items. After you're done taking your shower and putting on your blues, you will be taken to the second floor and wait for classification."

"Classification?"

"Yeah, you are classified by the level of your offense and your potential threat to others. That's how it's determined where you'll spend the night. You won't be put in a holding cell with the rapists and murders. You'll be in with the thieves and petty drug dealers, and maybe a lady of the night or two. But you'll be in there with all of them, so watch yourself."

"When do I get to use the phone to call someone? Don't I get my one phone call?"

"You'll get that right after you get in your blues. And we actually give you more than one call if you need it. We want you to speak to someone who cares, or someone that can bail you out. I'm just gonna go ahead and tell you, you ain't goin' nowhere tonight unless you know somebody like the Governor. You have a felony charge so you'll have to go before a judge tomorrow morning if you can find somebody who can come down here and help you out. So when you make that call you might tell 'em that, so you'll just ruin part of their night. Getting' up and comin' down here ain't gonna speed things up."

Following her shower, and decked out in her ill-fitting blues, the Detention Officer directed Lynn to a bank of phones where she punched in the cell phone number of Anne Wentworth. The clock on the bedside table showed 2:14 a.m. when the phone rang.

33

"ANNE. HELP ME. I'M IN jail."

"Lynn? You're what?"

"I'm in jail. It's horrible. The jerk I went out with tonight is some kind of big-time criminal. Into drugs I think. And he got arrested by the FBI and everyone else and they arrested me because that jerk gave me some money that wasn't mine and the police thought it was and they put handcuffs on me and I didn't do anything and they just wouldn't believe me."

"Wow! Slow down. Let's slow down. Take a deep breath. Now, where are you? Where in jail I mean. And talk slowly."

"I'm in the Fulton County Jail. This is crazy. The woman here said I would be spending the night and to let you know that it would do no good to come and try to get me out. They said I'll have a meeting with a judge tomorrow and could get out then, but I need an attorney. They took my phone, so I can't call out. Now the lady is giving me the cut-throat sign, so I better get off. Please help me."

"Why did they arrest you? What did you do?"

"I didn't do anything. They arrested me for money laundering. I have to go."

Anne turned on the table lamp by the bed and looked at Jason. Lying on his side with his back to Anne, he didn't move a muscle.

"Are you awake?"

"Yeah, what do you think?"

"Did you hear that?"

"Yes."

"Well, what are you going to do?"

"What do you mean, what am I going to do? She's your buddy, you get her out of this mess."

"Jason Wentworth, I can't believe you! That girl needs help and you're best suited to help her. She needs an attorney. You know all the lawyers. I guess I could help her out by sending Paul Passmore over there, but ya know what, she doesn't need a will drafted right now. I guess I'll get up and start calling attorneys. And I'm not calling one of those one eight-hundred scum balls who runs television ads at midnight. I'm starting with Preston Burt and working my way down. If he's good enough for Wentworth Construction then he's good enough for Lynn Gregor."

"Don't call Preston. He's a corporate litigator. He doesn't get people out of jail, and neither do the other lawyers at Spence and Burt."

"Maybe he can give us a referral then. You pay him enough money. I'm sure he owes you a favor or two. Come on. Lynn sounds scared to death."

"Okay, okay. I'll call him."

Jason rolled to the edge of the bed, sat up, scratched his backside, put on his reading glasses, snatched his cell phone from his nightstand, and hit the contacts icon.

"Preston, it's Jason Wentworth. Sorry to bother you at this hour, but I need some help. Yeah, my clock says the same thing. Sorry. But here's the deal."

Jason, as best he could, explained the situation to one of the top corporate lawyers in the South. He said a good referral would fulfill his needs and requested the same. Burt gave him the name of Mariano Valdez.

"Mariano and I went to law school together. He's a damn good guy and he's extremely successful. Criminal law only," Burt said. "A jail call is like eighty-five rungs below his pay grade and you'll piss him off if you call him. Do you have a pen and paper? Here's his number. Now this is his cell phone, so you are going to get him, not voicemail. If you call him, please record the call if you can because I want to listen to him chew on your ass for waking him up. Maybe over a scotch some evening at your expense. It should be very entertaining. And be sure and use my name, just to gripe his ass. Good night. Oh, wait. Get us a tee time for Sunday morning, okay?"

Jason thought for a few seconds and dialed the number. It rang four times before a sleepy-sounding voice came on the line with a quiet "Hello."

"Mr. Valdez, my name is Jason Wentworth. Your name was given to me by Preston Burt. I need your help."

"Preston Burt, huh. He gave you my number? I hope you woke that son of a bitch up too. This better be important."

Jason, once again, as best he could, gave all of the details he possessed. Valdez seemed to listen attentively and said not a word until Jason had finished.

"Jason," Valdez asked, "do you mind if I call you Jason? Oh, who gives a shit. Jason, here's the deal. First, asking me to make a jail run is like asking a top-notch heart surgeon to fix an ingrown toenail if you catch my drift. Secondly, I do know who you are and I appreciate what your family does for this community. Thirdly, because I owe Burt a big favor, I'll be paying it off. Fourthly, if I get within sight of that jail my fee is five grand, no ifs, no buts, no nothing. Fifthly, I'll take the case to help your friend because I haven't been on a jail run in many years and it actually sounds like fun. And lastly, you have to promise me you will call Preston Burt the minute we get off the phone and tell him I said he could kiss my ass but thanks for the referral. And I'm not kidding. What is your friend's name and what was the charge?"

"Lynn Gregor. Becky Lynn Gregor. She was arrested for money laundering," Jason responded.

"Now, if you agree to all of this, and this is your cell number in my phone, I'll call you tomorrow morning at seven, and we'll try to go get your friend out of jail."

"Deal," Jason said. "Thank you, and good night." He touched his phone to call Preston Burt.

34

AT SEVEN O'CLOCK SHARP, ON Saturday morning, Jason's cell phone rang.

"Jason, this is Mariano Valdez. You can call me Marty. Now, would you tell me everything you know about your friend being confined in jail?"

"Her name is Becky Lynn Gregor. She's a guest here at our house. She went out on a first date last night with a guy she just met, and surprise to her, he apparently is a drug dealer or something. He gets arrested and she gets arrested just because she's with him."

"Just being with him doesn't necessarily mean she gets arrested. You mentioned money laundering last night, or should I say early this morning. That can get you arrested. Is she in Fulton County? What about her date?

"Yes, she's in Fulton County Jail. I don't know anything about the guy and couldn't care less. If you will tell us what to do, we'll follow your instructions to the T. And how do you want the check made out, payable to you? Five thousand, correct?"

"Yes, that's correct. You can make it payable to the Law Offices of Mariano Valdez, please. Now, when you say 'we,' to whom are you referring?"

"That would be my wife, Anne."

"Okay. If she is there, can you put me on speaker so you can both hear me? You both need to hear what I'm about to say if you both are planning on coming to the jail."

Jason complied, and both he and Anne could now hear Marty.

"Your lady friend is lucky. To go to a first appearance hearing this morning, she must have been booked by two o'clock, a.m. I called the jail to find out when she was booked. She got in just under the wire. So she gets a hearing after eleven o'clock to consider bail."

"Well," Anne said, "I guess that's good news."

"The jail has very strict rules about visitors. I'm going to give them to you. Don't forget them and please comply. If you don't, it will just slow us down. Now, don't bring electronic devices, meaning anything like cell phones, laptops, or even smart watches. You can't wear open-toed shoes or bring in a purse or handbag. Leave all that stuff in your car. Do bring a valid form of identification. Your driver's license will work. Now, they may run a computer check on you to see if you have any outstanding warrants. I'm telling you this just in case, you know.

"Your friend has a felony charge of money laundering. Like I said, this means that court time will start at eleven a.m. It does not mean she will be heard at eleven, that's just when they have hearings for the individuals charged with felonies. We will have her out of jail by this afternoon, on bond.

"The jail is located at nine oh-one Rice Street NW. I would like for you to meet me there, in the parking lot, at ten-thirty. I drive a two thousand and five red Chevrolet Impala with big chrome wheels. It has a big dent on the passenger side. You can't miss it."

Marty Valdez was correct about his car; you couldn't miss it. He leaned against the left fender as Jason pulled his Escalade next to it and parked. Valdez held up his hand to motion 'stay where you are' and hopped into the back seat of the Cadillac.

After quick introductions and an exchange of funds, Jason said, "Nice looking car. I was expecting something like a Benz or a BMW."

"The Chevy is a real jewel. Don't be dissing my ride. My family car is a brand-spanking-new Lamborghini Urus. Now that's a sweet ride. Six-hundred and fifty horsepower. The Chevy just helps me blend in when I venture into the DMZ or some other treacherous location. It draws little attention and nobody wants to mess with someone driving a POS like that. Anyway, let's get to work.

"We are about to go into what is called the first appearance hearing, or bond hearing. This first appearance hearing is not a hearing on the merits of the case or a trial. The judge will not consider dismissal at this hearing. We will not be asked any questions about our position or the facts of the case. That all comes later. The only thing that matters today is getting Lynn released and getting her bonded. Are you willing to put up a bond if one is required?"

"Yes," Anne answered immediately.

"Okay. Now it's my goal to get her released on her own recognizance. I don't perceive a problem there. I've checked you out on the computer and your status in the community should win the day. Now Lynn lives with you, correct?"

"Yes, she currently lives in our guest house, but we expect that to be a temporary situation," Anne said.

"Temporary won't be mentioned. That's where she lives today. My research indicates that Becky Lynn Gregor hardly exists. I couldn't find a thing on her."

"That's correct," Jason said. "We had her investigated by a PI and he found the same thing, meaning not much."

"If she's your guest, why the investigation?"

"We don't have time to explain in detail. Let's just say we had our reasons. She's a sweet young lady," Jason said.

"Well that seems to be a change of heart," Anne said to Jason.

"When we go in, you will not be able to talk to Lynn. I will. It's a public hearing but family access to the defendant is not permitted. Once we get bail resolved, she will be released, but not immediately. She will have to change back into her street clothes and turn in her blues."

"Her blues?" Anne inquired.

"Yes, that's what they call the clothes the defendants are given to wear while in custody. She'll be wearing them at the hearing."

"So what happens after today?" Jason asked.

"A date will be set for what is called the preliminary hearing. That's where the court determines whether there is sufficient evidence to believe the defendant committed a crime. You might call it the probable cause hearing. If it is found that probable cause exists, the case will be sent to Superior Court because we are dealing with a felony.

"At the preliminary hearing the District Attorney, usually a young Assistant DA, will present evidence to show probable cause. If we get that far, we could call witnesses, but that's not often done. And we can cross examine their witnesses if they call any, like the arresting officers.

"After today, I'll be doing the groundwork to establish the lack of evidence and involvement in the major arrest and get this thing dismissed before the preliminary hearing. If I can convince the DA they don't have a case, it'll be dismissed because they don't want to waste the time watching and listening to me kick their asses all around the courtroom."

"That last part certainly sounds encouraging," Anne said.

"That's what I'm here for. Let's go on into the courtroom and play the waiting game. There's not a formal docket and it's not first come, first served. We just have to wait them out."

At 12:35 p.m. the bailiff announced the next detainee to be brought before the judge would be Lynn. Marty got up from his seat by the Wentworths in the gallery and proceeded to the defendant's table on the other side of the bar. Lynn, brought in through a side door that permitted access from the jail, wore the blues, along with a pair of handcuffs and shackles around her ankles. She looked gaunt and discolored in the blue cotton pullover top and baggy pants. Anne took a deep breath, shocked by Lynn's appearance. Jason sat calmly, showing no emotion.

Anne could not reconcile the need for the metal bindings considering Lynn's petite physique. 'These people are barbarians' Anne thought. She later learned the cuffs and shackles were standard protocol and were locked on Lynn's appendages for less than five minutes as she was transported from the jail facility to the courtroom.

Judge Lana Watkins looked at the paper handed to her by the bailiff and said, "Let's see, next on our list of things to do is hear Becky Lynn Gregor."

At this point, standing, Marty Valdez said, "Your Honor, my name is Marty Valdez and I'm representing Miss Gregor here today."

"Excuse me," the judge said, more surprised than not.

"Mariano Valdez, representing Miss Gregor."

"That's what I thought you said. Welcome to my court Mr. Valdez, it is an honor. I must assume that Miss Gregor differs from the normal clientele that come to my court. She must be important."

"Thank you your Honor for those kind words. All of my clients are important. My objective here today is to seek a release for Miss Gregor and with the Court's indulgence, have her released on her own recognizance. If you will permit, I would like to state that Miss Gregor poses no significant risk of fleeing. She is currently a house guest of Jason and Anne Wentworth here in Atlanta. They are well established and highly recognized in the business and philanthropic communities. Miss Gregor poses no threat to any person, to the community, or property. Miss Gregor poses no significant..."

"That's good counselor. Miss Gregor will be released on a signature bond. If you and your client will meet with the clerk to your left, she will provide the necessary paperwork to complete the bond and Miss Gregor's release. Good luck."

"If you will, wait for me in the foyer," Valdez said to Anne and Jason as he softly patted Lynn on the shoulder and started toward the clerk. A guard halted their progress and reattached the handcuffs and shackles to Lynn's wrists and ankles as required by jail protocol.

Within five minutes, Valdez entered the foyer. "It will take about thirty minutes for her to get out. The jailers have to go through their routines. She'll be given her clothing and personal items not being held as evidence. She'll have to change her clothes. Once she's out, you can take her home."

"We can't thank you enough for taking this on," Anne said. "I know it's beyond the call of duty for you at this point in your career. Although we truly appreciate your help, it's hoped that this will be a once-in-a-lifetime engagement."

As Jason and Anne escorted Valdez back to his car, he said, "She will be assigned a court date for the preliminary hearing, but I believe I can get her out of this mess before that date arrives. Since there's not much else for me to do today, I'll be on my way, and I'll be in touch. It was a pleasure to meet you both."

Valdez got into his Chevy and started the engine. The exhaust gave a quick roar, followed by a low rumble as the car idled. Valdez pushed a lever with his left hand that activated the hydraulic pump system attached to the front of the car's suspension system. The front end of the car leaped about three feet off of the pavement, and repeated the leap two more times. Both Valdez and Jason laughed aloud as Valdez dropped the gearshift into drive and sallied from the parking lot.

"Well, that was different," Anne said, surprised to see such a demonstration.

"Hey, what a deal. We get a top-rated lawyer and a side show. You can't beat that."

Anne and Jason returned to the foyer where they awaited Lynn's arrival. After about forty minutes, she came through the double doors that welcomed her to freedom. She looked a bit disheveled, but she smiled as she moved quickly toward the Wentworths. To Anne's astonishment, Lynn ran straight to Jason. His body, functioning as a backstop, ended her forward motion. She gave Jason a big hug. One of those big hugs, that in Anne's mind lasted about three seconds too long. Lynn then released Jason and gave a hug to Anne.

"Let's get you home," Anne said. "You are probably starving."

"I am. But the first thing I want to do is take a shower. I feel grimy and yucky."

35

BACK IN THE COMFORTS OF Reid Lane, and following a long, hot shower, Lynn ate a grilled cheese sandwich with tomato soup as she conveyed her experience to Anne and Jason, including being pulled by the neck. She returned to the guest house to sleep, and remained there for the balance of the day.

Sunday morning, Jason went out the front door of the house to retrieve his paper copy of the *Atlanta Journal-Constitution*. He had subscribed to the *AJ-C* since graduating from college. He could read the newspaper online, as so many of his friends chose to do, but he preferred the touch of the paper in his hand.

"Look at this," he said to Anne as he entered the kitchen. Anne put down the bowl she held and walked over to the nook. "Looks like we now have the story on Mr. Wonderful. Why don't you text Lynn and see if she's up? Tell her to come and look at this."

Anne tapped in the letters.

AW: *I know it's a little early, but if u r awake can u come over and look at what's in the paper?*

In less than a minute Lynn came through the door. Her physical appearance showed that she had slept restlessly. The incident from Friday night, and Saturday morning, had taken its toll.

"Here's the story on your date," Jason said as he turned the paper so Lynn could read it.

FEDS ARREST DRUG KINGPIN

Agents from the FBI and the DEA, supported by the Atlanta Police Department and the Fulton County Sherriff's Office, arrested Tatum Anderson, thought to be "Voxlow," the mastermind who organized, built and operated a deep web market for illicit drugs. Styled after the notorious "Silk Road" operation that was shut down in 2013, Anderson's delivery system was known as "the Cobbled Highway."

The arrest took place on Paces Ferry Place NW late Saturday night following Anderson's departure from The Sanctuary Club. A spokesperson for the Fulton County Sherriff's Office stated that warrants had been issued and served on Anderson at the scene of the arrest.

Anderson used cryptocurrency to launder more than $27 million of profits earned from brokering drug transactions on the dark web.

According to a news release, U.S. law enforcement reportedly initiated and closed multiple purchases of controlled substances from Anderson's enterprise, including methamphetamines, heroin and OxyContin....

Lynn's hands began to tremble as she read the article. Jason, standing behind Lynn, looked over her shoulder and read along. He would occasionally pat her on the arm or back to comfort her.

"I could have been killed. Oh, my God. He was a drug dealer! What happened to the computer business stuff?"

"He's a chameleon I guess. He has fooled a lot of people. If the Feds have the goods on him, and according to this article they do, he'll be in jail for a long time when convicted," Jason said. "How is your neck?"

Lynn pushed her hair up so both Jason and Anne could see her neck. Bruises had formed where Anderson had grabbed and pulled her. Tender to the touch, it looked like the bruises would take some time to go away.

"What an asshole," Anne said.

Lynn chuckled. "That's what I yelled at him before they put me in the police car. I called him an asshole. Mr. Valdez asked me if I wanted to press charges against him for assault and battery, but I said no. I never want to see him again. I like the lawyer. He said for me not to worry. That he would get me out of this mess when I have my preliminary hearing. I think that's what he called it," Lynn looked at Jason. "Can you come with me to the hearing?"

"Certainly. I'll rework my schedule. Just let me know when it is."

"I'm so sorry for what has happened. And there is no way for me to thank you, both of you, for what you've done for me. Can I take the newspaper with me?"

Anne knew a comfort level existed when someone had your back. It was obvious Lynn had that with Jason's support. But she was a little miffed with the fact that she, the benefactor, had been set to the side.

"Jason, we need to get ready for church," Anne said. "I assume you're still going."

"No, I think I'll stay home in case Lynn might need something."

Lynn carried the newspaper to the guest house and read the entire article. Lengthy and very detailed, it told the story of Tatum Anderson. He obviously had the intelligence to develop a network of on-the-street drug dealers and to establish relations with the cartels that provided product. Through a series of computer programs, he had managed to avoid detection for over three years while he amassed millions of dollars in cash.

About two-thirds of the way through the article Lynn took a deep breath. There, in print, flashing at her like red neon lighting, was her name. Becky Lynn Gregor. Arrested. Charged with money laundering. Only two sentences brought her into the story, but it seemed like front-page, headline news to Lynn.

The *AJ-C* made two interesting comparisons between Anderson and his jailed "Silk Road" predecessor, Ross Ulbricht. Like Ulbricht, Anderson utilized cryptocurrency, or Bitcoin, to transact his trades. Anderson basically provided a platform for trading, as a broker. When a transaction occurred on the Cobbled Highway, Anderson got a cut of the action. It is estimated that Ulbricht had accumulated nearly ninety million dollars in Bitcoin. Anderson, on the other hand, converted his Bitcoins to real currency. This reduced the risk of loss and also permitted him to function in the real world of commerce.

The other business characteristic that set Anderson apart from Ulbricht: He actually paid state and federal income tax. He didn't pay on all of his earnings, but he paid on a substantial amount. The specific information as to the amount of taxes he had paid could not be provided to the authors of the article. By paying taxes, it gave Anderson a semblance of legitimacy. He could open bank accounts, deal with attorneys, transact business with real estate title companies, and a wide variety of other business enterprises.

When Lynn finished the article, she knew the authors had been provided with a vast amount of detailed information, well before it became available to the public. She and Anderson were arrested after the *AJ-C*'s print deadline, so nothing could go into the Saturday edition about the arrests. But Sunday presented a different story, and the story contained explicit details that don't just pop up by interviewing an FBI agent for thirty minutes. That fact didn't particularly bother Lynn, she just wished she had known one of the reporters before she accepted a date with "Voxlow."

Lynn, sitting at her kitchen table re-reading the entire story, flinched when Ava knocked on the door.

"Come in."

"Oh, honey, I read the horrible story about how you got arrested for being in a car with a drug dealer. What is this world coming to? I've come over to see if there is anything I can do for you."

"Ava, it was terrifying. For a second I thought I was going to get shot. I just knew if that crook had pulled out a gun it would be like Bonnie and Clyde. Thank goodness he just threw up his hands like he knew he was at the end of the run."

"Well sweetie, some crazy things can happen in this world, in this life. You can always trust in the Lord because he is looking after you. But you have to trust in yourself and your own instincts. Nobody is going to look after you better than yourself."

"I now believe that, because I didn't feel good about that guy. I only went out with him because I was influenced by some of my friends at work. Well, maybe not influenced, but I felt like I would have been embarrassed if I hadn't accepted the date, him being Mr. Bigshot and all.

"Ava, you're really smart. Do you know that? You always think things through and give great advice. How come you work here? You could be a crew chief at one of those big hotels downtown. Or you could run a country club restaurant I bet. How come you stay here?"

"Well, I can't actually say that I'm all that smart, but I can for sure say I'm not stupid. I came to work for the Wentworths right after Cole was born. It's been sixteen years. The Wentworths are like family to me. They have always been so gracious with my schedule. I can say for a fact that I never missed a football game or a track meet for either one of my boys. And now, I only work three days a week, and as needed, but I still receive my full weekly compensation. And I'm provided a car. So, I don't think it would be a good move for me to seek employment somewhere else. Do you?"

36

On Monday morning, Anne sent a text to Lynn inquiring about her mental state. Lynn's response indicated to Anne that she was still disturbed about her experience with the notorious Tatum Anderson and the criminal justice system. Anne called Amber Sessions at Mercy, explained what had happened to Lynn, and requested that she stay home from work on Monday to get her wits back together. She assured Amber that Lynn was not at fault. Anne could sense that the trauma had impacted Lynn more than she let on. Amber told Anne she had learned of Lynn's ordeal in the newspaper and approved the Monday time off to recuperate.

By Tuesday morning, Lynn had spoken with a few of her colleagues at Mercy and felt comfortable returning to work. She just didn't know what to expect. Had she had any expectations at all, she would have been wrong. It seemed that everyone from the receptionist to the physicians were curious about her tribulations. Arriving at her small office, after a half-dozen inquiries, she called Amber Sessions on the inter-office phone system.

Amber saw Lynn's name on the digital display on her phone.

"Lynn, how are you doing? I just can't believe this has happened to you. Anne gave me the big picture as to what happened. You must have been scared to death."

"To say the least. It was horrible. I do have something to ask. Is there any way we could have a quick little meeting so I can explain what happened to everyone who is curious to know? I think it would save a lot of time and everyone could get to work. I'm just afraid people will be checking on me all morning long, and I won't be able to get anything done."

"Lynn, you are an amazing young lady. I don't know anyone who would have thought to approach your situation in this manner. You are just a blessing to our organization. I will announce a meeting in the big conference room at nine for anyone who would like to hear about it. I'll tell everyone the meeting will last about ten minutes. I don't know if you are up to Q and A or not. In the meantime it would probably be good if you shut your door to keep the traffic down."

"Thank you. That would be wonderful," Lynn said. She thought for the first time in her life she had become the focal point of everyone's attention. It was rather nice.

Roughly thirty-five Mercy employees shuffled into the conference room to hear what they thought might be a blow-by-blow description of the adventures of Lynn Gregor. Lynn did not get to tell much of a story because questions from the curious consumed most of the time. They seemed to be much more interested in Tatum Anderson's involvement as he truly set the scene for the Atlanta news coverage over the weekend. Lynn did get to expound on what she thought to be her compelling story of fear and misfortune. Everyone returned to work thinking they had been blessed with enough gossip-worthy fodder to pass along to others. After all, they did know the damsel in distress on a personal basis.

The day raced by. Her friends bought her lunch, and a drink for her afternoon break. Sympathy abounded, but curiosity prevailed. It seemed as though people couldn't get enough of the story and certainly enough details. All the while, Lynn reveled in her fifteen minutes of fame. She knew it was ephemeral.

As the end of the day approached, Lynn punched in Amber's intercom number once again.

"Yes, Lynn, how may I help you?"

"I have some questions, and maybe some ideas, about my job. Do you have a few minutes to meet with me, at your convenience?"

"Yes, I do. Why don't I come to your office? I've seen enough of mine today."

Lynn politely asked Amber to close the door and have a seat upon arrival to her office.

Lynn began with no small talk. "Since I've been here I've gotten to work on a few requests for funding, the grant requests. I've noticed a couple of things that I would like to visit with you about."

"Certainly. To hear about new views from a new pair of eyes is always worthy of consideration. What are you thinking?"

"This will only take a couple of minutes. I was just thinking that, so far, all of the grant requests I have seen appear to be geographically limited. I pulled a good sample of some requests just to test my assumption. All of them were directed to organizations, institutions, foundations, corporations, and individuals within a two-hundred-and-fifty-mile radius of Atlanta. I got to thinking, money from outside of that radius is just as green as the money within it. If you, and the board, would approve, I think we can materially increase our receipts by expanding our search to the entire country. There are foundations in this country whose sole purpose is to provide medical care for children. I feel like some of them might be interested in helping us provide those services. The worst that could happen is the loss of some paper, postage, and a little time.

"The second thing that has come to my attention is our use of the word 'we.' When a request is prepared, it describes 'us' and what we do. I think the body of every request begins with the word 'we.' I think we should, at least in the requests, sing the praises of the contributors. Say how they are making a difference in the lives of people. There's just nothing better than having someone sing your praises. That's all."

"Lynn, I guess that's what they call thinking outside the box. Those are wonderful suggestions. Would you please write what you just said in a memorandum so I can present it to the Board at our next meeting? I want you to get the credit if your ideas are accepted. You're doing a great job."

37

STANLEY GREGOR DIDN'T FEEL THE need to pack any luggage or overnight toiletries. It was only about 130 miles from Hollins to Atlanta. He estimated it would be about a two-hour drive because he could take Interstate 20 most of the way driving 75 miles per hour. He projected his arrival time in Atlanta to be around ten o'clock in the morning, if the traffic cooperated. He had cleared out the back end of the company delivery van in the event that Becky Lynn had accumulated anything that he might let her take back to Hollins. She had been gone for over three months now and it was just time for her to come home. God willed it. He also needed her experience in running the dry cleaning and laundry business. It was taking too much out of Stanley to cover all of the bases day after day. He now realized what a valuable asset Becky Lynn had been to the business. He planned on giving her an increase in pay, he just hadn't determined how much. He thought he would be open-minded with her and they could negotiate her compensation. Something he had never done with anyone.

As the miles clicked away, he gave thought to how and when he might approach Becky Lynn. Thanks to Teresa Jones from church, he knew Becky Lynn worked at Mercy Care, a poor people's healthcare provider located on Decatur Street. He knew Teresa had been in communication with Becky Lynn and she wasn't at all willing to give up any information about her. He had overheard her speaking about her to someone at church. To persuade Teresa to relinquish the information he needed, he threatened her by saying he would fabricate some wild stories about her sinful ways and enlighten the members at church of the wanton hussy in their presence. Since Teresa knew whatever Stanley said would be taken as gospel at church, she relented and divulged Becky Lynn's employer and work location. She didn't mention the Wentworths.

As Stanley drove, he practiced in his head the various approaches he might take to persuade Becky Lynn to return to Hollins. "I need your help. You were much more important to the business than I thought." "It's my duty to look after you. The family entrusted me to take care of you and that's what I'm going to do." "No, that's what I need to do." "No, that's what God wants me to do."

Stanley detested driving in Atlanta, even the few times he had. With the profusion of traffic and the abundance of people, he felt nearly claustrophobic. "Why do these drivers have to ride my back bumper?" he thought. His anger level had increased substantially by the time he arrived at the exit to approach his destination. He parked the Chevrolet Express van near the building housing Mercy Care. He said a short prayer thanking God for his deliverance and the courage to pursue his mission. He knew Becky Lynn worked in the financial outreach department, so she shouldn't be hard to find. He didn't expect that she would be out and about, as they say in Hollins. And as he had hoped, the young lady at the reception desk provided explicit instructions as to where to find her. She was thoughtful enough not to announce his arrival, as it was intended to be a surprise.

Lynn sat at her desk in the small room upper management had defined as an office and she was proud to be there. She glanced up for a second as someone had crossed the threshold of her door. She first saw a pair of white three-striped Velcro clasped sneakers. Uncle Stanley. A bolt of fear shot through her chest.

"It's time for you to come home!" he bellowed.

"No!"

"Yes, Becky Lynn, it is time."

"Uncle Stanley be quiet. Don't get me in trouble," Lynn said as calmly as possible. "I want you to leave me alone and quietly leave."

Stanley moved across the small office to the same side of the desk as Lynn. He grabbed her by her upper arm and yanked hard. In a quiet but hissing voice he railed, "What have you done to your hair? And what is that trash on your face? You look like a whore. Now let's go. I have a duty to take care of you and look what's happened to you. And how do you expect me to explain this to the people at church?"

Lynn forcefully pulled back, freeing herself. She reached across her desk and grabbed the heavy-duty Bates stapler she had been using to bind grant proposals. With all her might she slammed the stapler into Stanley's face, driving his glasses into the bridge of his nose and shattering a lens. He staggered back a step, sweeping aside his glasses and touching the cut on his nose.

"You indignant little harlot," he sneered.

He started lifting his right arm above his head to strike, but Lynn struck first. The second Stanley lifted his arm, she clobbered him again with the stapler, this time square in the jaw. Stanley went down like a pig on ice. Lynn felt a reticent satisfaction as she witnessed seventeen years of resentment and hate crumble to the floor.

On his knees, dazed and bleeding, Uncle Stanley felt a cool, solid object against the side of his head. "You move one inch asshole and I'll blow your fuckin' brains all over that wall. The only reason I haven't done it yet is that someone would have to clean up the mess."

It was Lashann Bronson. Like everyone else on the floor, she had heard the commotion. Unlike everyone else on the floor, she was well prepared and trained to do something about it. Lashann worked in the domestic relations group at Mercy. Not your namby-pamby domestic relations, but the domestic relations that involve broken families, broken bones, and jail time. Lashann had a heart of gold, but she had also spent nine years in the army as an MP and was tougher than a five-dollar steak. She could be as sweet as apple pie and as coarse as a burlap sack. She once told an irate husband over the telephone, "If you start some shit, I'm bringin' the toilet paper, and it's not biodegradable."

Stanley collapsed on his side. Lashann stood over him, straddle-legged like he was a hunting trophy, with her Beretta Px4 Compact nine-millimeter stuck in his left ear. He vaguely discerned something that included the phrase "stupid motherfucker," but passed out before she finished her statement.

Two people scurried Lynn away from the fracas and about eight more had already dialed 911 on their cell phones. Within minutes the floor swarmed with police, EMS personnel, and interested parties from other floors in the building. Mercy employees escorted Lynn to a staff physician and the police hauled Uncle Stanley to the back seat of a police cruiser.

Two officers came to see Lynn to question her and take her statement. They told her that Stanley would be charged with assault and battery, and that he would probably spend a few weeks in jail if found guilty at his trial. They assured Lynn that her testimony would be the foundation of the district attorney's case. When she asked if she would be expected to testify at trial, the response was a joint effort, "Yes."

"So, if I have to testify, then I have to see Uncle Stanley, correct?" asked Lynn.

"Yes," one of the officers said. "The accused has the right to see and hear the accuser."

"But I haven't accused anyone of anything."

"Ma'am, that man just tried to kidnap you as best we understand. And grabbed your arm and pulled it. The bruise is starting to form right now. I can see it."

The officer then turned to his partner and asked, "Is attempted kidnapping a federal offense? Do we need to call the Feds in on this?"

"Whoa, whoa, whoa," Lynn said. "If Uncle Stanley is convicted of a federal offense for attempted kidnapping, couldn't he go to prison, for a long time?"

"Yes, ma'am, that's what those prisons are there for."

"Well, then I don't want to press charges. I truly believe Uncle Stanley will never bother me again. If he goes to jail, then the people who work at his laundry will lose their jobs. Uncle Stanley is from a small town in Alabama and the jobs at the laundry are really important to several families. What happens if I don't press charges?"

"He'll be set free and won't be punished for what he's done to you."

"In Exodus, it calls for an eye for an eye, and a tooth for a tooth. I think I just about got an eye and maybe even a tooth today. He's been punished enough. I think it's fair to say that I won the fight, and I feel really good about that. So, I don't want to press charges. There is nothing to gain for me to have him spend time in jail. He'll never hurt anyone else."

Stanley Gregor was released and given his van, with the understanding that he would immediately vacate Atlanta. With one lens in his glasses and a couple of loose teeth, Stanley left the city. Mercy Care granted Lynn two days of paid leave to recover from the trauma. It had been a rough few days for Lynn.

38

ANNE SAT AT THE TABLE in the nook. On a normal evening, back in the good times, Jason would have been home by seven. Now, at eight, the dinner she had prepared continued to cool in the kitchen as she awaited his arrival. She had called twice to be shuffled off to voicemail. Her only meaningful option – wait. She had the option of storing the dinner in the big, expensive refrigerator and going to her office to review whatever she could find. Alternatively, she could dump the dinner, his favorite of chicken parmesan and au gratin potatoes which constituted entirely too much cheese, onto the middle of the kitchen floor just to get some kind of reaction. She knew better than that because she would just be creating a mess for Ava to clean up. So, she chose to wait.

At a quarter after eight Anne heard the garage door open. Jason parked the Escalade and came into the kitchen.

"Sorry I'm late. I should have called. Got caught up in a conference call and I just couldn't cut loose."

"Your dinner is getting cold, but it's your favorite. Do you want me to warm it for you or do you want it as is?"

"You don't have to warm it, I'm hungry. I'm sure it'll be fine."

Anne served dinner and it was consumed without a word. One serving of each item, with some asparagus and iced tea, and dinner ended.

In frustration, Anne began speaking to herself in a series of questions and responses, just to see what kind of response she could elicit.

"How was your day? Oh, it was fine. What did you do? I went to the gym to work out with Paige and then we went shopping. Did you buy anything? No. Then you didn't go shopping did you? No, I guess I just went looking."

Jason sat and looked at her like she had lost her mind.

"What are you doing, Anne?"

"I'm having a conversation Jason, like normal people do. But I can't be too normal because you choose not to participate. When was the last time we talked, about anything?"

"I think you're getting a little extreme to tell the truth."

"Extreme? What is extreme is the extreme lack of response I get from you about anything. And it seems to have gotten worse over the last few months. You're not happy; I'm not happy. It's time. No, it's past time for us to do something about how we are living. We need to see a marriage counselor."

"Oh boy, that's the answer. Let someone else tell us how to resolve our problems."

"You just admitted we have problems, didn't you? And it's time we did something about it."

"Whose idea? I mean, who came up with the marriage counselor plan, Paige?"

"What difference does that make? What I want to know is if you will commit to seeing a counselor. It's about our lives, Jason."

"Okay. I'll do it. And you're right. We're off in the ditch and need to do something about it. I'm guessing you have someone in mind to counsel us, or am I wrong about that too?"

"As a matter of fact, I do. A lady named Stephanie Botti. She's a Ph.D. and is supposed to be very good."

"And where did you get her name? Who's providing the review?"

"Erika Allen."

"Erika Allen? Isn't she the one who puts pyramids under her bed, believes those oils, essential oils, have healing value, and thinks Sedona, Arizona is a source of mystical powers? She's goofy as a loon."

"Well, yes and no. I'll admit that Erika can be a little enigmatic, but I wouldn't put her in the goofy category. She said Stephanie is very professional, very good, and gets great reviews."

"What, on Yelp? Right up there with the electricians and tree trimmers?"

"Jason, you said you would do it. So, are you on board or not?"

"Okay, we'll do it."

"Tomorrow I want you to block out a lot of time on your calendar so we can get something to match her schedule. Okay? This is something we need."

Three days later they stepped into Stephanie Botti's office. Located on North Highland Avenue NE in a four-story building near the Atlanta Medical Center, the office cried out for some needed maintenance. It had gone beyond the acceptable standard of normal wear and tear. The furniture and fixtures were dated. Probably cutting edge in the eighties, the charm had long since faded, along with the color pattern in the draperies. Stephanie met the Wentworths with a less-than firm handshake and requested that they have a seat on the chrome-framed white leather couch. She, in turn, sat on a stool with a star-shaped base on wheels. A diploma announcing her successful completion of the Doctor of Psychology program at some obscure university Jason didn't recognize, hung in prominent view on the wall.

She stood taller than Jason, by about an inch. Her short-cut blonde hair and thin face matched well with her slender body shape. She wore round glasses with thick, tortoiseshell frames, giving her the appearance of a hoot owl. Her earrings were long and dangling, consisting of strands of silver balls, each ball larger in size from the next, starting with the smallest ball at the bottom of the strand and increasing in size to the top. They swung to and fro as she moved her head.

Jason sat on the right end of the couch, crossing his arms over his chest and crossing his left leg over his right, away from Anne. Anne sat on the left end of the couch, rather erect, with her purse in her lap. After a few brief cordialities, the counselor jumped right in.

"Interpreting your sitting positions, I've concluded that you both have some issues. How can I help?" Botti asked as she rolled back and forth on her stool. "Please tell me what brings you in today?"

What Jason wanted to say was "You're the fucking marriage counselor, why do you think we're here today?" But he restrained himself to say they were seeking some help with their marriage.

"Obviously," Botti grunted. "Anne. Is it okay if I call you Anne? Can you please tell your husband, in your words, why you are here today and what you want to accomplish? And Jason, when Anne completes her statement, it will be your turn."

After a torturous fifty minutes and the payment of one hundred and fifty dollars, the Wentworths sat in the Escalade staring at the windshield.

"That was bullshit," they both said in unison. They laughed.

"Maybe Erika is a little goofier than I thought," Anne said. "But we still need to get some guidance. This was just not it. Will you commit to one more try?"

"Yes, if I get to pick the brainwasher. You've blown your shot at it."

"And you think you can find someone who will listen to both of us, and not some rubberstamp male chauvinist who'll support your position?"

"Hey, come on. I didn't question your choice, only the source of the referral. I'll be fair."

"Okay. But soon."

Jason obtained the name of Philip McDaniel, Ph.D. and marriage counselor, from Jon Sylvie, the controller at Wentworth Construction. Jason knew Jon and his wife had worked with a marriage counselor and appeared to have achieved success. Jason requested Jon keep their conversation confidential.

After a few days to build up his courage, Jason called McDaniel's office and spoke with his assistant. She told Jason an appointment would be scheduled after the Wentworths had completed a comprehensive and exhaustive questionnaire, which would be sent to the participants in separate envelopes and returned in separate envelopes. Jason, thinking the procedure to be over the top, agreed. The questionnaires were received, completed, and returned.

The initial meeting with Philip McDaniel occurred in his office on Barnes Street NW, near the Georgia Tech campus. Situated on a tree-lined street in an old neighborhood, a comfortable feeling emanated from the place. The office, more like a living room, consumed the front of the house. The furniture – couch, side chairs, and coffee table – compared with any that might be seen in a middle-class Atlanta home.

After the proper introductions, the Wentworths sat on the couch at the invitation of Dr. McDaniel, their positions comparable to their positions at the first counselor's office. Dr. McDaniel, seated in an armchair across the coffee table, immediately initiated the conversation relative to the essence of the meeting.

"Thank you for coming to see me. My practice is designed to assist couples in reconciling, or reconstituting their marriages. I take an approach that is called behavioral couples therapy. It's based on the concept that the environment of a person affects behavior. I believe that behavior is learned, and if that behavior is detrimental to the marriage, it can be unlearned. This is not a unilateral process. It takes two to tango. Action and reaction, or no action and no reaction. I'm not going to sit here and listen to the sounds of silence for fifty minutes. I will be nudging you along. I think my input is just as important as yours. I believe my patients come to me for help and suggestions, not to have me sit here and ask, 'how does that make you feel?' It's not a comfortable process. If both of you are willing and want to work with me, major improvements can be made in your relationship.

"I have read the questionnaires you submitted and I found several areas where we might direct our attention. But first, let's discuss the loss of your children. Would one of you give me their gender and ages, and a very brief description of how and when they died?"

Anne responded. Cole, the boy, age ten. Emma, the girl, age eight. Both killed by a drunk driver when his pickup hit the bus in which the children were riding. The accident occurred in 2012.

"So it's been six years, correct? As both of you know, the death of a child is a traumatic experience that can have long-term effects. The loss of two children, even worse. The grieving process takes time, sometimes long periods of time. Interestingly, a thorough study of the long-term effects of the death of a child was done by a group of psychologists right here at Georgia State about two years ago. They addressed the matter of marital disruption, which is certainly not uncommon in such situations. Their findings indicate that couples who find a meaning in life have the greatest potential for recovery. In other words, parents who pursue satisfying work or participation in community or religious organizations. Based on your questionnaires it appears that you both have found satisfaction with work and charitable participation. However, the grieving process can have hidden, lingering effects, and we will search these out.

"Now, I would like for both of you, together if possible, to tell me about yourselves, your backgrounds, how you met, when you married, what you assumed your futures would be like back then, and, in general terms, where you stand today relative to your marriage. This information, coming from you, is to help me so we can focus on you at our next meeting."

For the next twenty-five minutes, occasionally prompted by Dr. McDaniel, Anne and Jason relayed their historical background. They were direct and honest.

"Okay, and I know this may sound a little corny, but here's what I would like for you to do when you leave here. Both of you give some time thinking about how you felt when you first met. How you felt after your first date and the anticipation you had, at the time, thinking about seeing each other again or even speaking on the phone. Think to remember those feelings. And tonight, if you have no prior plans, I would like for you to go on a date. Go eat at a nice restaurant, have a glass of premium wine if you are so inclined. Put yourselves in the mental position you were in on your first few dates. Try to enjoy yourselves.

"Please, call my assistant to schedule your next appointment. I believe we can truly improve your marriage. And believe me, there have been times when I have told couples the healthiest thing they could do would be to file for divorce, and that has happened after just one meeting. That's not your situation."

That evening Jason arrived home a little earlier than usual. He and Anne, dressed more nicely than normal for a Thursday evening, enjoyed a fine meal at Bones Restaurant and returned home in good moods. That night they made love for the first time in four months. It would be the last.

39

Pledge sister Saturday. Time to head to Athens. Paige provided the transportation since Anne had chauffeured the year before. She had parked her dark blue Tesla Model S in Ava's spot on the east side of the house and entered through the back door into the kitchen as most of Anne's friends did.

"Morning all," Paige exclaimed with the enthusiasm of a camp counselor. "What's cooking?"

Anne had seen Paige park and head for the back door. After she entered, Anne said, "I see you're driving your electric car. Will it make it seventy miles to Athens before it runs out of power?" She finished off her glass of orange juice, rose from the table in the nook, and put her glass in the sink. Jason, wearing his Saturday morning golf gear, emerged from the pantry.

"Hey, stud-muffin, in there scrounging for food? Just so you'll know, when I left the house a while ago, Eric was stuffing twenty dollar bills in his pocket and telling me how he was going to, and I quote, 'Kick Jason's ass this morning.'"

"Right. And if he plans on kicking my ass, why does he need those twenties? If he thought he could win, he wouldn't need the money, he'd just take mine. Besides, he couldn't kick the shit out of a horse paddock."

Anne had her limited luggage sitting by the door, which she scooped up and said, "If you're waiting on me, you're wasting time. Let's go." She looked over to Jason with the expectation of a warm farewell, but received what had become the standard, not the exception.

"Have fun," he said, and walked back into the pantry.

Outside, Paige remarked about the farewell. "That was pretty raw. So it's obviously still touchy. You guys need to get your shit together."

"Save it for later. I just want to have a good time and enjoy the day. But since you brought it up, we're still doing the roommate routine."

"I'm sorry."

"We'll work it out. We've been working it out for some time now."

Paige backed the car around and headed out the drive toward Athens.

Two minutes later, Lynn gave the back door a couple of thumps and invited herself into the kitchen. "Hello?"

Jason stepped out of the pantry. "And hello to you."

"Is Anne here?"

"You just missed her. She headed to Athens about two minutes ago. Do you need anything?" Jason asked as he walked out of the pantry toward Lynn.

"Oh, I just had a question for her. It can wait until she gets back. What are you up to?"

Jason noticed that Lynn wore one of his old Georgia Tech T-shirts. Anne had given it to her, more or less as a joke, after they had seen the eighty-five dollar stretched and frayed T-shirt in Macy's on their first shopping excursion. Jason knew Anne had given the T-shirt to Lynn. It had seen better days. It sported the Georgia Tech gold color, with TECH in navy blue across the front. Stretched and frayed itself, and several times too large for Lynn's petite body, the collar hung off her shoulder and the bottom extended to her thighs like a dress. Jason assumed she wore shorts beneath the T-shirt. He also noticed the two protrusions on the front of the T-shirt, just to the outsides of the T and the H. She had not bothered to put on a bra.

"I'm getting ready to eat some cereal and go win a little money playing golf."

"You can't play a round of golf on a bowl of cereal. You need some real food. What do you say I whip you up a decent breakfast? It'll just take a minute and it would be a pleasure to do. You've taken care of me, so let me take care of you for once. I insist." She took Jason by the arm and guided him to the table in the nook where he sat down. "Here, enjoy your paper and let me make you an omelet. I know where everything is. I'll refill your coffee cup and get you some orange juice."

Jason, with a full cup of coffee, settled in to read the newspaper and Lynn began gathering the ingredients for breakfast. She brought Jason a glass of orange juice as she said she would, but when she handed it to him things got messy. Lynn extended her arm to place the glass of juice on the table. Jason raised his hand thinking she would hand him the glass. These movements created a collision that knocked the glass out of Lynn's hand and onto the table. Jason began wiping the pool of juice with his napkin as Lynn apologized and scurried to the kitchen to retrieve a handful of paper towels. As Jason assured her that accidents do happen and no harm had been done, she worked at cleaning the spill. As she cleaned, she leaned over to reach the middle of the table. In doing so, gravity, being a bit of an irresistible force, pulled the old T-shirt away from Lynn's chest, creating a sizable gap between the shirt and her body. Jason scrutinized Lynn's breasts, as both were in plain view. At that moment, he sensed a venereal sensation that had avoided his body for too long.

With the spilled juice removed and Jason back to the paper, Lynn retreated to the kitchen to prepare the omelet. She grated some cheese, cut some fresh mushrooms, and whipped three eggs in a stainless-steel bowl. She placed an English muffin in the toaster and put a pat of butter in the pan that sat on the cooktop. As she moved the butter around with a spatula, Jason came up behind her.

Being just a little too close, he leaned over her shoulder and asked, "Do you need any help?"

Lynn turned, leaned against Jason and looked up at him. "I can always use some extra help," she said. "Why don't you...."

She didn't complete her question. As she spoke, Jason kissed her and she eagerly responded. He reached over and turned off the burner. He then moved his hands up along her ribcage and onto her breasts. He cupped them in his hands where they fit perfectly. Startled, Lynn grabbed Jason's hands and pulled them down, but she didn't release them. Deliberately, she moved them back up.

Lynn gently leaned away from Jason. He ran his hand up her back and into her hair. He pulled her to him, and kissed her again on the lips. Lynn, standing on her toes, returned the kiss. Jason broke the embrace, stepped back, and lifted the T-shirt off of Lynn. There was no resistance from Lynn or the shirt. Underneath the T-shirt she wore a pair of gray cotton pull-string shorts.

Jason stood at the crossroads. His mind sprinted through his options. Is it best to turn around, go back and forget that anything happened? Is it smart to forge ahead, which could potentially lead to a dead end? What are the unknowns that await to the right or left? And there are unknowns at those corners. What if you turn right, abandoning the current situation and admit this indiscretion to your spouse? What if you turn left, monkey around a little, don't get too familiar, and forget it?

Jason took a step back and studied Lynn. Young and firm. Not pretty, but cute. That is where his analysis ended. She smiled at him. Not a broad, happy smile, but a smile of gratification, of willingness.

Jason picked Lynn up in his arms. Surprised by her lack of weight, he held her without effort. He carried her to the nook and placed her, seated, on the table. There, as she reclined, she lifted her hips and pulled the drawstring on the shorts. Jason removed them and his own in one easy motion. He pulled her closer, kissed her fervently and slowly entered her, watching her reaction. Her face initially indicated mild discomfort, but she smiled again and pulled Jason to her. She lay motionless momentarily and then she matched Jason's movement.

Jason's motion was slow and easy. He initially had no interest in rushing. But nature being what it is, that plan changed. He increased the speed of his thrusts and began to experience that feeling of weakness in the knees and the misgiven notion that he could support the world. He exploded inside of her and became motionless. It was over. For Jason, those feelings of lust, and exhilaration, and satisfaction were immediately displaced, rudely, by guilt, fear, shame, and self-reproach.

Lynn too knew she had materially erred. The ringing of the bell could not be undone. She had let her better judgement slip down as easily as that T-shirt came off. At a total loss of how to approach the situation, she looked to Jason.

"What do you say we get kinda cleaned up? I'll see you in a minute."

Lynn returned to the nook, and found Jason sipping coffee. She procured a cup for herself and sat down by Jason.

He looked into her eyes. "I guess we got a little carried away there, didn't we? I guess things like this happen when the situation is right. You hear about it all the time. But we're adults and I know we can handle this like adults. Right?"

Lynn reached out and touched Jason's arm. "Jason, that was wonderful. It's never been like that before. It's like the other three times don't even count."

"What do you mean by three times?"

"I mean I've only done it three times. Now four. Twice in high school and once with a man from church.

"A man from church?"

"I promised I would never say who it was, and I won't."

"That's not important now," Jason said, thinking now he had to ask her the question. "Are you on the pill or something? Some kind of protection?"

"No."

Now the pebbles of guilt in Jason's stomach turned into a brick. He couldn't let his mind go there. Worry would eat him alive.

"Don't worry. I'm pretty sure it'll be okay."

"Lynn, it goes without saying, Anne must never, and I mean never, find out about this."

"Yes, I know. We both have too much to lose."

Jason Wentworth was fifteen minutes late for his tee time.

40

THE CLUBHOUSE ATTENDANT MET JASON when he pulled into the portico. "Mr. Wentworth, your group is waiting at the first tee. I've taken your clubs over, so all you need to do is change your clothes if you're going to and put on your golf shoes. I'm sure you left your keys in your car so the valet can park it for you."

Jason thanked him, handed him a twenty and went into the locker room to change his shoes. He then hustled over to the first tee. There he found Eric, Scott, and Mark waiting.

"Uh, look who's fifteen minutes late," Eric chirped, alluding to the joke he told at an earlier outing. "I know your wife is headed to Athens, so what have you been up to?"

"Very funny," Jason said. "I had some business to take care of. You want your loans repaid don't you?"

"Hey, we're up," Mark said when he heard the starter toot his whistle.

Jason teed off last, trying to warm up a little as he waited his turn. He topped the first ball he hit, and it went only about ninety yards down the middle of the fairway.

"Hey, we'll give you a mulligan on that one if you want it," Scott said, with the other two nodding in agreement.

"That's okay, I'll make up for it on my second shot. At worst I'll get a bogey on this first hole."

He didn't get his bogey. Instead he wound up with a three-over-par triple bogey. On the second hole, a straight par four, Jason pulled his tee shot far to the left, over a line of pine trees.

"I don't think you kept that one in the one-nine zip code," Scott said. "Do you want to hit a provisional, or just chase that one down?"

Jason located his ball in the middle of the eighth fairway. From there he finished the second hole with a two-over double bogey. At this point his game collapsed. His scorecard reflected a ninety-two at the end of the round, twenty over par.

Back in the clubhouse, Eric asked if Scott and Mark would excuse them, as he wanted to talk to his friend alone.

"Let's go get a sandwich and a beer," Eric said.

"No, I think I'll just head to the house,"

"No, I think we're going to have a sandwich, a beer, and talk. You shot a ninety-two. It should have been a ninety-three since you used that foot wedge on fourteen, which I'll let pass. I bet you haven't shot a ninety-two since you were in the eighth grade. You didn't say ten words out on the course today. I think we need to talk."

"Isn't that line supposed to come from my wife?" Jason asked.

"Well, it's coming from me and I'm not feeding you a line of bullshit."

They talked little until halfway through their Reuben sandwiches. Finally, Eric spoke. "I know you well enough to know that something isn't right. Care to tell me about it?"

"Oh, I guess it's the same old shit," Jason said. "You know how it is around the house sometimes."

"Well, I do and I don't. Like sometimes I get pissed when a sprinkler head breaks. That's around the house. And sometimes I get pissed just because things aren't going my way because Kara has a swim meet and Parker has a ball game and Paige is riding my ass because I spend too much time at the office. That's around the house too. Entirely different kinds of stuff. On those days, sometimes I just want to say, 'fuck it.' But that's when I suck it up and change my way of thinking. Note I didn't say suck it up and take it like a man. So tell me about what kind of same old shit you're having?"

"I don't think it's a well-kept secret between the four of us that Anne and I aren't hitting on all eight cylinders. It's just been tough, for whatever reason. I know, you can sit there and tell me guys would line up from here to Savannah and back to be with Anne. It's not the looks, or the body, or the brains that everyone else sees. For me it's something deeper. I just don't know what it is. And it's just not her, it's me too. Maybe more me, I don't know."

"Look, I'm not smart enough to tell you how to fix what's going on, and I don't want to try. But I am smart enough to tell you that you and Anne should get some professional help.

Find a good therapist. Okay? Now this doesn't have anything to do with that young lady living with y'all does it?"

"Oh, come on Eric. Hell no. And as a matter of fact, now that you've brought it up, we have visited with a therapist. We're working on it, I promise."

"That's good to hear, seriously. Nobody knows it, but Paige and I have spent a few hours on one of those couches, and it made a big difference with us. We open up more now, and we don't let shit simmer like we used to."

After lunch, Jason sat alone in his Escalade and thought about what Eric had said. He also contemplated his relationship with Anne and what had occurred earlier that morning. Guilt started to permeate his consciousness. After thirty minutes he left the parking lot and drove to a small drugstore eight miles away from Buckhead. There he purchased a box of condoms, just in case.

41

PAIGE HEADED HER TESLA EAST for the roughly seventy-mile
drive to Athens, home of the University of Georgia. According to her iPhone, the estimated travel time was an hour and
twenty minutes, less if she pushed the pedal just a little harder.
She knew she could beat that time by fifteen minutes.

Bringing back the short goodbye delivered by Jason, Paige
inquired about the state of the marriage. She and Anne had
had more than one conversation about Jason's change in per-
sonality. About his traveling more to out-of-state jobs when
he once delegated the travel to the company's vice presidents.
About his staying up later, not coming to bed until Anne was
asleep. About leaving earlier for the office than in the past and
arriving home later, as well.

"I waited until today to tell you, but we went to see a psy-
chologist last week. We actually saw two. The first one didn't

quite cut the mustard, but the second has some promise. His name is Philip McDaniel. He's straightforward and doesn't seem to be all that interested in trampling through the swamp of our detailed marital history. His focus is on the future. I think he's a good pick."

"What happened to the guy y'all went to, what was it, five years ago? I thought he really helped y'all out."

"He did, and he was obviously my first choice, but he retired."

"That's too bad. But it sounds like this new guy may fit the bill. That's good," Paige said.

"True, but let's not talk about it now. I'm looking forward to getting out of Atlanta and having a good time visiting with old friends. I think we wound up with nineteen attendees. That's not a bad number for this time of year."

"It's actually twenty," Paige said. "Didn't you get the email from Ellen McNulty saying that Sarah Brooks was going to make it?"

"I haven't looked at my email today, but that's good. How many Sarah's did we have in our pledge class? Five, six? And who could have imagined that none other than Ellen McNulty, AKA Polly Perfect, would be in charge today?"

"Or Polly Prudent."

"Or Polly Punctual."

"Or Polly Planner. With Ellen, all we have to do is sit back and have a good time. You know everything will be in perfect order and timed to the minute," Paige said.

"Staying at the Hotel Indigo will be convenient," Anne said. "The little bus Ellen has chartered should make it easy for all of us to get around and stay together and not have to worry about the 'margarita effect.'"

And so the conversation went, until about fourteen miles east of Bethlehem, Georgia, where Paige, pushing the pedal a little too hard, received a visit from a trooper with the Georgia State Patrol. Paige pulled her car to the shoulder, stopped, put her hands on the steering wheel, and pursed her lips. "Son of a bitch! I had that fifteen minutes in the bag."

"Good morning ma'am. Could I see your license and your registration please? Is there any reason you are in a hurry? Is there a family emergency or a need to seek medical care?"

"No," Paige said, as she handed over her license and registration.

"Okay, ma'am. If you will stay right here, I'll be back in a couple of minutes." The trooper returned to his cruiser to run a check on the car and Paige Simmons Buchanan.

"Everything looks okay except that you were going eighty-five in a seventy-mile-an-hour zone. So I will be issuing you a citation."

Anne could see the veins in Paige's neck thicken as she gripped the wheel.

"Let me ask you a question, Officer. Why didn't you stop the red Ford pickup truck or the silver BMW that blew by me like they were goin' to pick up free gold nuggets somewhere?"

"Ma'am, have you ever been fishin'?"

"Certainly," Paige replied a little huffily.

"Did you catch all the fish?"

"Oh, just give me my ticket and I'll be happily on my way."

The trooper had Paige sign the ticket, assuring her it was not an admission of guilt, handed it to her, and wished her a safe and pleasant journey.

"How in hell am I going to do that Trooper? You've taken the pleasant part out of it."

"That's enough Paige," Anne said as she took the ticket from Paige's hand.

Paige ran up the window, put the car in drive, and left the scene, being mindful to turn on her blinker as she merged back into traffic.

Anne, reading the information on the ticket, informed Paige that, depending on her driving history, she would be paying a fine of one hundred and fifty dollars.

"But you get the bonus. Because you were going eighty-five, you are the winner of the Super Speeder award. For going fifteen or more miles per hour over the posted speed limit, you get dinged with an additional fine of two hundred bucks. Sucks to be you today."

Paige motored on into Athens and drove to the Indigo where she and Anne checked into the room they agreed to share. In the gift bags so properly left at the front desk by Ellen, they found a granola bar, a small bottle of Perrier, a seventy-two percent Ghirardelli dark chocolate bar, a small sack of jellybeans, and an extraordinarily detailed Reunion Weekend itinerary authored by Ellen. A notation included at the bottom of the itinerary suggested that, for old times' sake, maiden names would be used during the reunion. Everyone was to meet in the lobby at eleven forty-five to hop on the bus for lunch at Pauley's. Following lunch, for those who were interested, the pledge sisters would take a walking tour of downtown Athens to see what had changed and what had not. After the tour, the group would return to the hotel to rest before dinner at the Last Resort Grill, where nearly everyone agreed on having a piece of the white chocolate cheesecake. Following dinner, it was over to Milledge Avenue to gather in the chapter room at the Kappa Kappa Gamma house. Breakfast the next morning would be at the Mayflower Restaurant.

During dinner Anne's cell phone chimed the Ring doorbell sound. She had turned it on to be apprised of any activity, visitors or deliveries, coming to Reid Lane in her absence, particularly with Jason being gone several hours playing golf. The urge being too great to resist, Anne checked her phone to see what might be the cause of the alert. On her screen she observed a pizza delivery boy holding a large pizza box. The door opened, Jason paid for the delivery and the boy was on his way. Anne found this odd for two reasons. First, Jason hadn't ordered a pizza in nearly six years. Secondly, why would he order a large?

The Kappa House, a two-story Greek revival mansion, serves as the incubation facility for endless memories for the hundreds of young ladies who had graced its interior. The 1991 pledge class would meet in the chapter room located in the back of the house. Along the north wall, beneath the wide window, sat the long table with an assemblage of nineteen bottles of wine and one six-pack of Coors Light, just in case the urging for the good old days grew strong. Merlot. Pinot Noir.

Zinfandel. White. Red. Rosé. The Athens weather report for the evening: It was starting to look drunk inside.

"Good evening ladies," Ellen squeaked as she opened the evening's activities. "Everyone get a glass of wine if you are so inclined, or a beer. I understand the beer came from Jimbo's, so it will be especially refreshing. We're going to stand and chat for about forty-five minutes and then we'll sit in a circle and tell some stories and catch up. How does that sound?"

"When she said, 'about forty-five minutes,'" Paige whispered to Anne, "she means forty-five minutes on the fucking dot."

The conversations were fast and fun for that exact period of time, forty-five minutes, when Ellen said, "Everyone take a seat, please. We are going to tell old stories about being a Kappa at Georgia and catching up on current affairs."

"I can start this off," said Margie Horne. "Do you remember the night Sarah Brooks, or Sarah Number Three as she was also known, got just a little too comfortable with the margarita machine the KA's had after some football game? She wandered off into the neighborhood and woke up the next morning with a stranger in her bed. It was a beagle, and she just fell in love with it."

"I fed that beagle a good breakfast and got him back home by noon," Sarah interjected. "And he was not just any old beagle. His name was Carleton."

"Sarah, I never knew. Did you lower Carleton out your window from the second floor, or did you stroll out the front door with him?" Margie inquired.

This comment drew a laugh from everyone, as bedsheets and ropes popped into the conversation.

"Do you remember Keven Parker at the Halloween party our sophomore year?" asked Ashley Ward as she pointed toward Keven. "She dressed up like Dolly Parton. Big blonde wig, this plastic false front with boobs out to here," she gestured, "a checkered Daisy Duke's shirt tied at the navel and long fingernails. Guys were hitting on her like there was no tomorrow."

"What about the time Anne, Paige, Lisa Dittmer, and I went on Spring Break to Destin?" asked Tracey Morrison. "We get intercepted by these guys from Ohio State and they are looking to hook up with anybody. They ask us our names and Anne said we're all named Jane. But each name was spelled differently. Mine was just plain Jane. Paige was Jayne. Lisa was Jain and Anne was Jeign, rhymes with reign. Those guys just gave up."

And so went the evening, until perhaps a little too much wine had been served and inhibitions began to take a back seat.

Kelly Pringle stood. "Ellen said we were going to talk about old stories and current affairs. Well, let me tell you about my current affair. Todd and I are getting divorced. And oh, it's been a real shit show. And it's damn tough to get that through to two teenagers. I'll admit that I spent too much time at the office. It seems to be a professional malady. But while I was working my ass off in Louisville, Todd was boinking this homewrecker in Cincinnati about every chance he could get. Come to find out we had an open marriage. He just never bothered to tell me about it."

That's when the civility wheels came off the cart. Two more pledge sisters joined in the discussion to vilify their ex-husbands and update the group on how to approach marital discord.

Tracey Morrison stood. "Divorce can sure change your image. I was sitting in a meeting at my daughter's middle school with my ex. The meeting was about my daughter's medication she took at the time. He made some absolutely stupid remark and suggestion, which was not beneficial to my daughter. Right there in front of that school administrator I called him a fuckwad. I had never used that term in my life."

Cynthia Allen stood. "My two-legged shitbag of a former husband moved off to Delaware and left me with two teenagers. Try that on for size. My daughter, who's fifteen, has this boyfriend and they're hot and heavy. Since daddy pencil-dick isn't around to direct traffic, I get both roles. So my daughter and her beau, Evan, are in the den one night watching a movie. I walk in and find them on the floor, getting rather familiar with each other. I asked Evan if he could step out for a minute. I told him, 'Evan, you can play with her perky little titties all you want, but if you fuck her, I will hunt you down and kill you.' They're still an item, but Evan keeps an eye on me like I keep an eye on him."

Finally, Claudia Roche asked, "By show of hands, how many of us have been divorced?"

Of the twenty women in attendance, eight raised a hand. Anne made the simple math calculation in her head. Forty percent. She had recently read the divorce rate for first time marriages settled in at forty-one. Anne thought, "Are we heading into the stats, or will Dr. McDaniel help pull us through?" She didn't drink any more wine and made a mental note that she would call Jason when she returned to the hotel. But following a lengthy discussion with Paige, she decided not to call because of the late hour.

Earlier in the evening, at 1716 Reid Lane NW, Jason just happened to see Lynn in the back yard and asked her if she would like to join him for dinner. It was certainly no coincidence that he saw her. He had been watching out the kitchen window off and on for nearly an hour when he saw her park her car and walk across the lawn. Maybe they could get a pizza and watch a movie, he suggested. He said he didn't have anything else to do since Anne had gone to Athens. The pizza arrived about seven-thirty; the movie didn't hold their attention. At eight-fifteen Jason escorted Lynn back to the guesthouse. He was pleased that he had the foresight to stop by the little drugstore following his golf game.

42

AFTER A LEISURELY BREAKFAST AT the Mayflower Restaurant and some long goodbyes, Anne and Paige began the trek back to Atlanta. Due to Paige's moderate infection of the *vinum flu,* Anne drove. Both ladies agreed that the reunion had been a success, notwithstanding Ellen McNulty's obsession for punctuality and perfection.

They discussed the events of the weekend: the food, the sorority house, and their pledge sisters. They lamented about how some things had changed, always for the worse when compared to the old days, and how some things had surprisingly remained the same. Eventually, the conversation settled on the incidence of divorce among their group.

"I did the math," Anne said. "Of our twenty sorority sisters present, eight had gone through divorce, which is obviously forty percent. Do you know the national average for divorces for first-time married couples is forty-one percent? That's scary. And I sat there and thought about what really caused the demise of those marriages. I know screwing around is high on the list, maybe number one. But just lack of compatibility has to be high on the list too. People just grow apart sometimes. I'm genuinely concerned about my marriage. It's just not like it used to be, and I mean in a lot of ways. It seems like we have become friends without benefits."

"What is it that you think he's doing wrong?" Paige inquired.

"See, that's not it. He's not doing anything wrong, not that I know of anyway. It's not like back in two thousand one when he had the affair, or the Alabama fuck-a-rama as you liked to call it. That was a long-distance ordeal with that bitch from the architectural firm in Mobile. I believed it wouldn't last, and I forgave him. That took some doing, but I got over it. I just chalked it up to those changes in life that occur."

"Maybe your new doc, McDaniel, can get things back on track for you."

"I hope so. Then I look at you and Eric and think we should be just like that. I know all marriages have a rough spot now and then, but you just keep on rolling. And your eight-year age gap never seems to be a problem."

"I think it actually helps," Paige said. "Eric sowed his wild oats before we got married. He never has to sit around and think about what he's missed. I kind of guided him through his forties, you know, those middle-aged crazy years. Plus, I kind of run him on empty if you know what I mean. He's happy at the house."

"Jason doesn't seem to be unhappy, he just seems to be content with nothing. I'd nearly like it if he would get mad about something. I hate to say it, but it's nearly gotten to the point where he focuses more on the success of the construction company, and wants to compare it to Democycle, to see who can make the most money, percentage wise that is. That's what gets him excited, if you want to call that excited. I feel like our marriage is suffering from some kind of slow degradation.

"Okay, I know your head hurts. Why don't you try to sleep from here on in? You'll need the rest for when you get home. We can talk about this stuff later."

Arriving at Reid Lane, Anne found the house empty. Paige came into the house for a drink of water and a bathroom break, and then was on her way. Being two o'clock in the afternoon, Anne assumed Jason to be at the country club playing golf.

Thirty minutes later, Anne heard Jason park his car in the garage, and she saw Lynn walking to the guest house as Jason entered the kitchen. He offered up a marginal hello.

"What's up?" Anne asked, with no particular inflection in her voice.

"Oh, I was talking with Lynn and she said she missed the Dairy Queen in Sylacauga, so I took her to the one over near Tech. Since we were over there, I showed her the campus."

"My, your attitude toward Lynn has certainly softened since her brush with the law. Are you getting soft in your old age?"

"No, I wouldn't say that. Like you said, she's just a sweet young lady who needs a little help. I'm just trying to be nice."

"I wasn't snooping, but I saw on the Ring doorbell camera yesterday evening that you had a big pizza delivered. Did you eat the whole thing, because I didn't see any in the fridge?"

"Uh, yeah. I did. I finished it off this morning for breakfast. Why?"

"I don't know. It just seemed a little out of place for you, that's all."

With that, Jason told Anne he needed to run to the office to look over some bid numbers for a meeting to be held the next day. He did not return home until after eight.

Monday morning, Jason arose at six and got in the shower. Anne picked up his iPhone, opened it by entering 1716, moved to her contact information and tapped "Share My Location." She could now look at her phone and determine Jason's location, and she knew he would never know it or understand how it worked. Someone else's obliviousness of electronic devices can actually be a blessing, in a sick kind of way. Anne had no intention of abusing the function. Two days later, she did look at Jason's location and found him to be at the Hampton Inn, about two blocks from his office. She thought nothing of it, as Jason could certainly be meeting an out-of-town customer there for a drink. The company had out-of-town guests frequently stay at the Hampton Inn.

Early Thursday morning Anne's phone rang. Her oldest brother informed Anne that their mother had fallen and broken her collarbone. His report indicated no need for alarm and all was well, considering. Anne, regardless, told her brother she would be leaving for Mineral Bluff within the hour. She texted Jason to inform him of the same. She began her hundred-mile trip mindful of the "Super Speeder" bonus penalty Paige had received along with her speeding citation.

Anne found her mother in good spirits and ready to return home from the hospital. As is the case with broken collarbones, Mrs. Willis sported no cast or splint, just a sling. Her age-related healing time could take eight to ten weeks, maybe more. In the meantime, she would suffer discomfort, and Anne assured her she would be at her beck and call as needed. Anne remained in Mineral Bluff until Sunday, her time there being more of a short vacation than a trip of mercy. She visited, naturally, with her mother, but enjoyed seeing and talking to her brothers and old friends. She did on one occasion check on Jason's location. She found him at the country club.

Leaving her mother in good condition and in no need of additional assistance, Anne returned to Atlanta Sunday afternoon. The week that followed produced no variance from normalcy. She did, early Wednesday evening, check in on Jason's location. Once again, his phone at least, had found its way to the Hampton Inn.

Then again on Thursday morning, Anne received another call from her brother. Anne's mother had now, because of her inability to balance properly due to her left arm being held in the sling, fallen and injured her right shoulder. Once again, Anne rushed to Mineral Bluff finding that her mother had sustained a deep bruise and would mend with time. Anne, for the second time, extended her stay until Sunday.

On Monday morning Jason, with a meager goodbye, took off to the office early. Anne, feeling a little tired from her trip, looked forward to a long, warm shower. As she stood under the flow of the water massaging her shoulders and neck, she observed something out of place. Her hair conditioner. She was meticulous about the location and placement of the items she kept in her shower. Soap, shampoo, body wash, conditioner. The conditioner had been moved. Ava, being very particular herself, would have placed it back to its original position had she moved it, which was doubtful. Jason had his own shower on the other side of the room. This left Anne with one far-reaching conclusion, and one she didn't care to believe. Someone had been in her shower.

At this point, events, not coincidences, began to accumulate in her mind. The Hampton Inn, the large pizza, the trip to Dairy Queen, the hair conditioner. The sum of the items added up to profound questions, the answers of which she would solicit from Jason.

Anne checked Jason's location on her phone. Not to her surprise, she found him at the Hampton Inn. Holding the phone reminded Anne that the cancellation of the next meeting with Dr. McDaniel would more than likely be required.

Jason arrived home at eight-thirty. He ate a lukewarm meal and watched as Anne pushed her food around on her plate. Their conversation lacked any significance at all, as neither seemed to be willing to engage in any substantive topic. After dinner, Jason excused himself and departed for his home office.

At this point, Anne had had enough. She wanted answers. She had thought through her questions and had anticipated his responses. Somehow she thought it would turn out as she expected. Entering the office, Anne said, "Jason, I have some questions."

"Sure," he responded, not bothering to look up from his pile of papers. "What about?" He looked indifferent and dismissive at the same time.

"My first question is, why did you order a large pizza when I was in Athens? You haven't eaten a pizza in years, much less a large one."

"Well, I told you...

Anne held up her hand, with her palm facing Jason, "No, you don't have to answer yet, just let the questions accumulate. One answer might be easier than working our way through several.

"The next question is, why have you been spending so much time at the Hampton Inn after, say, five-thirty?" She again held up her hand, palm facing Jason.

"Next, why was my hair conditioner moved from its usual location in my shower when I got home?"

"Next, who is she?"

"Who's who?"

Then she asked the final question she had hoped she would never ask. "Who are you fucking?"

"That's the most ridiculous thing I have ever heard you say. Have you been drinking?"

Anne knew she was putting her marriage at risk. She knew she could have just squandered the trust, if any, that Jason held for her.

"No! The question is: Who are you fucking?" Anne yelled across the room at Jason as he rose from his chair and stood with his hands on his hips and looked at her hard.

"I don't have to put up with this kind of shit. This is ridiculous."

"Answer the question!" she yelled again, this time storming to his desk and slamming her hands down on top of it.

Jason looked at Anne for a few seconds, still with his hands on his hips. He looked at her as though she had just violated that sacred trust that had crossed her mind. Then he exploded, "Lynn!" If an unwitting stranger had heard his reply, it would appear that whatever had just happened would have been Anne's fault.

"That's all I need to hear. You need to get your shit and get the hell out of here. And take the apparent object of your affection with you."

"Now let's be reasonable. I understand you're mad. Why don't I just stay in the guest room tonight and we can address this issue tomorrow?"

"No! I don't have to be reasonable. I want you out of here and I want you out of here now! If you are not gone within the next twenty minutes, let me tell you what I'm going to do. I am going to run face first into a door jamb. And I mean hard.

And then I'm calling nine-one-one and your ass will be going to jail for spousal abuse. And if you don't believe my ass, just try me. And don't forget Lynn, Becky Lynn. She's all yours now. I want her out of here, too."

Jason gathered a few items and vacated the house within the allotted time.

43

AFTER A FRETFUL NIGHT'S SLEEP Anne awoke feeling troubled. She turned and saw the empty pillow to confirm she had not been dreaming. Jason was gone. Doubt and uncertainty reigned. She rolled over, hugged her pillow, and started to cry. "To what end," she thought. He's the one who screwed up. He's the one who brought this to where it is today. He's the one to blame. But there is always plenty of blame to go around. Yes, she could take some blame, she just didn't know why.

With nothing to be gained by lying in bed, she got up at seven-fifteen. Time to start the day, whatever it may bring. For the first time since the bus accident, Anne found it difficult to concentrate. Options swirled in her head. Then her mind focused on Lynn. Becky Lynn. Anne noticed Becky Lynn's car, the one she had bought for her, parked in its customary spot at the edge of the driveway. As part of the equation, Anne needed to get her the hell out too.

Rain began to fall when Anne opened the back door to make her way to the guest house. Screw the umbrella, the wet clothes will dry. Pounding on the door, she got no response, no answer. The lights were on so Anne believed her to be there. Anne returned to the house, grabbed the key and again traversed the flat river stones to the guesthouse. She inserted the key and opened the door.

"Hey! Are you in here? I want to talk to you!"

No response came. Anne looked into both bedrooms, both bathrooms and the small patio to make certain Becky Lynn had vacated the premises. Not finding her in the guesthouse, but seeing her car, reinforced her thought that she had left with Jason. The only other possibility was abandonment and flight, but Anne materially discounted that choice. Becky Lynn had advanced too far into a more comfortable lifestyle. Anne doubted if she would throw it all away.

Returning to her kitchen she started mentally processing the details of her next actions. She had to call Paige, but would wait until after Paige's day had leveled off, say ten o'clock. Next, she procured paper and pen and recorded the things she needed to address about Becky Lynn: cancel her cell phone service, cancel her credit card, cancel her automobile insurance, cancel her health insurance, and call Amber Sessions at Mercy Care. Maybe calling Amber demonstrated a bit of a revenge factor, but Anne could live with it. She had no intention of seeing the woman at a board meeting at Mercy. Besides, Jason could now be Becky Lynn's only means of support.

A few minutes after ten, Anne gave Paige a call.

"What's up?" Paige immediately asked when she answered.

"Well, it's certainly not the same old shit today. I sent Mr. Wentworth packing last night and he's not coming back."

"What? Don't move. I'll be over there in fifteen minutes. Make some hot tea. Stay put."

Within fifteen minutes Paige entered the back door into the kitchen and put a white paper bag on the granite countertop. The bag contained croissants, bear claws, cinnamon rolls, and an apple fritter the size of a salad plate. She gave Anne a big hug.

"I thought we might need something to snack on because it sounds like we have a lot to talk about. I'll get a couple of cups and spoons. Now, what in hell has happened?"

In explicit detail, punctuated by an occasional question from Paige, Anne recounted the events of the prior evening and the occurrences that merged to spawn the inquisition.

"Can you believe the audacity of that conniving little bitch? I have never been stabbed in the back like this. It's humiliating. What are my friends going to think of me now?"

"They're not going to think anything of you that's bad, that's for sure. But it will be a different story for the rip-roaring asshole who wandered off the reservation, and the two-bit home-wrecking bitch you tried to help."

"I hope you're right," Anne said softly.

"What's your next step? What are you going to do?" Paige asked.

"How should I know, I've never been in this situation before," Anne said. "I just stepped into a quagmire and I feel like my next step could pull my shoe off. I know I'm not going to sit around and let this thing fester. I need a lawyer. I want to file and I don't want to get caught up in the parking lot that lawyers call the legal system. Remember when Kaitlin Hammond got divorced? I bet it took a year and a half or more. That's not for me."

"Who are you going to hire?"

"Bryan Munday. He represented Amy and Melissa and they both sang his praises. I'm calling him today."

"Good, I'll try to check in with you later this afternoon, or you call me if I don't get you. Now, do you want a cinnamon roll, a croissant...?"

After Paige departed, Anne called Bryan Munday and made an appointment to see him the next day.

Munday's office, located on the second floor of a three-story building near the Fulton County Courthouse, didn't impress Anne. Most successful law firms seemed to flaunt success with opulent furnishings and artwork, at least in the lobby. The Law Firm of Munday & Fisher probably couldn't sell their furniture and artwork at a garage sale. Anne had met Bryan Munday a couple of times, but had never had a lengthy discussion with him. She did know the location of his home in Buckhead and it spoke well of his material success, unless he had happened to marry into some substantial wealth. Perhaps he and his partner followed the adage of some older, successful attorneys: small office, big house.

Anne announced herself to the receptionist who asked her to have a seat while offering her coffee or water. Anne declined and sat on an old brown leather couch built more for looks than comfort. Based on her skewed perception of antique furniture, she thought someone might pay several thousand dollars for the thing in years to come if it endured long enough. The artwork, or wall decoration as the accountants seemed to call it, could be hung in any funeral home in Atlanta without notice.

When Bryan Munday came into the reception area to greet Anne, her perception of him changed from what she expected based on the last time she had seen him. He appeared to have shrunk in stature, maybe a couple of inches from what she remembered. She estimated him to be about five-seven. He now sported a goatee, nearly all gray. His hair appeared thinner on the top and longer on the sides. Time changes everything.

"Anne, how are you? It's been several years. Why don't you come back to my little conference room next to my office? That way neither one of us will be distracted by the piles of paper I have sitting around my desk."

The little conference room, more of a chatroom really, measured ten by ten at best. It did feel better there than being in a normal, oversized, law firm conference room.

"I'm kind of surprised," Anne said. "How many lawyers work at Munday and Fisher?"

"There are two partners, we have two associates, two paralegals, our receptionist, and one secretary. That's it."

"I'm just used to firms like Spence and Burt, my husband's company's law firm by the way, where they have four or five floors of lawyers. I guess that's what I expected here."

"No," Munday responded, "we keep it small. Family law seems to function better that way. Big firms, like Spence and Burt, generally stay away from family law. They don't want to jeopardize a strong corporate client over an unhappy result in a divorce situation. They refer the work out to firms like ours.

"So much for that, please tell me what's going on in your life, and take all the time you need. And everything you say will be held in confidence."

With that, Anne began telling Munday about her marital situation, prompted frequently by questions from him. How long have you been married? How long have you been separated? Do you have any children? Do you feel safe around your husband? Does your husband want a divorce?

"I'm the one taking the initiative. I'm here today to file for divorce and get this thing over with. What's the first step? And I'm not changing my mind, and we're not going to any more counselors. I'm done."

"Then let's get to work," Munday said as he turned the page to a new sheet of paper on his yellow legal pad.

"Georgia has no-fault divorce laws. If you've been a resident of Georgia for over six months, and you have been, and you're not expecting where your husband is the father, you can divorce thirty-one days after the petition is filed."

"Can you cut that time down to an earlier date?"

"Very simply, no. That's the law, and I've never seen the time period modified. In the petition we can state the grounds to be irreconcilable differences. That's very standard and functional if both parties desire the divorce."

"Are there other grounds available?" Anne asked.

"Oh, yes," Munday replied. "There are many. Cruelty, drug or alcohol abuse, insanity, adultery...."

"Bingo!" Anne exclaimed. "That's the one I want."

"Now, you need to know the divorce filing and any court activity becomes part of the record. In other words, all of this is open to the public."

"That's exactly the way I want it."

"Grounds of adultery can be a two-edged sword. I must, and have to, ask you this. Any time during your marriage did you have an affair, a tryst, or anything that might pop up? Because if you have, it will probably be discovered and disclosed. And once again, this is public information."

"I can state unequivocally that I have not, in any form, had a sexual relationship during my marriage except with my husband, and that's been pretty limited for the last four years."

"Okay, here's what we need to do."

Munday began to run down a laundry list of steps required in the divorce. He explained the preparation and filing of the petition, the serving of notice to Jason, the need to mediate to possibly avoid the necessity of going to court. He covered the documents that would be required from both sides, such as tax returns and statements from banks, brokerage firms, and retirement accounts. The possible need for valuation reports of the businesses and the need of an appraisal for the Reid Lane property.

"Damn," Anne muttered, "this makes me tired and I haven't started yet."

"It's a lot of work, and nothing can be taken lightly. Tell me a little more about these businesses, Wentworth Construction and Democycle."

Anne provided a brief history of both, how the construction company came from Jason's grandfather and how she started Democycle in 2006.

"So it sounds like Wentworth Construction is Jason's separate property and Democycle is marital property, meaning owned by both of you?"

"No," Anne said. "Democycle was my idea and I'm the one who's been involved with its development and growth. It's mine."

"I understand your position, but under the law it's marital property unless we can prove where Jason made a gift to you of his half. But let's not worry about that now. Georgia isn't a community property state, but a spouse is entitled to an equitable share of the marital assets. And equitable does not mean equal. This is why you have me," Munday said.

"What else do I need to know today?" Anne asked.

"I usually save this little speech until after my client, male or female, has gotten over some of the emotional complications that come with divorce. You seem to be well-grounded, and there are no issues with children. Here's the deal. Your divorce is now a business transaction. There will be an emotional side to it, and there can be some sentimental issues, but all in all, it's now about money, assets, and debt. That's really all that remains. My job is to help you identify and retain all of the assets you can, and at the same time, reduce your share of any debts you must assume."

"Gee, that puts a whole new light on it, doesn't it? It's just a business deal."

"I don't intend for it to sound that simple, but that's what it is."

"Okay," Anne said with a show of confidence. "You draft the petition and I'll start gathering information. Fair enough?"

44

FRIDAY MORNING ANNE RECEIVED A phone call from Bryan Munday.

"Anne, I have drafted a petition for divorce citing irreconcilable differences and adultery as causes. It's ready to file. I have to ask, are you certain you want to move forward and are you certain that you want a cause of adultery?"

"As sure as the sun comes up every day."

"Okay, I'll send a paralegal to file the petition with the clerk of the Fulton County Superior Court this morning. Now, we haven't discussed how you want to notify Jason of the action. We can have him served in person, at home, or his office, or we can do it by certified mail."

"Mail takes too long and since I have no idea where he's staying it would be hard to serve him there. I guess I could wait until he gets to wherever he's staying and find his location on my phone."

"Anne, I want you to text him and tell him to turn off the locator function. And send the text now before the petition is filed. Is he aware that you can follow him?"

"Oh, hell no. That's how I got part of my evidence on his cheating ass."

"Send him the text now. And if he responds to your text, good, bad, or indifferent, ignore it. Don't respond. You are not to call him, see him, talk to him, or talk about him. If he has a desire to communicate with you, it needs to come through this office. Text him my name and number, inform him you have retained me, and if he needs to communicate...."

"Hold on a second, I'm recording what I need to text him."

Bryan continued, "Tell him all communications need to come through me. Got it?"

"Okay, yes. Now, let's have him served at his office. I think that would be great," Anne said with a touch of excitement. "Today's June twenty-eighth, so July twenty-eighth will be thirty days. So we can be divorced by July twenty-ninth."

"Listen, you need to crank it back a little. For you, look at it this way. The thirty-day waiting period for you means you can't get divorced until thirty days have passed, not that you will get divorced after thirty days have expired. Your divorce has the potential of being complex, regardless of how anxious you are to get it done. Any questions?"

"No, I'll get to work," Anne said with an air of confidence.

The first text from Jason came at one-twenty: *What the fuck?* Anne ignored it. Then the second and the third, also ignored. Finally, the call, that Anne let go to voicemail and then deleted without listening to it. Anne sent Jason the information on Bryan Munday as he had requested and then she blocked Jason's number.

Anne called her attorney. "From the text messages I have received it's obvious that he has been served. Now, can I change the locks on the doors?"

"No, the house still belongs to both of you, and his belongings, I assume, are still there. You can't deny him access to his belongings, but we can restrict his access by limiting them to appointed times agreed to by you. In other words, if he wants to come and get something, I don't want you there. And don't mess with his belongings during the pendency of the divorce.

"Jason will be hiring an attorney sooner than later. When that happens, his attorney will contact me and then all communications can come through us, the attorneys. Also, don't open his mail if your name's not on it. You need to focus on the financial data we discussed, not Jason."

That's when Anne realized, at the current time, she had access to all the financial records other than Wentworth Construction. The records should be in Jason's study. She found bank statements, brokerage accounts, and retirement accounts. At least nothing that she was aware of would be disappearing. She carried the statements to her upstairs office and made copies on her small copier.

Ava arrived on Monday morning at her usual time, eight o'clock sharp. Before she began her day, Anne asked that she come and sit in the nook so she could be informed of the situation.

"Friday afternoon I had papers filed that begin the process of divorce. Jason and I are getting divorced. If you have any questions, I'll try to answer them. And I know that you will show enough discretion not to ask too many. But here's what I want you to know. You are still in my employ and you will continue to be in my employ. I want you to have no concerns or reservations about your position here.

"Now, I want you to take this hundred dollar bill and go to the U-Haul store off Piedmont Road, there by Peachtree Creek, and buy however many storage boxes that will buy. When you get back here, I want you to go into the guesthouse and box up anything and everything that you know doesn't belong there. If it's a toss-up one way or the other, send it packing. We don't have a house guest anymore. Put the boxes just inside the door when you're done. We don't want anything to happen to her stuff."

Anne walked Ava to the back door where she noticed that Becky Lynn's car had been removed. "She must have taken it in the still of the night," Anne thought.

That afternoon, Munday called Anne and asked if she could come by his office.

"I know this is short notice and I appreciate you coming in. I need to tell you that Jason hired an attorney and the impact that has on our strategy. He has hired Jenny Beard."

"I didn't know we had a strategy yet."

"We did. It was pretty broad-based. Now we have to step up our game. Are you familiar with Jenny Beard?"

"I've heard of her. She has a reputation for being a bit of a ball-buster doesn't she?" Anne asked.

"Yes, but in this case she's representing the balls, if you will, your husband. She can smell money like a beagle can smell bacon frying from a mile away. She learned her negotiating skills from reading General Sherman's memoirs about his trip through Georgia. She will try to drown us in paper and drag this out as long as she can. Translation, more fee income for her. I don't understand why Jason hired her, but it is what it is.

"And here are the highlights from her first salvo, which I'll email to you. Don't get mad. We won't put up with this nonsense, but here it is. You are to vacate the house and turn the keys over to Jason. You are to remove your signature authority from all bank and brokerage accounts. You are to turn over all credit cards. You are not to contact Mr. Wentworth by any means and if you do she will seek a restraining order against you."

"Well isn't that nice? Do you recall how General Anthony McAuliffe answered the Germans' request to surrender during the Battle of the Bulge? He had a one word reply, 'Nuts.' I'm going to double that with a two-word reply, fuck off."

"I'm impressed with your knowledge of history and your spunk. However, I have to be a little less direct. And on the subject of communications, do not, let me repeat, do not use your text or email functions to send anything that might be used in court. Those things are open books. It's best if you just call me on the phone."

"What are we going to do about her demands?"

"I'll schedule a hearing before a judge and request relief from any of her cockamamy demands. There's not a judge in Fulton County who would expect or make you comply with any of her nonsense. This is just one of her methods to get the fees up. More paper to chase and more hearings to attend."

"What if he doesn't comply with our request that I not be bothered and that he's not supposed to come to the house when I'm there?"

"I'll request a restraining order against him and it will be granted. Remember, he's the one with the balls. And the one with the balls has to toe the line a little closer."

Munday handed Anne a piece of paper. "On there you will find the names of three certified public accountants who provide expert testimony in divorces, three business valuation experts and three real estate appraisers. Unless you have some-one else in mind, interview them and pick the ones you like. They will need to get to work."

"I just assumed Jason would be the one to get everything appraised. Won't we be paying twice for the same work?"

"A lot of times single appraisers will work if both parties agree, but not when Jenny Beard is involved. She has her pet accountants and appraisers who invariably seem to have everything tilted to the benefit of her clients. We're talking about thousands, maybe hundreds of thousands of dollars. Remember, now it's all about the money."

"You said the experts would testify. Do you mean testify at a trial? I thought we were going to mediate our divorce."

"We will mediate the divorce. But because of Jenny Beard being involved, the likelihood is great that we will have to go to trial. She considers a mediation a warmup for trial. And somehow, she seems to be able to convince her clients that the best results come from a trial. Unless Jason can get her sidetracked, a trial is likely."

"If that's the way they want it, saddle up cowboy. We're going to ride them to the ground. And let me tell you. Based on the request that I turn the house keys over to Jason, that means he wants Reid Lane. He loves that house. He designed it, he built it and he can have it. But it's going to cost him dearly."

After her meeting with Bryan Munday, she returned home and began calling experts.

45

PAIGE BUCHANAN'S NAME FLASHED ACROSS the screen of Anne's cell phone in conjunction with the vibration that immediately followed.

"What's up?"

"Eric took the kids to some deal at the College Football Hall of Fame. There are supposed to be a couple of Falcons there and all three wanted to go. They won't be back until after nine I'm guessing. So I've been sitting here listening to this bottle of Yellow Tail merlot beg me to drink it and I thought you might be able to help. Can I come over?"

"Oh, I wish you would. You know it'll probably end up being our wine and whine routine. I'm just sitting here digging up bones."

"Listening to a little country, huh? What happened to George? That's not one of his songs."

"No, it's not. But even George Strait has to have a warm-up band, and Randy Travis and his bunch are doing a wonderful job. George is waiting in the wings. And by the way, Elton just happens to be here, too. He's sitting over in the corner and starting to act a little pissy. So you need to get on over here."

Paige opened Anne's back door and entered the kitchen in less than ten minutes. Anne, busy putting together some munchies to share, gave Paige a nod and a quick hello.

"Bring me the wine and grab a couple of those wine glasses from the cabinet," Anne said.

As Anne pulled the cork from the bottle, Paige asked, "Did you hear what happened to Kendell Blevins yesterday morning?"

"Oh, no. What has Kendell done this time?"

"You may know her husband, Rob, is a big-time cyclist. He rides a lot. Well, Kendell decided she was going to take up the sport. Maybe spend a little more time with Rob. She goes out and buys a new bicycle, shorts, jersey, helmet, the works. She also buys a pair of those clip-in pedals and shoes. So she's all clipped in, without practicing, and she's riding in Chastain Park. She was going to cross the bridge on Nancy Creek, the one you've been over a thousand times running, and she has to make a pretty sharp right turn. She was going slow, and there were people coming toward her. About halfway up the incline she was going so slow she just fell over. She couldn't unclip in time. She skinned her elbow and her knee, but no real damage. It made her so mad that she got up, picked up the bike, and threw it in the creek. She called an Uber and went home. Rob went over after work and fished the bike out of the creek. She's lucky someone didn't steal the thing."

"Why am I not surprised? Let's go into the Great Room. We can hear our voices echo a little, and I think it's the cleanest of all the rooms in the house, if you know what I mean. I don't know if they ever made it to, or should I just say made it in, my bed, but I've been sleeping in the guest room."

"Fuck 'em," Paige replied. "I entirely agree."

In the Great Room Paige plopped into a big, soft leather side chair and Anne took up residency on the couch. They both removed their shoes.

"Ya know, it's nice to be in a room without a television or a computer. I get so sick of those things. Great, it's just us. Got anything in mind to discuss?" Paige inquired. "Let's put on Elton."

"Okay, but you only get to listen to *Crocodile Rock* one time, as in once."

"I don't know why you don't like Elton John. He runs circles around George Strait."

"I don't think so," Anne said.

"Elton John has fans all around the world. Does George Strait?"

"I don't know, but George is more productive. He's had more gold and platinum albums than Elton."

"Oh, bullshit."

"You can look it up. George Strait has had seventy-two and Elton John has had sixty-five. And that *Candle in the Wind* thing shouldn't even count. That was sympathy."

"Okay, changing subjects. That trip to Athens was fun. We should do the meeting again, but invite everyone to Atlanta. There's more to do here and it's easier to get to."

"But you know what? We actually had the most fun just sitting in the chapter room talking and exchanging stories."

"After we left Athens I thought of a story I should have told on you. It just didn't come to mind at the time," Paige said.

"Like what?"

"Like the guy you went out with a couple of times who was from Meridian, Mississippi. The one that wore the eighteen-pound gold Rolex. Said his family owned a jewelry store, and a music store, and a gun shop, and an art gallery, and an electronics store and something else. Come to find out his father owned a pawn shop. What was that lying sack of shit's name?"

"Oh, what was it? Jay. Jay Oakley!" Anne exclaimed.

"That's it," Paige said laughing. "He would rather lie on credit than tell the truth for cash."

"Well, what about you? I should have reminded everyone about the night you bet three Phi Delts you could outdrink them. Straight shots. They were drinking Jack and you were drinking vodka. Y'all stayed even for quite a while, but they finally started to fall. You drank them under the table. But they never knew your vodka bottle held about eighty percent water. There was enough vodka in it to produce the vodka smell, and they fell for it."

After two glasses of wine, Paige's irresistible strong Southern accent seeped out like the golden sugar droplets atop the meringue on a lemon pie.

"Do ya think y'all will be gettin' anywhere with that mediation?"

"Nope, not according to Bryan, who I really like, by the way. And for that matter I don't intend to settle it in mediation," Anne said quite calmly. "I think I'd like to see his butt in court. Kind of a showcase for Atlanta. He dicked me around, no pun intended, and I'm guessing everyone is saying this stems from the accident with the kids, even though it's years old. I think it would be fair for all of his friends and colleagues to know that he's the one who got the itchy britches. Remember, 'Thou shalt not play hide the wiener with someone else when you're married.' Or something along those lines."

"Ya know," Paige said, "this whole thing started out like *My Fair Lady*, and turned into *Pretty Woman* for Jason. Maybe the sequel for him can be another version of *Fatal Attraction*."

"You're being too kind to Jason."

"What's the biggest issue you have to resolve?"

"This house. I'm letting on like I have to have it, and I know he really wants it."

"What would you do with this big ole house?"

"Sell it."

"Sell it?"

"Absolutely. There's no way I'm going to live in this house. For starters, it's nearly seven thousand square feet. That's just a little more than I need. Believe me, the only reason I'm saying I want it is because Jason wants it. Remember, he built it. He takes a lot of pride in this place and he really wants it. I'll let him have it, but it'll come at a price."

"So you think that shitweasel and his gutter slut of a girlfriend will live here?"

"Paige, you just have such a wonderful and expressive way with words. Can I use that line?"

"Sure."

"And to answer your question, yes, I think they will live here, if she's still around. He won't have to get a new driver's license and she moves up quite a few more rungs on the social ladder. Maybe she can show off my new kitchen again next spring."

"What are you gonna do? Have you thought that one through?"

"I'm looking at townhomes or garden homes."

"Where have you been lookin'? I hope it's close to here."

"My realtor has been pretty good with show and tell. She says she knows a couple who are about to move out of town and they are putting their townhouse on the market. It hasn't been listed yet. It's at the Watkins Enclave development, in the twenty-two hundred block of Woodward Way off of Peachtree Northwest."

"I know where they are. Those are really nice, and pretty new. They vary in sizes from twenty-five hundred to four thousand square feet. The smaller ones are still a lot of house for one person."

"I know. But they're very private, with a gate. Also, you just never know. I may want to take in a bunch of Vietnamese sometime."

"Have they given you a price?"

"No, but the realtor thinks it'll be around a million two. She says it's in fabulous condition and needs no work. But I can't buy it while I'm still fussing with Jason over pots and pans. How can I argue that I want to keep Reid Lane and be purchasing another house at the same time?"

"Well, I can," Paige said.

"You can what?"

"I can buy that house," Paige chirped. "That way you can buy it from me after the divorce is final. Or better yet, I'll enter into a binding contract to buy, make it assignable, pay a big ass deposit to hold the property and then assign the contract to you after you finalize the divorce. That saves closing costs and shit like that."

"Would you do that?"

"Are you kidding me? Hell, yes! I'll do it, and you know it. I'm as serious as..., as..., oh, whatever. Tomorrow, let's talk to your realtor and get this underway. And I mean it."

"Yes, ma'am."

"What are you planning on taking out of here?"

"I just don't know. I guess I'll have to hire the design bandit so she can pick out the stuff that is just darling and I can't live without."

"No, what you need to do is change horses. You should talk to Patrick Ables. He's helped me with some stuff and he's really good. And I'll bet you he'll yell bullshit when you mention taking anything out of here to a new place. He's a no-go on antiques. Says they've lived too long. But he's not one of those super contemporary, all glass and chrome and black leather kind of guys either. Black leather furniture, that is."

46

ONE AFTERNOON FOLLOWING THE WINE and whine summit at Reid Lane, Anne and Paige met with Anne's realtor at the Watkins Enclave townhome development. Situated on Woodward Way NW, two blocks off Peachtree, the project hugged Peachtree Creek to its southwest. The French Regency style of architecture permitted maximum utilization of the properties' footprint. The stand-alone dwellings were owned by a comfortable mix of successful young professionals, and retirees looking to downsize their living accommodations while remaining close to their former neighbors and friends.

The townhouse available to Anne comprised thirty-two hundred square feet and held exactly what she wanted. The two-story floor plan incorporated a living room, a study, two bedrooms, two and a half baths, a family room, a small dining room, kitchen and a breakfast area in perfect functionality, especially with the two-car garage. The dark red brick exterior of the building highlighted the striking gray granite that enfolded the front door to the house. A small plot of land lay out the back door providing an unimpaired view over Peachtree Creek onto the Bobby Jones Golf Course, hopefully never to be spoiled. The price, as the realtor had previously expected, sat at one million two-hundred thousand dollars.

"Anne, you couldn't draw up anything more suitable for what you need right now," Paige said. "Obviously it's going to look a lot different when you get your furniture in here. And it's certainly big enough that you won't be tripping over yourself."

"Since the owners are moving out of state, they want to sell the property as soon as possible. I have to put it in the multiple listings tomorrow," the realtor informed Anne. "How interested in this property are you? I have four more options for you to see."

"I like this one a lot, as is. It's just a timing issue as to when I can buy it."

"Anne, if you're sure you want it, let's get it." Paige, turning to the realtor said, "Draw up a contract with me as the purchaser, full price, one point two million. Do the sellers have a mortgage on this place?"

"Yes, about seven hundred thousand."

"Okay, they'll want to pay that off and have a little money to work with. Ask them if they'll accept a contract, that is assignable, with a deposit of one million in cash and the balance paid at closing. I will escrow the balance of the sales price so it will be available at closing. Closing must take place within six months of signing the contract. I'll guarantee that closing date. I'll be responsible for all operating costs, HOA fees, and taxes from the date of possession until closing. Would you get them on the phone and ask them?"

"Paige, I can't expect you to do this. That's a million dollars, with more at risk."

"What's money good for if I can't use it the way I want and help out my BFF? Besides, I know you're good for it and this deal is going to work."

"I think the whole world needs a friend like you."

After a ten-minute conversation with the sellers, the realtor said the plan would work if the deposit could be one million one hundred thousand with the balance held in escrow. The sellers needed the additional money to invest in the new home they had found. About the only part of the conversation Anne and Paige heard was when the realtor chuckled and said, "Oh, they're good for the money."

"Deal," Paige said, "let's draw it up."

"You can take possession on September first," the agent said.

"Paige, how are you going to keep this from Eric? He is a banker after all. Won't he be aware of your check clearing the bank for over a million dollars?"

"He will never know it. I'm writing the check on my trust account in Savannah. I don't bank the trust at T Bank."

After writing and signing the real estate contract, Anne and Paige departed to the Swan Coach House restaurant for lunch, a piece of Key lime pie, and perhaps a celebratory glass of wine.

"You've taken a pretty big bite out of, what do they call them, life changing events? This is adding up for you to have some high seas ahead. Lord, just moving would be enough to drive me crazy. You have the divorce to contend with, plus moving. I can't be more than a cheerleader with the divorce, but I can certainly help you with moving. I'm volunteering to be your 'girl Friday.' I can do a lot of running around for you if you don't have the time.

"Now would be the best time to engage Patrick Ables. He can evaluate what you have at Reid Lane and draw up some ideas for your new place."

"You know Paige, if I had two of you, I wouldn't have to do a thing. Thank you."

Paige picked up her cell phone and called Patrick Ables. She made the complimentary over-the-phone introductions and handed the device to Anne. Patrick agreed to meet Anne at Reid Lane the next afternoon. Then Anne called the realtor to secure a time for a walk through with Patrick at her new home.

At home, later in the afternoon, Anne received a call from Bryan Munday.

"Anne, I've gotten the preliminary values from the valuation experts so I called Jenny Beard about scheduling a date for the mediation. She actually agreed. To me this means Jason is putting pressure on her to get this done. I went ahead and scheduled a mediation at the end of the month, on the twenty-ninth, if that's okay with you. Since it's the end of August, everybody's back from vacations and ready to go to work."

47

PATRICK ABLES ARRIVED AT REID Lane a few minutes after one. He wore skinny blue jeans, a four-button, light gray, cotton, long-sleeved Henley shirt – not the picture of professionalism that Anne had expected, but he did think with the other side of his brain.

"Paige Buchanan speaks very highly of you," Anne said.

"I appreciate her confidence, especially considering her strong character."

"Oh, so you think Paige has a strong character?" Anne asked with a chuckle.

That seemed to get things off on a good footing. Patrick told Anne his best effort comes from getting to know a little about his client's background and tastes. He asked if they could sit and talk for a while so he could get Anne's preferences and ideas into his head. They retired to the nook where Anne served coffee and Patrick served up questions.

To Anne's surprise they talked for nearly an hour. Patrick asked about her upbringing, how she got to where she is, her family, and what she couldn't tolerate in furnishings. She obviously told him about the children as she knew he would be seeing their rooms, and she told him about her marital situation. She said the time for big changes in her life started now. Why else would she be moving? She also told him about the purchase arrangement on the new townhome and showed him a picture of the front exterior. She assured him she would be moving there. Move-in day could begin September first.

"Now you know my life history pretty much, I'd like to hear about how you approach your job."

"Your home needs to be a reflection of you, not what other people want or expect to see. If you go for the magazine layout style, chances are good that you will be uncomfortable in your own home. But you will have a copy of a glossy mag that everyone else will throw in the trash when the next edition gets printed. Like they say, 'It looked good on paper.'

"You and your guests need to be comfortable in every room in your home. That's what I'm about, comfort and livability. Don't misunderstand. I'm not going to suggest putting bean-bags everywhere. I'm not that Bohemian. Your interior will be elegant, in keeping with the beautiful exterior portion of the structure of your new home.

"Why don't you take me room-to-room for show and tell? Let's see what you have. There is one thing you should know about me. I can be a little sarcastic. So be sure and let me know if I step on your toes."

They started in the kitchen and circled the downstairs reviewing the nook, the family room, the formal dining room, the foyer, the study, the master bedroom and baths, a sitting area, the Great Room, and back to the kitchen. Patrick took notes and pictures as they went. Upstairs they visited the two bedrooms that were the children's, an upper study, additional bedrooms, the large family room, and Anne's office. Patrick inquired if the upstairs part of the house was currently being used. The answer was no, except for the office.

After completing the tour, they recessed to Anne's small office over the garage. She sat in the swivel chair behind her desk, and Patrick in an old rocking chair, the only other chair in the room. Patrick asked a few questions about some of the items in the house, but generally seemed to be non-committal on anything.

"This is a beautiful old rocking chair. It feels like I'm gliding," Patrick said.

"It was my grandmother's chair. It's very dear to me," came the reply.

"Sweetie, you have a mess in some respects and some big decisions to make. I'm just going to put it right out here. I believe the only item of furniture you need from Reid Lane is the chair I'm sitting in. Everything else stays with the house. You've made it clear, and in no uncertain terms, that you are making a new start. So, that's what you need to do. All this stuff here is just outdated, literally and figuratively. Here's a question for you. When you played tennis in college did you use a graphite racket or an old wooden one? Now, is there anything in there you can't live without?"

Anne stared off into nothingness for about a minute as Patrick quietly rocked. "No," she said, "except for the rocker."

"Did you rock your babies in this beautiful chair?"

"Yes, I did."

"This is all you need from the past as far as furniture. Now let's go take a look at your new place."

Upon arrival, Patrick immediately expressed his liking of the complex. He adored the architecture and the open space along the creek. He took pictures, measured spaces, and asked questions. He told Anne about the budget spreadsheet he would prepare and asked what the budget limitations might be. He discussed the possibility of minor remodeling, if Anne was interested. He asked about accent lighting and wall coverings. He asked about her taste in art and area rugs.

"Let's start with 'the new you' in home furnishings and design. I will come up with a plan. Pictures, ideas, floor plan layouts, color schemes, and lighting. No chic eclectic crap. We're too old for that. When do you think you will really need this place?"

"I would say early October. We are trying to get the divorce trial scheduled as soon as possible, and my attorney is going to request the judge give me possession of Reid Lane for up to six months after the final decree is entered to find a new place to live. He's pretty convincing that he can pull that off. I want to get out of there, but I should have a good cushion if needed."

"In regard to this new place, the majority of the items we will be buying can be procured right here in Atlanta. That's another big joke with some designers. They think if the furniture doesn't come from at least one thousand miles away, it has no character. What a bunch of crap. Let's get busy and decorate this new home."

"My soon-to-be ex knows nothing of this house. And I want it kept that way."

48

A WEEK BEFORE THE SCHEDULED mediation Anne met with
Bryan Munday to review the accumulated documents, including the valuation reports and appraisals, to formulate a plan
of attack.

"Anne, the mediator's name is Ryan Parker. He's in his
mid-sixties and practiced family law for years before getting
into the mediation game about five years ago. He's skilled,
knows what happens when you wind up in court, and does a
good job of explaining what will happen in court if you can't
settle the matter in mediation. We will all meet at Parker's
office. He has a setup that's designed for everyone's needs.

"The cost for Parker is four hundred dollars per hour,
per party, with a minimum of two hours, even if you cancel.
There's also an admin fee of two fifty per side. We'll have some
complex things to discuss, so I said it would probably be an

eight-hour day. Then again, if Jenny is her normal horse's ass, it could be over in ten minutes. We are required to mediate, but nowhere does is say we have to accomplish anything.

"I know I brushed by this earlier, but you need to remember Ryan Parker is not your attorney; he's more like a combination negotiator and salesman. He's probably going to tell you that whatever it is you want is out of the question. He'll tell Jason the same. Then he'll start to whack away at what each of you want and try to have you agree with what is acceptable given the law and the courts.

"It's not uncommon for the parties to meet together with the mediator before the mediation starts to go over the ground rules and open things up in a civil manner."

"Nope," Anne said. "I will not meet with Jason before the first pitch. If you want to talk to what's-her-face, have at it. Can Paige Buchanan attend? I could use the moral support. She is my North Star. I set my compass off of Paige."

"No, only the parties involved, the attorneys, the experts, if needed, and the mediator will participate. So Paige won't be able to attend. She can be available by phone if you feel like you need a little moral support."

The accountant retained by Anne had compiled the financial data and valuations that had been prepared. His Statement of Net Worth presented the assets and liabilities of the Wentworths. Using the statement as a starting point, Anne and Bryan identified the assets she would like to receive in the settlement, if that goal could be attained. All of the information shown on the statement was current.

Jason Wentworth & Anne Willis Wentworth
Statement of Net Worth
As of July 31, 2018

Cash in banks	$ 297,231
Brokerage accounts	14,763,445
Limited partnerships	12,400,000
Retirement funds, JW	2,811,180
Retirement funds, AWW	103,416
Democycle, LLC	11,000,000
Porsche automobile, JW	92,000
Land Rover automobile, AWW	75,000
Residence, 1716 Reid Lane NW	3,600,000
Furniture, art and personal items	800,000
Total assets	$45,942,272
Deferred income taxes	$ 8,200,000
Net worth	37,742,272
Liabilities and net worth	$45,942,272

Note: Wentworth Construction, LLC is the separate property of Mr. Jason Wentworth and has a fair market value of $34,700,000.

After a discussion of the assets and their values, Anne listed the assets she would like to have. She told Bryan she could be happy with all of Democycle, one-half of the cash, one-half of the brokerage accounts, her car and her retirement account, and one-half of the furniture. She said she wanted to list Reid Lane as hers to make it a big negotiating point, and to irritate Jason. She repeated her position that she had no desire to own the house but she felt as though Jason would fight for it. She said she would accept her share of the deferred income taxes, whatever that meant.

Bryan multiplied, divided, added, and subtracted.

"With your share of assets that you have listed, less a reasonable share of the deferred taxes, your request comes in at about nineteen million. That's just a hair over fifty percent of the net worth. I don't see how they could argue with that. But then we are not dealing with reasonable people. You may think Jason might be reasonable, but by the time Jenny Beard gets through brainwashing him, you'll experience an entirely different person."

"That's going to take some doing, because he is already an entirely different person."

Anne and Bryan arrived at the mediator's office a little later than scheduled. Anne knew Jason would be prompt, so to avoid seeing him and his attorney, she purposefully created a time void between arrivals. Bryan had told Ryan Parker there would be no meeting of the minds prior to the commencement of the mediation. Parker escorted Anne, her attorney, and her box of files to a moderate-sized conference room with a table that sat six. Parker offered a variety of pastries and beverages, both of which were declined.

"I've visited with Mr. Wentworth and his counsel, setting the ground rules for today's mediation. I'll do the same with you."

"Ryan, if you don't mind, we can dispense with that. I've been over it a couple of times with my client and she is comfortable with what we are about to do."

"In that case, let's get started. Ms. Wentworth, since you are the petitioner, you get to go first. Do you have any strategies as to what you would like to accomplish here today?"

With that, Bryan laid out a brief history of the marriage and the assets to be divided, assisted by Anne to fill in some details. Parker was given a copy of the net worth statement marked up to indicate the assets Anne sought. Both Anne and Bryan clarified the source of each asset, item by item. Anne presented her proposal of the assets she would like to have. All of these, half of these, and none of those. As she had originally projected, her offer amounted to just a hair over fifty percent of the couple's marital net worth, or roughly nineteen million dollars. Anne's share included the house on Reid Lane. She over-emphasized the importance of her obtaining sole possession of the house. And she assured Parker that Wentworth Construction would remain in Jason's possession as she understood it to be separate property. She said she thought her offer to be fair and equitable. With his yellow legal pad and Anne's documents in hand, Parker exited the room to meet with Jason and his attorney with the proposition.

It didn't take long for Jason to counter-offer. Parker returned to Anne's room with copies of Jason's documents and his proposal in hand.

"Here's the deal," Parker said. "He wants the house. Also, as you can see on his workpaper, his position is that most of the stock accounts are his separate property. He is also taking the position that Democycle is marital property and he wants half of its value added to his side of the equation. In a nutshell, his offer to you for your share of the marital assets is around ten million. You can see on the paper what he suggests."

Anne picked up the paper and compared the amounts line by line. She found some material differences, none of which favored her side of the ledger. Besides the variances in valuations, Jason had requested a greater percentage, seventy-five percent, of the brokerage accounts and one-half of Democycle.

"I'm a little befuddled right now Mr. Parker. How do you spell delusional? It has only one 'S', correct?"

Anne took a pen and wrote on Jason's proposal in big capital letters: "I'M DONE. YOU ARE DELUSIONAL!"

"Please take this back to Jason and tell him to prepare for court. We are wasting time and money here today. Mr. Parker, thank you for your time and I'm sure you have something more constructive to do with the rest of the day. But before you go back to give him that, let me see it please." Anne took her pen and placed three additional exclamation marks by her comment.

After Parker left the room, Anne turned to her attorney. "Tell me about the Speedy Trial Act. I want to get this over with. What's our next step?"

"First of all, the Speedy Trial Act does not apply in your case. It's a federal law for federal criminal cases. We're stuck on the slow wheel of justice. We have two obstacles to contend with, our worthy opponents and their desire to move forward quickly with a trial, and the Superior Court's docket. I'll make an inquiry with Jenny. If she and Jason agree to speed things up, then I'll start working on a court date. Let me go down the hall and see if they're still here. If so, I'll talk to Jenny about it right now. We'll leave after I speak with them. I'll be right back."

To Bryan Munday's surprise, Jenny Beard agreed to try the case as soon as the parties could get a setting. After lunch Bryan set about to twist the arm of the scheduling clerk at the courthouse. Once again, he had a surprise in a case that he anticipated taking months to resolve. He called Anne.

"You are not going to believe this, but we have a trial date set for September sixteen and the other side has agreed to it. The catch is that both parties have to agree to limit the trial to two days. It seems that Judge Coates is leaving on Wednesday of that week to go on a fishing trip. Since he had an opening on Monday, he agreed to hear the case if it would be limited to two days. I can't tell you how shocked I am that Jenny has agreed to this. She would generally drag a case like this one out for months to jack the fees up. Jason must be putting pressure on her.

"Now, what you need to understand is that Judge Coates is a cantankerous old cuss. He's probably eighty or so. He's been on the bench for years and he very rarely gets overturned on appeals. As is said, 'He does not suffer fools gladly.' Translation, he's not going to put up with any of Jenny Beard's customary shenanigans, which helps us. Now we need to schedule some depositions to find out how Jason's experts came up with their numbers."

49

ANNE RECEIVED THE KEYS TO her new home on the first day of September. With the intention of christening the property, she looked around Reid Lane for something appropriate. She found it in her little upstairs office. The heavy chestnut rocking chair that she received from her grandmother's estate. Ironically, the chair represented one of the more significant items from the estate and everyone decided Anne should have it, being the only granddaughter. She wrestled it down the stairs, through the foyer and out the front doors to her Land Rover. Anne took pride in her physical conditioning, but the chair pushed her to the limit. It seemed to get heavier with each step and fitting it into the back of the SUV presented a challenge.

The new townhome, new to her anyway, seemed so much more spacious without furniture. It appeared to be much bigger than when she first saw it. But she knew this to be an illusion. Once her furniture found its way through the door, the size would diminish to the human eye.

Earlier in the day she and Paige had transferred the utilities into Paige's name and informed the property management company of the change in responsibility for fees. In the afternoon, before going to the house, Anne stopped by the management company to introduce herself where she was provided with page after page of the rules and regulations of the closed community.

Ignoring her garage, Anne parked in front of the townhome to deposit the rocking chair. After opening the back door of the SUV, she looked at the chair and thought, "This is going to be your final habitat for a long time." And with that thought she reached for the chair to pull it out.

"It looks like you could use a hand with that thing," a male voice came from out of nowhere, startling her slightly.

"No thank you, I've got it," she said as she started to extract the chair from the Land Rover. But instead of actually reaching for the chair, she stopped to turn around and face the source of the voice.

By Anne's estimation, he stood about six-foot-four or-five based on being around her brothers. He had a dark tan that emphasized his bright blue eyes. His hair, brown with a mix of gray, appeared to be in need of a cut, but it fit him well at its current length. A slender body, and his long arms extending out of a green T-shirt, presented the characteristics of an athlete. His superb physical appearance did not reveal the fact that he was fifty-five years of age.

"To me, it looks like it has you. My hands have been hanging around all day just looking for something like this to do. You're not going to deny my mitts the privilege of assisting, are you?"

"Okay, if you insist," Anne said quickly, relieved of the task.

The man extracted the chair from the SUV like it was balsa wood. He lifted it to the side so as not to obscure his vision and started walking toward the front door. Anne had scurried over to unlock and open it.

"Ma'am, why don't you scoot on in there and show me just exactly where you would like me to put it?"

"Okay. Oh, just anywhere, put it right there. As you can see, I haven't moved in yet."

"This is really a nice chair. American chestnut. Handmade and looks to be about a hundred years old based on the darkened color of the wood. And look, the rockers are cambered out a little so the chair won't shuffle sideways when you're rocking. This is nice."

"You seem to know a lot about wood and rocking chairs."

"I grew up in the backwoods, so I guess it comes natural to me. I'm no expert. By the way, my name's Jack Masterson."

"Jack Masterson? Masterson. I've heard of you. Baseball. Did you once play for the Braves? Pitch for the Braves?"

"Yes, ma'am, I'm that Masterson. But that was a long time ago. Today I'm just simple old Jack. And who might you be, if you don't mind me asking?"

"Oh, sorry. I'm Anne Wentworth."

"Never heard of you," he said with a broad smile.

Anne laughed. "There's no reason why you would have. I never got an at-bat against you. And where in the backwoods did you come from because I bet I have you beaten in that department?"

"Then you go first because I bet I can beat you."

"Okay. How about Mineral Bluff, Georgia, population one hundred and fifty. It's about one hundred miles north of here near the Tennessee border. And there are lots of trees. It's in the middle of the Chattahoochee National Forest."

"I'm going to tell you where I grew up, but you have to promise not to laugh. I'm from Pumpkintown, South Carolina. It's so small there's no reported population. The folks there are just lumped in the census count for Pickens County. Pumpkintown is not incorporated as an actual place. If I guessed, I'd say the population of the community is around sixty. It's located in the upper northwest corner of the state, nearly in North Carolina."

"You win. How did you get out? My ticket was a tennis scholarship to Georgia."

"About the same thing for me. I was fortunate enough to get a baseball scholarship at South Carolina. That was my ticket. I played ball there for two years and got drafted by the Reds after my sophomore year. I was twenty years old."

"How did you wind up with the Braves?"

"I played ball for ten years. Since I was a lefty and pitched as a middle reliever I had a good chance of staying with a team. Left-handed pitchers are hard to come by. I made the big club in Cincinnati, then was traded to the Rockies. I spent a year in Denver and then got traded to the Braves where I pitched for six years. I've been out of baseball now for twenty-four years and I can say I don't miss it at all. It's a young man's game."

"How long have you lived here?"

"I bought my house three years ago when this complex was brand new. My place is on the opposite end from yours. It's more room than I need, but I have two daughters and four grandchildren. Throw in a couple of sons-in-law and I need the room occasionally. You'll find this place to be safe and pretty friendly. There are a couple of computer geeks who live here. I think they're hermits, but other than them, everyone seems to know one another."

"I guess you could say I'm downsizing, home and family. So it's just me."

"I'm sorry," he said apologetically. "I'm standing here bending your ear and I know you have things to do. I didn't mean to distract you from what you're doing."

"Jack, the absolute opposite of that is true. You have made my day. Are you going for a walk?"

"Yeah, there's a little bridge behind your house, about two hundred yards downstream. I cross over there and walk the back nine of the golf course. I don't play the stupid game, but I enjoy the scenery. It was a pleasure to have met you, and I look forward to seeing you again. And like I say, I'm the last house on the other end if you need anything else moved. Okay?"

"Okay. I'm going to be rather busy for the next few weeks. My plans are to be moved in by October first."

And with that he wished her a pleasant afternoon, walked out of the door, and turned left.

50

THE DATE OF SEPTEMBER SIXTEENTH turned into a paradox for Anne. The trial preparation time seemed protracted: gathering information, consulting with experts, meeting with appraisers, and attending depositions. Then, seemingly in an instant, she found herself, with her attorney, at a long table in the courtroom of Judge Ralph Coates. Surrounded by boxes filled with files, the files filled with bank statements, brokerage statements, business valuation reports, financial statements, and other documents, Bryan Munday thought he had everything necessary to sway the judge's determination. Anne's experts, decked out in their finest gray suits, crisp white shirts, and blue ties, sat in the public seating area and conversed quietly amongst themselves.

Across the aisle sat Jason, with his pompous attorney, Jenny Beard. They too had boxes holding files with reams of paper and experts seated in the gallery. Jenny appeared to have recently wrapped up another round with the plastic surgeon, sporting protruding lips, a high forehead, and a permanent Botox expression. Endeavoring to retain the spirit of youth is one thing; trying to chase it down in a plastic surgeon's office is another.

Except for the parties involved, their attorneys and paralegals, court personnel and the experts, the only other person in the courtroom was Paige Buchanan.

Anne had assured Paige she did not need to attend, but she insisted.

"Anne, you may need someone to testify what a dumbass Jason is, let alone being a philandering asshole," Paige said. "What are friends for? I've got your back."

Everyone stood as Judge Coates entered the courtroom. He positioned himself behind the bench, surveyed the attendees and requested everyone to have a seat. His black robe showed some wear and appeared to be a bit large on his body. It probably once fit perfectly before the ravages of age diminished his stature. His glasses were thick, making his eyes appear large behind the lenses. His hair, or what remained of it, was cut in the same fashion as the day he had graduated from law school fifty-six years before. After some perfunctory announcements and clarifications with staff, he got down to business.

Both attorneys declared to the judge they were ready for trial. Anne noticed a slight amount of perspiration on her palms.

"Counselors, you did mediate this matter, did you not?" Judge Coates asked.

Bryan stood. "Yes, your honor. This matter was mediated on August twenty-ninth."

"Apparently to no avail."

"That's correct, your honor."

"Okay, I'm giving y'all two days to complete this trial. And when I say complete, I mean complete. Experts will be given twenty minutes each to present their testimony. Cross will be twenty minutes each. Rebuttal will be limited to ten minutes with a smattering of time for follow-up questions. The petitioner and the respondent will each be given two hours to testify. Cross will be limited to thirty minutes with fifteen minutes for rebuttal, and then a few more minutes for follow-up questions. Any witness time not used will expire. There will be no carryover time applied to another witness. By my calculations that should get us done and out of here by tomorrow afternoon."

After brief opening statements from the attorneys, Judge Coates looked toward Anne.

"Ms. Wentworth, as the petitioner, you will go first. Mr. Munday, call your first witness."

And with those instructions the trial was off and running. Each of Anne's expert witnesses testified regarding their specific engagements. The value of Democycle. The value of Wentworth Construction. The value of Reid Lane. The accountant testified to his net worth calculation and explained the evidence supporting each amount shown. Ms. Beard barked her way through the cross examinations of each witness trying to find chinks in the armor, but none were found. Anne's witnesses had presented viable and probative facts. The judge now held in his hand Anne's request for the division of property.

After lunch Anne testified. Well-designed questions from Bryan provided the basis for Anne to establish a concise history of the marriage, the reason for the petition of divorce, the background of the development of Democycle, and a discussion of the other assets in the marital estate. She testified that she understood Wentworth Construction to be the separate property of Jason and she sought no interest in it. After a few cross examination questions from Jenny Beard, Anne stood down.

"Ms. Beard, we are moving right along now, and I would like for you to call your experts to testify until we run out of court time today. That will assure us of the ability to finish tomorrow without cutting anyone short. I don't want to do that," the judge said.

Jason's experts testified to the values of the same assets as Anne's experts had, except for Wentworth Construction. All of his experts had finished testifying by ten o'clock the next day. Ms. Beard told the judge that since Anne had stipulated the construction company to be the separate property of Jason, she saw no need in incurring the cost of the valuation. All of Jason's experts provided valuations and appraisals that were materially different in amounts from Anne's experts, as expected.

After a short break, the court reporter swore in Jason. His testimony went quickly as did the cross examination. By agreement, in order to reach a quick settlement, each side agreed not to bring the issue of adultery into the court.

"Before you are excused Mr. Wentworth, I do have a question," Judge Coates said. "I noticed on the petition for divorce filed with the court that there were two causes. One being irreconcilable differences, very standard, and the other adultery. Mr. Wentworth, did you engage in adulterous conduct?"

"Yes, your Honor, I did. But at that point in time in my marriage, I believe the irreconcilable differences had all but terminated the marital relationship."

"So, Mr. Wentworth, while you were married, and you still are married by the way, you had extra-marital sexual relations with a female. Is that correct?"

"Yes, your Honor."

"Well Mr. Wentworth, in Georgia, we call that adultery. You may be excused."

At the petitioner's table Bryan leaned over to Anne and very quietly whispered in her ear, "On the record. I knew Judge Coates wouldn't let that one slip by."

"Let's now break for lunch. We will reconvene at one o'clock sharp, separate the pots and pans and be on our separate ways."

At lunch Bryan told Anne the introduction of the adultery charge could make a significant difference in the way the judge allocated assets. "He's old, and he is old school. His view of women, although a little outdated, if you will permit me, is that they should be held in high esteem and respected. This plays well for the decisions he will be making after lunch."

Everyone had returned to their respective places as Judge Coates opened court after lunch, with the exception of the experts who had already testified and whose presence was no longer required. Paige Buchanan had her place in the spectator's seating directly behind Anne.

Bryan Munday stood and addressed the court. "Your Honor, before we began the process of allocating assets, Ms. Wentworth would like to present a modified schedule showing she has no interest in keeping the home on Reid Lane, but instead she seeks a greater allocation of the securities held in the brokerage account. Additionally, your Honor, she requests an occupancy period of six months to permit adequate time to locate new living accommodations."

Jenny Beard quickly stood, dropping a three-ring binder she had held in her lap which broke apart scattering paper across the floor. "Objection, your Honor."

"Ms. Beard, this is not the time for an objection. No one is currently giving testimony and we are merely trying to settle the marital estate. I would be glad to give the attorneys a few minutes to discuss and resolve the matter."

Jason reached over, grabbed his lawyer by her arm and very firmly said, "That's okay. You know I want the house."

"Thank you Mr. Munday for bringing this to the court's attention, and you also Mr. Wentworth for being so agreeable. I'll make a notation here. Since Ms. Wentworth is being inconvenienced with the burden of having to move and find a place to live, I am now ruling that she has a period of six months from today before she has to vacate the property. Now, I have in hand the asset allocation proposals entered into evidence by both parties with the one modification which is now on the record. Ms. Wentworth, your schedule indicates that you believe your share of the marital estate should be roughly nineteen million dollars. Mr. Wentworth, your schedule indicates that Ms. Wentworth's share of the marital estate should be around ten million dollars."

The judge had an old calculator in front of him, into which several times he punched some numbers and pushed total. He then proceeded to make further notations on the papers.

The judge looked at his notations and then said to the attorneys, "I'm not defacing the documents admitted into evidence. I'm writing on some copies. Now, since that's a difference of, let's see, nine million dollars, or forty seven point four percent, we have some reconciling to do. Let's start with the liabilities. It appears the only liability listed is deferred income tax. Both of you testified that no sales of assets are expected, so I don't see any reason to factor in an unknown tax. Liabilities are zero. Now let's move up to the assets and start with cash in the bank."

The judge meticulously compared each asset on the schedules, reconciled the differences through questions to the parties and made his decisions regarding final distribution. He split cash in the bank evenly. Anne had requested one-half of the brokerage account and in addition, the amount needed to offset the value of Reid Lane. Jason had requested seventy-five percent of the account, arguing that seventy-five percent of the value in the account came from his separate property, making the seventy-five percent solely his own. Anne's accountant had testified that the funds in the account had been comingled, making separate recognition impossible. He demonstrated that millions of dollars of earnings from Democycle had been deposited into the account, along with Anne's guaranteed payments. He also testified that distributions from the account, amounting to over eight million dollars, had been used to invest in the real estate partnership interests that were going to Jason. The judge sided with Anne.

One of Jason's experts had testified that Democycle had a value of nearly twenty million dollars. Anne's expert testified the value to be only eleven million. Her expert testified the business had a limited life because the quarry pit, as it filled up, limited future revenues, ultimately to zero. He explained how Jason's expert had failed to consider the depleting value of the property, but instead had capitalized the company earnings into perpetuity, which caused an overstatement of value. The judge accepted the valuation provided by Anne's expert.

Finally, after considering each of the remaining assets, the judge made his ultimate decision.

"Mr. Wentworth, your construction company is separate property, as agreed to by everyone here. However, you didn't bother to provide a value for the company. Ms. Wentworth provided an appraisal of the company indicating its value to be thirty-four million, seven hundred thousand dollars. Understanding that Wentworth Construction is your separate property, I cannot award Ms. Wentworth any of the company's shares. However, since the State of Georgia believes property settlements should be not equal, but equitable, separate property can be considered in the division of the marital estate. Therefore, I award Ms. Wentworth the assets she has requested totaling the twenty-three million dollars, plus an additional five million dollars in cash provided from whatever source you deem appropriate Mr. Wentworth."

Anne could not resist looking at Jason to observe the expression on his face, which was one of befuddlement. She could plainly read his lips when he spoke to Jenny Beard, "Why am I paying you?" Anne had just been awarded more than what she thought she deserved, which did not cause her any angst.

From behind the rail, Anne heard Paige say, "Hot damn, pigs can fly."

Bryan Munday again leaned over to whisper into Anne's ear, "That was not a marital asset decree, that was the rendering of a verdict."

51

FOLLOWING THE TRIAL, WHICH HER attorney assured her to be a big win, Anne now had the time to focus on her new home. She had the purchase contract assigned to her. She repaid the money that Paige had advanced, with interest, to Paige's objections. She closed the purchase, paid the balance due and got busy. Piecemeal, she had moved her personal belongings from Reid Lane. Philip Ables had done his part. Just as he had said, the new furniture made the home warm and inviting. The only item of furniture in the house that attached to Anne's past remained the rocker.

On October first, Anne sent a text to Jason, the first communication with him since the night she called his hand.

AW: *I have vacated the house. I believe I have removed all items in which I have an interest. My key and my garage door opener r on the table in the nook. Ava is there and she will lock the door behind her when she leaves.*

Anne had much earlier assured Ava that she would continue her employment at the new house. Her employment arrangement would remain the same, working MWF as needed, and remain on stand-by for Tuesday and Thursday with her compensation enduring.

At last, she was home. Just about everything had found its place. Moving gave her the chance to shrink the size of her wardrobe, something she had been intending to do for years. With Philip's selections, Paige's suggestions, and Ava's assistance, settling into the new home felt like putting on a comfy bathrobe.

On her first day of residency she noticed Jack leaving on his walk. Thinking back as to what he had said about his walk, Anne estimated the golf course to be about seventy-two hundred yards long, hole-by-hole. That would make the back nine about thirty-six hundred yards. Adding the two hundred yards to and from the bridge, the total yardage should be in the range of four thousand yards, or about two and a quarter miles. At a rate of six miles per hour, the speed at which Anne estimated Jack would walk, the time to complete the course would be approximately twenty-two minutes. Anne went to her pantry and found a new jar of Grey Poupon mustard. She removed the plastic seal and held the lid under hot water until the molecules in the metal were sufficiently heated to permit microscopic expansion. But instead of removing the lid, which would be the normal procedure following the heating process, she turned the lid clockwise as hard as she could, putting it on more tightly, and set it aside to cool.

Carefully observing his path, she saw him returning twenty-two minutes later. Yes, he walked at a speed of about six miles an hour, fifty percent faster than the normal gate. As he walked by, she spoke to him from her front door.

"Jack! Excuse me. Could you do me a favor? I can't get the lid off of a jar and I bet you're just the guy who could do it."

Jack, more than willing to assist, followed Anne into the kitchen where he removed the lid with no apparent effort at all.

"Got anything else you need me to do?"

"No, but I do have a question."

"Which is?"

"Since you've finished your walk, would you like some ice cream? I bought a container yesterday and I'm going to have some. You should join me."

"That sounds like an excellent idea."

Anne collected two never-been-used bowls along with two never-been-used spoons as Jack removed the lid and dug out two scoops each. They sat at the breakfast table and enjoyed their treat.

At that table they talked for three hours. For whatever reason, Anne found Jack Masterson fascinating. She felt compelled to question him about his career, on and off the field, his family, his beliefs, his likes and his dislikes. He answered her questions in a straight-forward fashion without reluctance.

Jack left college to sign a professional baseball contract at the age of twenty. Following two years of minor league ball, the promotion came to the Cincinnati Reds. After two years, the Reds traded Jack to the Colorado Rockies where he pitched for one year, and then moved over to the Braves where he finished his career with a six-year stint.

At age twenty-two, in 1987, he married his high school sweetheart, Connie, who made the commitment to be a ball-player's wife. Jack and Connie, anxious to start a family, had two girls, Ashley in 1989 and Lauren in 1991.

Jack retired from professional baseball at the age of thirty-one. To stay busy, he started coaching high school baseball and Connie became a middle school teacher. They both enjoyed Atlanta and had no plans to leave. Jack's six years with the Braves afforded him some limited privileges that he would not otherwise enjoy in another city.

Jack briefly, but with obvious emotion, explained that Connie developed breast cancer. She fought the disease off and on for six years and ultimately succumbed to its tenacity at age forty-eight. She got to see two of her grandchildren before she died. Two more would never meet their grandmother.

"Considering the fact that you and Connie both worked in the school system, baseball must have been very good to you. You seem to have done quite well," Anne said.

"Not really. My biggest contract was one hundred and fifty thousand, and that was for one year. I played back in the days when the big name stars got the big bucks and a left-handed middle reliever got much less. I'm not complaining, it was a good living.

"Now, I'm going to tell you something that not many people know. In nineteen eighty-six, I received a signing bonus of thirty thousand dollars. After taxes, twenty-one thousand remained. Connie and I were very conservative, so we put the money in the bank. One of the guys I played with, also a pitcher, had graduated from the Stanford business school. He spent a lot of his time studying financial stuff and the stock market. He told me one day that a Seattle company was about to go public and all of his research indicated it would be wildly successful. It was Microsoft. The initial public offering came out at twenty-one dollars per share. I had twenty-one thousand dollars that remained from the signing bonus. I had read the biography of Ty Cobb. Cobb was a multi-millionaire, and he didn't make all of his money playing ball. He had bought Coca-Cola stock and made a fortune. So I thought 'why not?' I bought one thousand shares of Microsoft. Considering all of the stock splits, I have about one-half of what I would have had if I never sold a share. Had I kept it all, it would be worth about thirty-one million today. But I'm comfortable with what I have. I don't have to be concerned about money."

"What makes you happy?" Anne asked.

"Today, it's my girls. Ashley, who is twenty-nine, and Lauren, who is twenty-seven. They both married fine young men, and they each have a little boy and a little girl. They all live here in Atlanta, so those four grandkids keep me hopping."

"Jack, I'm sorry. I seemed to have intruded with too many questions. That's generally not my nature."

"That's all right. I don't tend to sit around and blab about everything under the sun, but you are easy to talk to. But now it's your turn. Tell me about you."

She concisely enlightened Jack about everything Anne Wentworth. She threw it all out there for him to hear. The highs and lows, and a few things that went sideways.

"Looking back on my marriage I guess I shouldn't be surprised at where I am today. I have to admit that the lug nuts had been loose for a long time, but finally the wheels fell off.

"Now, you've been so nice, is there anything I can do for you?" Anne inquired.

"As a matter of fact, there is, if you're going to be around. Tomorrow morning I'm leaving on an Alaskan trip. I'm going to do some hunting and fishing, and panning for gold, believe it or not. I will be gone until the nineteenth. Would you get my mail while I'm gone? It would be easy since we have the neighborhood cluster boxes. One of my daughters had agreed to do it, but it would sure save her a lot of time if you would get it instead."

"It would be my pleasure."

"Great, I have the key right here in my pocket."

When Jack left to go home, it dawned on Anne that she had not felt better in years. She once again enjoyed the feeling of hope. And that hope did not solely attach to Jack Masterson, although he did remove the lid.

52

ON MONDAY MORNING IN MID-OCTOBER, Anne set about to go shopping for some new artwork. Patrick the Designer, as Anne referred to him without the "bandit" addendum, had provided her with the names of two galleries and a few pieces to consider. She planned on calling Paige to see if she could join in the fun. Then her phone rang. Paige had just called her.

"What are you doing? We need to get together. What are you doing right now?"

"First of all, I was about to call you to see if you wanted to go art shopping, but this sounds important."

"It's not life-shattering, but I don't want to discuss it over the phone."

"Well, get your butt over here."

"Great. I'll swing by CamiCakes pastry shop and grab some goodies. See you in a few."

Paige arrived about twenty minutes later carrying a bag stuffed to the top with pastries.

"It looks like we are going to make a day of it based on the size of that bag. I've made some coffee. Let's go to the breakfast table."

Talking as she walked, Paige said, "You are just not going to believe this shit."

"Well, why don't you have a seat and enlighten me. I'm all ears."

"I wanted to tell you this yesterday, but I just didn't have the time. And I wanted to tell you in person."

"Okay, tell me."

"Saturday afternoon Eric and I went to watch Tech lose to Duke. Can you believe that shit? Duke? Anyway, before the game we went to the bank's tailgate party to eat and drink beer, or as Eric calls it, 'customer relations.' It was a full house. Lots of folks. And here comes Jason with you-know-who, that little bitch. Anyway, I did my best to avoid her, and succeeded. Eric did go over and greet Jason and Miss Alabama at the opportune time of my trip to the Chem-Can. Thank God I didn't have to talk to her.

"But just ten minutes later I'm standing there daydreaming about being at a Bulldog game and really enjoying myself when I hear that Alabama twang go off behind me. She was chatting it up with someone I didn't know. Jason was entertaining the husband, well I guess they were married because sweetie britches and her new-found friend were talking about, of all things, kitchens. At a damned tailgate party.

"Anyway, I hear the little slut telling her new-found friend all about 'her' kitchen. Oh, she had solid oak cabinets, thick granite countertops, a Sub-Zero fridge big enough to hold food for an army and a pantry so big you could shoot skeet in it. Not exactly her words, but you get the point. Can you believe that shit? HER kitchen?"

"That back-stabbing little bitch. She's damn lucky I wasn't there to hear what she had to say," Anne injected.

"I wanted to reach across and slap the shit out of her," Paige continued. "Little bitch, talking about your kitchen like she designed it. It really griped my ass. I bet she couldn't cook a TV dinner. Or being from Alabama, she can probably make some biscuits and gravy, but I bet that's about it. And those biscuits would probably come out of a can.

"And she was wearing a Georgia Tech sweatshirt with the big GT on the front. I'm thinking, since she's from Alabama, she should be wearing a sweatshirt with a big red A on the front. After all, red is their color," Paige said, reaching for the pastry sack.

"That finagling strumpet. She's got the nerve. I know it's not my kitchen anymore, but it's certainly not hers in my opinion. She just walked into it, or shall I say, I just invited her in. What am I going to do about it? Follow her around pointing out the times she should be keeping her big mouth shut? I'm genuinely trying to get past that mess, and I think I'm having a pretty good go at it. But something like this just picks at the wound."

"Now get this," Paige said. "Eric told me Jason said he and his little tart were leaving for Paris this afternoon. I hope it rains the whole time they're there."

"Hey, we've got to change the subject. You have been just a bundle of interesting news today, but enough is enough. Now don't make anything out of this, or start having wild ideas, but let me tell you about the man who lives at the other end of the complex. His name is Jack Masterson..."

After Paige left, Anne proceeded to the art galleries, but her heart and mind just weren't in the mood. Paige's rampage did rekindle a fire. It was like having a serious bout of the flu, nearly recovering, and then getting hit with round two.

Becky Lynn's kitchen? "No, it was my kitchen," she thought. Anne pushed for an answer. She grasped the fact that she had abandoned everything in that house. Why? To start over. To leave the baggage behind. Should she be concerned over the baggage she didn't want? But it was her kitchen. She had designed it. She loved to use it.

That evening, after eating half of a cinnamon roll and feeling a little guilty about it, Anne went to bed with her old kitchen on her mind. And Paris. Screw Paris.

53

ANNE GUIDED HER LAND ROVER into a parking space close to the Dick's Sporting Goods store located at Lennox Marketplace off Piedmont Road. She sat there for a few minutes contemplating, and rethinking her plans. To move forward was the question in her mind, or perhaps just to go home and continue to wallow in her own self-pity. Concluding moving forward with her plan would be the most satisfying, but not the most logical from a common-sense prospective, she got out of the vehicle, locked the doors, and headed toward the sporting goods store.

The young man greeting her as she entered the store was enthusiastic to assist her. "May I help you find something today ma'am?" he inquired.

"Yes. I need a baseball bat."

"Okay. Are you looking for a baseball bat or a softball bat today?"

"There's a difference?"

"Oh, yes, ma'am."

"Well, I believe I'm looking for a baseball bat," Anne said. "My father played baseball."

"The bats are back over here. Let me help you make a selection. Who are you buying the bat for? That will help me get you to the right place."

"The bat's for me," Anne replied with moderate reservation.

And with that, Anne and the salesclerk, or sales associate as they preferred to be called at Dick's, trekked their way through the T-shirts, running shoes, football gear, and basketballs to come to the racks of bats that lined the wall.

"We have a great selection of Eastons and Louisville Sluggers. This is the light-weight Easton Ghost X Evolution-Ten. A very popular model. It carries a five-star rating across the board. Great feel, lots of pop, limited vibration, durability."

"You're telling me there's a difference in baseball bats? I just thought a bat was a bat. However, Connor," Anne said after looking at the name on his identification badge, "what I would like to have is a bat like my father used. You know, one made out of wood. That's what I'm looking for."

"Yes, ma'am, they're right over here. I'm sure we'll have one that meets your needs. Are you going to play baseball?"

"Yep," she replied without looking at the clerk, but looking over the rack of bats, "I'm going to be the designated hitter."

Anne walked to the middle of the rack of wooden bats and picked one up. It was a Louisville Slugger Model T141, made of rock-hard maple, thirty-three-and one-half inches long, and weighing thirty-one ounces, according to all of the information available right there on the bat. This had to be the one. After all, it said "Genuine" right there on the head of the bat above the imprinted name of John Gall.

"This looks like the one," Anne said.

"That's a lot of bat ma'am. You might want to go with one that's a little lighter."

Anne gripped the bat at the handle and made two slow and deliberate swings, more or less like she was chopping wood. "Well, I have a lot of hitting to do. I think this will work just fine. I'll buy this one."

"The customer is always right," said the clerk, reserving the comment that actually popped into his head. "Can I interest you in something else today, ma'am, maybe a new glove?"

"Does a designated hitter need a glove, Connor?"

"No, ma'am, I guess not. Let's get you checked out."

She purchased the bat for eighty-nine dollars. An investment in her future.

Bat in hand, or actually in the back cargo space of her SUV, Anne made the ten-minute, two-and-one-half-mile drive to the Home Depot store at Piedmont Road NE and Morosgo Drive. Her shopping list for this stop was short and simple. It was just a matter of selection. She wandered around the aisles for a few minutes hoping to stumble upon the location of her needed items. She thought, "Jason knows what all this shit is used for" as she looked at all of the items on the shelves. After several trips of "frustration shopping" back and forth on too many aisles, she yielded to professional help. She button-holed the next available, orange-aproned, associate and inquired as to the location of gloves and masks. He took her directly to the aisle for the selection of a mask.

"What type of mask are you looking for ma'am?" asked Charles, as his name appeared written in Sharpie pen ink on his orange apron. "What are you gonna use it for?"

"I would like to buy one of those plastic visor type masks that covers all of your face. Something that protects the face from flying objects, like shards of glass or pieces of brick if you were knocking down a wall."

"Then I suggest this model ma'am. It's made by Three M and is a top seller. It's a clear acrylic full-face shield with a ratchet headgear. It fits about any size head."

"I do believe this will do," Anne said as she turned the knob on the ratchet mechanism. "Now, I need a pair of gloves to protect my hands. Let's say I was swinging a sledgehammer or something like that. A pair of gloves that will give me a good grip and protect my hands."

"Come with me," Charles said. And together they passed by the plethora of hardware goods to the glove display. Charles extracted a pair of gloves from the bunch and said, "These should probably cover your needs, based on your description."

Anne inserted her hand into the right-hand glove. "This is kind of stiff and bulky, and just feels rough. What else do you have?"

He then handed her a pair of DeWalt premium-grain goatskin gloves, size small. The texture of the gloves was extremely soft. And the scent of the leather was strange to her, but somehow refreshing. She slipped one on her right hand, astonished as to how it fit and felt. She thought if this information got out, women would take a different view of the big, tough construction workers who wore them.

"I'll take these also," she said.

"Are you needing anything else that I can help you with? Would you like to look at some safety helmets? It sounds like you might need one. Or how about an apron to cover your clothes?"

"No, I don't think those items will be necessary. I'll be extra careful, how's that?"

"Fine ma'am. Now will there be anything else? Now's the time to get it to avoid another trip."

Anne thought for a few seconds and said, "Yes, there is. I need a small can of spray paint, if you have it."

"Yes, ma'am. We have a wide variety to choose from. Let me show you what we have. What do you need?"

"Do you have some gold paint? Something like the Georgia Tech color of gold."

"As a matter of fact, we do. And it's called Tech Gold. If you will follow me, it's about six aisles this way."

They found the small can of Tech Gold spray paint, and along with the mask and gloves, Anne thanked Charles and headed for the self-checkout line.

Anne had one more task to complete to finish her day's work. She returned to her townhouse and sought out the cell phone number of Marty Valdez. Marty had given Anne his business card when she met him at the Fulton County Jail. She found the card in her booklet made to hold and store business cards. She dialed the number.

A strong male voice answered the call. "Marty Valdez."

"Mr. Valdez, this is Anne Wentworth. I had the pleasure of meeting you at a very unpleasant event a few months ago."

"Certainly, I remember Ms. Wentworth. How can I help you?"

"I need to know your immediate availability and your standard retainer for criminal representation."

"That's an interesting request. When you say immediately, just exactly what do you mean?"

"I mean, say, within the next twenty-four hours."

"Okay, let's assume I'm available. What would be the nature of the representation you are alluding to? And please, call me Marty."

"Okay, if you will call me Anne. And why do lawyers always talk in code? Assumptions and hypotheticals. It's a real deal. And what is the retainer amount?"

"The retainer is twenty thousand dollars, but let's focus on the matter. Just exactly what has happened?"

"That's an issue. Nothing has happened...yet."

"Anne, what do you mean by yet? If you know of a potential or suspected crime, you have a civic duty to inform the police of such an activity. I can't represent someone, or anyone, who might be contemplating the commission of a crime. I might be viewed as a conspirator. I actually like my bar card and I intend to keep it. Does all that make sense?"

"Yes, it does. Your law license will not be threatened. Is your office address still as shown on the business card you gave to me?"

"Yes, it is. Now tell me that you have not committed any form of criminal activity and you are not planning to do so."

"I promise you I have not committed a crime."

"What about planning?"

"I'm not planning on committing a crime today, I promise."

"Do I need to send someone to perform a wellness check? Are you okay?"

"Marty, I haven't done anything wrong and I haven't felt this good in a long time. Everything is fine. I'm just looking for a little information, that's all. For a friend."

"If I call you tomorrow at this number, will you answer?" Marty asked.

"I will if I hear it ring. Thank you, and have a good evening, Marty."

Following the call, Anne wrote a check for twenty thousand dollars payable to the Law Offices of Mariano Valdez and prepared it for mailing the next day.

She had work to do.

54

ANNE PULLED INTO THE CIRCULAR drive at 1716 Reid Lane NW like she owned the place. Parking her Land Rover at the front door of the house, she pushed the button that released the back door of the SUV to permit access to the way-back. Anne got out, put the keys on the floorboard and walked to the back to gather her equipment. One Louisville Slugger baseball bat, a pair of soft leather gloves, a plastic face shield, and a spray can of Tech Gold paint.

Anne stopped for a minute to admire what was once her home. She and Jason started construction on the house in 2000 before she became pregnant with Cole. The construction finished three months before she gave birth. She loved the house because she had turned it into a home. The bold Georgian style of the house, accented by twin chimneys and dormers, fit comfortably in Buckhead. The two-story columns at the magnificent entrance supported a beautiful conical cap unique to the neighborhood. The house was the envy of many, and she took pride in this fact.

As she climbed the steps to the front door, she wondered if Jason had taken the time to change the locks. She had tendered her key earlier after moving what belongings she wanted out of the house. She believed the baseball bat would have to serve as an alternate key to open the leaded glass front doors. Then she thought of the house key that she had occasionally left in a false sprinkler head for workers to use in her absence. The thought paid dividends. She found the false sprinkler head and inside of it she found a key to the front door. Did Jason change the locks or not?

The key slid into the lock like a hand into a well-worn glove. When she turned the key, the latch opened. Bingo. Once inside the house she knew she had to work fast because of the burglar alarm, which, with its blinking red light, indicated that it was active. But what the heck, if he didn't change the locks, perhaps he failed to change the code on the alarm. 28-27-2016. The final score and the year the last time Georgia Tech defeated Georgia in a football game. Go Yellowjackets. The blinking red light stopped blinking. "Come on, Jason," she thought, "take care of business at home. Dumb butt."

Having disengaged the alarm, she had what she didn't expect to have, all the time she wanted. With her redesign equipment in hand, Anne did a general walk-through of the entire house, beginning with the first floor. There had been some changes since her departure, but not many. She walked back to the kitchen and observed that the cooking utensils she had taken had not been replaced. Thanks to the glass front on the refrigerator, she could see the limited supply of food available. Those facts, along with the lack of staples in the pantry, helped explain why Jason, according to Paige via Eric, had gained several pounds. The new couple apparently enjoyed their meals in restaurants and at the club.

Anne walked by the nook and rubbed her hand across the top of the antique table. Had she known what had transpired on that wooden surface just months before, she would not have touched it. Passing by the family room, she noted a new larger television, but nothing else. She strode through the Great Room, into the foyer, and up the curved staircase on the right, the one she descended to open the door for Becky Lynn. She first went to her little office above the garage and found it as it was the day she vacated. She left the office and entered Cole's bedroom. It was just as it was the day he had left for camp. She then crossed over the large playroom situated above the Great Room. Pausing there for a moment, she could nearly hear the laughter. On into Emma's room. Once again, nothing had changed.

The second floor had become a museum. She left it untouched.

She returned to the first floor contemplating the foremost important question at the time, where to start? The kitchen won hands down. Anne had loved her kitchen. She had spent hours and hours with the interior design bandits coming up with the right mix of fixtures, cabinets, tops, appliances, and lighting. Working in her kitchen, she felt content. What a better place to start than the kitchen, since it's where most things get cooked up. Anne donned her plastic face shield and gloves. Gripping her bat, she walked over to the glass fronted Sub-Zero refrigerator and took one healthy swing. To her astonishment, the tempered glass broke into thousands of tiny squares and scattered across the kitchen floor like ice chips. She thought it might have taken three or four swings, but one swing did the trick. With three more strategic swings, she decommissioned the granite countertops. The granite broke much more easily than she had expected. She passed on the faucet. She had no desire to damage the structure of the house with water. In order, Anne took out the cooktop, the upper and lower ovens, and the microwave.

The lower cabinetry created a bit of a problem. A solid hit on an oak door just didn't bring enough satisfaction. Opening the door and taking a hard downward swing against the top edge seemed to do the trick. The doors just didn't want to close as flush as they once had following the adjustment. Those swings did put dents in her bat. Battle scars.

The upper cabinetry posed no problem. With doors containing panes of antique glass, demolition came easy with each swing of the Louisville Slugger.

Anne entered the formal dining room. She paused for a moment to admire its magnificence. She adored the reclaimed oak floor with its herringbone pattern. And atop it sat an antique bespoke handmade, burl walnut dining table, and twelve antique chairs. The interior design bandit had told Anne the table and chairs were stunning, and she had to agree, although she did remember thinking it was a lot to pay for used furniture. The floor, being part of the house, received a pardon. She just couldn't bring herself to take her feelings out on the dining table. She did take a whack at three or four of the antique chairs, but found them uninteresting. Anne stopped to think that the room had not been used at all since the children's passing. Maybe everything in the house died that day.

Now she stood toe-to-toe with the antique claw-footed breakfront which still held the beautiful fine china she and Jason had received as wedding gifts from the affluent population of Atlanta, twenty-two years earlier. She had forfeited all of the china when she vacated the house. Since she thought it would probably never be used again, she let it rest in peace, and not in pieces.

From the formal dining area she strolled into the family room. There she examined the new 52-inch wall mounted flat screen television. Since no part of it was ever hers, she let it remain intact. She did, however, lay waste to a couple of floor lamps that at some point in her life had just been "darling." The coffee table in the middle of the room deserved a good whack or two, and did receive them. Beer and pizza just won't taste the same. So much for the family room.

Next on the agenda, the Great Room, as it was named by the architects on their schematic drawings. Happy times had happened here. Guests with drinks and hors d'oeuvres standing and chatting about all things appropriate at such gatherings. The Falcons, if they were winning, the Braves, interest rates, politics, construction, or the new Whole Foods being constructed on Peachtree. Hardly an echo could be heard, but the thud of a wooden baseball bat against a cherry side table – unmistakable.

After taking out a few more relics from the past in the Great Room, Anne moved on to the master bedroom. "The chickenshit doesn't even have the decency to buy a new bed," she thought. But why would Becky Lynn care, since she had skirted a few of the rungs on the ladder of success? And, oh yes, the name was Becky Lynn once again for Anne, not Lynn. Becky Lynn, the country bumpkin who rode into town in a pumpkin carriage, or was it a Greyhound bus? Becky Lynn, who wittingly, or unwittingly, drove the final nail into the coffin of what most Atlantans thought to be the perfect marriage. The remodeling of the headboard would certainly give Jason the impetus to procure a new one. Whack! Whack! Whack!

She looked to the right side of the room to see the entrance into Jason's bath and closet area. She had no beef with anything there. To the left, she saw the entry to her former bath and closet. That area held a little more attraction.

Anne felt a bead of sweat running down the side of her face. Sweat that she had earned. Proper Southern ladies don't sweat, they perspire. Not today. Anne raised the plastic face shield, grabbed a hand towel, wiped her face and dropped the towel on the floor. She lowered the face shield and proceeded to her old closet.

She entered what was now Becky Lynn's closet and took a mental inventory of the items warehoused there. The inventory included a few items purchased post-Anne, but she could quickly identify most of the garments she had so generously purchased. Anne reached her hand around searching for the can of Tech Gold she had shoved into a back pocket of her blue jeans. Its time had come. Each garment she identified as having been purchased for Becky Lynn received a two-inch wide stripe of gold paint, top to bottom. Go Tech.

At this point, Anne sat down on the floor exhausted. She didn't feel any great satisfaction in what she had done, not like she had expected. Conversely, she felt no guilt, shame, or remorse. Had her heart become callused? No, she thought, her heart had not become callused, nor had her hands, protected by the soft goatskin gloves. No, she thought, not callused, just betrayed.

Anne rose and went into the bath area. There she again used her spray can of gold paint to write in bold, capital letters "ANNƐ WAS HƐRƐ" on the mirror above the basin. She ended her name with the script Ɛ that she had used most of her life. As a final touch, she drew a circular smiley face and finished up with an exclamation mark. Jason had often asked why she, and a lot of women, used the exclamation mark in their texts. Now he would know it was to make a point.

Exiting the bedroom she happened to notice the vintage mahogany highboy dresser chest that had cost thousands of dollars. Once having held her fineries, it now held Becky Lynn's. One swing to the middle of the chest produced little damage or fulfillment. She took a couple of steps back to survey her quarry. Focusing on the left front leg, she gave it three hard blows with the bat. The third swing, solid and unyielding, took the leg out from under the chest. Come to find out, an antique highboy doesn't function very well with only three legs.

Anne, her day's work done, began her trek through the house to the front door. In the foyer she observed the antique, red-stained, beech and pine Shaker meetinghouse bench she and Becky Lynn had sat on when she invited Becky Lynn Gregor into her home. If anything needed to be redesigned it was that damn meetinghouse bench. She pushed it away from the wall with her foot and squared up to present it with an introductory offering. Whack! Right in the middle of the solid wood seat. The effort appeared to be for naught as the seat showed no willingness to succumb to the blow. Anne found that addressing the spindle back produced acceptable results. The curved frame, made with care to hold the spindles, splintered at the point of impact. She turned the bench upside down to expose its tender underbelly, the wooden rungs that held the legs in place. Two more blows put the piece to rest.

Anne raised her plastic face shield, pulled off her gloves, hoisted her Louisville Slugger over her shoulder and headed out the front doors, to both of which she did no harm, but she didn't bother closing behind her. Standing on the porch, she noticed the Ring doorbell camera set to pick up the images of anyone or anything coming within its range. Just in case someone might care to review the video being recorded of her standing there, she gave the camera the finger and proceeded to her Land Rover.

Anne, being one who never put off the inevitable, had one more task to perform before she finished her day's work. She picked up her cell phone and dialed 911.

"Atlanta nine-one-one, what is your emergency?"

"I'm reporting a breaking and entering incident. It's more breaking than entering, although entering appears to be an integral part of the activity. I'm telling you about the property at seventeen-sixteen Reid Lane Northwest."

"Ma'am, are you inside the property, and are you being harmed or are you in danger?"

"No, I'm not inside the house and I'm safe from harm. Is there anything else you need to know?"

"I'm sending a unit to seventeen-sixteen Reid Lane Northwest. Is that address correct, just to confirm?"

"Yes."

"Ma'am, if you are not in the house, please remain outside. An officer will be there soon."

"I'm going to head on home now. I feel like I've done my civic duty in reporting what appears to be a crime. Goodbye."

55

ANNE SAT IN A COMFORTABLE chair in the living room of her townhome. Yes, Patrick Ables, her new interior designer, did have good taste and a good understanding that furniture should be sat in and enjoyed, not observed. In her mind she repeated the steps that would surely ensue with her impending arrest. She thought about the detailed descriptions Lynn provided following her arrest. There would be a tunnel of sorts, the fingerprints, and a shower, and a health check, and forfeiture of clothing. She tried to remember everything.

As best she could recall, she worked her way through the discussion she had with Marty Valdez the day he came to get Lynn out of jail on bond. He talked about clothing and personal effects and evidence. What do I wear, what items do I take, what things do I leave at home? Anne was pleased that she had finished her remodeling project and notified the Atlanta police by ten in the morning. If the police were on their game, they would certainly discern the culprit to be Anne. After all, she had left her autograph on the mirror in the bathroom and she had posed for a picture on the Ring doorbell. Certainly she would be apprehended and booked before two o'clock in the morning. To be released the day following the arrest she knew she had to be booked no later than two o'clock a. m. She concluded if the police had not arrested her by five that evening, she would simply turn herself in at the police substation near Buckhead. She wanted to get that ball rolling.

She didn't bother to change from the old blue jeans, sweat-shirt, and running shoes she had worn to do her handy work on Reid Lane. She knew all of the clothes would be going into a plastic bag until her release on bond. Going to jail was not a red carpet event. She then remembered that mug shots are accessible by the public and her mug could be put on Facebook by anyone. Such is the life of a criminal. After all, the notorious Bonnie Parker seemed to be quite popular and had a fan base, of sorts.

Holding the expectation that she would be home tomorrow, she didn't reset the temperature level on her furnace. The high temp in Atlanta had been running around fifty for a week and she didn't want to come home to a cold house.

"Am I supposed to throw some kind of 'divorcee gets set free party?' Invite a few of my friends who have been down this path, divorce, not arrested, and exchange stories?" she thought out loud. "Nope. That's stupid."

At eleven-thirty Anne summoned up the cell phone number of Marty Valdez with her index finger and hit call.

"This is Marty Valdez."

"Hi Marty, it's Anne Wentworth.

"Anne, I was just about to give you a call, seriously. Like I said I would. How are you doing?"

"First, I want you to know that I put a twenty thousand dollar retainer check in the mail to you today. If you don't get it today, it'll be there tomorrow. And in other news, I'm about to get my first ride in a police car. Is it true that I have to wear handcuffs all the way to jail?"

"What have you done?"

"Oh, I did a little remodeling. In some respects I could say I took out the trash."

"Have you physically harmed someone?"

"No, no. I just retired some pieces. Pieces are what the interior design bandits call furniture and fixtures, stuff like that."

"Anne, tell me exactly what you have done."

In the matter of five minutes she provided an excellent overview of what had transpired earlier in the day. She might have missed an item or two, but in the order of occurrence, she presented a concise blow-by-blow description of the demise of the interior of 1716 Reid Lane NW.

"Anne, listen to me. What you have done, the destruction of property in excess of five hundred dollars, is vandalism in Georgia. It's a felony in the second degree and is punishable by one to five years in prison. This is really serious."

"It sounds like I met those requirements on the first swing."

"Anne, this can draw a felony conviction. There is no humor here. I have to be present at a hearing at one, and I need to prepare. It sounds like you are fully convinced you will be arrested and jailed today. Call me and leave a message, or text me. Let me know what's happening. Because of the felony nature of the crime, you will spend the night in jail. I'll get you bonded out tomorrow at the eleven o'clock hearings. In the meantime, don't say a word other than your name and your medical conditions."

At noon, Anne prepared herself a ham and cheese sandwich, half an avocado, and a small glass of milk, which she enjoyed at her breakfast table. It may not have been the greatest pre-jail meal ever eaten but she felt it would be better than the one she might get behind bars. She put on some George Strait music to enjoy with her meal.

Knowing the mailman delivered around one o'clock, Anne went to the neighborhood cluster of boxes to retrieve her mail, and Jack's, as she said she would. Among the fliers and other advertising pieces she found a first-class letter, which she opened. The letter announced that she had been selected by *Atlanta Magazine* as one of twelve honorees for the annual Women Making a Mark program. She thought, "I've made a mark all right, and the magazine's selection committee will probably be rethinking its decision."

At one-fifteen she heard a knock on the front door. The walk from the breakfast table to the front door was substantially shorter than the similar trip at Reid Lane. Opening the door, she observed two individuals, a man and a woman, wearing civilian clothes but both holding police badges in their hands for easy inspection.

"Ms. Anne Wentworth?" the man asked.

"Yes, why don't you come in?"

"Thank you. I'm Lieutenant Frank Isaacs with the Atlanta Police Department. This is Sergeant Ja'Mee Smart. We are here to make some inquiries regarding a break-in at a house on Reid Lane this morning."

"Yes, you've come to the right place. Come in and please have a seat. Can I get you something to drink? Coffee, water, a soft drink?"

"No, ma'am, that's fine. Let's get on with our questions if that's okay?"

"Certainly. Ask away."

"Do you have any knowledge of a break-in at 1716 Reid Lane this morning around ten o'clock?"

"Do you mean the break-in where someone remodeled some of the furniture and furnishings in the house? Yes, I'm familiar with that. What would you like to know?"

"I think we will have a seat," Ja'Mee said. "This might be interesting. We rarely get such a direct response."

"Now Ms. Wentworth, just in case...just in case we have to arrest you today, you do understand that we will be reading you your Miranda Rights? That's where we tell you that whatever you say can, and will be, used...."

"Oh, yes. I'm very familiar with that. I used to watch a lot of *Law and Order.* So sure, I understand my rights."

"Like I said, we aren't arresting you right now, but your rights are important to you in the future."

"Let's get something straight, and save some time. Because if you're going to book me, I want to be sure to have it done in time to have my bond hearing tomorrow."

"There's no record of you having been arrested before. You appear to be pretty well informed about the happenings around the jail," Ja'Mee said.

"We learn a few things the hard way once in a while. You know what they say about experience, that she's a hard teacher; she gives the test first, then the lesson. That's the way I've learned a few things."

"Is there anything you'd like to tell us about Reid Lane, just to cut to the chase?" Detective Isaacs asked.

"Let's see. Like the fact that I went over there this morning and walked right in because my former philandering husband isn't smart enough to change the lock or the security code. My lying, whoremongering ex, bless his heart, is extremely intelligent, he's just not very smart sometimes. Once I entered the scene of the crime, I began remodeling, that's what I prefer to call it, remodeling all around the house. And that's how y'all wound up here today."

"From what I've seen of it," Ja'Mee said, "it looks like you did a number on that place. May I ask what you used?"

"I used the baseball bat that's leaning against the wall right over there. It worked like a charm. I got very little vibration or discomfort. The Louisville Slugger makes a nice bat. I assume you'll be taking that with you as evidence?"

"Yes, ma'am. Now what I'm hearing is that you are confessing to the crime of breaking and entering, and vandalism of the house on Reid Lane this morning. Would that be correct?" Isaacs asked.

"That would be correct. I'm not hiding from my sins."

"Ma'am, do you understand that we now have to place you under arrest? You have the right to remain silent...."

"Really? I think I've already blown through that one. But I understand my rights. Are you the ones who will be taking me to jail and do I have to wear handcuffs?"

"Yes, and yes. Normally a couple of uniforms would take you in, but you've been so cooperative, we'll do it. The handcuffs are required procedurally, so you'll have to wear them. Maybe Ja'Mee could make a couple of mistakes when she puts them on you, like having them fit real loose and placing your hands in your front instead of behind your back. The ride's not all that far."

"I have a couple more questions. One, can I call my attorney right quick and let him know where he can find me, and do I need to take a coat or not?"

"We will permit you the phone call, no hurry. And I think you can skip the coat. Our vehicle is warm and the guards will take the coat when you are processed."

Anne punched up the number for Marty Valdez and got his voicemail.

"Marty, Anne Wentworth. I'm heading off to jail now with a couple of very nice detectives. It's a little after one-thirty. I trust I'll see you tomorrow since our line of communication is being severed. Later.

"Okay, let me lock up and we'll be on our way. The only thing I'm bringing with me is my house key, so I can get back in tomorrow."

56

THE SALLY PORT, THE THING Becky Lynn had described as a tunnel, loomed like a cavern as the unmarked police car approached. The huge garage door rolled up and open, and then closed behind her with little more than a moan from the metal track wheels. When the rolling steel door met the concrete floor, Anne realized she had been incarcerated. Detective Isaacs stopped the car at the foot of a long ramp and Detective Smart got out of the car to open the door for Anne.

As Anne stood at the base of the ramp, Detective Smart removed the handcuffs as Isaacs walked around the back of the car to join them.

Under her breath, Detective Smart said, "Honey, I can feel your pain, because I've been there. My ex was running around on me like a stray tomcat. So, personally speaking, not professionally, I think you've done a bang up job, if you'll excuse the pun."

"Thank you," Anne said. "At least now I don't feel like the Lone Ranger."

"No, I think you are representing a lot of us women who wish they had the nerve to pull off something like you've done. Good luck."

Detective Isaacs, in a very uncharacteristic move, extended his hand to Anne. "Ma'am, it was a pleasure to meet you. Take care of yourself."

Two detention officers then escorted Anne up the long ramp into the receiving area. Anne observed that only she and one other person occupied the room other than jail personnel. Criminal activity must be pretty limited on a Wednesday afternoon, she thought. Her first introduction into the jailing procedures, the strip search, loomed ahead.

"We have to perform a strip search. Officer Nelson and I will accompany you into this room. You will remove all of your clothing, squat down, and cough. This is not a cavity search, no one will touch you," the officer explained.

Finishing the search, and enduring the humiliation that came with it, Anne dressed and proceeded through the rest of the process. Initial health check, electronic fingerprint analysis to check for outstanding warrants, into formal booking for fingerprinting and her mug shot, followed by an in-depth medical screening.

"Let's go get you a shower and some new duds, and you'll be all set," the officer said.

"I took a shower just before I was arrested," Anne informed the officer.

"Well, since we don't have any evidence of that, you'll be double clean. When you're finished, put on this new outfit and give me your clothes. We'll trade back tomorrow after you bond out."

After changing into the "blues," the jail clothing referred to by the officer, Anne followed a deputy into a holding area where she was classified and told, that because of her charges, it would be the following day before she could seek bail.

Anne spent the night with her colleagues who were classified as low risk. This is not to say there are no risks at all in such situations, but far less risky than sharing a big cell with murderers and rapists. Petty thieves, drunk drivers, and a hot check artist seemed tame by comparison. Sleeping very little, Anne assured herself, with a prayer thrown in, that Marty Valdez would be at hand the next day to extract her from Fulton County's own little inferno.

At ten-thirty Thursday morning, in a small room, Anne met with her attorney.

"You very distinctly told me you were not going to commit a crime," Marty said, with a disgruntled look on his face.

"Not exactly," Anne said. "You asked me if I had committed a crime or if I was planning to commit a crime. I said I had not committed a crime, and then you asked, 'What about planning?'

I very distantly said, 'I'm not planning on committing a crime today.' And that's how we left it. I don't think you're in trouble."

"Really? You were mincing words."

"Isn't that what you do for a living?"

"That's beside the point. We're not talking about me. Now let's look at getting you out of here. When it's time for the eleven o'clock bail hearings, I'll be with you. All you have to do is stand there and look innocent."

At twelve-fifteen a deputy escorted Anne, wearing the jailhouse "blues" and the customary restraint jewelry, into the courtroom. Marty joined her at the defendant's table.

"Your Honor, if I might beg the court's indulgence, my client, Ms. Anne Wentworth, is a stellar citizen of Fulton County who got a little out of line yesterday. She is a pillar of the charitable community in Atlanta and ..."

"I know who Ms. Wentworth is," Judge Kelsey Cannon said, "I subscribe to *The Atlantan* magazine. I'm just guessing you will ask that Ms. Wentworth might be released under a personal recognizance bond, which I am granting. Please follow the court's procedures for release."

"I do have a question," Anne said to Marty before the deputy reattached the jewelry. "Will you give me a ride home?"

"It's either your home or my office, but we have to discuss your future."

"I'm voting for home. I want to take a quick shower."

Anne gladly returned her "blues" as she now wore her own clothing. With her house key in hand, she and Marty proceeded to Woodward Way.

"You have gotten yourself into a pickle. As Dr. Phil would say, 'What were you thinkin'?' or something like that."

"And I have you to get me out. I have the utmost confidence in you and your ability."

"Anne, I'm a lawyer, not a magician. You could spend years in jail for what you have done. Do you understand that?"

"I do now. I guess I should be remorseful. But guess what? I'm not. I wouldn't do it again if I could turn back the clock, but I can live with what I've already done. I just wish I could get a video of when they return home."

"Let's set the parameters right quick. You're guilty. I got a copy of the detective's report. Did you write it for him? And I distinctively remember telling you not to talk to the police, or was I just mincing words? So, when it comes time for trial, you will plead guilty and it's my job to reduce your sentence to what the court will allow."

"Can we move this thing along and get it over with? I'm prepared to accept whatever punishment fits the crime, and get on with my life."

"Your case will be assigned to an assistant district attorney. A lot will depend on who pulls your file. I'll start negotiating on day one to get the sentence reduced."

"I know you're not a magician, but I'm willing to bet you will pull a rabbit out of the hat."

After Marty departed, Anne tuned into various news stations on her television. It lit up like a Christmas tree. Apparently she had made the news, at all local levels. '*Atlanta Philanthropist Jailed,*' and '*Scorned Ex-Wife Goes to Bat,*' along with some other choice headlines, filled the news.

Her phone rang as she held it in her hand, and seeing Paige's name pop up, she answered it.

"Wentworth Crime and Destruction," Anne said, answering the phone.

"Are you out of your mind? How could you do that and not ask me to come along?" Paige roared. "I'm coming over."

57

"I HAVE BEEN WORRIED SICK about you," Paige said, with a bit of a tremor in her voice. "What in the world is going on? I saw this news story last night on television, and there you were. It was a good picture though. One of the newshounds had gotten it out of an old Junior League roster book. And there was a picture of Reid Lane, but just from the outside. The television anchor reported a police officer saying it looked like a tornado hit the inside of the house. Now, tell me what happened."

"I just did a little remodeling over at the old house, that's all. The police seem to have taken exception to my craftwork, but I knew they would. After you told me how sweet cheeks was yakking about my kitchen, it kind of got in my craw. So I went over there with a baseball bat and rearranged a few things. There's not that much to tell," Anne said.

"Oh, yes there is," Paige said, as she held her coffee cup in both hands to enjoy the warmth. "From what little I've heard, and you better believe everyone is talking about it, you could write a book."

"Maybe not a book, but a very interesting short story," Anne responded with a smile.

"Start at the first. I want to hear it all."

Anne explained, how after Paige's story from the tailgate party, she couldn't get the thought of her old kitchen out of her head. She thought a good night's sleep would restore civility to her brain, but she woke up Tuesday morning angrier than when she had gone to bed. Remembering about the departure to Paris, she felt as though that afforded her the opportunity to take a little wind out of Becky Lynn's sails regarding the kitchen.

She told Paige how she had gone shopping for her "remodeling paraphernalia," and described what she had purchased. She said it made her feel confident.

Anne talked about how she kept her plans to herself, as she wanted no co-conspirators. She had driven over to Reid Lane, addressed the issue at hand, and went on her way. She had not planned for the scope of her engagement to expand as it did, but once inside the house, she said she couldn't pass up the prospect of tidying up some raw feelings. She told Paige, as best she could remember, about each swing of her bat.

"Tell me about the jail," Paige requested.

"It's no place you want to go, I can assure you of that."

Anne described the jail and the admission process, the fear of spending the night in the holding cell, and told how Marty

Valdez swooped in and saved her. Then she passed along what Marty had told her about being neck deep in some hot water.

"But you know what? I think Marty is going to keep the damages to a minimum. I don't know how, but I think he will."

Later that afternoon, Anne received a call from Marty Valdez.

"You seem to have created quite a stir around the DA's office. You may be more popular than you thought. It's not every day an assistant DA gets to prosecute a high society criminal. Fortunately, your case has been assigned to an experienced prosecutor, Melanie Edwards. She's got a good head on her shoulders and I've been able to work with her in the past. When I get my hands on everything in the government's possession, I'll start twisting arms and calling in favors. Having said that, I can't overemphasize the peril you are facing."

On Friday, in the early afternoon, Anne's doorbell rang, reminding her that she needed to install a Ring video doorbell. Looking through the peephole, she observed the grizzly face of Jack Masterson. It was painfully apparent the Jack had not shaved since the day he left.

"Hi, are you here to borrow a razor?" Anne asked when she opened the door.

Jack looked at her for a second and said, "I'll be right back."

He returned fifteen minutes later, clean shaven, carrying a very small cylindrical glass tube and a brown paper sack.

"Oh," Anne declared in a louder than normal voice. "It's Jack Masterson. Please come in."

Otto L. Wheeler

"Hi. Does this look better?" he asked. "It's good to see you. Look what I've brought you."

"Come in and have a seat, and let's see."

Jack opened the bag and extracted an airtight package of salmon. Anne guessed it weighed two pounds.

"Jack, this is lovely, but I have a problem. I can't eat all of this by myself. Could I persuade you to come over later for dinner? I'm having fresh salmon."

"That sounds like a great idea. So, have I missed anything around here?"

"Things got a little crazy while you were gone. Clearly you have not been reading the newspapers or watching the news online. I went on a little adventure and got thrown in jail. So you will be dining with a criminal this evening. Do you have a problem with that?"

"I guess not, unless you're packing a gun. What happened?"

Anne enlightened Jack of all the details, much more concise than her explanation to Paige because she had to envelop Becky Lynn and the divorce activity into the story.

"I swung that bat until my arms were tired. It did a great job though."

"Where did you get the bat?" Jack asked.

"Dick's Sporting Goods. They have quite a selection."

"You didn't have to buy one. I would have given you one of mine."

"You weren't here."

When asked where she thought it would head, she said she didn't have a clue.

"But, I've got the best criminal attorney money can buy in Atlanta, and I've got plenty of money. I know I was just a little out of bounds, like three miles, but I'm optimistic that the results won't be too bad."

"So I can look your mugshot up online?" Jack asked with a grin.

"Don't you dare. I don't think it's one of my better pictures and they didn't allow retakes. So, to change the subject, what's in that little bottle you brought with you?"

"This?" Jack said as he dug the small vial out of his pocket. "It's gold. Just half an ounce. It's worth about six hundred dollars at today's price. I'm guessing it cost me about three thousand. Pretty good deal, huh? Gold is very malleable. Maybe I can have a charm made for you that looks like a little bitty pair of handcuffs."

"Very funny. Let's go into the kitchen and put this salmon in the refrigerator. How would you like a piece of banana nut bread? I made it this morning."

They talked for nearly two hours when Jack said, "Let me go call my girls, unpack and look through my mail, if you have any to give me. When do you want me to come back?"

"I don't know. Let's just say as soon as you can. I'll be here."

58

A WEEK PASSED AND THE end of October approached. The weather cooled. Anne had not had any communication with Marty Valdez for several days. She had always heard that "no news is good news," but in this case she had her doubts. Then, as it nearly always seems to happen, he called.

"Anne, I want to give you a little update on your case. I have gotten all of the evidence the DA intends to use against you in court. The pictures from inside the house are substantial. I must say you did a job on that place. Anyway, I have a meeting with assistant DA Melanie Edwards on Thursday afternoon, November the first. I'm going to present my position to her and try to get your charges reduced from a felony to a misdemeanor. I feel confident."

"That's good. I was wondering what was going on since I haven't heard from you for a spell."

"Believe me, I'm working on it. I truly appreciate you not being pushy. The wheels of justice turn slowly, and there are some things that I have no control over. But I am speeding things up and actually getting help from the DA's office. I know you want to get this behind you. Do you have any questions?"

"Yes. You just said you're trying to speed things up. What does that entail, and is there anything I can do to help?"

"The only real way to get this resolved quickly is for you to plead out and avoid a trial, which means you plead guilty. Now let's be real here. There is no question of your guilt. It's a question of punishment. If I can get the charges reduced, and soon, we can avoid the trial and get the first step over with. The second step is the punishment phase, but let's go one step at a time. I will call you after my meeting."

"Marty, thank you."

Marty's meeting with Melanie Edwards on Thursday afternoon, cordial and rather brief, produced results that put Anne in as good of a position as Marty could have expected.

"Your client nearly destroyed every piece of furniture inside that house," Melanie Edwards said as she turned the file around so Marty could observe Anne's handiwork. "There was some really nice stuff in there."

Pushing the file back around to Edwards, Marty said, "I've seen the pictures. Yes, it's a mess."

"What are your thoughts on this? Where do you think we should go from here? Your client is guilty of trespass and destruction of property valued in excess of five hundred dollars. That carries a penalty of one to five years."

"Yes, I'm aware of the penalty, and the crime. But I think we need to take a hard look at the perpetrator. Anne Wentworth is a pillar in the Atlanta community. She has done as much as anyone regarding the health care and education of under-privileged children. She has never gotten more than a traffic ticket, and I'm not even sure that she's gotten one of those."

"Mr. Valdez, I know you're angling for a wobbler offense. Go ahead and state your case. I'm all ears."

In Georgia there exists the opportunity for a felony to be converted to a misdemeanor. In criminal law a wobbler is a crime that can be punished as a felony or a misdemeanor. The flexibility of the wobbler permits the consideration of unique circumstances that can still carry significant penalties but allow the defendant the opportunity of not being convicted as a felon.

Prosecutors can consider several factors in determining how to charge a wobbler, and Anne fit the bill in numerous categories: severity of the crime in terms of physical harm to the victim, the defendant's prior criminal record, the likelihood of the continuance of criminal activity, possible eligibility for probation, and the level of cooperation with law enforcement.

"This is a picture-perfect scenario," Marty said.

"I won't disagree with you, and just between us chickens, the DA's office wants to move this along, and put it all behind us. So, here's the deal. We reclass the charges as misdemeanors and Ms. Wentworth pleads guilty. She will pay restitution of five hundred thousand dollars and do some time in jail, natu-rally to be determined by the judge. Our recommendation is one year subject to early release for good behavior."

Marty took the Monte Blanc fountain pen from his pocket, removed and reset the cap several times and leaned forward. "Restitution of half a million dollars? You do realize Mr. Wentworth will be well compensated by his homeowner's insurance coverage?"

"Yes, I am aware of that. Then let's change the wording from restitution to punitive damages."

"Okay, let's do that, but money isn't going to solve anything here. How about two hundred and fifty thousand? It sounds worse if we say a quarter of a million. And I won't agree to jail time of one year, or any time for that matter. We'll see what the judge has to say about that."

"I'll accept the quarter of a million, but she has to do six months of sensitivity training, one day a week, and two hundred hours of community service, in addition to the jail time to be set by the judge."

Marty smiled to himself, "I think my client can agree to that. Now, can we get this done at cattle call next Tuesday, that is if you can get it scheduled?"

"Stay right here. Let me go check the schedule."

After five minutes Melanie Edwards returned.

"Next Tuesday will do, the two-thirty time slot. It opened up this morning."

Completing his notes on his yellow pad, Marty said, "I will have this typed up and returned to you today. I don't want any misunderstanding."

"There will be no misunderstanding, Mr. Valdez."

Marty placed a call to Anne from his car in the parking lot. "Anne, clear your calendar for next Tuesday afternoon; we're going to court."

He explained the deal he had cut with the assistant DA. A wave of relief came over Anne, but she still had a possible year of incarceration ahead of her.

"We will get that reduced. Or I feel confident that we can. That decision will not be made until the sentencing hearing, which will not be set until after you plead. In the meantime, I'll see you next Tuesday for cattle call. All you have to do is appear and plead guilty. Don't wear any jewelry or dress like a million. Keep it simple."

"Okay. But what, may I ask, do you mean by cattle call?"

"It's the time on a judge's docket set aside to hear guilty pleas. Since the hearings take very little time, there may be ten defendants pleading out on Tuesday, so that's why it's referred to as a cattle call."

Anne immediately informed Paige of the advancement of the case, then she called Jack.

"I have some good news, I think. Why don't you come over for dinner this evening and I'll tell you all about it. I'm not going to tell you now, as I don't want to spoil the excitement. But don't get too excited, I'm still on the hook big time."

A week earlier Jack had invited Anne to join him on one of his walks. He promised he wouldn't "drop her." On their first outing together she matched his pace stride-for-stride until they crossed the bridge over Peachtree Creek and started ascending the short hill to Anne's house. Jack's stride carried him more quickly, so Anne lunged forward grabbing his right forearm. As he immediately slowed his pace, her hand slid down his forearm into his hand. When her hand crossed his palm, he grasped it and didn't let go until they arrived at Anne's back door. As they walked, Anne had applied a bit of pressure to make sure his hand wouldn't slip away. They later often held hands as they walked.

That evening, while Anne prepared roasted chicken, sweet potatoes and asparagus, she told Jack about the status of her case. The conversion of the charges from a felony to a misdemeanor preserved several of her rights. At least she wouldn't be tagged as a felon the rest of her life. She considered the punitive monetary payment reasonable considering the circumstances, the public service hours as something she would be doing anyway; and the sensitivity training a nuisance. Her only concern now, the incarceration phase.

After dinner, Anne and Jack talked for about an hour and then watched a corny old movie from the fifties. As Anne opened her front door for Jack to return home, a lightning bolt flashed across the sky, immediately followed by a tremendous thunderclap. A deluge of rain began falling from the sky.

"Wow," Jack exclaimed, "that was close. Smell. You can smell the ozone created by the lightning."

Looking up at the sky, Anne said, "That is some really nasty stuff out there. You are going to get soaked, and you might get struck by lightning." Anne closed the door, locked it, and looked up at Jack. "I think you better spend the night here tonight."

59

ANNE DRESSED IN SIMPLE BLACK cotton slacks, a light blue long-sleeved blouse, and flats. No jewelry, as instructed. The hearing, scheduled for two-thirty or "thereabouts" as Marty put it, was to take place in the Lewis R. Slaton Courthouse, home field for the Superior Court of Fulton County. She arrived at his office exactly at one-thirty as directed, and as expected. She sat in the reception area for ten minutes before being ushered into Marty's office.

"It's a big day," Marty said as he pulled on his suit coat. "It may not be a giant step for mankind, but it's a giant leap for you. Believe me, compared to the alternatives that exist out there in 'Justice Land,' you are working on a good deal. The courthouse is just two blocks away, do you object to walking over? It's impossible to find a place to park."

"I'm okay with walking. It'll do me good. I guess the next time we do this you'll walk back by yourself."

"No, you'll be with me. Our next trip will be the sentencing hearing. That's where your confinement period will be determined. Your incarceration will be on a date subsequent to that hearing. But my goal is to have you serve no time at all."

"Confinement period?" Anne questioned. "Go ahead and call it what it is. Fulton County is going to put my butt in jail."

The Beaux Arts architectural design of the building projected the image of how a courthouse should look. The six, recessed, five-story columns that adorned the front of the building expressed both strength and balance. Anne had previously entered the building on two occasions, once to procure a marriage license and again to more or less hand it back in. The hallways were teeming with people. "Could there be this many problems in Atlanta?" Anne thought. "And is it like this every day?"

As they entered Courtroom 122, they observed several groups of people huddled in different areas of the room. "These are probably friends and family members here to support the individuals going up before the Court today. Let's just have a seat and wait our turn. It could be ten minutes, or it could be an hour or so."

"I guess 'or so' is the same thing as 'thereabouts?' I know how you legal folks like to get picky over words and context."

"Let's just go with a few minutes, how's that?"

Three defendants pled guilty as Anne awaited her turn. Then her name was called. "The State of Georgia versus

Anne Willis Wentworth, Judge Sterling Chalmers presiding," the Court clerk read.

"Gee, I thought I was just up against Fulton County, but now it's the whole damn State of Georgia? You better be on your toes," Anne said as she nudged Marty with her elbow.

"Sit down and be quiet," Marty said.

"Are they going to swear me in?" Anne whispered to Marty.

"No, you are pleading guilty, not testifying. Now hush."

Assistant District Attorney Melanie Edwards presented a brief oral explanation of the case to the Court. She described the offenses committed by Anne. She explained the punitive assessment of two hundred and fifty thousand dollars, the sensitivity counseling obligation, and the hours of community service requirement. She notified the Court of Anne's intention to plead guilty, and upon such a plea, the State would modify the charges from a felony to a misdemeanor as agreed. She stated that the confinement period would be determined at a sentencing hearing to be held at a later date. She said the State currently sought a one-year term of incarceration.

Judge Chalmers thanked the assistant DA and turned to Anne. Marty told her to stand.

"Ms. Wentworth, you have heard the charges brought against you and the suggested punishment sought by the State. How do you plead to these charges?"

"Guilty, your Honor."

"Having so pled, you are now instructed to appear again before this Court for sentencing, at an appropriate time to be determined in the future. You are now dismissed."

Marty, standing beside Anne said, "Thank you, your Honor." He then turned to Melanie Edwards across the aisle and said quietly, "May I have a word?"

Marty told Anne to wait in the hallway across from the courtroom door. He then exited a side door with Edwards.

Anne stood in the area as instructed, shifting from foot to foot for ten minutes. She had some reservations about the cleanliness of the available bench and chose to stand. As she texted an update to Paige, Marty all of a sudden stood beside her.

"Do you really want to get this over with fast, as you have requested?"

"Absolutely!" Anne replied with her enthusiastic response.

"Here's the deal. Melanie Edwards checked the schedules and conferred with Judge Chalmers' clerk. He will be presiding over several sentencing hearings next Wednesday, the fourteenth. If you want to go then, I'll confirm the date with Melanie."

"Marty, that's great. I'd do it this afternoon if I could. I'm ready to move past this whole mess."

"Okay, I'll confirm and we'll be set."

Anne later received a text from Marty confirming the court date of November fourteenth for the sentencing hearing.

MV: *Anne, next Wed has been confirmed. This is moving really fast. I want u in my office tomorrow at 3:00. That gives us a wk to prepare. C you tomorrow. Marty.*

The next afternoon Anne met with Marty in his office.

"I don't understand what we have to get ready for. Don't we just go over there and play 'Let's Make a Deal' with the judge?"

"It's not that simple. We are fighting for you to stay out of jail. As I've told you before, this is a serious matter, and you don't seem to be buying into it."

"Certainly I do, I'm guilty. I'm willing to face the penalties for my actions."

"Now is not the time or place for a stoic Nathan Hale routine. You don't want to go to jail, let me assure you."

"Okay, I'll get off of my good citizen high horse. What do we need to do?"

"I want you to write, by hand, an allocution statement. For you, it can easily be, and should be, at least three pages long. Tell every good point you can make about yourself. Charitable works, church involvement, your company, your clean history of obeying the law, why you feel sorry for the crime you committed and some details of what led you to do it. Put in there everything you can think of. I need it by Monday morning so I can get it to Judge Chalmers.

"At the hearing, you will make a verbal allocution statement to the Court, along the lines of what I just told you to write, but not too long, say four minutes. The prosecutor is not permitted to cross-examine you.

"I'll get you the estimated time of your hearing. Before it starts, I want a few people in the courtroom to speak on your behalf. They will be trying to persuade the judge that a light sentence, or even no jail time, would be appropriate for you. Your friend Paige is an excellent candidate, and maybe the guy who's president of your company. Two or three people like that.

"There's one other thing. The victims, Jason Wentworth and Becky Lynn Gregor, have a right to speak against the Court rendering you a light sentence. It's their right."

"They wouldn't dare!"

Anne did her homework. She recruited Paige, David Gallimore, and Amber Sessions of Mercy Care, all of whom would have been furious had she not. When Anne's day of reckoning came, the table was set.

The appointed time, more or less, had been determined to be ten o'clock in the morning. Anne met Marty in his office and, as before, walked to the courthouse. Jack tagged along with Marty's permission and stated his willingness to speak in her favor. When they entered the courtroom, there appeared to be one other defendant awaiting sentencing. He sat with his attorney at the defendant's table, his wife and son behind him. Nearby, behind the bar, on the opposite side of the aisle sat Paige, along with David and Amber. But in addition, to Anne's astonishment, the courtroom was packed with people she knew. Among those present were the board members from Mercy Care, a large gathering of fellow sustaining members of the Atlanta Junior League, three elders from her church, and the arresting detectives. But most surprisingly, next to David sat five employees of Democycle, LLC, dressed in their best clothes and sitting erect. Jason and Becky Lynn were nowhere to be seen.

The other defendant present in the courtroom went first. He pleaded his case with the Court, as did his wife and son.

The judge gave him a sentence of eight to ten years for armed robbery.

Anne and Marty crossed the bar and took their positions at the table. The prosecutor sat across the aisle at the other table. Judge Chalmers addressed the Court as to the case and cause, then requested the State's position on sentencing.

"Your Honor, as you can plainly see, the defendant has seemingly unlimited support here today. I'm certain you will hear not only a persuasive position from the defendant, but also from a multitude of these individuals behind me, time and you permitting. The defendant's standing in the community should not be an excuse for not serving a reasonable period of time in jail. The magnitude of her crime warrants a reasonable penalty your Honor, and the State believes a reasonable period of incarceration should be one year, subject to early release for good behavior. The law, to be meaningful, must be administered evenly, regardless of social stature. Thank you, your Honor."

Anne presented her allocution statement to the Court. Quick, concise, and meaningful, Anne recited her history in Atlanta for the past twenty years. It was compelling. Next Paige gave her statement, shorter than anyone would have thought, but very descriptive of Anne's nature and conduct. David made a short statement, as did Amber. Following Amber, the first Democycle employee stood behind the lectern.

"Your Honor, I'm former Georgia Department of Corrections inmate five zero five, six seven nine." He then eloquently told the Court how Anne Wentworth provided him with a job when he left prison. He told of his hopelessness, and how the job at Democycle had changed his life. He was fully convinced that had it not been for the opportunity afforded him by Anne, he would probably be back in prison.

"Sir, can we get your name for the record?" Judge Chalmers asked.

"Yes, sir. Tyron Lister." Tyron returned to his seat.

"Your Honor, I'm former Georgia Department of Corrections inmate number seven four one, four three six. Because of Ms. Anne, I'm proud to say I'm a taxpayin' citizen for the first time in my life. I vote, and I go to church with my wife and my two boys on Sunday. If there's no one who don't deserve to spend any time in jail, it's Ms. Anne. Thank you for listening, your Honor."

"And sir, can we get your name for the record?"

"Yes, sir. My first name is Herman, and my last name is Chalmers, just like yours."

Judge Chalmers tapped his sounding block with his gavel. "I believe we have heard enough statements to establish the defendant's worthiness to this community. But we must still give consideration to the magnitude of the crime she committed and the appropriate punishment that must be borne because of that criminal act."

"Your Honor, it is still the State's position that one year would be appropriate," Melanie Edwards said as she stood.

"Your Honor, my client has experienced some time in Fulton County Jail, and she is contrite regarding her violation of the law. The State has little to gain in placing her in jail. I request that the Court order a probation period of two years without incarceration, along with the other penalties assessed."

"I believe some incarceration time is appropriate, but I agree the one year is too long given the circumstances," the judge said, leaning back in his chair.

"Your Honor, I hate to use the term miscarriage of justice, but to let this defendant go free with a proverbial slap on the wrist would set a bad example. The State now requests an incarceration period of eight months."

"Your Honor, then one month should certainly be an appropriate time to serve," Marty stated.

"But your Honor..." the prosecutor started to say before being interrupted by Anne.

"Your Honor, let's get this over with. Why don't you put me down for three months? Will that make everybody happy?"

"Ms. Wentworth, you have a deal. Three months it is, with early release for good behavior. Your date of incarceration is to be determined by you, but it must start no later than three months from today. This court is adjourned."

Once again the judge tapped the sounding block with his gavel, a little harder than normal to express finality. The cherrywood gavel he used once belonged to his great-grandfather, a Supreme Court justice in Georgia. No one knew, not even the judge, that the white granite sounding block, seated in oak, came from a mine just west of Sylacauga, Alabama.

60

In early November Anne placed a call to Ed Bumpass, the in-house CPA at Democycle.

"Good morning Ed," Anne said. "First of all, I want to tell you how much I appreciate what you do for the company. We always know where we stand with the financials you provide. And just so you will know, I do read them every month. You've taught me a lot. Now, here's my question, and I don't intend to be pushy. What's the status of the financials year-to-date through October?"

"We're waiting on a couple of bills on the Charlotte job. When those are accrued, we'll be ready to print."

"Would it be possible for you to call the vendors and see if they can get you those invoices sooner rather than later?"

"Sure. I don't expect the amounts to be very big anyway."

"If you can't get the actuals, please estimate the amounts. If possible, I'd like to see the financials by this afternoon. Also, would you please let me know our number of employees at this time? And I would like to know all employees, including office staff and executives."

At three o'clock, Anne received a buzz on her cell phone indicating the receipt of an email from Ed Bumpass. She hustled up the stairs to her new, larger office in her new townhome. Open, click, print. There they were. The Democycle balance sheet as of October 31 and the year-to-date income statement. According to the income statement, the net income for the company sat at $2.6 million. Anne studied economic trends, and after reading a report from a highly respected economist from Waco, Texas, she felt Democycle would be very profitable for at least the next two years. Inflation remained low, interest rates were the lowest they had been in history. Real estate developers had projects waiting to be started. With the low interest rate, states, cities, and educational institutions were floating bond offerings and spending the money on their physical plants. All of this activity, commercial and governmental, most often required the demolition of the old to bring in the new. Democycle's future looked bright.

Anne placed a call to Ed after reviewing the financials. "Ed, I know you've done a forecast for November and December's operations. What do you think the numbers will look like, on a conservative basis?"

"Things kind of slow down in December because of the holidays. It seems to be a growing trend that more people take off during December and January than they used to. Anyway, I project an income for November and December to be around three-hundred-sixty thousand. And you asked for the number of all employees. That is eighty-seven, counting you."

"So if I assumed that two point nine million would be a safe estimate for income this year, I should be okay, right?"

"Yes."

"Great. If David is in the office, would you please transfer me to him?"

After a short pause, she heard "David Gallimore speaking."

"David, it's Anne. Do you have a few minutes to talk?"

"Yes, ma'am."

"Would you stop that. I'm going to start calling you Captain Gallimore if you don't. We're partners."

"Sorry. Some habits are difficult to break."

"It's not a bad habit at all. You just don't have to say it to me. Now, here's what I want to talk about – a Thanksgiving party."

"A Thanksgiving party?"

"Yes, I'd like to have it on Saturday evening, the seventeenth, the weekend before Thanksgiving Day."

"Okay. That seems a little extraordinary, but okay. What brought this on?"

"We all have a lot to be thankful for and it's time to celebrate that."

"Yes, you're right. We do have a lot to be thankful for."

"I would like to have it at a nice location. Have Hailey call the Evergreen Marriott over by Stone Mountain and see if they have a banquet room available. This party will be for everyone and their significant others. So I guess it will be around one hundred and seventy-five people if they all come. And on the menu, I would like a choice of filet mignon, grilled salmon and, I guess, some kind of vegan dish just to make sure we've covered the bases. Everyone can wait until Thanksgiving Day for the turkey and dressing."

"Okay. Is that it?"

"No, I want to meet with you to go over a few things with the financials and get your opinion about something. When do you have time?"

"I can meet with you this evening if you want. Just tell me when and where."

"No, that won't be necessary. What do you have going on tomorrow?"

"I'm free tomorrow afternoon."

"Great. I'll come to your office at two. And would you ask Ed to be available in case I need to ask him a question?"

As anyone would expect, the meeting started exactly at two o'clock in David's office. He and Anne sat at the small, round conference table David had in the corner of his office. He preferred meeting people at the round table instead of meeting them separated by his large office desk. His theory was the desk created a barrier, both physically and mentally. Avoiding a barrier is easier if the barrier is never put in place. He often recalled what his grandfather had told him, "It's easier to plow around a stump instead of over it."

After an update on the jobs-in-progress and the contracts in the pipeline, Anne got down to the purpose of her visit.

"According to the financials through October, and Ed's projections for November and December, we are conservatively going to enjoy a profit of around two point nine million this year. Here is what I want to do. As a ten percent partner, your cut of that profit would be two-hundred and ninety thousand. I would like for you to take a draw for that amount and we'll have Ed treat it as a guaranteed payment. We'll work those differences out later if we need to. After your payment, the income will come in at a little over two point six. Now, according to Ed, we have a total of eighty-seven employees. When we subtract you and me, that leaves eighty-five. I want to allocate four hundred thousand for employee bonuses. That will leave a year-end profit of over two point two million. Who wouldn't be happy with that?

"Let's get Ed in here to see how this puts a wrinkle in his program."

With Ed joining the meeting, Anne explained her plan for the bonuses. Both men knew Anne to be fair and charitable, but her approach to the bonuses took them both by surprise, although they tried not to show it.

"Ed, we are going to have a Thanksgiving party. I would like to hand out bonus checks to everyone. The total bonus amount will be around four hundred thousand. Can we afford it?"

"We can afford it. That could strain our cash flow. We have to pay bills and make payroll through December, and we need a cash cushion for the same thing the first half of

January. Additionally, we had budgeted the purchase of a new dozer before the end of the year so you could get the tax benefit this year. That income you see on the income statement is not representative of cash in the bank. Our accounts receivable balance is a little over two million, which has been recorded in revenue. The cash won't come in until next month or later."

Anne asked, "According to the October balance sheet, we have a little over one million in the bank. How much would we need to make this work and not screw up your numbers?"

"We could be about a quarter of a million short on cash today, plus the cost of the dozer."

"Okay, call Eric Buchanan and borrow four-hundred thousand, plus enough to pay for the dozer. That will bridge the gap until we collect the receivables. We can repay the loan in January. In the end, it will all come out the same since I won't be taking profit distributions of the same amount as the bonuses, correct?"

"Yes, that's correct. There would just be a little interest cost, but not much."

"Great. Okay, here is what I want to do. First, make a bonus check payable to David for two-hundred and ninety thousand. That would be his ten percent share of the income before the employee bonuses. Not counting David and me, we have eighty-five employees. Get your little calculator out please. Now Ed, divide four hundred thousand by eighty-five. What do you get, rounded up to the next five hundred?"

"That's five thousand," Ed said.

"Great. Now each employee, not owners, will receive a bonus check in the amount of five thousand dollars, including you Ed. But don't tell anyone. Can you get the checks written and keep this under your hat?"

"Yes, but let me get this straight. I've heard what you said, but I want to confirm. You want each employee to receive this bonus amount regardless of seniority, position, or anything? In other words, you want Marqise Treadwell, who started here in August, to get the same size bonus as our longest-employed people? And, just to make damn sure, these bonuses are in addition to the bonuses we have already accrued in the normal course of business?"

"Ed, I don't think I can make it any plainer than that."

At the Thanksgiving party, Anne, escorted by Jack Masterson, immediately became the focal point of the evening, not by her design or desire. The outpouring of thanks, gratitude, and kindness was overwhelming as the guests mingled, enjoying drinks and hors d'oeuvres. Anne was so charming, and delighted in meeting the wives and husbands of the employees who made Democycle spin. Jack got a firsthand look at the real Anne Wentworth.

Anne had a little competition for the limelight as one of the employees, a former inmate, recognized Jack. This caused a minor stir of excitement among the prior internees. They explained to Jack how they were all Braves fans and how they followed the team during incarceration. Baseball, one more diversion from isolation. Several sought his autograph.

Following an exceptional dinner, enjoyed by some who had never eaten so well in their entire lives, Anne took her position at a lectern that had been set up at the side of the banquet hall. Carrying what appeared to be a shoebox, she thanked everyone and discussed what a good year the company enjoyed. Then she got down to business.

"Tonight, unbeknownst to you, I will be passing out bonus checks. First, you must understand these checks are not Christmas bonuses. They have nothing to do with Christmas, although I do hope your Christmas will be a little more joyous this year. These are Thanksgiving checks, nothing more. We have worked hard and we have a lot to be thankful for, especially here at Democycle.

"Let's start with DeVarri King. DeVarri will you come up here please? DeVarri is our first frontline employee. He drives a Cat and pushes stuff around. DeVarri, in this envelope is a check for the gross amount of five thousand dollars. Now Uncle Sam and the State of Georgia got their cuts, but you get to keep what's left."

A single sound could not be heard in the room. If someone had tried, perhaps DeVarri's tears could have been heard rolling down his cheeks.

"Okay, let's move on. Is Marqise Treadwell here? Yes, please come up. Marqise is Democycle's most recently hired employee. You have been here what, Marqise, two and one-half months? In this envelope is a check made payable to you in the amount of five thousand dollars, less the government withholding. It's all yours."

Marqise accepted the envelope, opened it right there and gazed at the check. He stood straight and looked at Anne. He very softly said, "Ma'am, people don't do this for people like me."

"They do now Marqise," Anne said as she touched his shoulder. "You can go show that check to your wife, and I'll bet she's already making some plans as to what to do with it."

"We have now established a benchmark," Anne said. "All of these checks are the same gross amount, so you can compare notes and talk about them all you want. I want to hand each of them out, so you are just going to have to sit there and wait your turn."

If feelings had texture, they would have been palpable at the Evergreen Marriott that night. Everyone returned to their homes with more on their minds than turkey and football. Indeed, there was much to be thankful for.

61

ON THE WAY HOME FROM the Thanksgiving party, both Anne and Jack rode along in Jack's Tahoe for a few miles without saying a word. A flavorful steak, a good dessert, and a couple of glasses of wine had numbed the conversation nerve. After a few minutes, Jack spoke.

"That was pretty amazing what you did tonight. Most of your employees will talk about that party for the rest of their lives. Your approach was very non-conventional."

"I wanted it to be. I felt like it would remind everyone we are all in this together. Next month we will pay our regular bonuses, which are determined on specific contributions to the bottom line. So the heroes will get their rewards."

"I don't know why I haven't asked you this before, but what are your plans for Thanksgiving?" Jack asked.

"I'm going to run up to Mineral Bluff to see my mom and brothers. I need to see them and tell them about my jail situation, if they don't already know. Why do you ask?"

"I would like for you, if you can, to come to Thanksgiving at my place. I want you to meet my daughters. And sons-in-law. And grandkids."

"Yes, I would love to. I think that would be wonderful. What I'll do is run up to Mineral Bluff on Wednesday, spend the night, and then come back to Atlanta. What time do you want me to arrive?"

"Why don't you come over about eleven. I'm going to deep fry a turkey in the backyard. Peanut oil, propane, and a turkey. Simple. See, I may live in the city, but I'm still from the backwoods. The girls will prepare everything else. Their mother did teach them how to cook, so expect some good stuff."

"It sounds like so much fun. What do you want me to bring?"

"I think bringing yourself should do it."

Anne found her visit to Mineral Bluff relaxing. Leaving Atlanta for just twenty-four hours provided some relief from what pressed on her mind. She updated her family on the results of her trial and impending jail sentence. Glad to see her mother nearly recovered, and all of her brothers and their families healthy, she left to return to Atlanta early Thanksgiving morning. The trip consumed only an hour and a half. Showered, dressed, and ready to go, she began making cookies just before nine, giving her plenty of time to be at Jack's by eleven.

Two things came flying out the door of Jack's home after she knocked. One being sound. Not noise, but the sound of a family having fun. Following the sound came a red-headed boy who looked to be about four years old.

Jack, grabbing up the little one and swinging him up to his shoulder, said, "Come in, come in. Welcome to the Thanksgiving Day madhouse." Jack returned the boy to the floor, closed the door, took the plate of cookies from Anne and said, "Follow me, if you dare."

As the family gathered for introductions, Jack placed the cookie plate on a table near the door.

"To everyone first, this is Anne Wentworth. Anne, this is my daughter Ashley and her two young'uns, Andrew, age six and Ellie, age four. And this is Lauren and her two rug rats, Kate, five, and Connor, the one who nearly ran you down, age four. Husbands, lurking in the background, that's Matthew, attached to Ashley, and Sean, Lauren's husband."

After a round of handshaking and "nice to meet you" greetings, everyone settled into the routines being enjoyed before Anne's arrival. Matthew and Sean, with all of the kids, off and on, watched the Macy's Thanksgiving Day Parade and everyone else occupied the kitchen.

"Oh, Anne, thank you for these cookies," Ashley said. "Look Lauren, they're cut out in Thanksgiving Day silhouettes. There are shapes of pumpkins and maple leaves and a football and a turkey. And she has written each kid's name on a cookie. Oh, here's a squirrel, and it has dad's name on it."

"I heard that. How come I got tagged with the squirrel?"

"Purely coincidental Jack, I just had one type of cookie left when I got to your name," Anne said to Jack. Turning to the sisters, she said, "I baked those for the kids for dessert if they want one."

Anne rolled up her sleeves and got to work in the kitchen, naturally at the objection of the sisters. But Anne's willingness would not be subdued. She was eager to help, but not to direct. She understood the rules of being in someone else's kitchen.

The parade turned into a football game and Jack heated up his cooking vat in the backyard. By one o'clock the adults were seated around Jack's formal dining table and the kids, as best they could, occupied the breakfast table. After a delightful meal and some minor cleanup, everyone settled into the living room to watch football and talk.

Anne sat in an armchair and relished the chatter. How wonderful, just to have the privilege to share the day with this family. She looked down to see Kate, the five-year-old, standing to her side holding a child's storybook.

"Would you read to me?" she asked in a voice that no one could refuse.

"I would be delighted to read to you," Anne said as she stood. "Let's go right over here."

Anne and Kate went just into the dining room, where Anne sat down on the floor and began to read a story about an Arab prince and his magic sword. As she read, Ellie came over and sat in Anne's lap. Both boys, Andrew and Connor, joined the group, but not too close. By the end of the first story, Ellie had fallen asleep, resting her head on Anne. Before Anne could complete the second story, about a bear that could talk, all four children were sound asleep. She could not help but recall her children. Cole would be 16, Emma 14.

Anne eased herself out from under Ellie, and looking at Ashley, asked if she could lay her on the carpet with the others.

At four o'clock, Anne said it would be best if she returned home. Jack escorted her on the walk where she thanked him for sharing the day with his family. Jack, feeling quite content, returned to his home where his daughters and sons-in-law eagerly met him at the door.

"Dad, you had better hang on to her," Lauren expounded. "She is wonderful!"

"Yeah," her husband chimed in, "and, I mean, she's really..."

Lauren quickly, and jokingly, interrupted Sean and poked at his ribs. "If you say 'hot,' I swear I'll slap your ears off."

62

THE MONDAY AFTER THANKSGIVING WEEKEND Anne called Marty Valdez to discuss her jail term.

"When's the best time to enroll?" she inquired.

"You're already enrolled. The question should be, 'When does class begin?'"

"Then let me rephrase the question. What's the best day to go to jail?"

"That one's easy. There is no best day to go to jail. Why are you asking?"

"I want to get this over with. Today's the twenty-sixth. Would it be possible for me to go in on December third, a week from today?"

"I can arrange it, but why, with the holidays coming?"

"Because I want to get it over and done."

"Okay, I'll arrange for your arrival on Monday to begin your sentence. I'll confirm it with you later. But I'm already working on getting you out of there sooner rather than later."

To stoke the movement for early release, Marty immediately called Melanie Edwards. She recognized his voice.

"Melanie."

"Hi, Marty. How can I help you?"

"I want to let you know Anne Wentworth will begin her sentence on December third, and I'd like to add a comment or two."

For five minutes he bombarded her with reasons why holding Anne Wentworth in custody did more harm than good. "She was contrite and will follow through with every detail of her punishment. Fulton County can save money by cutting her sentence short to make room for another more deserving candidate. Ms. Wentworth can do better for Fulton County outside of jail than in...."

Finally, Melanie Edwards broke into the conversation. "Alright, already. Let me see what I can do. Maybe, if she demonstrates good behavior during her incarceration, maybe we can shorten her stay."

"I won't accept maybe. I'll be back in touch in two days. That should give you enough time to run your traps and think about it. Goodbye."

Marty called Anne to confirm her "move-in date."

After talking with Marty, Anne gave Paige a call.

"Right now, I'm planning on beginning my sentence a week from today. That gives me enough time to get things in order. I want you to come over to the house between now and then. What night is good for you? Any is good for me."

"Any? I'll be there on Wednesday?"

Later that day, Anne and Jack left Anne's house for their now daily walk around the golf course.

"Do you think you could get my mail for me starting Monday, say, for about three months?"

Jack stopped in his tracks. "What do you mean by three months? Are you starting your sentence on Monday?"

"Yes, I just want to get it over with. The longer I put it off, the harder it is going to be for me. I look at it like getting a shot. Putting it off won't make it feel better."

On Wednesday, Paige arrived with a bottle of wine and a forlorn expression. She gave Anne a big hug.

"Cheer up. You look like your dog just died."

"Why are you going to start your sentence on December third? You are going to miss Christmas."

"Yes, I am. But if I wait until after Christmas, I'll miss New Year's. If I wait until after New Year's, then I'll miss my birthday. Then it's Valentine's Day, then it's Presidents' Day, then St. Patrick's Day. It goes on and on. If I start Monday, I'll be one day closer to being done every day. And that's what I want to be, done."

They sat in the living room and sipped their wine, the usual banter and laughter missing. Paige wanted an update on Anne's developing relationship with Jack. Anne skated across the subject, not willing, or ready, to tell Paige she was falling in love. Paige promised she would come to visit Anne in prison, to which Anne responded, "It's a jail, not a prison. There is a difference. Not much, but there is a difference. Prisons exist for the more serious-minded criminals."

"I know you broke the law, but I don't see why you have to spend time in...jail. It reminds me of when I was in law school. My last semester, if you want to call it that, I took a course in estate and gift taxation. I remember studying about gifts, and the term 'charitable intent.' I look at your situation and all I can think of is charitable injustice. For all the good you've done for Atlanta, not to mention that conniving little Becky Lynn bitch, you get put in jail for breaking a couple of chairs. Well, maybe more than a few chairs."

"Sam Houston had a saying for my situation," Anne said, "Do right and risk the consequences. Well, maybe I didn't do right by the law, but I feel like I did right by the situation."

On Thursday morning Anne drove over to the CVS near her home where she purchased a Mead college ruled, seventy page, spiral notebook and a roll of brown wrapping paper. She returned home, inserted a ballpoint pen into the wire spiral, and wrapped the notebook for mailing – to herself. Not to Woodward Way, but to the Fulton County Jail. In the lower left-hand corner she boldly wrote "Recipient To Arrive On Monday, December 3." She took the package to the post office and mailed it.

Returning home, she called Jack.

"Do you have any big plans for this weekend?"

"You know the answer to that quiz question. What's on your mind?"

"How would you like to go to the Barnsley Resort? It's north of here, about sixty miles up IH seventy-five. It's near Adairsville, if you know where that is."

"Absolutely I'd like to go. Now tell me what we're going to do at the Barnsley Resort?"

"All sorts of stuff. We can ride horses, go fly fishing, clay shooting, canoeing. Lots of things. They have a golf course and a spa. But you're certainly not going to play golf."

"Oh, hell no. Wouldn't think of it. Besides, you know I can't stand that game," Jack assured her.

"And this is on me, period," Anne insisted. "I'm not going to be spending any money for a while. So just come along for the ride and enjoy yourself. We'll leave tomorrow morning, spend two nights, and come back Sunday morning. I should probably be going to church, but I don't think they'll miss me that much."

The next two days were days of bliss; the drive home more somber.

Monday came, like it or not. Anne and Jack had arranged to meet Marty Valdez in the parking lot at the jail. Anne wore running shoes, blue jeans and a University of Georgia sweatshirt.

Before leaving her house, Jack had inquired, "Aren't you taking anything with you?"

Anne said, "There's some pretty good proof that you've never been in jail, at least here. They won't let you bring anything in, at all. And in fact, they will take away my clothes. So that's why I'm going without anything. And let me give you my mailbox key."

After locking her front door, Anne said, "And here's the house key. I'm hoping you'll pick me up when I get out, or released, as they like to call it."

He chuckled and said, "Hush."

They met Marty at the jail and walked inside together. There, a deputy came to escort Anne into the receiving area. She gave Marty a quick hug and Jack a long embrace.

"I'll be here for you when you get out," Jack said. He watched her walk through the doors that would separate her from the rest of the world for who knew how long, but not more than three months.

Marty patted Jack firmly on the shoulder. "I'll have her out of there in two weeks. You just watch."

Anne entered the receiving area with less than enthusiasm. She knew, and dreaded, the first stop in the process, the strip search.

To the officer in charge she said, "I did this routine not too long ago, and passed. Do you think I could get a walk today?"

"Oh, sweetie, I have some good news and some more good news. The Sheriff's Office sprang for a big x-ray machine, like you see at some airports. So the good news is, you don't have to take your clothes off, just walk through that tunnel. The other really good news is, we don't have to see you people buck naked."

When Anne arrived at the fingerprinting station, the young lady in charge looked at Anne and said, "I remember you. We don't get too many ladies in here that are as pretty as you."

Anne thanked her politely and moved on to the next station.

After being "processed through," Anne stood in a holding area waiting to be ushered to her cell. Two female officers presented themselves and asked Anne to lead the way as they gave directions from behind.

Once inside the cell, an adorable fourteen-by-nine with gray bars, bunkbeds, and a fashionable chrome toilet, one of the guards filled in Anne on protocol and told her about her cellmate.

"First, we got two pieces of mail for you. A package and a letter. You have to open them in front of us because we have to observe you opening them. Someone must have known you were coming."

Anne opened the package and displayed the notebook and pen.

"I want you to leaf through the notebook so I can see the pages," the guard instructed. "Now let me see the pen."

Anne did as she was instructed.

"The notebook looks okay, and the pen is plastic. We'll let you keep them."

Next she opened the envelope containing a letter. The return address showed to be Northwest Presbyterian Church. She pulled out the letter and unfolded it.

November 27, 2018

Dear Anne,

    I received word this morning that you are to commence your confinement next Monday. I'm attending a conference in the Smokies where electronic devices are not permitted, hence this letter. Otherwise I would give you a call.

    As a congregation, and personally, you will be in our prayers. May God comfort you during this time.

Yours in Christ,

Darwin Scott

The physical letter, not the message, was haunting to Anne. The bold script, written in blue ink, triggered a flash in her mind. The seven in the date, November 27, carried a slash through its middle. Anne held the stationery up toward the light to check the watermark. Strathmore Writing, twenty-five pound bond. Identical as to what Becky Lynn had handed her just months before. She lowered the letter. It was her minister who referred Becky Lynn.

"Now, your cellmate is Twila Thompson. You may have heard of her. She's a big country singing star in here for a visit. Seems she worked over her boyfriend with an electric guitar after she caught him with some, shall I say, seeker of love. That was in the Hyatt downtown. But we've found her to be harmless in here, so you don't need to be worried. You're on the top bunk. Your roomie is on the roof right now getting some sunshine and exercise. She'll be back in about fifteen minutes. Stay out of her shit over there. We don't snoop in jail. Okay?"

Anne had heard of Twila Thompson, winner of last year's Young Artist Award at the CMA show and currently enjoying one of her songs being in the Top Ten. It sounded like they could compare notes and get along just fine.

The cell door closed with a clank, locking Anne inside. She noticed there were no marks on the wall counting down the days. Apparently, that was not permitted.

Anne hopped up on the top bunk and crossed her legs. She took out her notebook, opened it, clicked her pen and wrote, "Once upon a time...."

ACKNOWLEDGEMENTS

FIRST, TO MY WIFE SUZY, whose suggestions, comments, encouragement and corrections made for a better book and a better me. Next, to my editor, Pam LeBlanc, whose guidance has made this book possible. Without Pam's direction and encouragement, the book would not exist. Now, many thanks to: Atlanta Police Department Officer Ryan Chandler who enlightened me about the criminal arrest process in Atlanta. Austin attorney Chris Gunter for sharing his knowledge of the nature of felony crimes. Austin attorney Matt Dow for suggestions regarding the plot development. Atlanta Fulton County Sheriff's Lt. Col. Adam Lee, for providing the booking and holding procedures at the Fulton County Jail. University of Georgia graduates Brooks Leavell and Meredith Withers for their input regarding the college experience in Athens. Atlanta criminal attorney Kevin Fisher for his contribution to details of judicial process in Georgia. Atlanta family law attorney Beth Garrett for her clarifications of family law in Georgia. Austin attorney Joe Cain for sharing his knowledge of court procedures. United States Federal District Judge Lee Yeakel for instruction about the process of allocution.

www.ingramcontent.com/pod-product-compliance
Lightning Source LLC
Chambersburg PA
CBHW030546260626
47157CB00006B/2206